"STUNNINGLY ORIGINAL."
—*Atlanta Journal-Constitution*

"A combination of inquiry, skepticism, and sympathy voiced with a zany appeal . . . What gives *The Sweetheart Season* its distinction is the delicate comedy with which Fowler creates her townspeople. . . . They make an alluring crew for her time-travel venture into the mysterious universe that lies half a century behind us."

—*Los Angeles Times*

"[The] narrator is imagining the life of her mother, Irini Doyle, when she was nineteen years old. . . . When the person doing the imagining is as singular, as wise, and as talented as Ms. Fowler, it's easy to see how ordinary lives can acquire such incandescence."

—*The New York Times Book Review*

"[Fowler] has outdone herself in *The Sweetheart Season*. Readers will smile their way through this one and at times break out in gurgles."

—*Detroit Free Press*

"*The Sweetheart Season* is a pleasant read and a touching tribute from daughter to mother."

—*San Jose Mercury News*

"CHARMING."
—*The Cleveland Plain Dealer*

"[Fowler] is a true original, and one of the funniest people currently writing in English."

—*Minneapolis Star Tribune*

"*The Sweetheart Season* is sly and witty and grand fun to read, remarkable when you consider that it involves a reasonably nasty hick town, gobs of breakfast cereal, an Anne Pillsbury clone, women's baseball, and a lady ghost who looks like the Indian death goddess, Kali. Karen Fowler interweaves the elements in splendid style. She knows her baseball and she also knows what Red Smith used to call 'the mother tongue.'"

—Roger Kahn
Author of *The Boys of Summer*

"Quirky characters worthy of Dickens . . . Fowler depicts our nation's past as more surreal than real, while at the same time slamming her novel out of the ballpark."

—*Publishers Weekly* (starred review)

"Witty . . . Haunting."

—*The Anniston Star*

the sweetheart season

BY KAREN JOY FOWLER

the
sweetheart
season

a novel

KAREN JOY FOWLER

Ballantine Books • New York

A Ballantine Book
The Ballantine Publishing Group

Copyright © 1996 by Karen Joy Fowler

http://www.randomhouse.com

Library of Congress Catalog Card Number: 97-93935

ISBN: 0-345-41642-2

This edition published by arrangement with Henry Holt and Company, Inc.

Manufactured in the United States of America

Cover design by Kristine V. Mills-Noble
Cover photo © FPG International
Book design by Paula R. Szafranski

First Ballantine Books Edition: March 1998

10 9 8 7 6 5 4 3 2 1

For the *good* child

the sweetheart season

Foreword

A limestone rainbow hung over the gate to Margaret Mill. The topmost section of the arch was ornamented with a crown of wheat. Beneath this crown, carved in an arc, was a motto in Latin. "Spinning straw into gold" was the official translation. And a date: 1898. The date, the crown, and the motto were only visible while passing under the rainbow on the way into the mill. On the way out, the limestone was blank.

My mother showed me this one day when I was a very small girl. We took our bikes and a fried chicken lunch from my great-grandfather's house to the falls. It was a day in a dream, cloudless and full of light. My mother wore denim shorts and hiking boots. We stopped to rest at the mill gate. White and purple morning glories coiled about the wrought iron, and a flock of invisible birds sat among the flowers. I remember this because my mother pointed out to me how each bird was calling only its one or two repeated notes, but how, taken as a whole, they made a melody.

A car passed us on its way out of the mill. A woman leaned from the window. "You're Irini Doyle, aren't you?" she said to my mother.

"I used to be."

"I recognized you right off. You had a great arm." She turned to me. "She had a great arm, kid," she said. She drove on through.

Inside the mill I was given a tiny metal airplane. My mother identified it as a P-38. Under ordinary circumstances I would have had to eat an entire box of cereal to get it.

The Date

Eighteen ninety-eight was the year Henry Collins fled his Bostonian creditors and the shock of his mother's death to hide in the tiny community of Magrit. In 1898 he walked the stony path behind the Magrit Falls and put a curtain of water between himself and his past. He was not a local; he couldn't know that in 1882 Miss Opal May had thrown herself over the falls on the day of her own wedding, all dressed in white, and that her veil had been found more than five miles downstream with two fish netted inside it, and that Jeb Tarken had eaten one of the fish and from that day forward suffered from nightmares of suffocation that startled him awake, making him clutch the blankets and gasp for air. But Henry did sense that the spot was touched by some longstanding sorrow.

It suited his mood. The sound of the falls was a steady scream, obliterating all other sound. The space behind the water was cold and dark. Henry had forgotten how hot and bright the day was. When he emerged on the other side of the falls, he was momentarily blinded by the glare. It was in that moment, deafened by noise and blinded by light, that he was visited by a phantom. The hallucination was entirely aromatic. Henry Collins, in a wilderness of savage water, a man as thoroughly alone as any man has ever been, strongly and unmistakably smelled bread baking.

Magrit was too far north to be wheat country and the closest area to the south that might have served was already seriously over-wheated. But an omen is an omen. Less than a year later Margaret Mill stood just downstream from the spot where Henry had first smelled it. He had named the mill for the falls and for his mother.

The mill was the first of Henry's projects to prosper. It would remain the basis of his fortune for the rest of his life. In an age when the world seemed to be made for the sole purpose of providing room to vigorous and propertied men, men with that extra little bit of go and the capital to feed it, Henry Collins found himself, at last, in the breakfast cereal business.

This was a fortuitous fit. It combined his love of science with his love of conquest with his love of invention with his love of philosophy with his love of money. Breakfast cereal was the wilderness, first tamed, and then eaten. It was family, it was America, it was a wholesome and American alternative to grain's other uses, a point that Henry made clear in his 1906 pamphlet, *Barley, the Janus-Faced Seed*.

During his long career Henry made several contributions to milling in general and to the breakfast cereal field in particular. He introduced the concept of the Scientific Kitchen; he created Maggie Collins, a lady in a red-checkered apron who represented the Kitchen. Maggie authored a line of cookbooks, then branched out into etiquette manuals, and by the 1940's was a magazine columnist, combining household tips with family counseling. Three letters taken from an issue of the magazine in the early forties illustrate the range of concerns on which Maggie was considered expert:

Dear Maggie,

No one in my family will eat the end pieces of a loaf of bread. I have always eaten them myself, because I believe waste is wicked, particularly when so many in Europe are going without, but I don't really like them either and eating them makes me feel put upon. Any suggestions?

and

Dear Maggie,

Every time I pick up a magazine I am told how much easier the American housewife's life is in these modern times. If this is true, then why are we still mixing the coloring into our oleo by hand? Can't somebody market yellow oleo? How hard can this be? Does it take a rocket scientist?

and

Dear Maggie,

I was recently at a dinner party where Jews were discussed. I had no wish to be rude, neither did I wish to listen to the conversation. What should I have done? Do you think we will ever see an end to intolerance?

Maggie herself was a fiction—over the years a variety of men and women at the mill wrote under her name, which explained the unevenness of her marital advice—but in a poll taken in 1945, she was named the most admired woman in America. She was not eclipsed until the late forties, when her star set quite suddenly as Eleanor Roosevelt's continued to rise.

In the 1940's, well past the age of retirement, Henry invented Sweetwheats, America's first puffed *and* sugar-coated cereal. According to the ad campaign, the puffing resulted when the germ of the wheat was forced through the barrel of a special cereal gun on which Henry held the patent. In fact, the gun had been abandoned when an early prototype exploded, leaving Henry, who was operating the gun at the time, with the permanent sensation of hearing bells ring, a condition he gamely described as festive. The introductory campaign continued with a ten-gun salute in ten targeted cities in the Midwest, although the equipment involved in the process now bore a closer relationship to today's popcorn popper.

The crown in the limestone was made out of wheat, but was shaped like the laurel wreath.

The Motto

As a young woman my mother worked at Margaret Mill in the Scientific Kitchen. Her father had worked there as well, as the staff chemist. My mother left the mill and the town of Magrit sometime before I was born. We rarely went back and my mother was vaguely unhappy whenever we did—things were wrong somehow, things were not as she remembered them, this was not Magrit. Magrit turned out to be a hard place to find again.

But the motto continued to have a particular importance in our family. It was quoted often as I was growing up and always in reference to me.

By way of shorthand my mother would call me a spinner. This was a polite way of saying I told whopping lies. My mother always did this, always put the best face on everything, filtering the world through her own generous and charitable spirit. This was not lying, not the way that I did, although the results were often far from truthful. "I'm just fine. You go and have a nice dinner" were the last words she ever said to me.

She was a good parent for the kind of kid I was. Another mother might have believed, and might even have convinced me, that I was untrustworthy, tricky, or evasive. In fact, I was all these things. But I was driven primarily by a love of drama. My mother always made it seem like a gift.

She hardly believed in evil at all. When confronted with undeniable evidence of malice or cruelty, her fall-back position was that it would be punished. She was not a religious person; she was not talking about the afterlife. "I wouldn't have his nights for anything," my mother would say sadly. Or "I wouldn't want to dream her dreams."

The story I want to tell now is a story my mother told to me. It takes place in a time before I was born, a time I must work to imagine. When my mother told it to me, it was a very short story. I have been forced to compensate not only for her gentle outlook, but also for her spare narration.

You would do well therefore to keep always in mind that this is a story told by two liars. It is possible, our fictional impulses being so opposite, that we may arrive together at something clear-eyed and straightforward, the way two negative numbers multiplied together produce a positive value. If this happens it will be by accident. It is not my intention. I will go so far as to say I would consider it a disappointment.

1

In 1942, with much ceremony and sentiment, a new portrait of Maggie Collins was hung in the entryway to Margaret Mill. *The Margaret Mill Story,* a thin pamphlet given out to mill visitors all through the forties, identified the artist as Ada Collins, Henry's second and final wife. The portrait was an anniversary present to Henry, done between the wars. It differed from every other depiction of Maggie in two obvious ways: it was the only portrait in which she was not wearing an apron but was instead in evening wear, and it was the only portrait done entirely in the medium of breakfast cereals. It was the highlight of the Margaret Mill tour. The skin tones Ada coaxed out of flakes and farina were nothing short of remarkable. Henry in the flesh had never looked so lifelike.

Page 2 of the Margaret Mill pamphlet contained a vaguely erotic look at wheat. The individual grain was described as hairy at the apex, with a small embryo and a large development of endosperm. A sample grain was pictured in cross-section, in the very act of germination. There was also a list of wheat pests, illustrated by a pen-and-ink drawing of the adult chinch bug with an ambitious, predatory look on its face. The list ended with the fungal killer, stinking smut. The pamphlet's forgotten author achieved an astounding degree of drama, given the inherent limitations of the subject matter; the title of this section was "Wheat!"

Sometime in the early forties, Henry iced the portrait of Maggie over with shellac in an effort to preserve it against a sudden infestation of chinch bugs or stinking smut. Maggie's colors suffered in the process and the portrait took on the yellowish tones of an old photograph. This had its own charm, but was not the effect intended by the artist. It irritated Ada whenever she saw it and she saw it until the late forties, when Maggie had her troubles, and the portrait was quietly removed from the mill and stored behind Collins House, in the potting shed.

The work was rediscovered in 1982, intact, thanks to its coat of varnish. At this time it was reinterpreted as a radical statement on the role of women and rehung in a show in Chicago whose theme was the kitchen, next to a recent painting of an oven through whose glass door a well-groomed woman's head could be seen, cheerfully roasting. But this is the happy end of Maggie's story.

The beginning is in 1947, when the portrait still hung in the mill. This is the year that Irini Doyle graduated from high school and took a job in the Scientific Kitchen. Of course, a lot of women all over the country were going back to the kitchen after the war, but for Irini it was a promotion.

During World War I the troops had been fed primarily on cereal grains; by World War II these had been demoted in nutritional importance in favor of meat and dairy. Margaret Mill spent the early days of the war producing breakfast cereal for the troops, but it was a devalued effort that could be accomplished by the almost entirely female staff. In 1943, with manpower and gasoline both in short supply, the milling and the production of cereal were moved south. By the end of the war, only the Scientific Kitchen part of the operation, only Maggie's part, remained in Magrit, where the emphasis was on R and B— research and baking. Irini was assigned to the B team.

Later Irini would become my mother, but in 1947 she was only nineteen and this is not my story in any other way except the largest possible one, that I am the person telling it. You must keep in mind that I've not been nineteen myself for many years now. If, from time to time, a more cynical, more fatigued tone creeps into my mother's teenaged voice, you'll know I've slipped up, and that's me, not her. She's the mother and I'm the daughter, but she is young and I am not; this is one of those time-travel paradoxes and we just all have to deal with it.

Irini Doyle's great arm was the right one. It was larger than her left. This is true of most right-handed people, but in Irini's case the difference was pronounced. She attributed this to her stint in the Scientific Kitchen. Nineteen forty-seven was, she always told me, a whale of a good time. The fighting was over, the air-raid drills were over, rationing was over. "You can't imagine what VE Day felt like," she said to me, more than once, and it's quite true that I can't. And that I resent this, just a bit.

In 1947 Magrit was a world whose every aspect was touched, however lightly, by victory. They had all been hearing about victory for so long—there was the victory garden, the victory coat, the victory penny, the victory salute, Victory cigarettes, and Elizabeth Arden's Victory-Red lipsticks. But this was the real deal, the capital V with the thumbs pointing out and the arms like wings, not the later unhappy, close to the body, sixties version. The simplest, most ordinary tasks—mowing the lawn, folding the laundry, dusting the sideboards—took on a temporary luminescence.

These people had just fought and won a war. Everything they later learned about this war affirmed the necessity of it. Perhaps uniquely in the history of American warfare, it was a war with popular support. But even beyond that, as it was performed on the radio and sent home in dispatches, it was a war that seemed to provide an entire generation with evidence of their essential goodness, their innocence, their generosity. It seems to have been a war waged in an almost total absence of doubt. To us today, of course, this might as well be fairyland. The people who raised us are no more like us than the fairies are.

Irini was nineteen years old, and even though she'd lived through a whole war, nothing yet had hurt her enough to leave a mark. This makes her even harder to imagine.

She had dark hair that changed color with the seasons. In the fall it had a red tint, in the summer, gold. Her eyes were brown. She accented her full lower lip with dark lipsticks, curled her hair with home permanents, and wore it fastened back with bobby pins. She made herself earrings by attaching golden sequins to her lobes with clear fingernail polish. She padded her shoulders, tweezed her eyebrows. She wore stockings with a seam down the back, when she could get them, and made the seam line with eyebrow pencil on her bare leg when she couldn't. She used a peppermint-scented soap, so she always smelled of peppermint, overlaid with whatever other spices they might have been using that day in the Kitchen; some days peppermint and thyme, some days peppermint and cinnamon. And after several months in the Scientific Kitchen, the muscles of her right arm were so enlarged that once, just outside a Chicago trade fair, a sculptor begged her to model for him, just her arm, for a Winged Victory. "Your arm is like something by Michelangelo," he told her. "Your arm could be in the Sistine Chapel." At her peak she could mix fourteen loaves in a single morning, best record in the Kitchen by three.

The Scientific Kitchen was a sea of stainless-steel sinks and spotless white counters. It smelled of yeast and caramelized sugar and was kept always at the perfect temperature for growing bread—warm. Its purpose was to see that no woman, whatever her lack of talent, judgment, or experience, would ever again suffer the humiliation of a failed meal. The Kitchen combined the technology of the home with the procedures of the laboratory. Ingredients were measured with pharmaceutical accuracy. Temperatures were checked with scientific precision. Results were noted in lab books and shared in weekly meetings.

The linkage of housework to science was Henry Collins's particular pet. In the collective mind of Margaret Mill, the typical housewife was intelligent, methodical, and forward-looking. The Platonic idea of housewife was Maggie Collins, a tidy, indefatigable, even-tempered, ageless woman with a working knowledge of the chemical properties of gluten, a penchant for standardized weights and measures, and a proselytizing impulse when it came to the seven basic food groups. She dressed in an apron rather than a lab coat; she relied on measuring spoons rather than graduated cylinders; but she shared the scientist's obsession with reliable, predictable results and she might have made pipettes an ordinary everyday kitchen item if they hadn't been so hard to clean.

She was as interested in innovation as she was in codification. During the war she was magnificent. Food shortages brought out her creative side. She published a meatless spaghetti recipe using half a pound of pureed breakfast cereal rolled into balls and browned quickly in hot grease, and also a four-part piece on raising rabbits in the home. "Contrary to popular belief, they can be housebroken," she wrote. And suggested, "After you've eaten them, a lovely coat can be made of the pelts." She created "flurkey," a sort of wartime turkey dinner with stuffing and potatoes and relishes—with everything, in fact, except the turkey itself.

"Don't talk to me about the French," Henry Collins sometimes said, as if anyone in Magrit was likely to. "Don't talk to me about the genius of the male chef. There's no one so willing to take a chance on a spice she's never heard of than our Maggie Collins. She was using saffron in the thirties."

Henry's retirement years coincided with the shrinking activities of the Magrit part of the mill, but he continued to take an interest in the Kitchen. He didn't come in often. He would get absorbed in something else, space travel or bird migrations, but then he would suddenly be back, showing up at the odd moment, wandering through, and taking in deep breaths of yeast. A hand-painted sign was hung over one of the sinks as guidance and inspiration to his employees. "What would Maggie say?" it asked enigmatically.

"He's in love with her," Fanny May warned Irini when she first started in the Kitchen. Fanny ran the Kitchen. She was ten years older and built to a much larger scale than Irini. There was enough difference in their size to make them look incongruous together, a dachshund and a shepherd, a canary and an emu.

The Mays were an old Magrit family, descended not through but around the same Opal May who went over the falls rather than marry. Their offspring tended toward the female. Fanny was particularly female. In fact, she was a dish.

Fanny showed Irini a blue ceramic cookie jar on the counter in a corner. "If you say out loud that Maggie isn't real, and Mr. Henry hears you say it, you have to pay a fine. You have to put money in the cookie jar. And then Maggie gets to spend the money on something she really wants."

This would be a practical item. Maggie had lived through the Depression.

The blue cookie jar was in the shape of a grinning pig whose head came off. Irini looked inside. She saw seventy-six cents—three quarters and one zinc penny. "It's not the problem it once was," Fanny added. She was referring to Henry Collins's reduced hearing.

In 1947, people believed that no two snowflakes were alike. Current research has thrown this into doubt, but holds it to be true for ears instead. You'll be surprised, I bet, to hear that even identical twins do not have identical ears. But I digress.

Henry's ears were quite large, with lobes as big as thumbprints. From time to time he would stick a finger into the hole and vibrate it alarmingly. "His brain itches," his wife, Ada, offered as explanation. It was fondly said. They all knew that Henry had a busy brain.

Fortunately his ears did not stick out, but were nicely folded back. In shape they resembled the leaves of an exotic tropical. But they were all show. By this time Henry had persuaded himself that his hearing loss was an actual asset, that it gave him an additional cunning, making him that much harder to deceive.

We are often told to value our eyes over our ears—seeing is believing, and don't believe everything you hear, and one picture is worth a thousand words—but these aphorisms are only words themselves and therefore testify against their own validity. In fact, it is as easy to show a lie as to tell one and maybe easier. Henry's own large and capable-looking ears were a case in point.

One evening in early April Irini's father asked Cindy May, Magrit's telephone operator and Fanny May's littlest sister, to call her. "Your pop wants you at Bumps," Cindy May said. "Again. He says you're his little love and it won't take but a minute." Bumps was her father's most frequent location, a bar within easy walking distance from home.

"How far along is he?" Irini asked.

"Somewhere between pensive and patriotic."

Irini's father's patriotic stage was usually short-lived. Uniquely in Magrit he had had difficulties with the war. Too old to serve, and too honest to pretend he minded, Irini's father was uncomfortable with the national spirit of elevated morality. He found the war as reported at home preposterously glossy. "Just because the Nazis were bad, that doesn't automatically make everything we did good," he might suggest when no one had said that it did.

Or he might want to talk about the bomb. "The human race is hanging by a thread," he would shout, not without a certain relish. He had a superior tone, as if he were the only one in Magrit who was concerned, when Maggie Collins herself had addressed the issue in a column published back in 1946. "Over and above all else you do, the prevention of atomic war is the thought you should wake up to, go to sleep with, and carry with you all day," Maggie had written, and you couldn't get much more concerned than that.

But let's be fair. The Japanese military had behaved despicably at Pearl Harbor and even worse throughout Asia. And the bomb *had* ended the war. The Hiroshima maidens would come to the United States for the best plastic surgery the world could offer, all bills to be paid by Uncle Sam. American lives had been saved. In fact you could argue, as Vannevar Bush of the Carnegie Institute had already argued, that Japanese lives had been saved as well. Without the bomb, Bush pointed out, Japan might well have faced its eventual defeat with a nationwide orgy of ritual suicide.

And then there was the Atomic Energy Commission, already predicting a future of atom-powered cars, cheap and abundant food, plenty of leisure time for all, and no more wars, ever, as the new critter, Mr. Atom, worked his magic. Irini's father was stubbornly refusing to see the bright side. This was so like him.

Fortunately, his drinking gave Magrit a way to be forgiving. "It's just the liquor talking," someone would say, buying him another, pushing him quickly out the back of his probing stage and into his pain-free.

Soon after this, he would begin to sing. "Lili Marlene," perhaps, if he was nostalgic, or his personal favorite, "Take a Leg from Any Old Table," if he was playful. Songs in which love was hopeless or had gone bad and you either died of it or had expected it to turn out this way all along.

And yet, from his mother to his wife, whom he'd married late, to his daughter, his own life was rich in women who loved him.

Irini put on a heavy coat, blue with leather buttons, and black knitted gloves. Crusts of tired snow lay on the grass along the streets. There were no sidewalks in Magrit except for those in the two blocks constituting the downtown. There the walks were the kind that glitter. "Step lightly. You're walking on diamonds, Irini," her father said once and for many years she took this literally.

The day was just past sunset, still light out but extremely cold. Sometimes, but not often, April was spring. This year it was the dead end of winter. There had been snow that very morning, big flakes but not many, so they only stuck in the hollows and the shaded sides of trees where there was already snow to hold them. They had performed the kind of spring cleaning of which Maggie Collins does not approve. Not a real cleaning, nothing that involved muscle. Just a new clean layer over the soiled old one, the way you sweep dirt under the rug, cover a stained tablecloth with a fresh.

This was not a pretty effect, merely a tidy one. The snow was as dry as Styrofoam. The grass on the hills was the color of straw, tall but dead and brittle. Even the evergreens were gray. In contrast, the birches were more beautiful than ever, with their thin, elegant trunks and the white of their bare branches lacing against the evening sky.

It was hot inside Bumps. Her father was seated at the bar, talking animatedly to a man she didn't know. With one hand he gestured to Norma Baldish, the Bumps evening bartender. With the other hand he drank. "Norma's great-grandmother once subdued a violent lumberjack with nothing but a potato masher. Just drew it, never even had to mash with it," he was saying. "In this very bar. Isn't that so, Norma?" Her father was a poetic, sentimental man, a wonderful storyteller who often moved himself to tears.

Behind the bar was a sheet of polished brass, pressed with a pattern of flowers. It was a piece of the original bar, saved by the original Baldish family from the fire of aught-five. Irini's father saw her approaching in it, warped and repeated in the petals, a daisy with eight Irini faces, all growing large as they headed his way.

"Irini!" He took a gulp and spun around on the bar stool. He didn't look like a corporate chemist. He had the thin, lupine, four-o'clock-shadowy look of a partisan. "What a delightful and totally unexpected treat. What a surprise! This is Thomas Holcrow." Her father gestured to his drinking partner. "He's from Los Angeles. He plans the train schedules. Can you imagine how methodical the man must be? So many people depending on him. Can you imagine? Thomas, this is my daughter, Irini."

Irini attempted without success to smooth her father's hair, still rumpled from the winter cap that now covered one knee. Holcrow watched her with an unsteady gaze. She stood five foot three and weighed 105 pounds. The heavy coat probably made her look even smaller.

"You're on," Holcrow told her father.

Her father had bet his bar bill Irini could beat Holcrow arm wrestling. Irini took off her coat, but not her gloves. Holcrow's breath was wet and inflammable. His hand was much bigger than hers and even through the gloves she could feel how warm it was. The match lasted less than a minute. "Holy mackerel," he said as he went down for the count.

"Isn't she something? A face like Maureen O'Hara and an arm like Jack Dempsey." Her father's spirits were unbearably high. "Cheer up, Holcrow," he said. "I'll buy you a drink." To Norma Baldish he said, "Two beers." To Irini, "You run along home now. This is no place for an impressionable young girl. Does your father know where you are?" To Norma, "Just put them on my tab."

He did not come home for supper that night. Just before midnight she woke to the sound of his voice. "I will not wake my daughter," he was shouting. "Not for anything." He stood on their front step and she could hear him through the window just as if he were in the room with her.

Holcrow had followed her father home and was demanding a rematch. Irini inferred this; she could not hear Holcrow at all. "She is not some sideshow exhibition. She is a growing girl." Her father's voice was crisp with indignation. "Go ahead. Break the window. Break down the door! I'll never get her up. She has work in the morning!"

Irini heard the sound of smashing glass. Two minutes later her father knocked on her bedroom door. The knock was ever so soft, a knock designed to bother her as little as possible. "Irini, can you help me? I seem to have cut myself."

Irini put on her bathrobe. "Did Mr. Holcrow break our window?"

"No. I dropped my bottle."

Irini went to look out the front door.

"He's gone," her father said. "He had an engagement. Just as well. What a sore loser. I swear, it almost makes a man afraid to ride the trains." Her father held out his hand. He had cut across the tips of two fingers and was bleeding. "No need to put anything nasty on it. Some of the whiskey splashed over it on the way out of the bottle. It's as clean as can be."

Irini went to the medicine cabinet for the iodine. Her father closed his eyes. "I'm just a little sorry everyone at Bumps saw you win," he said. "I could have lined up the matches if I'd thought it through more. It was just a happy inspiration and I didn't think it through. You were a trump, though. You were beautiful. Two seconds and you had him pinned. Did you hear that little squealing sound he made? If I'd thought it through more I would have told you to make it look more difficult. Ouch, Irini! Ouch, my love!"

Maggie Collins writes: "No open wound, however small, can be considered trivial. Bacteria gather at the site and begin to enter the body immediately. The quick use of an antiseptic is the first priority."

Maggie Collins writes: "Every girl must learn early not to compete in sporting events with men. It is not the possibility that she might lose that must be avoided. It is the very real possibility that she might win."

"No good ever came to me from arm wrestling men," my mother always told me, and these are the words I've tried to live by.

2

Upper Magrit:

The history of the mill was outlined on the back of the Margaret Mill pamphlet. This brief account told you that Lewis Collins, Henry's father, was a schoolteacher and amateur ornithologist, that Margaret Collins, his mother, was the daughter of an alderman, and that this happy union had produced a visionary. Confirmation was provided by Henry himself. He gazed soberly out from the back page in a photograph taken perhaps in his fifties, straight out so you hardly saw his ears, and captioned, "I have always been a man who sees things other men don't see." The pamphlet concluded with the statement that Henry chose Magrit Falls as the site of his mill because of its special human resources, as well as its perfect aspect of water.

To some small extent this was even true. The water around Magrit had a temperate effect on the climate. Magrit had fewer subzero days than many places far to the south.

But in fact, Henry Collins had to change the landscape some considerable amount in order to build his mill. Before 1898 the town had been divided into the Upper and the Lower, a few big homes below the falls, a few small homes above. The water above the falls ran through a deep shale ravine called the kill. Henry wanted a millpond and a dam. To get them on the scale he envisioned, he had to drown Upper Magrit. He did it with dynamite and politics.

Of course, the families of Upper Magrit were compensated. Ten cents on the dollar, as the Upper remembered, but generous, said the Lower, since, according to the Water Dam Act of 1840, no compensation of any kind was required. In addition to this, Henry put the project to a vote. He wouldn't go ahead unless the community wanted the mill. And of course, the residents of the Upper had ample time to pack and relocate. It was a tiny community back then, the Lower said. Hardly anyone lived there at all. And among those who did, some wanted the mill as much as anyone, the Lower said.

Still, when the residents of the Upper resettled into the Lower, they brought, along with their belongings, animosities that lasted for generations. Their lost homes continued to exist in their memories, fully furnished and actually seen, very occasionally, by moonlight. It was as if the surviving town had a shadow, preserved under the water of Henry Collins's millpond like a trout under aspic.

In Upper Magrit streets were rivers; beds were boats. A wintry lake wrapped itself around the trunks of apple trees, spread over parlors and kitchens like a cold, green carpet twelve feet deep. Books floated off the library shelves and settled to the floor, their pages rippling. Fish circled the legs of parlor chairs, glided over the dinner plates. Cups and saucers rattled against each other—half speed, double volume. Corked wine bottles popped to the ceilings of kitchens.

You must think of the Magrit that remained in the same way you think of other divided lands—Ireland and Ulster, the North and the Confederacy, India and Pakistan. You wouldn't expect a little thing like the complete and permanent drowning of Pakistan to stop the troubles there and you mustn't expect it in Magrit either.

When she heard the matter would be decided by vote, Madame Nadeau sent for her five sons. The Nadeau brothers were in Canada, following the pine. They came hurrying home. This was not just a matter of five votes. The Nadeau boys, as a group, were remembered as persuasive. "Persuasive" was my mother's word, although the Nadeaus barely spoke English and rarely spoke at all to anyone but each other. Joe Nadeau had once eaten a live snake, tail first, to settle a bet.

Their boat capsized on Lake Superior. Since it was Superior, the bodies were never found and word was slow getting to Magrit. The boys weren't there for the vote, but their mother clung to the hope that they would still arrive in time to be persuasive. Henry Collins sent south for a crew to set the dynamite and Madame Nadeau sent north with a second message for her sons. When the dynamiting began she had to be forcibly removed; by this time she knew her sons were not coming and was determined to drown with her house. She died anyway within the month, on a stuffed chair in her daughter's home, of grief.

It was three years later, in the spring, that Tom Baldish was doing the supper dishes and thought he heard the first of the geese passing overhead. He stepped outside to watch and wave but saw instead, in the sky right above his house, the bottom of a boat with five oars dipping and pulling through the air. The apparition of the flying boat had been seen before; the residents of Magrit called it the Chasse Galerie, because that was what it was called in Canada, where it appeared more often. It floated down to Magrit roughly once a decade. But it had never had five oars before. Clearly the Nadeau brothers were still trying to get home.

All of this had kept Henry Collins from being as popular locally as he might have been. Every misfortune that befell the Collins family was said to be caused by the curse of Upper Magrit in general and the Nadeau family in particular. Madame Nadeau, whose mousy manners had been quite overwhelmed by those of her sons in real life, was remembered as a woman with unnatural powers. When lightning struck the Collins home and caused a fire throughout the second story in April of 1928, no one was surprised. The Nadeaus had been attacked with water and responded some thirty years later with fire. It made perfect sense.

Magrit in 1947:

After the dynamite, the small remnant of Nadeaus who survived, all female, left Magrit, but the Upper families who stayed—the Mays, the Leggetts, and the Kinsers—continued to speak on their behalf and to hold Nadeau grudges loyally along with their own. The Doyles moved to Magrit when Irini was four and were often oblivious to these ancient tensions, but no one could mistake the animosity between the Mays, who lived on the Doyles' right as you faced the house from the street, and the Tarkens, who lived on the left, and all because the Tarkens were Lower Magrit and the Mays were Upper.

When she was little, Irini's father used to tell her that Magrit was right on the border between America and storyland. "There's you, princess, always losing your shoes," Irini's father would say, as evidence. "There's Rapunzel of the river." Rapunzel was her father's name for Margo Törngren, a schoolmate of Irini's who now worked with her in the Kitchen. Margo was a capable girl with a broad, pleasant face and magnificent hair. She was one of Irini's closest friends.

Irini's father drew Irini a map once with colored pencils. When I was a girl this same map hung on the wall in a succession of my bedrooms, more permanent than any home I ever had. It showed a troll's bridge over Glen Annie Creek. A Hansel and Gretel cabin out in the woods, which was called the Sweet place. The castle was Collins House. In a leap of imaginative cartography, the castle moat contained the drowned city of Upper Magrit. And in the very center of the map was the Doyle home on Brief Street.

It was the smallest house on the block, as the Doyles were the smallest family. It was made out of brick, with apple green shutters and a peaked roof. It was built along the same lines as the most successful and final house of the three little pigs and was, as a matter of actual fact, the only house on Brief Street to survive the Big Blow of '88. Or so Mr. Henry had said when he sold it to them.

Henry had bought it for a song from the widow Kinser, added indoor plumbing, and offered it for the same song to Irini's father as part of an employment package. It was too hot in the summer and too cold in the winter, which meant that was comfortable enough. People didn't expect as much of their houses in 1947.

And truthfully there hadn't been another option. Before coming to Magrit Irini's father had taught chemistry at Lewis High School in Indiana at the same school where her mother taught English. Irini's mother had died the day Irini was born and Irini's father began to drink the day after that.

Four years later, with his teaching career gone south, he brought Irini north to Magrit and Brief Street for a new start. She couldn't remember Indiana at all, except, she told me once, for a water-colored recollection of following her father's shoes out of a tobacco store, only to realize they weren't her father's shoes at all. What she really remembered was the way the shoes looked, worn and creased over the toes, and that moment of being lost. She never forgot that part.

In Magrit Irini had her share of ordinary neighborly troubles. The Mays traveled frequently to Florida up until the war and left Irini in charge of the house. They'd come back in the summer of '42 to find their basement flooded in the last downpour. Irini had somehow failed to notice. "I never went down there," Irini said, which seemed reasonable enough to her, if now regrettable. The Mays' basement was as dark and unpleasant as anyone else's basement. It smelled of spiders.

"I would think six feet of water would be hard to miss, missy," said Mr. May, although Tracy May said she'd waded across it, so either it was no six feet or Tracy was lying.

The Mays had brought Irini a conch shell, with a sandy outside and a polished pink curl that disappeared into darkness. They decided not to give it to her. "You can hear the ocean in it and everything," Tracy informed her to make certain she regretted the loss. Tracy was the middle daughter, ten years younger than Fanny, two years older than Cindy, and the May girl closest in age to Irini. She was just as annoying as most middle children. Irini told her she already had a conch shell anyway, even though she didn't, and Tracy, of course, said, "Show me," and Irini climbed up into the apple tree instead and had to be coaxed down for dinner just like a cat.

And then, years later, Mrs. Tarken had spent an entire day planting a victory garden, and Tweed, Irini's collie, spent the entire night digging up the bulbs and potatoes. She left an easy trail of footprints to the Doyle porch, where she had laid the vegetable matter out in a neat line. She had even arranged the items by size. Irini's father had been enchanted. "It's an amazing effort," he'd said. "For a dog."

But Mrs. Tarken said it was unnatural, and of course it was, even for Magrit. She all but accused Tweed of being a Nazi agent.

The point being that these arguments were transitory and niggling compared to the hostility the Mays and the Tarkens had for each other, and all because the Mays were Upper Magrit and the Tarkens were Lower. Local legend had it that the name Magrit was created out of the first letters of the family names of the six original inhabitants. The M stood for May. And then, as far away as possible, was the T, which stood for Tarken. The Tarkens had for several generations referred to the town as Tirgam, but no one else did, and eventually even they forgot to. When Margaret Mill opened, Magrit became the indisputably right name.

The Mays and the Tarkens passed each other on Brief Street for the whole of Irini's life there without once speaking except for the week of the telegram. The telegram arrived in a black car, in the gloved hand of a soldier. It said that Jimmy Tarken had disappeared in the jungles of the Solomon Islands.

It came in a hush that everyone heard. The Mays had never expected Jimmy Tarken to die for them or they would have been nicer to him. They joined the rest of Magrit in leaving cakes and sandwiches on the Tarken porch. It was a momentary truce, forced on them by the war. When VE Day came, hostilities recommenced. "I don't think she even ate the sandwiches," Mrs. May told Mrs. Leggett who told Mrs. Kinser.

"We didn't eat the sandwiches," Mrs. Tarken told Mrs. Baldish. "You know tuna. It's not really a gift spread unless you know exactly what you're doing."

3

On the night of the Thomas Holcrow–Irini Doyle arm-wrestling match, when her father stepped back outside, a towel wrapped around his sliced and iodized fingers, Irini put her coat over her bathrobe and followed to make sure her father hadn't woken the neighbors. The windows next door were shuttered, except for one room upstairs at the Tarkens' where Jimmy had slept. The glass in Jimmy's window had a dull gleam. The room was just as Jimmy had left it, except that his mother had made his bed. She'd done this the day he left, of course, not the day of the telegram, which spared Irini having to think about Mrs. Tarken making her dead son's bed. Even as it was, she didn't like to think about it. She supposed it would have been even worse to think of the bed unmade.

The air was icy. Irini put her bare hands into her pockets. "Ah, Irini," her father said. "You're not a gentle nurse. Fortunately, I took the precaution of anesthetizing myself first. And I forgive you. I more than forgive you. Come outside and turn off the porch light. You've never seen such a sky for stars."

The moon had already dropped beneath the horizon, untouched as yet by boots and nationalism, and made up only of poetry and metaphor and cold, reflected light. Without it, the stars blossomed

25

above her. They had always made Irini think of the dead, with their distant, icy, unreachable fires. Once this had meant her mother, but since the war Irini's ideas of dead people had grown to encompass more starlike numbers. The Tarkens had a gold star in their window for Jimmy.

The sky was brighter in 1947. This must be why our parents' songs are so celestial: "Stardust," and "East of the Sun and West of the Moon," and "Deep Purple," and "Blue Moon," and "Shine on Harvest Moon," and so on and so on. In Magrit, where there were few houses and no street lights at all, the stars were crowded into every corner of the sky, thick as summer clover.

The stars have always made people feel small. Depending on what size you think people ought to be, this message is either cold or comforting. It is only us and only now, after all those centuries, finally drowning them into silence with our own innumerable lights.

The more fragile constellations have been the first to go. "There, Irini. There spins Cassiopeia, round and round the Maypole. See her? She's never looked lovelier."

"Um," said Irini. She had no idea where Cassiopeia was. When she was younger, she used to try.

"See the two stars there." Her father would point. "The pink one is Shedar. The blue is Caph. Caph is her hand. Take a line, down and then east and then down again. They form a W. See? Just up from Pegasus. Not the dim little clump of blues. Just past it. See?"

How could she see? There was a sky full of stars and her father expected her to find one by finding another. She didn't know where to start, so she couldn't know where to finish. The only constellation she could find with any assurance was Orion and that was only because the belt was so astonishingly bright.

Her breath was painting the air, she was shivering, and her teeth were beginning to click. "It's very late, Dad," she said. "The sky is beautiful and all, but why don't you come inside?"

Looking up was apparently making his head spin. He took a sudden, shaky step, then sat down on the porch. "And just listen to them, Irini. Can you hear? Thank God for all their little bell-like voices."

Irini closed her eyes and stilled her teeth in order to listen. She willed herself to be warm. She could do that, but only briefly, so it was rarely worth the effort.

She heard water. Every few winters or so, the falls froze. You knew immediately when this happened. Once it woke Irini up from a dream—that eerie absence of noise. Otherwise, you always had to listen around the water. So she listened harder and perhaps there was another sound underneath, something at the very bottom of her hearing. Not a discrete or sequential sound, not a tune, not bell-like voices, but the way bells might sound if there were so many of them that they overlapped and ran together. A soft sound, continuous and watery, like the falls, but lower. The stars were sighing.

Of course, they were so very far away. Those sighs could have been explosions—deafening, deadening, screaming—but by the time the sound reached Magrit how would she know the difference?

And maybe she didn't hear it at all. But just the thought of hearing it filled her with a blurry sort of longing. She kept her eyes closed and a stream of stars poured over her.

"Of course, they were even better during the blackouts," her father said. "Remember? What stars we had then." He got with some difficulty to his feet. "Thank God for darkness," he said. "Thank God for a sun that goes down."

My mother told me the story of Cassiopeia once when I couldn't get to sleep. Cassiopeia was a beautiful queen, she told me. But she angered the gods of the sea, who sent tidal waves and typhoons and sea monsters against her kingdom. To stop the devastation, they demanded the highest price imaginable. They demanded her daughter. At the last possible moment Perseus saved the girl, and in gratitude Cassiopeia allowed him to marry her. The ending was a happy one. Perseus was handsome and royal and desperately in love. When Cassiopeia died, she was turned into stars.

Like all my mother's stories, this one was long on love and short on detail. There is more to the story. If I were telling it I would point out that Cassiopeia's great crime was pride. She had claimed to be more beautiful than the sea nymphs.

Her daughter was named Andromeda. When Andromeda was, as per instructions, chained to a rock in the ocean, her mother and father came and lamented over her. A great sea monster with a serpent's head rose up before them. It opened its enormous mouth; green saltwater and white foam flowed out.

It was just then that Perseus appeared. He was wearing Mercury's shoes, early precursors to the Nike line, so his hang time was birdlike. And all he asked was that the daughter be given to him instead, along with a suitable dowry. There was no time to quibble. The foam from the monster's mouth had reached Andromeda's feet.

There they were—the guilty mother, the desperate father, the eager monster, Perseus hovering, Andromeda, her maidenly beauty set off to its best advantage by chains, and the sea. Yes, said Cassiopeia. Please.

So it was a happy ending, just as my mother said, although the wedding party was a raucous one, spoiled by some unpleasantness on the part of Andromeda's previous boyfriend. Half the guests had to be turned to stone. Eventually, Cassiopeia landed in the heavens, but she still spends half her time on her head as a reminder to be humble. The sea nymphs have long memories.

Which is why you hardly ever hear women claiming to be more beautiful than the sea nymphs anymore. Women used to say, I can weave better than Minerva, or Minerva's hair is not so beautiful as mine, or my fourteen children are better than Latona's two. Not, I need to lose ten pounds before I buy a bathing suit, or I hate my thighs. Those ancient women had some self-esteem.

In fact, it must have been an enormous problem, since so many cautionary tales were generated against it. Just try to picture an entire society of boastful women. Who's doing the dishes? Cleaning the toilets? Nursing the sick? How amazed the ancients would be if they could wander for a bit through any contemporary bookstore, reading the current stack of be-your-own-goddess books.

Irini did know one exceptionally confident young woman. This was her next-door neighbor, Tracy May. There was no accounting for Tracy's assurance. She was a middle child in an all-female family. There had been a silent sort of father around there somewhere, before he went to work at Willow Run, where, corrupted by the salary and the city, he fell in love with a barrel-shaped, black-haired woman who owned her very own gas station and he never remembered Tracy's birthday again.

So nothing in the family dynamic explained Tracy's confidence. In fact, the three May sisters picked at each other constantly. They were all attractive, and Tracy was no exception, neither was she exceptional. She had the same coffee-colored hair as her sisters, maybe even thicker, but she was not as large and toothsome as her older sister, nor as petite and wholesome as her younger. Her nose humped slightly and her lips were thin enough you'd think she'd notice. At school she was an average student, and in the Kitchen she was an average cook. She had tried out for the lead in the school play for three years and for three years it had gone to Arlys Fossum.

Arlys Fossum was so shy she was the last person you would think of for the lead, but she was strikingly pretty with red-blond hair and light blue eyes and fragile, perfect skin. And even in the first grade, when Arlys could hardly read at all, Miss Curry, the teacher, praised her for the way she read with expression. You only had to give her something to say and she metamorphosed into someone you didn't know. That last year she'd sung "How Are Things in Gloccamorra" and there hadn't been a dry eye in all Magrit. Tracy was given a part with no dancing and no talking. So there was no reason for Tracy to feel particularly good about herself, but she always did. This is a gift worth having.

"I met a new man yesterday. Right here in Magrit," Tracy told Irini. They were working with flour blends in the Kitchen. Henry Collins had the ad copy from Bisquick posted to inspire them. "He: You're a wizard, honey. Boy, look at that biscuit. Mother can't match that! She: Yes, she can . . . if she uses BISQUICK! Just think, darling . . . all you do is add milk or water!" It was the boiled down essence of all Henry's aspirations. Bisquick was modern, fast, and foolproof. She was happy, He was happy. If only Bisquick hadn't belonged to one of Margaret Mill's competitors.

Outside the window the sun blinked the bits of persistent old snow on and off like a neon sign. "He had lunch at the Paree Nuits Supper Club and then he went bowling. He got four strikes," said Tracy. Bowling had come only recently to Magrit when Norma Baldish had hammered and sanded in a single lane, behind Moodey's grocery store. You still had to set up your own pins, which was a definite disincentive to knocking any down.

As for the Paree Nuits Supper Club—it was half an hour out of town and most of Magrit gave it a miss. Maggie Collins's heartfelt and often published belief was that those secret French flavors were produced by not washing the pots between meals. Maggie was a fastidious woman. And Magrit was innocent enough to believe that the food at the Paree Nuits was French. The club stayed in business because of its owners, a Mr. and Mrs. Blount. Mr. Blount was only five feet tall. Mrs. Blount was six foot four. Mr. Blount cooked and Mrs. Blount served. People drove all the way from Chicago just to see them. The food was quite incidental.

"What did he have for lunch?" Irini asked. She was being sarcastic, but Tracy missed it.

"Coq au vin. He once had Hunt Club sandwiches with the Countess de Forceville of New York. He told me. His name is Tommy. He works for the railroads. He was an ensign in the Navy."

"Thomas Holcrow?" Irini asked.

"A really dreamy guy," said Tracy. "I can just see him in whites. Like a magazine ad. But I had to back him off a bit. You know what I mean."

Sometimes Irini was charmed by Tracy's confidence, sometimes she was irritated. This time she was neither. She was too busy trying to think. He'd been drunk. Had he been young? Had he been dreamy? Like a magazine ad? Not so she noticed. But it would be like her, it would be so like her to beat some really dreamy guy arm-wrestling before she saw how really dreamy he was. "When I met him he was having the vin without the coq," she said. "I backed him off a bit, too. I backed him way off." Now Irini was in a bad mood. She put her hands into the bowl to mix. There wasn't enough flour. Her hands came out in mitts of dough.

"What do you think he's doing in sleepy old Magrit?" Tracy asked. Tracy was dying to go to Paris, but not the postwar Paris, where no one had enough to eat and the streets were filled with orphans and collaborators. Some Parisian mirage she had gotten out of a radio play or magazine story before the war. Some place where women wore their hair in a curtain over one eye and left the dark red imprint of their lips on their cigarettes. Some place where the women all had pasts and the men loved them helplessly in spite of it. The real Paris.

She would have settled for Detroit. "He doesn't know a soul. He told me. He's living in the room over Bumps. He can hardly be on vacation. In April? In Magrit?" Tracy held out her hands. "I gave myself a manicure. Deep purple. What do you think?"

Irini rubbed her own hands together to clean them. "Deep," she agreed. "Try not to leave any of it in the dough."

Fanny May, Tracy's older sister, came into the Kitchen. "Tracy," she said. "Are you the one who tested the recipe for Rhubarb Grunt?"

"It was requested," Tracy May said. "A Tuckahoe housewife."

"Did you put pepper in it? Several teaspoons of cayenne pepper?"

"No one would put pepper in grunt."

"Sort of a ridiculous name, isn't it?" said Irini.

"It's a kind of cobbler," Tracy told her.

"And that's a ridiculous name, too. So shoe-ish."

"Well, it was published with seven teaspoons of cayenne pepper. Can't you be more careful? Now we'll have to run a mea culpa for Maggie. You know how he hates that."

"I don't think I was the one who made the mistake," said Tracy. "I very much doubt it."

"And what do you have on your hands?" Fanny asked Tracy. "You look like you've been killing ticks."

This may have been the beginning of Maggie's troubles, though Irini didn't notice at the time or remember it later. Probably it was the innocent misprint it appeared to be.

"Cobble, cobble," said Irini. "Grunt, grunt."

4

After work Fanny drove Irini to Collins House, where Ada Collins was giving a small dinner party. Claire Kinser had gotten the day off from the Kitchen to work in the kitchen. When the household had been large, when the children from Henry's first marriage had still occupied the upstairs bedrooms and later when the grandchildren had come back, Claire's mother, Rose, had cooked all the Collins's meals. The Kinsers were an old Upper Magrit family; Rose had braved considerable censure to take the job. But now when Claire was hired on special occasions, it was accepted as an inherited post and no one even thought about it. Irini had been asked to help serve and clean up.

In the summer Irini would have walked and enjoyed walking. This April was too dark, cold, and soggy. She knew, from listening to the radio, that spring had arrived in other places. In Radioland June was busting out all over. But in Magrit, on this particular evening, a fog had risen off the river and rolled over the roads. It was as if Magrit had risen right into the clouds.

Nothing slowed Fanny down. She wiped a small circle on the glass with her mitten and accelerated through a puddle that was just starting its nightly freeze. Ice and mud hit the windshield. Fanny flipped on the wipers, diluting the mud and smearing it around. Irini couldn't see at all, but there was no one else on the road. In 1947 there were no seat belts to remind her that riding in cars was a dangerous thing to do.

They hit a new spring pothole. "Ouch," Fanny said, on behalf of the car. "Time for Norma to put away the snowplow and get out here with her little bucket of tar." Fanny never touched the brakes until she reached the Collins House driveway.

Collins House was in lower Lower Magrit at some distance from the rest of the town and was unlikely to get closer, since Henry owned all the land between. No place else in Magrit was anything like Collins House. It was actually fenced in wrought iron as if it were an estate. On the grounds there were statues of naked cupids with tiny, elegant penises that really pissed, and a goldfish pond Henry always said was shaped like a cereal bowl. Round. Irini let herself in the front gate by lifting the lion's head handle.

She spoke soothingly to the dogs, who'd come running at the sound of Fanny's car. There were seven dogs in all, although it seemed like more. They were a pack of orphans, an exultation of dirt, saliva, smells, and noise. They varied in shape and size and color, but matched in temperament; they all had hybrid vigor and they had it in spades. One had an obvious corgi heritage; another, Dane, another, boxer; there was an unearthly Pomerian–Boston terrier mix. Henry had picked them up at the pound for an experiment on the effects of nutrition on learning.

If he'd had his way, there would have been many, many more. The scientific method required large samples and large control groups: any experiment was valueless without them. But Ada was adamant. You could not bring a dog home, spend six months teaching it to beg for grains, and then simply return it. Any dog they took was theirs to keep.

In point of fact none of the dogs had been able to learn to beg. The corgi distracted Irini, while the Dane immobilized her, while the boxer drooled on the toes of her boots. They were all sporting new collars, the very latest thing, collars treated with chemicals to kill fleas. In 1947 people still thought the war against fleas was winnable.

"Very scientific," Henry had told the girls in the Kitchen the day the collars arrived. "Very exciting. They actually turn the animal's blood into a flea-sized dose of poison. Wouldn't it be something if we could do the same thing for humans vis-à-vis mosquitoes?"

"I don't want poisonous blood," Fanny had objected. "I'm so funny that way."

"Nonsense," said Henry. "Would you prefer malaria?"

"Are those my choices?"

"It may become a matter of us or them. You put all the people and animals of the world, and I mean the fish, too, the gray whales and the giant squid, put them on one end of a large teeter-totter and all the insects on the other, and the insect side would be heavier. It's a scientific fact."

"Has it been done?"

"It's been done with statistics."

"I don't see how," said Fanny, but quietly, underneath Henry's hearing. He had a strong need to explain anything anyone didn't understand. He couldn't seem to control it; it was almost Pavlovian.

Although Henry insisted the dogs were now flealess, they were still scratching the old bites. Irini was grateful. It prevented them from closing in and finishing her off. The pungency of their collars rose even above the odor of wet fur. She picked her way over the icy gravel toward the house.

Inside more science was running amok. Henry had built an ant farm in an old aquarium so that he could study the effects of nutrition on social organization at the most purified level. He'd kept it in the dining room so that he could observe and take notes while he ate.

Sometime in the night, rather than eat their cereal, the ants had made a ladder of their little bodies so that some could climb over the others and escape into the kitchen. The escapees were in the process of stocking a new home in the pantry wall with sugar granules when Ada got up in the morning. She had mopped and scoured, but this had merely moved the ants around and cleaned them up. "Just try to keep from serving them tonight," she'd finally told Claire.

Claire was a tall, thin girl with a high forehead, thin, feathery hair, and a pronounced rosiness that flamed across her cheeks when she was embarrassed. "I'm peppering everything lightly," Claire said to Irini, who was at the sink, washing the traces of dog off her hands and aiming the stream so as to send a few dozen ants down the drain as well. "That should cover us for any small, brown specks in the food. We're having lamb." She consulted a stained, handwritten recipe. "Maybe Norma can get out tomorrow and fumigate."

Irini had smelled the lamb the moment she walked in. Lamb and bacon. Claire was the best cook at the Mill. She was five years older than Irini, had been briefly engaged to a soldier she met in Detroit. One week she was showing everyone her ring—a modest affair with a diamond chip—and his picture—a blond man, about Claire's age, with an embarrassed smile—and the next week her hand was bare. Fanny took her out for drinks and to talk, because that was Fanny's role and because you could tell her anything; she was never shocked and she never told anyone else. The rest of them were left to imagine the worst. Broken hearts, previous marriages, terminal illnesses, unsightly wounds, unnatural demands. The world is rich with tragic possibilities. It would have been nice to know.

Irini moved along the stove, lifting lids and looking underneath them. Small boiled potatoes with ham. Carrots in cream and dill. And on the breakfast table a salad, an exotic innovation whose ingredients were imported from California. Irini wasn't sure when to serve it. She would have to ask Mrs. Ada.

Collins House had the very latest model of gas range. The oven was insulated, ventilated, heat-controlled, and automatic time-controlled. It buzzed to tell Claire the pie was done. She lifted it out and set it to cool on the cutting board. Real mincemeat, made of spiced venison.

Norma Baldish had taken the deer herself, one shot in the head, from a stand of pin oaks by Upper Magrit. She was an enthusiastic hunter. One wall at Bumps was filled with Norma's antlers.

At Christmas the customers embellished them with tinsel, beer bottles, and Santa hats. It was Irini's father's idea. "Camouflage. I'm just hoping the reindeer won't guess what they are," he said, finishing off a bottle for purely ornamental reasons. "I'm just hoping no one here was a special friend of Blitzen's."

Norma Baldish hated it. She refused to wire them for lights and no one else in Magrit was capable of it. "It makes it look like I killed them all during their Christmas party," she complained to Irini once. "How sporting is that?"

"Who're the guests tonight?" Irini asked Claire.

"Guest. Only one. A lady journalist from the *Tribune*. I think Mrs. Ada went to school with her mother. I saw her arrive. She looked nice."

This meant nothing, coming from Claire. Claire thought everyone looked nice. To think someone unattractive would have been cruel, and she had the kindest heart imaginable. She was fidgeting over her pots and preparations, and Irini concluded that she was nervous about the lamb. It was surprising that Claire had even attempted it. Everyone knew that Mr. Henry was very fussy about lamb.

Claire cut a small, sickly hothouse tomato into the thinnest slices imaginable and fanned them over the top of the salad. She crumbled bacon onto them. Irini put on an apron embroidered with violets. Radish roses in ice water bloomed at her elbow. Crumbs of dried mint lay on the cutting board next to the pie. She picked them up, looking closely to make sure they were mint, and rubbed them between her palms. She opened her hands and closed her eyes to smell. She had a moment of instinctive contentment brought on by the warmth and the smells and a woman at the stove.

Working all day in the Kitchen made Irini reluctant to cook when she got home. She and her father lived on crackers and canned soups, cold sandwiches, and breakfast cereal. Irini was not a cook herself. But she was something of a connoisseur when it came to kitchens.

Ada entered the room. "Twenty minutes," she said to Claire. "Henry is just finishing one of his stories. His bear hunting story. Maybe twenty-five minutes. Irini, thank you for coming. Claire, dear, try to keep the lamb warm, but don't let it dry." She smoothed her hair, turned to leave. "His mother was just a whiz at lamb," she reminded them.

In fact, Henry's mother was the original Margaret Collins. She'd been a superb cook whose recipes no one could duplicate. She cooked by impulse and intuition. "Use a handful," she might have said when pressed for an amount. If asked to be precise:

"Scoop flour in your hand, palm up. Don't close your fist.

"A lump of butter the size of a walnut.

"Enough water to moisten, but you don't want it wet.

"Cook till thick, but don't overcook, it'll clot. Reduce the heat if you have to.

"Stir it till it looks right.

"You'll know when it's done." When she died she took the world's most perfect lamb sauce with her to the grave.

She was Henry's inspiration. Imagine a world where every woman was able to cook the way his mother had. Imagine his mother, only make her more stylish, beautiful, but in a regal rather than a sexual way. Make her more modern than his mother, certainly. Make her immortal. And maybe just a little bit more forgiving than his mother had been, though what was he thinking? His mother had certainly loved him. Why else cook all those wonderful meals?

It was unclear whether Henry's mother's namesake had children or not. "Ask Mr. Henry sometime if Maggie is married," Fanny May once told Irini. "It puts him in such a spot. He can't stand to think of her as a spinster, but he can't imagine a man worthy of her, either. And it makes him jealous. He doesn't know what to say."

"Try the mint sauce, Irini," said Claire. "Tell me if it's all right."

Irini put a finger in the sauce and licked it dry. It was delicious—faintly sweet, perfectly fresh. "It's wonderful," she said. "Everything looks wonderful. Do you want me to test anything else?"

"Here." Claire put together a plate for Irini. "Eat. You've got thirty minutes, at least, if it's the bear hunting story, and this way you won't be serving and starving at the same time."

The sauce was even better on the lamb. The potatoes crumbled invitingly under Irini's fork. She moved them into the range of the cream and dill. The only things she didn't eat were the salad, which was too carefully arranged, and the pie, which was too hot.

"They're going to love everything," Irini said. She was trying to think of a way to turn the conversation to the new man in town, but really what was there to say? He bowled four strikes and ate coq au vin?

With the end of rationing, what the American palate craved most was meat. Roasted, baked, braised, stewed, fried, gravied, ground, chipped, creamed, sliced onto toast, wrapped in pie crusts, stuffed into peppers, boiled into soups, dipped into horseradish, smothered with caramelized onions, pounded and breaded, but best of all, plain. Meat, with salt. Meat, dripping with butter and blood. Great, glistening slabs of meat. In 1947 Americans ate 155 pounds of meat per person. It was more than a craving. It was a personal best.

So the Collins's dinner guest, Miss Schaap, was all the more a surprise. "No. Thank you. I don't eat meat," she told Irini, who stood to her left, offering the serving platter. "Not since India." Miss Schaap was a middle-aged woman, plainly dressed, with, contrary to Claire's description, pinched, ferrety features. Irini had never seen anyone anywhere who looked more carnivorous. Miss Schaap turned to Ada. "Ahimsa," she said as if this explained something. "It's one of Mr. Gandhi's principles. It means no harm. It includes not eating meat."

"Oh dear," said Ada. Irini looked over the serving board. Bacon in the salad. Ham in the potatoes. Perhaps the carrots in cream?

"Or dairy," said Miss Schaap. "No dairy either."

"Mother's lamb sauce had a kind of thymy taste. That's what made it so different. You would have loved it, Miss Schaap," Henry Collins said. He was being the host, which meant good-humored and avuncular. If not attentive. But let's be fair. The man had trouble hearing. "Irini, bring that over."

He'd slicked his hair with hair oil in honor of a company dinner.

Irini held the plate for him and looked right down the glistening strands to the freckled scalp beneath.

Ada glanced at Miss Schaap, then took a single, compromised slice of lamb for herself. "Irini, go and tell Claire our guest doesn't eat meat. See what she can do."

"I don't want to be any trouble. I can have the potatoes. I'll just pick the ham out."

Irini brought the potatoes. "Don't they look delicious?" Miss Schaap said politely. They made a small pile on her otherwise empty plate. She separated the chunks of ham into a second pile, picking through the potatoes with her fork.

"Irini, go tell Claire," said Ada.

"Please don't. I don't want anything special. I love potatoes."

"Starch is for shirts," Henry observed. He turned to Ada. "This sauce is nothing like Mother's. Hers had just the merest hint of thyme."

"It tastes fine to me. Just slightly thymy. It's delicious." Ada took a big, showy, irritated bite. "Your taste buds have atrophied. That happens when a person hits your age. There's thyme in there. Maybe your mother left something else out of the recipe. A certain kind of woman does that on purpose." She turned to Miss Schaap and her tone brightened accordingly. "I thought it was just cows they didn't eat in India."

"I thought they ate whatever they could get," said Henry jovially. "Irini, fetch me the carrots."

"There are holy men in India who sweep the sidewalk ahead of them with every step so they don't accidentally crush a bug. I've seen them."

"Do tell," said Ada. "Irini. Go and speak to Claire."

"Nothing more for me, please. I'm getting rather full. They were the best potatoes. Anyway I never eat much. Mr. Gandhi fasts to achieve clarity of thought."

"There must be a lot of clear thinkers in India," said Henry. "Though in all seriousness, I must tell you none of my experiments would support Mr. Gandhi's hypothesis. I am interested in vegetarianism, though. Apes are vegetarians. And, since we're merely their descendants, it's likely our nutritional needs are similar. It wouldn't hurt us at all to eat less meat and more cereal. I once wrote a pamphlet entitled, *Feeding the Ape Within You*. Now this"—he indicated the salad—"this is cow food. We're not so closely related to the cow."

"I've been reading about satyagraha," said Ada.

"Have you?" Miss Schaap's voice expressed pleasure and definite surprise. She put down her fork and smiled. Her teeth were little and pointed. "Have you really? What have you read?"

"Well, Mr. Schweitzer, of course. And some of the campaigns."

"Bombay?"

"The thirties. Satyagraha and taxation."

"Please pass the salt," said Henry.

"You must eat something else," said Ada. "You must let me ask the cook."

"Really, I'm fine. If you made something extra I wouldn't eat it." The two women looked at each other. "I'm saving room for dessert," Miss Schaap insisted.

5

Irini's father was supposed to pick her up around ten. Claire had already left, sometime between the salad and the dessert, having thoughtfully piled the pots into the sink to soak. It was a good thing Claire was not there to see the plates come back. She would have taken it badly, all that time spent over the stove, all that food left on the plates. She would have seen no excuse for not eating. Claire wasn't interested in politics. "I can't see that they have much to do with people," she had once told Mrs. Ada.

"Wouldn't you give just anything to live in a nicer world?" Mrs. Ada had asked back; this conversation had taken place during the war, before they knew about the concentration camps and the bomb, back when Irini had still hoped the world was a pretty nice place.

Ada already knew better. Ada was a political animal, as she was the first to admit. Maybe the only one they had in Magrit.

Irini scraped the leftovers off the lamb platter, uncovering a painted pattern of California poppies. She could give the leftovers to the dogs, unless Henry was still monitoring their food. If he made her weigh and log each helping, then she would forget the whole thing. The dogs could just have their Sweetwheats.

A line of ants led to the uncut pie. Irini fetched the sponge. Some of them had made it up onto the crust. Irini brushed the piecrust off with her hand. "We're the Seabees of the navy," she sang, the way an ant would sing it, like John Wayne on helium. "We can build or we can fight."

She swept down the line with the sponge, but when she turned it over and she saw all those bodies, she felt guilty. And then the song had made them rather heroic. She shook them into the scrapings as compensation and filled the dishpan with soap and water. She didn't mind doing dishes much. She thought of it as an activity faintly related to the bubble bath, which was, after all, the height of luxury. The water was just as warm and the smell of dish soap was as nice. Glasses first, of course. Pots and pans last.

Irini liked the sound the glasses made when they touched one another under water. She didn't worry about her hands, although clearly she ought to have, you only had to read the ads in any magazine. Maggie recommended olive oil as a cheap way to deal with dish damage, but it made your hands so slippery you couldn't turn doorknobs or fasten buttons for at least a half an hour. It's surprisingly hard to find a half an hour when you don't need to do one of those things.

By the time Irini got to the pots, and no amount of soap and water could make this part of the process pleasurable, it was ten after ten. Miss Schaap had left. Ada and Henry had gone upstairs. Fifteen minutes later, the dishes were back on the shelves, the counter was clean, the trash was trashed, the food was wrapped and stowed in the refrigerator. Irini had run the carpet sweeper over the dining-room rug and rubbed the tabletop with a special dust cloth treated with wax. She couldn't think of anything else to be done.

She left the kitchen and went to sit on the top step of the stairs. She couldn't actually see the road from there, even on a clear night, but the headlights from any passing car would reflect into the high mirror over the fireplace in the dining room, and she would see that. The clock over the fireplace chimed once for the half hour.

In a story we can make a half an hour go very quickly. Irini waited a long time. At about eleven, Ada reappeared. Ada was wearing a long satin nightgown, a chenille robe, and bed socks. The sheen of cold cream was on her face. She sat down next to Irini, smelling of powder and soap. It was chilly, but Irini wasn't the sort of girl you put your arm around easily, and Ada wasn't the sort of woman who would do this, even if Irini were.

Irini admired Ada, because she had held up so well compared to Henry, but in fact she was more than twenty years younger. Irini knew this, but didn't entirely comprehend it; they were both so old.

Ada had spent her married life in a sort of public isolation. She was too young to socialize gracefully with her husband's contemporaries. When people her own age came to the house, they generally came to visit Emily, Henry's daughter, or Oscar, Henry's son. Although Ada had once been a friend of Emily's, there was no way to include the stepmother. It was too awkward all around.

The town didn't know what to make of her. She was deaf to appeals from the church and the school, who felt that, as the mill owner's wife, she had an example to set, a standard to maintain. At the wedding she had been so shy she hardly spoke, and in her sixties she was still a quiet woman, but this was probably not so much a function of shyness as it was of lack of practice. She was an avid reader, which is almost the same thing as having friends.

She'd enjoyed the war, although of course no one could admit to this. There'd been so many things to feel deeply about and be part of. She'd papered one wall of her studio with maps, positioned colored overlays to represent troop movements. Black for the Axis, blue for the Allies, red for Russia. Battles were shown by overlap. A lot of this information was classified, so she was only guessing.

Embarrassed by the bad faith of the Second Front negotiations, Ada had briefly converted to communism. Within Magrit she had constituted a cell of one. Too many people remembered or had been told how Leon Czolgosz, who used to live right over in Seney, went down to Cleveland in 1901 to hear Emma Goldman speak and then straight on to Buffalo, where he shot President McKinley dead.

Still, Ada's communism surprised and upset no one. Ada was an artist, and Magrit was sophisticated enough to know that there is little distance between art and Marxism. Ada's specialty was painting flowers on china.

On her latest serving set, the flowers were falling from their stems, burned into ashes. She'd been in a kind of depression ever since the bomb. Henry simply couldn't understand it. He tried to cheer her up with tidbits of scientific prediction. The National Education Association was telling high school students that atomic energy would save them from cancer and heart disease as well as infectious diseases. "Most of the current generation can expect to live to be a hundred," Henry read to Ada. This was good news!

But the bomb had turned Ada implacably against science and scientists. She was confusing the message with the messenger. She was misunderstanding the political neutrality of technology. She was starting to speak to Henry with less affection and more impatience. There was a tiny little fault line running through the marriage.

Ada had become an advocate of the World Government Movement. But this was large, abstract, and unlikely. She couldn't put her heart into it.

"You don't have to wait with me," Irini said. "I'm sure it'll only be a few minutes."

"I don't mind," said Ada. She rubbed the cold cream deeper into her cheeks. "I don't think I could sleep anyway. Miss Schaap has really set me thinking."

"What would you think about getting an ape?" Henry asked. This was just the sort of thing Mr. Henry would ask. Exuberance, my mother called it. Joyousness. Money and a lively brain.

If it wasn't heedlessness. Henry stepped out of the shadows of the landing, found a place to sit, one stair down. He was very elegant, in striped pajamas with navy piping. His ears were red from his bedtime ablutions and bloomed on either side of his head. "Not to keep, you understand. I've been thinking of borrowing an ape so that I can run some studies on it."

"I have a kitchen full of ants," said Ada. "What if they were apes?"

"Just one ape," said Henry. "Of course, only one."

"Ants I don't want, but ants I don't want to hurt," said Ada. Ada recognized a bargaining chip when she saw one. "It puts me in a difficult position. I'm sure you can see that."

"A female ape," said Henry. "A docile ape with a pleasing personality. You would like her."

During Ada's communist period she had tried to get the girls at the mill unionized. Henry had been genuinely astonished. "I never exploited anyone in my life," he'd said. He'd had some justification for the statement. He took a paternal interest in the workers at the mill, was a soft touch for hardship loans and helpful without being asked in cases of unexpected medical costs. He built his enormous house far away from the falls and the mill, but he hosted a Christmas party for the mill workers in it every year, complete with generous Christmas bonuses and free of alcoholic beverages. The Collins children and grandchildren attended the public school along with everyone else, at least until they turned twelve, and then they were sent back East to be finished.

The issue had lost its political urgency but remained in Ada's mind as an irritating defeat. Or perhaps she wanted to do something for Irini, sitting on the steps with her arms around her knees, and her head on her arms, staring into the shadow made by her own legs so that no one could see her face. The fireplace clock chimed the half hour.

"I just can't see my way clear to an ape," Ada said. "The girls at the mill should be unionized."

Thus opening negotiations. Mr. Henry caught on immediately. "I can't see my way to a union," he said. "I'm not antiunion, as you well know, but I honestly can't see the need for our girls. They would benefit more from some activity that gave them fresh air and exercise."

"They could picket," said Ada.

"Or they could play baseball," said Henry. "I could provide equipment. They could use the school field."

Irini lifted her head.

"I could see a benefit to baseball."

There was a long pause, while they all thought about this. The longer the pause went on, the more benefits Henry could see.

The first was exercise. This was obvious. This didn't even need to be said.

The second was publicity. Henry Collins had always taken an active role in marketing decisions. He had been quick to see the possibilities of radio time, and wrote the Sweetwheats' jingle himself, with input from the Kitchen staff:

> *Every mother's day starts*
> *With Sweetwheats for her sweethearts.*
> *Mother really shows she's smart*
> *With Sweetwheats for her sweethearts.*

But in the forties there was no doubt that the breakfast battle of the airwaves was being easily won by the Breakfast of Champions. A team of attractive girls eating Sweetwheats daily and exhibiting an innocent, healthy glow might be just the ticket.

Third, if there was a team, then the team could travel. This would give Margaret Mill girls a chance to meet prospective husbands. Marriage was less and less likely for girls in Magrit and they were all painfully aware of it. Magrit was suffering from a drastically reduced male population.

Only Jimmy Tarken and Mr. Floyd were actually lost and only Jimmy in the actual fighting. Geb Floyd died in a war-related incident, on VE Day while trying to set off a celebratory fireworks display. Geb had survived the First World War, but had developed a taste for gunpowder. He had mourned Pearl Harbor with the whirlybirds. He had solemnized the Normandy Invasion by sending up seven rockets containing seven hooded rats, all male, in parachute harnesses.

All seven floated back down, and were caught again, easy as could be, because of the parachutes. Then it was back to the daily grind of exercise wheels and mazes and nutritional studies. Eventually they came to look back on their wartime experiences with nostalgia. "Those were the days," they told their children. "Weren't those the days."

No one knew what Geb had planned for VE Day, but Geb had already entitled it "The Triumph of Law and Reason over the Forces of War and Chaos," so it was obviously going to be big. Just before noon, Irini's collie, Tweed, was suddenly strangely agitated, whining and following Irini about and trying to keep her from going outside. Then there was a lot of smoke and noise as if the Floyd place had taken a direct hit. The white noontime sky sparkled for five solid minutes with golden petals and silver flakes. Irini watched from her backyard. She was embarrassed later to remember how much she had enjoyed the display, troubled enough to confess it to her father.

"I'm sure Geb would have wanted that," he told her. "You just think of that enjoyment as your final tribute to a great master."

The sonic blast took out the back window of the Baldish's truck and destroyed every bottle in the Törngren's medicine cabinet. No body was ever found. It was a miracle that the kitchen, and Mrs. Floyd in it, were spared.

Today there is a monument to Jimmy out in front of the copy shop, one solemn stone with his name on it and the words: MAGRIT REMEMBERS, but the plain fact is that Magrit remembers Geb Floyd better. There is always the Fourth of July to remind them of both.

The rest of the Magrit men married Filipino or Italian girls, or went to college on the G.I. Bill and were never going to be mill workers or marry mill workers again. Even those too old or unfit to be drafted had gone to work in the Willow Run bomber factory or the Rouge Plant in Dearborn. The salaries were big there; they stayed on. Magrit had those tearful, joyful, awkward homecomings, just like the ones they saw in *The Best Years of Our Lives,* but the boys flew into their mother's arms and right back out again. The demographics in postwar Magrit resembled those in postwar Russia.

For those members of the baseball team who did not find husbands, travel was broadening and provided one with memories and photo albums. Memories and photo albums were good for everyone, but they were imperative for old and unmarried women.

Fourth and finally, Walter Collins, the male heir, could be enticed home to manage the team. Milling was not romantic enough to tempt the Collins children. They had been happy to take the money Margaret Mill provided and use it to live in London or purchase government positions or learn to fly airplanes. Tom Baldish was helping manage the mill now, but Henry refused to die until it was safely back in the family. And yet he had not produced a grandchild to whom the wheat laurel could be passed.

Among the grandchildren, Walter was his favorite. Walter's dad was Henry's youngest son, Oscar, a fitful entrepreneur who appeared on Henry's doorstep from time to time requesting seed money. A fortune could be made by the man who had a product everyone wanted, he told Henry once. He had figured this out all by himself. And this was the beautiful part—you didn't even have to invent this product. All you had to do was market it. The difficulty came in knowing what this product was. Oscar was looking for it everywhere, except at Margaret Mill. His last fantasy had been computer sales. Henry had to show him right there in black and white how the president of IBM had said there was an international market for maybe five computers, tops.

But Walter was the dividend that made it all worthwhile. Walter was a second lieutenant in the Army Air Force, specially trained at the Scripps Institute of Oceanography in California as a wave forecaster. He had just been ordered to Japan to forecast a landing there when the Hiroshima and Nagasaki bombings made the landing unnecessary. Because he had not gone overseas, his discharge was delayed a year. Perhaps he was disappointed not to see Japan. Perhaps he thought a wave forecaster could have little future in Magrit. Whatever the reason, he had not come home.

Walter had always loved baseball. If he would agree to manage the team, then soon he would be managing the Kitchen. If he managed the Kitchen, he could mature by the time of Mr. Baldish's retirement into the manager for the mill itself. Under fresh, energetic leadership it could be brought back up to capacity, back up to prewar productivity. He could live right there in Collins House in the meantime. And if he wouldn't coach the team, then Norma Baldish would have to.

The wheat crown from the mill entrance could be reproduced on the uniform pockets.

"Wouldn't it be nice to have Walter home?" Ada said, glancing Irini's way.

"Of course, I would want the girls eating Sweetwheats," said Henry. "We'd have to be pretty strict about that. We wouldn't know how to assess their victories otherwise." He stood and shook out his pajama legs. "Irini, let's have that pie now, shall we? Let's repair to the kitchen for a piece of pie."

Irini cut two pieces, looking carefully at each for ants. If they were there, they were cunningly disguised as cinnamon. She poured three glasses of milk and sat with Ada and Henry at the breakfast table.

"Nine girls on a baseball team," said Ada. "Nine girls, all eating Sweetwheats. Isn't that better than one ape?"

"The ape could be a mascot," said Henry. "A smallish ape. An ape would really fill the seats."

One minute there was no baseball team; there was only the ape, the union, and some ants; the next minute he had reasoned it into being, created it out of the sheer force of logic. The Sweetwheat Sweethearts. He was obviously smitten. There was no reason for Ada to waste the bargaining power of the ape on it now. "I've been thinking of going to India," she said. "I just have a feeling that the things Mr. Gandhi is doing in India are going to be important even to us here in Magrit."

Henry looked stricken. Ada wasn't Maggie, of course, but he missed her dreadfully whenever she was gone. He took a swallow of milk, a big bite of pie. "There's a kind of sharp taste to the filling," he complained. "Mother's pie never had that bitter taste."

"Have a piece, Irini," said Ada. "It's delicious," but Irini said no, thank you. The clock struck twelve.

Maggie Collins writes: "There is no doubt that the war will take its toll on the marriage prospects of young American women. With that in mind, there are things a determined girl can do to improve her chances. Those occupations least likely to marry remain librarians and teachers. Polls have recently confirmed what has long been suspected; most men do not want brainy women. Stewardesses have turned out to be that occupation blessed most often with marriage. The key elements appear to be uniforms and travel."

6

Irini learned to play ball by playing it in Arlys Fossum's back-yard. She learned to play catch from her father. He bought her a mitt for her sixth birthday, showed her how to oil it a little at a time. "It was so huge my hand would slip right out," my mother said. "It was like an oven mitt, like a clown's shoe. Only it smelled so wonderful. The best smell in the world. Better than White Shoulders perfume. Better than vanilla extract. Better than a new book or the minute before it rains. Neatsfoot oil and leather. Leather and freshly cut grass."

They tossed the ball around on weekends and her father took to inviting her to play whenever he had something difficult or embarrassing or female to talk to her about. "Get your mitt, darling," he'd say. "I'll throw you some pop-ups."

The word "pop-ups" was the key. If he had nothing awkward to discuss he'd say, "Let's play catch." Irini would station herself at the far end of the yard. If what he had in mind was a chat, he'd motion her in. "Not so far off, Irini. I don't want to have to shout."

"But you said you were going to throw to me."

"Pop-ups. Really high. Move in." Her father would force her even closer with his first throw. "Easy does it, Irini. Steady on. Just wait underneath it. Good girl."

He would begin to speak, all in a rush. "Now, Irini," he said one day when she was twelve. "You're growing up and there are some things your mother would want me to tell you. I wish she were here—this really should come from her, but she's not and there's no help for it. There are two kinds of people in this world. Toss the ball back now. Whoa! Nice and easy. Don't forget how close you're standing. Men and women. Sometimes they fall in love and get married, and that's what your mother would want me to talk to you about. The facts of life."

"All right."

"I'm going to pop-up to your right now. Catch it on the right. Don't move over. Good girl. Good glove. People who are in love want to touch each other. They want to hug and kiss. So the closest people can be is when they take off their clothes and lie down together. Oh, unlucky. You took your eye off the ball. You'd be surprised how much of baseball is really just a matter of keeping your eye on the ball."

"Sissy told me that's what married people did, but I didn't believe her. She said she had both her parents so she should know, but I said you and Mother would never have. I said had she ever really seen her parents and she said no, but Jimmy had. So I'm supposed to believe Jimmy Tarken. You and Mother wouldn't have ever. Would you?"

"Let's try to focus on the big picture, Irini. When I say these are the facts of life, I don't mean the facts of someone's little life, like me and your mother or the Tarkens. This is the big story, the story of humanity. Throw in a few wars and a few diseases and a few acts of God and you have the history of the world."

"I just can't believe that everyone would do that. I don't believe it. I can't believe that you believe it."

"Irini, if you're so shocked by people taking off their clothes, I'm not going to be able to finish this."

"Don't. Do you think I want to go to school tomorrow and sit at my desk and suddenly during history be thinking about Mrs. Tarken taking her clothes off with Mr. Tarken? No, thank you. Give me a really high one."

"So the man makes a lot of sperm and he makes it in his penis. You took your eye off the ball again."

"Did you say peanuts?"

"No."

"Oh. I thought you did. Throw me another high one."

"The woman makes an egg inside her body, but she needs sperm from the man. When the sperm reaches the egg, the egg can begin to grow into a baby. Every baby starts with sperm and an egg. No other way. No exceptions. On a high fly, you have time to move to the right like that, but it's a good idea to practice catching on the right so you learn to catch across your body. On a line drive you won't have the time to move."

"Do you really believe what you're telling me?"

"I'm telling you the truth."

"So you really believe the Tarkens do this. You can picture the Tarkens doing this."

"Nice catch. Let's not focus so exclusively on the Tarkens. Let's imagine a man and a woman we neither of us know. A married couple in Italy. The Giovannis. Mr. Giovanni wants to be as close to Mrs. Giovanni as he can possibly be, because he loves her."

"It's easier to picture the Italians, because of all the art. I believe you when you talk about the Italians. That doesn't mean that everybody would. I can give you the names of a dozen other people here in Magrit besides the Tarkens I don't think would, right off the top of my head."

"Softly, Irini. Underhand. I'm standing right next to you. It could be a couple in England. Mr. and Mrs. Peabody."

"I don't mind the kissing and hugging. I like to think about kissing."

"Mr. Peabody puts his penis in Mrs. Peabody's vagina. I'm sorry, Irini. I don't know any other way to say it."

"It taught me great powers of concentration," my mother said. "I was pretty resistant to the facts of life, but I did learn to keep my eye on the ball no matter what. I would face the pitcher, I would watch the ball start in her mitt, then move to her shoulder, then leave the mound, sailing right at me, getting bigger and bigger, waxing like a moon. And the infield would be riding me the whole time. Hey, batter. Swing, batter. But I wouldn't even hear it. Somewhere deep and quiet inside I would say to myself, 'Mr. Peabody,' just for the timing of it and then the ball would be leaving my bat on its way out to the fence, getting little again, but I couldn't stop to watch, I'd be running, and whatever they'd been saying, they weren't saying it anymore."

7

My parents' generation thought the great American art form was the Rodgers and Hammerstein musical. They spent their impressionable, formative years in the Depression and faced World War II as young adults, all the while sucking in frightening amounts of nicotine. Naturally they are quite mad. Or perhaps it was those ubiquitous hats pressing, always pressing down on their heads.

But then look at *their* parents. World War I as teenagers and the Depression as adults and pretty soon our grandparents had convinced themselves that there was nothing sexier than a man who could tap dance.

Irini sat in the Collins kitchen and waited for her father. She had cleared up the second set of dishes and wrapped the remains of the pie. Henry Collins nodded over the table, coming to now and then with a start, only to doze again. It embarrassed Irini. "Please don't feel you have to wait up with me." She would much rather have been by herself anyway.

"I'm not asleep," Henry said peevishly.

"No one said you were," said Ada. "Farthest thing from our minds." She invited Irini to play casino with her. She kept a deck in the drawer with the tablecloths. Ada was quite the shuffler. She did bridges and waterfalls, riffs and twists. She dealt with the speed of a much younger woman. The cards, when Irini got them, were slippery with cold cream.

Irini's hand was heavy on hearts. She waited for Ada to take her turn, wrapping her feet around the legs of the large breakfast table chair. Everything in Collins House was slightly oversized. It had a subtle, Alice-in-Wonderland effect on Irini. The longer she stayed, the smaller she got. If her father didn't show up soon, she would be a very little girl.

No one in the Collins family really fit the house. Ada was a medium-sized woman and Henry was a small man. Walter's height had been tracked on the kitchen doorjamb. The final mark put him at five feet seven inches, but the measurement was at least six years old.

Irini tapped her cards, rearranged them. Ada was building kings when they heard a car motor and the dogs barking. "There goes the game," said Ada. She managed a graceful note of disappointment. Irini was holding big casino, and *she* wasn't disappointed.

She was angry. She hadn't realized this until she stood. She was so angry her legs shook. Outside she heard the dogs coming as a unit up the gravel path.

"Car trouble?" she asked sarcastically as she opened the door. Or she started to say it. She lost the last syllable in surprise. The man at the door was Thomas Holcrow. She recognized him instantly, even though he was bundled for a blizzard and wore a red scarf across his mouth. He lowered it.

"You could say that," he said. "Your dad was having a little trouble inserting the key." He removed and replaced his hat, stooped to pick up Irini's cards where she had dropped them. "The jack of hearts," he said, handing them to her. "That's a lucky card. You're about to win." His gloved hand brushed her bare one.

She pulled back and closed the door on him. Ada was in her nightclothes and, anyway, who was Thomas Holcrow? "Don't worry," she said to Ada, loudly for Holcrow to hear. "Even if he tries to force the door I can hold it, no problem. I'm much stronger than he is." Her voice was higher than she would have liked. She had spun from anger to surprise to disappointment too quickly and now she was going to cry.

He was not forcing. "Miss Doyle," he said. "I told your father I would drive you home."

"The dogs are highly trained," said Ada. "Highly trained watch-dogs." Irini could hear the sound of panting and licking. "Who is the nice young man?" Ada asked her.

"Thomas Holcrow. He works for the railroads."

"And who are his people?"

"I don't have a clue," said Irini, in a voice that would starch shirts. "He may not even have people, for all I know."

"Your father is in the car," said Holcrow through the door. "And I have more people than you could shake a stick at. Please, Miss Doyle, do me the honor of allowing me to escort you home."

It was 1947 and haven't I spent my whole life hearing how safe it used to be? Yet a quick perusal of the nation's newspapers for April of that year shows us that in 1947 there was a serial killer stalking Los Angeles and murdering young women; there was a shocking double murder in Bloomington, Indiana, and an ordinary 1990's number of children were missing all around the Midwest.

Nothing at all untoward in Magrit, though, and apparently Irini could not think of a really good reason not to get in the car with a strange man. She fetched her coat and followed him through the yard. She had never seen him standing up before. He was taller than her father and had more bulk, but most of that might be the coat.

The fog had thickened to a roux. Irini could not see ahead to the car and couldn't have looked up to do so anyway. Snow had melted during the day, and then refrozen into ice. She had to watch every step. Her mouth steamed like a teapot, adding to the general cloudi-ness.

She was blindsided into a pin oak by a large dog, actually knocked to the ground. Holcrow was from Los Angeles and ice wasn't his terrain, but even in California they must have dogs, Irini thought angrily. A gentleman wouldn't have left her behind. Not that she would have taken Holcrow's arm, even if he had offered it. She picked herself up and stumbled through the gate, tripping into the backseat of the LaSalle. Holcrow was holding the door for her.

"How are things at Collins House?" her father asked heartily. Someone who knew him less well might not have noticed immediately that he was drunk. His words were clear; he was upright in his seat, his eyes were wide. But there was more than a trace of effort involved in these activities. He was blinking too often. Looking into his eyes by the overhead light, Irini saw red. Holcrow closed the door and the light went off.

"You're two hours late," she answered. Her own voice was even and matter-of-fact. What he could do, she could do.

He seemed amazed. "Am I? That doesn't seem possible. I was keeping careful track." Already he was losing control. His posture softened. His words blurred around the edges.

Holcrow lowered his scarf. It was crusted with bits of frozen smoke-colored breath. He started the engine. He turned on the wipers. They scraped unpleasantly over the glass and then they stopped. "I can't believe how quickly the windows ice up out here," he said. "I can't believe you people *live* like this. Dog my cats!" He pulled the scarf into place and got out to chip.

"Mr. California," said Irini's father jovially. He was sharing the moment with her.

"More than two hours late."

"You must sleep in tomorrow," her father said. "Have a nice long visit with the sandman. I won't even hear of you getting up to go to work."

Holcrow got back in the car. They eased away from Collins House. Irini was very tired. She lay back and let the curves and turns press her body this way and that. There was something about a moving car and fog that had always made her feel safe. This was ridiculous, of course. In her conscious mind, she knew it was ridiculous. But deeper than that, in her body instead of her mind, she felt as though she were wrapped for packing, wrapped in cotton.

Her father had a different attitude. "Steer into the turn if you start to slide," Irini's father said. "I mean just in case that should happen. Don't slam the brakes."

Holcrow hit the new pothole Fanny had found on the way in, although at a much lesser speed. Irini bounced against the door. "There go the shocks," Holcrow said.

"Norma Baldish'll have that fixed right up," Irini's father assured him. "Norma's just whizbang with tar." He turned politely to Irini. "What is Mrs. Ada up to these days?" He was trying to gauge how angry she was. She could smell the liquor now.

She wasn't really mad at him. She blamed Holcrow. If her father hadn't had a companion, he wouldn't have forgotten her. He never drank so much unless someone else was paying. "She's going to India. All of a sudden she's interested in Mr. Gandhi. She says we're just going to have to find a different path now. She says the bomb has changed everything."

"She's got that right. She could certainly do worse for causes," Irini's father said. He leaned tipsily into the front seat. "Like the first Mrs. Collins," he told Holcrow.

The first Mrs. Collins had been celebrated for her spiritedness, not to be confused with spirits, of which she did not approve. In her youth she drank occasionally and occasionally excessively. In those days she was referred to as high-spirited. When she joined the temperance movement, she became public-spirited. She stood out among the other like-minded, like-dressed women in her particular troop, because she loved the raids and conducted herself without the customary solemnity during them. There is, of course, no zealot like the convert, or maybe she merely liked to bust things up.

After she died, when Henry married Ada, he told people he wanted a young wife, someone unformed and malleable, someone, it is to be suspected, who would not be celebrated for her spiritedness.

"I was hoping to meet Ada Collins," Holcrow said. "And Mr. Collins, too. And Maggie. They sound like swell people. Perhaps Irini would introduce me sometime."

"I could introduce you," Irini's father offered. "To everyone but Maggie. Can't help you there." He gave Irini a delighted look. "Not that she wouldn't be a treat. And Mrs. Ada's all right. But the first Mrs. Collins, now, she was a corker. She was the berries. A black-bonneted woman with a wicked overhand. A woman who loved the sound of breaking glass. As who among us doesn't?" Irini's father observed. "Take a left here. It's the house in the middle. As if you didn't know."

Tweed came running outside to chase the car. It was a surprise and a delight to her when she caught it and Irini and her father got out. She panted great gusts of enthusiasm into the air, her long fur damp on top and jeweled with fog.

All three of them stood a moment on the porch, watching until the flickering brake lights of Holcrow's car disappeared. It was hard to say exactly when this happened. There were ghostly red echoes.

"I confess I liked him better tonight," Irini's father said. "A little too regulation, for my taste. A little too fill-out-your-forms-and-wait-in-line. But you can't blame him for that. No, it's the war has made our young men so starchy. A very salutary experience for all of us, I'm sure, except the ones who were killed or maimed or went completely nuts. And maybe those parents who are never going to be grandparents. But he's still a sore loser and I don't trust that in a man. Now, Walter, Walter's a man who knows how to lose." He turned to smile at Irini. "Tell you what, muffin. You just let me take care of everything tonight. I'll feed the dog and clean the kitchen. You go to bed and straight into the arms of the sandman. Just as quick as you can now." He was all consideration.

Maggie Collins writes: "To prevent snow from sticking, cut an onion in half and run it over the windshield of your car.

"To avoid tears while slicing onions, hold an unburned match (wood end) in your mouth."

Back at Collins House, Henry Collins was having trouble sleeping. He lay in bed and passed the time, as he often did on sleepless nights, happily dreaming of the kitchen of the future.

The kitchen of the future was made of a metal that didn't exist in 1947, a man-made metal cooked up in a chemistry lab at a major university on a federal grant. Henry didn't know the elements, but it had a glossy, ceramic finish that cleaned up nicely. It came in any color, but Henry himself preferred traditional white.

The kitchen of the future was on the moon.

The woman of the future resembled Maggie Collins in every detail. Whatever had happened with fashion and hairstyles in the interim, Maggie was too self-confident to care. She had a natural elegance; her look was classic maternal. Rembrandt could have captured her essence just as easily as Ada had.

She was absolutely at home in the kitchen, moved as gracefully through the reduced gravity as a swan on a lake. She wore no apron. There was no longer any need. The measuring and mixing, the paring and slicing were already done. Every dish from potato salad to baked Alaska was made in the future by opening a box and adding water.

A row of pinholes circumscribed the room. At the end of a meal, the entire room could be vacated, locked down, set on "wash." Water would pour from the holes and drain from the floor. Light would pour off the scalded surfaces.

Henry was asleep now. The kitchen of the future boiled inside his dreams with a steady, lullaby sound like rain on the planet Earth.

8

Ada made Henry give her the next day off, so it annoyed Irini to wake at the usual time. The sandman had compensated for the lack of hours with extra sand. Her eyes were scratchy and she had to rub them open. Just before waking she had had a dream. It involved the three May girls, which could be distressing; they could come off like the Furies or the Fates or something they clearly weren't during the daytime. The details were gone, but the distress remained.

The sun filtered in through the curtains with a halfhearted, underwater light. Irini looked about, relocating herself, shaking off the dream. The bedroom was preadolescent, prewar. There were dog books on the shelves, and dogs as well, miniatures made of china and plastic Irish setters and German shepherds. Irini had completely skipped the horsey stage; she took no small pride in finding her own path.

There was the start of a collection of dolls from around the world, but she had never been much into dolls either. The entire collection consisted of one Irish colleen in a stiff green dress, with bright red curls, and one Indian maiden in beads and soft leather and black braids. There was an antique doll with a china head and an elaborate christening gown that had belonged to Irini's mother. Their colors were dampened with dust. It would have saddened Maggie Collins to see it, all of it, from the dust to the lack of follow-through.

Irini had often thought of redoing the room. She cut pictures out of magazines for inspiration, priced white wicker bed sets and yellow-checked spreads. It could be done on the cheap if she sewed and painted herself, and would surely look it. It seemed all too likely that she would take a decorating misstep. She imagined that her mother, had she been there, could have helped her. Her mother would have had opinions on gingham and chenille. Her father, who had opinions on everything else, was useless.

Anyway, redecorating the room at this date would suggest that she was staying. She couldn't live with her father forever. It was hard to imagine how he would get along without her, but as long as it all remained in the future somewhere, she didn't have to dwell on this. She was secretly appalled at the way Fanny still lived at home at twenty-nine, and Claire Kinser and Norma Baldish, too, at twenty-four and twenty-five. But especially Fanny, who was so old and had so much energy and drive. If Fanny couldn't get out of Magrit, then how on earth could Irini?

She rose and opened the curtains. Perversely, Magrit had never looked more beautiful. Last night's fog had curled itself around each tree trunk, brushed over every branch, coated all the dead straw-colored grasses and then, sometime in the night, frozen into a thin skin of ice. Outside her window, Brief Street glittered like the crystal-line insides of a geode. Everything was glacéed. As far as she could see, everything was dressed in light.

The temperature was rising. It was a day to be alone, and a day to be outside. Irini decided on a hike to the top of the falls. She celebrated the day off work by wearing snow pants. Step lightly, Irini told herself, but her waffle-soled boots shattered the shining blades of dead grass beneath her feet.

By the time she reached the falls, the jewels had melted away. The glittering turrets became trees again; the rainbowed ground softened into an April patchwork of old snow and new mud. Sometimes Irini stepped on the first, sometimes the second. *Crunch, shloop, crunch, crunch, shloop.* Winter, spring, winter, winter, spring.

A deer had passed the same way earlier this morning; Irini saw the occasional print where the mud was. She picked up a tiny pine cone with the tight unfolded shape of a rosebud. She picked up a buckeye, because a polished buckeye was always a nice surprise when you found it in your pocket.

As the landscape about her turned to mud, so did her mood. Down in the Kitchen they were baking thumbprint cookies, singing along with the radio, and gossiping about her, even though Maggie did not like a gossip. "Where's Irini?" someone would ask, sticking their fat thumb into the raw dough. "Got the day off," someone would answer. And someone, Irini didn't know who or how, but someone would know why. "Mr. Doyle was at Bumps again. Irini waited two hours," someone might say. "Poor Irini." Or else, "She thinks she's too good for the Kitchen. They eat soda crackers with jam for dinner and she thinks she's too good for the Kitchen. No wonder he never goes home. Poor Mr. Doyle."

They might be talking about Walter coming back. They might know that Thomas Holcrow had come to fetch her last night. It drove Irini wild just to think about it. She hated being talked about. "Oh, well, we all have a skeleton or two in the closet," Tracy May had said one day to Irini when they were gossiping about Claire, and this thought had taken her completely by surprise. Eventually she dismissed it as typical Tracy bravado. Irini had no secrets and she very much doubted that Tracy did either. Someday Irini would go somewhere where no one knew her and no one talked about her. Someday she would give them all something to talk about.

Or not. She was definitely not going to think about this today. She walked into the chilly dark behind the falls and then emerged back into the sunlight on the other side. She kept walking until she hit the barbed-wire fence intended to keep children from swimming in Upper Magrit during the polio season.

Swimming in Upper Magrit was absolutely forbidden to Magrit

children. Once a year, on the Fourth of July, Henry stroked across to prove that, due to his excellent diet, he still could. But just because a man in his eighties could make it didn't mean that an eight-year-old would. Hadn't Opal May gone over the falls back in the days when the water was nowhere near so swift nor the current so strong? And along with the current and the threat of polio, there were the submerged houses to worry about as well.

In most kinds of light, little was left of the houses, beyond the occasional algae'd foundation. But every once in a while, usually by moonlight, someone reliable would see Upper Magrit just as it had been, intact and inhabitable, except for the water. Mr. Törngren hiked up every year and spent the night on the first full moon after the ice melted. It was the local variation of Groundhog Day. If he saw Upper Magrit, there would be good fishing in the summer.

Others found the apparition less benign. Maybe it was the sunlight that played tricks on people's eyes; maybe the hallucination was that the buildings were *not* there. Maybe the houses had returned, built entirely of malice this time. Even a good swimmer lured into entering a window at the Nadeaus' might lose his bearings and drown in the living room. The area was fenced off and posted with many signs.

At the end of every winter there were new places where the fence could be easily got through until Norma Baldish got up there to fix them. Or it could be avoided altogether by the simple method of walking farther upstream and then floating down. It was understood by all the children that one part of the bank was reserved for the girls and another for the boys. The boys' bank had a large tree with a branch that served for diving. The girls' had a little gravelly beach where they could lay their towels. Even without boys, it was hard for the girls to break this habit.

It wasn't only the fun of swimming or the prohibition against it that made Upper Magrit irresistible. There was also the lure of buried treasure. Arlys Fossum had once found a fork with a monogrammed handle in the rocks close to the shore, although the monogram had rubbed off and couldn't be deciphered. Jimmy Tarken had cut himself on something in the mud that turned out to be half a coffee cup. They never did find the other half.

And as a final inducement, there were the ghosts. Opal May haunted the falls, although people were too polite to say so when the May girls were present; since there were three of them, at least one of them always seemed to be.

Madame Nadeau haunted the millpond.

The Baldishes, who lived the closest to Upper Magrit you could live and still be Lower Magrit, were particularly tormented. Norma Baldish's mother had once hung her husband's heavy coat in its usual place, on a hook made of a severed deer leg. The Baldishes had been among the first to explore the possibilities of decorating with deer.

But when Mr. Baldish went to fetch the coat, it was nowhere to be seen. A thorough search of the house did not produce it. Then one day, twelve years later, there was the coat, back on the deer leg, but ripped and stained, as if it had undergone twelve hard years of wear and tear. "It gets pretty cold under the waters of Superior," the residents of Magrit said knowingly.

It got pretty cold under the waters of Upper Magrit. Irini found a spot where the wire was down and stepped across. On the far side was a line of white birches. The top of the millpond had been frozen since Christmas. Even frozen it still looked like water. The ice was a pale cloudy blue, the occasional drifts of snow were like whitecaps. Only the lack of motion gave it away. It looked like water the way a picture of water looks like water.

To the right, the falls flowed out from under a ledge of ice whose edges dripped with icicles. In the years that the falls froze, Irini would hike up to see. There was so much air in them, they had the look of whipped egg whites. This winter had been long, but not particularly deep.

Irini walked through the brittle cattails on the bank and onto the ice. During the war Maggie Collins had written a column in which she recommended picking unripened cattails, removing the sheaths, and boiling the spikes in slightly salted water until tender. Properly prepared, cattails could be eaten like corn on the cob.

Irini had never actually tried this. The response had been uniformly disheartening. It proved hard for the average housewife to determine when the cattails were done and the average husband seemed to have no sense of adventure when it came to food. But corn had once faced similar prejudices, and it had caught on eventually. Maggie was laying low on the issue, but she was far from giving up. She had, as Henry once said, stick-to-it-ivity and she had it in spades. "You'd be surprised at how much of the world is edible," Maggie Collins says. "If you only learn to prepare it properly."

The ice itself was the color of clouds, so perhaps it looked more like sky than like water, after all. As you stood on it you could forget for a moment, if you tried, which way was up and which was down. Somewhere beneath Irini's feet was the site of the Nadeau house; she was suspended above it, walking on water, walking through air.

I like to picture her this way. When she was little, she used to think she might fly. Her father told her stories about Charles Lindbergh, who once flew an emergency medical mission right over Magrit, and Amelia Earhart, only the way Irini heard it was Air-heart, a name so full of poetry that she pretended to be Amelia Airheart sometimes when she sat astride a branch in the apple tree in her backyard and it was sort of a plane and sort of a pony.

No later pilots ever matched the poetry of Lindbergh and Earhart, certainly not the astronauts, but when I was little, the sound of an airplane passing overhead was still extraordinary enough to bring children out of their houses. We would stand outside and search the sky, one hand cupped over our eyes in a gesture that resembled a salute. We would wait and watch as the thin line of cloud left behind by the jets turned feathery and dissipated into the blue. Now the sound is so common our children don't even hear it.

The air around Magrit seemed always to be full of exotica. There was heat lightning and lightning bugs, flying boats and flying squirrels. There were geese arranged in arrows and stars arranged in stories.

There were red-eyed vireos and ring-necked ducks. There was Lindbergh and there was snow. Above the drowned city of Upper Magrit, the air was particularly jammed. In addition to Opal May and Madame Nadeau, balls of light sometimes rolled through the sky. In foggy weather, the Baldishes claimed to see the little men known as the lutin dancing and flickering like candle flames just at water level.

People in Magrit had a gift for seeing things. It was the price you paid for living on the edge of nowhere. But the war changed everything. For the last few years people had seen Nazi spy planes instead of flying boats, or the coded messages from agents provocateurs instead of the dancing lutin. Magrit made every effort to stay current.

And if there was a loss of magic, there was a gain in purpose. During the war there was a reason to do everything. Maybe your job was to put on a uniform and go to London. Maybe your job was to clean your plate and do your homework and not sass your parents. Either way the object was the same. You did it, you did all of it, just to whip the Nazis.

You never knew what it would take. You saved the tin foil from gum wrappers and went south on buses with your classmates to help with the cherry harvest. If the government asked for milkweed fluff, to be stuffed into life vests because they could no longer get kapok, then you spent your spare time hunting out milkweed pods.

The Irini floating over Upper Magrit was nineteen years old. By the time she was nineteen, Mary Shelley was finishing *Frankenstein*. Joan of Arc had defeated the English and was already dead. By the time she was nineteen, Irini had defeated the Nazis, and was a lot older than she wanted to be. She had missed five years of her life because of the war and now she wanted them back. She put her hand in her pocket and there, left over from last winter or the winter before that, was a message Arlys had written her. It was in code and you needed the Sweetwheats' decoder ring, 1945 model, to decode it. This was the special Atomic Bomb Ring Henry had designed, with the sealed atom chamber and the genuine atoms. "Look inside the gleaming aluminum warhead and see them smash to smithereens!" the ad on the Sweetwheat box back had said. "Absolutely safe for kids." Cost fifteen cents and two box tops, unless your father happened to work at the mill and brought one home in his pocket.

Fortunately, Irini owned that ring. "Stop eating Sweetwheats! I already surrendered!" the message said. It was signed Hirohito.

The war was over. Everything was better again, except for those things that were worse. She had defeated the Nazis, but she never got to London the way some people who defeated the Nazis did. Now she was just a mill worker and the only way she could see to ever be anything else was to marry someone she wouldn't ever meet, stuck in Magrit as she was. "It was my mistake to expect so much for you," her father said on the day she started working at the mill. It was the only cruel thing he had ever said to her, in her whole life. That being the case, it seemed unfair and unkind of Irini to remember it so often.

The war was over and the magic was gone and there would never be a good reason to ever do anything again. Irini had lost her childhood and her hopes for the future all at the same time, all when she beat the Nazis. She felt for Arlys's note and she was crying, remembering that she had once thought she might live in a world of spies and codes; that she had once been Amelia Airheart. "I surrender already," she said aloud and saying it made her cry harder.

But it was only a nineteen-year-old kind of despair, and not to be confused with the despair a person can feel at forty-two or at sixty. What Irini was really feeling was a late night and a winter hanging on and a small town and her period coming. She tried to skate, but the waffle soles caught. She spun in circles, right over Upper Magrit, taking fast, tiny steps on the blue ice, spotting on the line of birches, faster and faster until she lost her spot, became dizzy, and fell down.

9

In the thirties, Henry had been able to handle Maggie's correspondence by himself, but by 1947 the task had grown enormously. With the end of the war, Maggie began to receive letters from all over the globe. It was a point of pride as well as common courtesy that she answer them all, so writing letters and tracing Maggie's signature in Maggie's own beautiful penmanship was added to the other duties of the Kitchen. Some letters required discretion and these Maggie answered privately.

Some were edifying for everyone. These she printed in a weekly column in *Women at Home,* between the ads for Fibbs tampons ("Don't miss out!")—a giddy slogan my mother once admitted to me she first read as meaning the tampons were the thing not be missed) and the ads for Clapp baby foods. ("Clapp for it"). *Women at Home* was a postwar magazine with an obvious agenda. "Aren't you lucky to be back at home?" it asked the postwar women. "Aren't you lucky to be a real girl?" The editorial staff was primarily but not exclusively female. These women, of course, all had jobs.

Henry took first pick of the letters. Sometimes he answered several himself. If something caught his fancy he could go on at some length. But other weeks, when he was occupied setting up timed mazes for

his rats, or growing vegetables in centrifuges, or hobnobbing with other men of science in hotels in Chicago and Detroit, he paid no attention at all.

The letters to be used in the magazine were collected in an old milk box Ada had tarted up with painted violets. Any girl who thought she had a letter and answer worthy of publication put it into the box. Fanny read through them, when she had the time, and chose from among them. They were then mailed to the editorial staff in New York.

Fanny was in charge of the mailing and of soliciting participation in a slow week. She was also stuck with the letters no one else wanted to answer. She got hazard pay for this. It was richly deserved.

No one oversaw the letters that went out privately. There were simply too many and it was more important to Henry that Maggie answer all of her letters than that he know what every answer was. He trusted his girls. And he believed in Maggie. She was so real to him, she was real. Like Pinocchio. He didn't have to watch her every moment. She could take care of herself.

My mother saved some of Maggie's columns from this period. "I was so touched by the letters," she said. "All these people in all these different countries, convinced that Maggie had missed them during the war."

Dear Maggie,

I have a tiny farm outside Oslo with one cow, one horse, one pig, one sheep, and six hens. Compared to others, such riches! Yet I think it will take a little time for us to forget and go on as before, with the evidence of such terrible things all around us.

Norway is too little to be a country, more like a big family. For five long years our family home was lost to us, like Tara in your wonderful American book *Gone With the Wind*. You cannot imagine how proud we all felt on that

day in May when we recovered our country. Now our beloved crown prince is back and the Norwegian colors fly everywhere. When can I begin to get *Women at Home?*

and

Dear Maggie,

My daughter is now in India doing physiotherapy at a military hospital while I am in Argentina doing missionary work. We write often and speak of you in every letter. She has asked me to tell you how many friends you have in the British-Indian community. May the sun never set on *Women at Home!*

and

Dear Maggie,

Now the Japanese have gone and even the American liberators are leaving. They used to be more than the population of Manila itself, now GI's are rare. Before the war I always read you for advice and encouragement. I always thought, someday I will have a problem and I will write to Maggie Collins. Before the war I had a piano, a radio, and a beloved waffle iron. Now I have only three wobbly chairs. All else was sold to keep us from starving, but no word could be gotten to you. And after the war it was still several months before civilians were allowed mail for the States. This letter will go out in one of the first posts.

These days in the Philippines, you don't ask people 'How is So-and-So?' You ask, 'Is he still living?' So I am wondering, my old friend, as I send you my greeting from the Philippines. Are you still living?

Maggie was gracious and international. "Someday I will be flying down to see the beautiful city of Rio for myself," she wrote her fans in Brazil. A rare letter from Finland persuaded Maggie to overlook their temporary alliance with Germany and focus instead on the sad conditions of the peace treaty with the USSR. *"Kaikki menne mita tulle eika pusaken.* Everything goes that comes, and it isn't enough." The Finnish was provided by Margo Törngren's mother.

Food was the immediate postwar problem. Herbert Hoover had been appointed by Truman to deal with the difficulties of feeding Europe, and Hoover had begun by asking Americans to voluntarily eat less. In the British zone of Germany, the British reduced the daily caloric allotment to an involuntary one thousand, well beneath the fifteen hundred in the American zone, which was the minimum recommended by nutritionists. In the French and Russian zones there were allegations that the Germans were not being fed at all. The French and the Russians cited the Potsdam Agreement. "Why should the Germans be eating better than the Poles?" they asked.

France needed cheese and electricity. Just try to imagine France without cheese.

America wallowed in meat and sugar again.

The goal in the domestic sciences escalated from clean to disinfected. Maggie Collins was equal to anything. A column on the wastefulness of the milk industry demonstrates her ingenuity. "Almost half the milk products produced in this country," she wrote, "leave a creamless milk by-product. Although nutritionally top-notch, millions of gallons of this by-product are dumped annually as a matter of taste. When so many are hungry, this is insupportable. Few foodstuffs have the versatility of milk. It can be used to make plastics, adhesives, fabrics, drugs, and penicillin."

She included a modest list of proposals. The fashion industry could use the milk by-product to make the plastic coated furs that were currently fashionable; the postal department could use it to make the gluey backs of stamps; the average housewife could use it to make the paste for papier-mâché. Papier-mâché could in turn be used to transform old picture frames, old lamp bases, old vases into brightly colored objets d'art. And housewives with less time or talent but plenty of sugar could cook the milk by-product. The column ended with a recipe for Maggie's own Skim Milk Almond-Cherry Nougats.

In early April she ran her salute to the brave people of Holland. It included recipes for tulip soup, tulip mash, and tulip cookies. Don't make substitutions, she warned her readers in bold-faced type. Serious consequences can follow the ingestion of crocus, hyacinth, daffodil, or gladioli bulbs. She was arguably at her very peak.

In the mid-April issue, *Women at Home* ran the following letter from Salem, Massachusetts:

> Dear Maggie,
>
> Now that the war is over, why not total peace? Tell the beauty experts in your magazine to quit making war on overweight women. Strange as it may seem, there are some women who work to be attractive, but do not see weight reduction as a key to this. Stranger yet, some men admire them. Yours is supposed to be a magazine for women, yet again and again in the columns, not to mention the ads, you attack overweight women in an endless variety of subtle ways. You could use your influence to show these same women in an attractive light. You could build their pride and self-assurance. Instead you try to shame them. You're the ones who should be ashamed.

The response ran as follows:

> Dear Salem, Massachusetts,
>
> I am only a columnist for *Women at Home* and have nothing to say about editorial policy or advertisers. For what it is worth, I couldn't agree with you more. Don't let my offi-

cial portrait fool you—it was done some years ago. I am
sure I weigh as much now as you do.

The same issue carried, on page 6, an ad for the AYDS Vitamin
Candy Reducing Plan. "No exercise, no drugs, no laxatives. Soldier's
wife loses 57 pounds, becomes a slender beauty," was the headline,
illustrated with a "before" and an "after" swimsuit picture. It is interesting to note, although completely beside the point, that 1947's slender beauty wore a size 14.

The letter to Salem, Massachusetts, was easily determined to have
come from the Scientific Kitchen. After publication the original was
recovered and examined. It had been typed on the mill typewriter and
gave no clues as to its author.

Among the girls, suspicion rested primarily on Fanny May. Fanny
remembered having taken the last stack of letters to the mail herself.
She admitted as much. And Fanny was also the woman in the Kitchen
who weighed the most. Only Henry Collins, set on blaming the
incident on youthful high spirits, refused to consider her, because of
her age.

By 1947 standards, Fanny was not fat so much as she was big.
Although she was almost thirty and had never even flirted with marriage, Fanny in no way fit the stereotype of the spinster. She was a
vivacious, prankish person who attracted male attention at will. Irini,
who had given the matter considerable thought, believed her chief
attraction was her mouth. She had a very erotic mouth, although Irini
would not have put it quite this way. The hollow leading to the top
lip from the base of the nose was unusually deep; a man could run his
fingertip down it. The lips were heart-shaped when she pouted and
very full even when she didn't. And the things she said with them!

"Bold as brass," Mrs. Tarken complained, even though Fanny
never spoke to her at all—she didn't know the half of it. But hadn't
Fanny, all by herself with the opposition of every Lutheran in town,
fought to have *Duel in the Sun* screened in the school auditorium? She
thought she'd won, too. Irini went to see it with her and her sisters,

but then Henry had *Lost Horizon* shown instead. "A delightful surprise," he called it, and then, catching sight of the three May girls, "a sensible compromise."

Henry Collins actually owned a copy of *Lost Horizon,* so they were delighted with it often. And it did have that one sexy swimming scene with Jane Wyatt, worn a little pale, as if someone had run the footage of that a little more often than the rest. It had that poetic image of the bright, shiny plane and its silly but steadfast shadow. I remember that much and I haven't seen it anywhere near so often as my mother did.

Even so, no one was happy, not the Lutherans and certainly not Fanny May. But then this is the nature of compromise, as I don't have to tell you. You live in a democracy, you know about disappointment.

Henry called all the girls into the Kitchen and read the letter aloud. He confined himself then to a brief speech reminding them all of how much they owed Maggie. "Maggie is a generous and gifted woman with none of the jealousies or pettiness that tarnish the sex. If she discovers a new use for an old spice, this discovery immediately belongs to women everywhere. A woman in faraway Switzerland can set it on the table before her delighted husband and claim it as her own." He pulled on his meaty earlobe. It stretched to an inch or more, then bounced back when he released it.

"The main point is that Maggie is not a stout woman. If she were stout," Henry said, "she would be the first to admit it. She is not in the habit of dissembling. But she is not. Not by any stretch of the imagination. She has a very pleasing figure." The ending was all charity. "If we refuse to suspect anyone, we avoid the risk of injustice. Accordingly, let us agree to consider the matter closed."

He commissioned a new portrait of Maggie to amplify the main point. She was wearing her usual sashed apron, only the sash was tied more tightly. The bow peeked out from behind both sides of her tiny waist, resembling little wings. Her figure was exaggeratedly hourglass. "And we all thought," my mother said, "that was the end of that."

10

 The whole episode hurt Henry more than he let on. It came at a particularly bad time. Some man up in Alaska had just developed fish sticks.

Fish sticks were exactly the sort of thing the Kitchen should have developed. Bits of fish with no bones, no scales, and no unpleasant fish taste, rolled in cereal, and cooked in minutes. Fish so transformed that even children would eat it.

Henry exhorted the Kitchen to produce a rival product. It wasn't merely or even mostly profit that motivated him. He wanted Margaret Mill to be a part of the bold new world waiting to be built on the rubble of the war.

Of course the rubble was in Europe and not in America, but you really couldn't have pictured it any other way. Americans were born lucky; it's just part of being American. So Henry wanted Margaret Mill to be part of what Americans had fought for. The most intimate part. The part that you ate.

Cooking fish, as Maggie is fond of pointing out, generally exceeds the grasp of the ordinary cook. It had once stood as a line of demarcation. And now some man in Alaska had brought it all within reach. Since nothing could be added to fish sticks in terms of taste or convenience, Henry focused on shape. "What's so great about sticks?" he said. His own inspiration was to make fish sticks in the shape of fish. He told Claire to choose her team and work on it.

Claire Kinser had always been the Kitchen girl he liked best, even though the Törngrens had named their daughter Margo in a delicate homage to Maggie, just to please him. Margo was bright as copper and dependable, too, but no one was sweeter than Claire.

Claire had chosen Helen Leggett and Tracy May to be on the fish-sticks team. Irini was left on the sidelines. It was nothing personal; she just wasn't Upper Magrit. She didn't mind. Irini knew she was well liked, but she also knew she had no intimate friends. She was closest to Arlys Fossum and Margo Törngren, but they were closer still to each other. Sometimes she thought she didn't know how to be close to people and that this was because she'd had no mother to teach her. She had grown up defending herself from pity over her motherlessness and so what she had learned instead of intimacy was self-defense.

Henry could have used a bit more of this. He persisted in taking the Salem, Massachusetts, incident personally. "Which just wasn't possible," my mother said. "We would as soon have hurt Santa Claus."

In fact, the two were strongly associated in my mother's mind. Every year at the mill Christmas party, Henry dressed as Santa and entered in some surprising way. "I'd go down the chimney if I could. But I seem to be fatter than the real Santa," he told Irini's father. This was a joke. Henry wasn't fat at all. "Since I can't be traditional, I aim for memorable."

Once he had popped from the dumb-waiter in the dining hall. Once he slid down the bannister on a large red pillow. One year when Irini was so small she just barely remembered it, he hid inside an enormous box all wrapped with silver paper that the children had been told to open together.

One year he had a sled made specially, a Flexible Flyer propelled by a motor and a drive wheel, with cloth-covered runners for the wood floors. He entered through the library doors, belly down. He was clearly unpracticed. The motor roared and filled the hallway with smoke. Excessive movement on the steering bar resulted in only small adjustments to the runners. After a brief period of wild and noisy tilting, he ran aground on the Oriental rug.

This was the year my mother turned thirteen. She wore a pine-colored velveteen dress from Sears with a gathered skirt, puffed sleeves, and a rhinestone medallion set into the bodice. Her coat was old and stained and crushed her puffs. She didn't want to put it on, not even to walk up the snowy, faintly lit path to Collins House, but her father insisted and insisted on galoshes, too.

Because they were guests, they went to the front door, up the steps of the porch, and between a pair of stone lions. Her father had been to New York in his youth and seen the public library there. "Reading between the lions," he had called it. Every social, front-door visit to Collins House afforded him a chance to retell the joke. It was not, to Irini's thinking, good enough to survive repeated wearings.

Her father was already weaving, but scarcely noticeably. He asked her to ring the doorbell. Three chimes sounded inside the house, each higher in pitch than the last. Inside the entrance was an enormous tree. It was decorated all with angels, every ornament an angel, and none of them the same.

And the lights! There were still a lot of people in Magrit made nervous by electricity. They all had it, because of the mill. They were all glad to have it. But to use it in such a frivolous way was to court disaster. Hadn't Madame Nadeau made her last attack with lightning? Had the Collinses ever stopped to ask themselves what she might do with electrical wiring? Upper Magrit came to the Christmas party, ate and drank fast, and then went home again.

It was too elegant to miss entirely. Even the littlest children were given their punch in thin glasses with gold around the rims. The punch was cranberry. Next to the gold, in the sparkling glass, it was as pretty as an ornament. Her father said she was a vision in her green dress with her shining hair, holding her red and gold glass. It made Irini think of her punch as a fashion accessory. She didn't want to drink it. Her father didn't want to drink his either. He told her to behave herself with the other children and wandered off looking for a place to set his drink down.

If the house seemed oversized when Irini was nineteen, it had been more so at thirteen. The ceilings were high, the steps on the stairs were tall. The yule log burned in an enormous tiled fireplace. The room smelled of pine. The fire hissed and spit and tossed shadows into the corners. Irini looked at everything through her glass of punch, which not only miniaturized the scene, but colored it red. The fire flickered rosy and far away.

A tiny face appeared in the liquid, altered by the curve in the glass until it was all nose. When Irini lowered her drink, the face's features normalized into Sissy Tarken. Sissy was also thirteen, but immature even by Tarken standards. She grinned at Irini, lifted her own glass and took a bite out of it. There was a crunching sound. Sissy spit a dime-sized piece of gold and glass onto the floor. For just a moment, Irini thought it was a tooth. Bright red liquid dripped from Sissy's mouth to the collar of her dress.

It was only cranberry punch, but it would be harder to soak out than blood. Sissy tried to cover the stain with her hair. She had stopped smiling.

"Why did you do that?" Irini whispered. She couldn't imagine a reason. She had been frightened when she thought Sissy was bleeding, so now she was irritated to have been frightened for nothing.

"I didn't think I could." Sissy wiped her mouth with her sleeve, watching Irini. "I wouldn't have done it if I thought I could." She looked as if she might cry. Irini turned around to make sure no one had noticed them. Then she stooped down, picked up the small bite of glass and dropped it into what remained of Sissy's punch.

"Hide it," she advised.

Sissy looked around in confusion.

"Oh, for goodness sake." Irini opened the door to the library and stepped inside, gesturing for Sissy to follow. She pulled two volumes, the comedies and the histories, of a four-volume Shakespeare from a shelf, and Sissy set the glass behind them.

Walter Collins entered the room just as she was replacing the books. He was home from school for the holidays. When Irini had seen him last, they had been the same height. He must have grown at least two inches. It made him skinnier as well as taller. He was wearing a thin, green sweater, very Ivy League and not at all appropriate for winter in Magrit, a season that demanded bulk. He had an out-of-town haircut, so a clump of dark blond hair was continually falling into his eyes. It was just a bit Hitlerian, even with the blondness, and he had stopped cutting it this way during the war. But now he pushed it back with one hand. "You're not supposed to be in here," he said.

This was rather rude, even if true, since he hadn't seen Irini in months, since he hadn't even said hello first, since it was Christmastime, and he could easily have said Merry Christmas instead. He didn't speak to Sissy at all. Irini's irritation shifted smoothly from Sissy to Walter.

"Then we'll leave." Irini took hold of Sissy's shoulder.

"You don't have to. As long as you're with me."

"We were leaving anyway." Irini pushed past Walter, pulling Sissy with her.

So it was a shock when Henry Collins, dressed all in red, made his entrance from the library. He threaded his way slowly through the library doors, his sled smoking beneath him. What if he had seen her with Sissy in the library? What would she answer if he asked, in that loud voice, had she been a good girl?

"Are you having fun, Irini?" her father asked her. His words were sloppy; he must have brought a bottle to the party. The combination of drink and Christmas made him impossibly sincere. Soon he would be singing carols. He would insist on a solo—"Silent Night" in the original German or something long and Latin. The Collinses would indulge him and his voice would shake with honest sentiment. Irini edged away, choosing a place off to the side of the rug where she could not possibly be suspected of being his daughter.

The room was becoming uncomfortably hot and the continual sound of the sled motor was unpleasant. She moved even farther off from the rest of the partyers. She was halfway up the stairs when

Walter Collins caught up with her. "You're not allowed up there, either," he said. "But I could take you. Gramps has got a ham radio set. We can get Greenland. I'll show you how."

He was being so pompous, as if they had not known each other for years, as if he had not once put peanuts in his ears just to amuse her and then had to have Dr. Gilbertsen come to the house and fish one of them out.

One step on the stairs was taller than the others. Henry Collins had designed this as an antitheft feature. If it worked as planned, the burglar, negotiating his way in the dark, his arms full of valuables, would be surprised by the sudden drop and fall and break his neck and they would find him at the bottom of the stairs in the morning. Years later Ada would worry about a way to reconcile this karmic design feature with the principles of ahimsa. This was the step Irini sat down on, ignoring Walter. He sat beside her.

At the party beneath them, the sled coughed twice and hiccoughed once and was silent. "I could probably fix that for you," Norma offered, but she was in her good clothes so Henry said no.

For a moment, no one else spoke. The silence was lovely. "An angel is visiting," her father would have said to her, had she been near enough to hear him. There were few enough silences when he was around.

Walter spoke. "Same old Christmas. Same old Magrit."

"Same old Walter." It was a suggestion, not an observation.

"You bet." Walter leaned back on his elbows and stretched his legs. His hair fell forward. He pushed it back. "Do you like the punch? Here." He picked up her juice from the step beneath her. "You better hold on to this. The glasses are heirlooms. Ada would be hysterical if you broke one." Ada wasn't his grandmother and he never pretended that she was.

"So you saw."

"Saw what?"

"You know perfectly well what."

"I don't know what you're talking about, Miss Doyle." Walter took a sip out of her glass and grinned at her. "Good punch. Refresh-ing."

"Sissy did it. I was trying to help out."

"Kiss me and I won't tell," Walter said.

This seemed fair enough. Irini looked around to make sure no one could see them and then she let him kiss her. It was her first kiss and it was a silent, lip-bumping affair. There was nothing particularly nice about it. She wondered if she was supposed to have made the smack-ing sound or if he should have. He appeared more satisfied with the result than she was. When he smiled, his upper lip rose so high you could see the pink line of his gums.

"I wouldn't really have told," he said. "I never tell on you. Do I?"

"I know."

"Kiss me again."

"No," said Irini. Enough was enough.

The sound of Irini's father's voice drifted up the stairs. *"Stille Nacht, heilige Nacht."* He needed Irini to pitch his songs for him. This one was way too high. He was never going to hit the *himm-* in *himmlicher Ruh.* But she didn't feel as embarrassed in front of Walter as she would have in front of anyone else. When her father came to the word "virgin" it would be in German and Walter probably wouldn't even recognize it. Her father had sung in church choir as a boy and always been given the solos. His voice was not so sweet now, but even Irini, who was only thirteen and also didn't really listen, because it was her own father, could hear how sweet it might have been once, before he started to smoke, before he lost his wife, before he knew he would spend his life working at Margaret Mill.

This was the last song in German Irini's father would be singing for quite some time. The date of the party was December 6, 1941. Henry Collins made a toast. "As we meet tonight, may we meet again. Each and every one of us. God bless."

Maggie Collins writes: "In the unfortunate event that, as a guest in someone's home, you should break a dish or stain a tablecloth, or do another sort of damage, you enter at once into a negotiation similar to the bidding process in contract bridge. You must offer, of course, to repair and repay. This opens the bidding. Your partner in the affair, the host, must refuse the first such offer, no matter how treasured the item, no matter how heart-breaking the damage. The first offer is merely pro forma.

"The second round separates the experts from the amateurs. The courteous guest will repeat the offer. It may be that repair or replacement is not actually possible, but this determination is not for the guest to make. This judgment belongs to the host, who must ask himself not only if it is possible, but the more delicate question, is it within the means of this particular guest? It is on these points that your partner, the host, chooses to accept or refuse.

"In the case of refusal, negotiations may move to a third round. The guest may offer again. Here, timing is critical. If the offer comes immediately after the second refusal, it suggests that you as guest feel the host has misjudged your abilities or your pocketbook. Perhaps you have a cousin in the antique business who specializes in matching patterns. Perhaps you have an aunt who tats. If the offer immediately follows the refusal, your partner is free to accept. But if the third offer comes later in the evening, if it comes, for example, as you are putting on your coat and saying your farewells, then it is merely another expression of regret and not to be mistaken for a serious offer. It ought again to be refused. Mind you, by making it, you risk acceptance. It may well be that your partner is not as sophisticated in these negotiations as you are.

"In any case, the matter is settled in three rounds and a fourth is not only unnecessary, but also rude."

That night after they'd returned from the party and Irini had gone to bed, her father sat up with his bottle in the kitchen. If he drank enough, he saw things, heard things. Only they were never the things he wanted to see or hear. So he had been forced to keep drinking all those years, until he got it right.

Someday he might find himself, just for a few minutes, in an older kitchen. There was a clock on the wall. He had broken it himself years ago, just because the sound was such a heartbeat to him, but someday he would hear that tick again, follow it to a woman standing at the sink, drying dishes.

Her voice would come next. She was singing and she couldn't carry a tune at all. She flipped the dishrag in his direction, came to sit beside him. She stretched his arm out onto the table, and laid her head and hair over it.

"I miss you," he would be able to tell her then. Never so drunk he couldn't get that out. The kitchen would smell of pot roast, caramelized onions, strong coffee. "Don't leave me here."

But then we all have someone we miss. No big deal. Nothing special about that.

11

I have already told you how Henry Collins drowned Upper Magrit, but there is more to the story. He had to hire outside help to do it. There must have been men in Magrit at that time who had the disposition for the job, if not the expertise. There must have been men who, for a paycheck, would have followed instructions. They were already doing so up in Canada—felling trees, digging mines, laying steel, blasting and paving everything they could touch. And keep in mind that the project in Magrit had community support.

Still, there were obviously going to be hard feelings. Better, Henry reasoned, to bring someone in, have him blow the place, and then leave again. The bad feelings might just settle on him and leave when he left.

Henry sent south for Jim Nedd and his crew of colored engineers. Jim Nedd was a freed slave who'd been highly thought of until he published a paper offering to straighten the Mississippi. Most of his work had involved the river; he was quite familiar with its notorious curves and shallows.

After publication, he was generally regarded as a crackpot. There hadn't been a job offer since. But it was this same paper that drew

Henry's attention to him. Henry was impressed with the audacity of the project as well as beguiled by the project itself. A Mississippi River that ran straight as the crow flies from the top of the country to the bottom. It was beautiful. It was farsighted. Someday, if the unruly river couldn't be brought to heel, someday there would be hell to pay.

Henry and Nedd were men of vision—visionaries, both of them, surrounded by myopics. Jim Nedd was asked to come and look at Upper Magrit.

Compared to straightening the Mississippi, it was a simple enough project. The pay was good. The crew could camp on land Henry had purchased for the purpose and not mingle too much with the locals. Jim Nedd had accepted the job and sent for his crew before he began to have second thoughts.

He was out one morning, pacing off the area under the baleful eyes of Upper Magrit, when he noticed the Dumas place. The Dumas had been Quaker converts and had lived in a white house with a brick chimney. It was the chimney that caught Nedd's eye. Down the side of the bricks, someone, long, long ago, had painted a white stripe.

It was 1898, but Nedd knew what that stripe meant. Friends here, it said. Safety. Shelter. Food. Many years ago the Dumas House had been a stop on the Underground Railroad. Nedd walked away quickly, careful not to speak to the current occupants.

Nedd's crew arrived, and they spent several days setting up their camp. Henry spent the same time overseeing the evacuation of Upper Magrit. He sold off lots he'd just purchased in the Lower to the displaced families of the Upper. There was a profit involved, of course, and Upper Magrit noticed, but it was not a large profit, as Lower Magrit was quick to point out. Building a mill was bound to cost money; naturally Henry would need to turn a profit wherever he could. The first payments went immediately into the wages of Nedd's crew. Henry occupied himself quarreling with and cajoling Madame Nadeau. It was several days before he noticed that no work was being done. Any delay gave the Nadeau boys that much more time to get down from Canada.

Henry bicycled up to Upper Magrit. The whole country had been gripped by a great bicycle mania, and Henry was one of the first and most severely hit of the victims. The day he saw his first bicycle, he swore he would never own a horse again. "What a steed!" he had said, even after his first attempts at riding landed him in the dirt. "What a steed!"

"Work starting soon?" he asked Nedd, swinging off the cycle and dropping it.

"Soon," Nedd answered. "It's simple enough. Place the dynamite in the right spots and the whole thing will flood. Then we just blast a channel where we want the water to fall."

Two days later no dynamite had been placed. Henry pedaled up the hill again. "Everything ready to go?" he said. "You have everything you need?"

"Setting the dynamite is delicate," Nedd told him. "It's not just a matter of placing it correctly. The men who light it, they have to be in the right mood. It's too dangerous to ask a man who's not in the right mood to do it."

"Who's not in the right mood?" Henry asked.

"I'm not," Nedd answered.

"I see," said Henry. "And I'm not in the right mood to pay a man who's not in the right mood to work. Shall we start tomorrow? I'll come up and watch."

The next day Nedd paced off Upper Magrit again. "I'm going to have to dismantle the chimney," he told Henry, pointing to the Dumas place. "It's too high. It's going to affect the cross-flow."

"Dynamite it first," Henry suggested. "Then dynamite the rest."

"No need," said Nedd. It took him two additional days. He chiseled the bricks carefully apart, trying not to break any. Then he stacked them on the high ground. When Upper Magrit was underwater and the crew had been paid for their work and sent home, Nedd stayed on. He made a tower of the bricks, two walls that sloped upward and met in a corner. He mortared them into place. When Henry asked, Nedd said it was a signature; he was signing his work. From the air, the bricks were an arrowhead, pointing due north.

Nedd returned south. Magrit decided that he had been a crackpot after all. But no one could quarrel with his work. Upper Magrit was deep and silent and dangerous. The falls had more than trebled in size and strength.

Irini had never wondered why there was a brick tower on the shores of Upper Magrit. She had never heard anyone else wonder either, not even the Leggetts, who were the only surviving descendants of the Dumas family. Helen Leggett worked right there in the Kitchen and even she had never heard the name Jim Nedd.

For the children of Magrit, the bricks were there to be climbed over, there to be jumped from, there to be written on. Years ago Walter had painted his name and Irini's among the other pairs. It had made Irini so angry he had never renewed it. Year after year it grew fainter and fainter and this year, when she looked, it wasn't there at all.

Irini took it as an omen that Walter was not coming home. In California Walter lived right on the ocean and dove for abalone. He pounded and breaded the meat and used the shells as ashtrays, the sort of thrift and ingenuity that Maggie Collins was always encouraging. He'd seen the grunion run. He'd surfed on canvas sheets filled with wind and tied off to hold the air as long as the ride lasted. Did you return from this to a town where winter never ended, and to someone who didn't love you back? Irini hoped that even Walter had more pride than that.

I told you that Walter had not come back to Magrit after being discharged, but there is more to the story. Once Walter had thought he would come home from the war and marry Irini. He'd made the mistake of asking. Ironically, the fact that he was willing to come back to Magrit had worked against him. Irini couldn't imagine that anyone with anything on the ball would come back to Magrit. And she had turned out to be right, although she could have eliminated the qualifying clause.

When Irini said no, she had thought she would have other options. She'd thought the war itself would give her other options. It wasn't that she planned never to marry. But someday Irini expected to be sick with love for someone. Even now, with prospects so demonstrably bleak, Irini expected passion. She thought that everyone got to fall in love. She thought that this was just the way things worked. The Master Plan. She didn't imagine that even a war could stop it.

Irini could already make herself feel this way, even though she had never felt this way. She had learned from books and movies and songs. She practiced now and then to keep herself in shape, and she tried it again that day, standing at Nedd's tower, looking at the unmarked bricks where her name had been. Sure enough, she could make herself so weak with love, her legs would hardly hold her.

She reset herself to simmer. She was nineteen. Simmer was her normal temperature.

Irini never told anyone that he'd asked. They all thought she was still waiting for him, and they all felt sorry over it. Irini told herself it was only right that she look a little pathetic on Walter's behalf, since he suffered the drawbacks of actually being pathetic. It evened things up a bit.

So she was surprised a week later to see Walter walking toward her down Church Street. It was just after noon. Out past the end of the street the purple edge of distant trees faded upward into the white sky. He was whistling and he was not a good whistler. His whistle was thin and off-key, but pleasantly buoyant.

She was happy to see him, but this was because she was happy. The water over Upper Magrit was finally beginning to melt in the middle. Behind Irini's house was a gully and at the bottom of the gully was a thicket of thin trees. Around those trees, in the depressions created by the trunks, there was still snow, but everywhere else the snow was gone. The cardinals were giving up their sulky winter silence. The wind rattled through the pine needles and you still needed a jacket, but you could already forgo the gloves and scarves.

Spring was so close you could smell it. Everyone's spirits were high. "You picked the right time to come home," Irini told him. His hair was sun-blond and his skin was browner than anyone's in Magrit with just a white strip across his forehead where his hair shaded it. It made him look slightly surprised, as if his eyebrows were up when they weren't. "Or is it still home? Are you just visiting? If you've come back, then you're the only one who has."

"I'm here for baseball season," Walter said. "And to spend some time with Gramps. Does he look old to you, Irini? He looks so old to me."

"Mr. Henry never changes. You're going to coach?"

"You're going to play? I remember that you were a good ball-player."

"I remember that you never picked me first," said Irini. She looked away. She could feel Walter watching at her, but she wouldn't look back to be sure.

"I always picked you first of the girls."

"Well, exactly," said Irini. "You boys all picked each other first. You'd take Wayne Floyd and Scott Moodey before you'd take me, and you know I was better than they were. The field in the Fossum backyard was the place where I first learned that no matter how hard I tried or how well I played, I was only a girl."

Out of the corner of her eye she could see him comb through his hair with his hand. She was making him nervous.

"You were a girl," said Walter. "No *only* about it."

She decided to push it. "And now you want me to play for you. Ironic, isn't it? Now you need a girl who plays ball."

"If you and Arlys won't play, we don't have a team."

"Arlys was better than you were. How come she never got to pick? And Scott Moodey was so bad, he had trouble getting into his glove. He was always the last of the boys to go. He married an Italian woman, by the way. He's going to college in Madison."

"I heard," said Walter.

"She probably didn't know what a bad catch he was. Why don't you ask Scott Moodey to play for you?"

"I haven't laid eyes on you in two years, Miss Irini Doyle, and you're already mad at me." She risked a direct look. He was smiling at her, that gum-revealing smile. She liked it, in spite of the pink edge.

He had ordinary ears and the nicest teeth. They were the nicest teeth that money could buy. Irini remembered the recess he'd lost his front two originals ski-jumping off a snow scaffold the boys had built in the school yard. Henry came right to the school and took him immediately to Chicago to buy a new pair. He told Walter he could pick them out, but when Walter chose something in a nice silver, Henry intervened.

"I'm just teasing," said Irini.

"No, you're not," said Walter. "But you don't have to start a fight with me. I want you to feel quite comfortable that I've come home to help out Gramps and not to see you. When I lived here before, I knew so few girls. I had no one to compare you to."

"There must be a more graceful way to put this," said Irini.

"I'm just trying to tell you that I'm ready to be friends. I'll always have friendly feelings for you. I'll always love you in a friendly fashion. But you needn't worry that there's anything more and, given a little time, the rest of Magrit will see it. No one will be bothering you about me."

"Well, good." It occurred to Irini that she had quite misinterpreted the omen on the bricks.

A few steps later Walter was waylaid by Mr. Baldish. She left the two men talking about the war. How the men loved to do this! "We're just so doggone proud of you boys," Mr. Baldish said and Walter was accepting the thanks, just as if he hadn't spent the war in La Jolla, California, lying around the beach getting tan.

Irini had gone about half a block when she noticed the buds of leaves on the dogwood tree at the corner of Church and Mill. In a few days they would open into the brilliant, translucent green of new growth. It happened so fast, like time-lapse photography, or like that moment in the movie when Dorothy stepped into the Technicolor Land of Oz. One ill-timed day of excessive introspection and you could miss the whole thing. Irini turned back. "Walter," she called. "Walter!" He looked up, with that mirage of surprise on his face, and waved. "Of course, I'll play on the team."

Irini's feelings about baseball were pretty simple. Once upon a time when she'd been very little, baseball had been a fairy-tale place where pirates fought with giants. It was too exciting for girls; only boys were allowed. Like most closed clubs, once you gained admittance, it was nothing so exciting as it had sounded. Baseball turned out to be just a game that anyone could learn to play. The Senators played the Indians, the Tigers shredded the Sox, but it wasn't as epic as the names would suggest. Irini found it sort of sad, how sedentary men tried to make do with stats and standings; their admiration for anyone who could tell you over beers who'd won the 1932 Series, how many games it had gone, and who made the final out, even when they didn't play themselves. Irini didn't listen to the games much. She didn't think it was much fun to watch, even when you got to go in person, but it meant a trip to the city so she never said no. And she had always loved to play.

Now, suddenly, when she was nineteen and hadn't played for years and never expected to again, suddenly she had a team. She had never noticed how much she wanted one. It was her childhood coming back after the war, just the way she'd hoped it would.

Thomas Holcrow came out of Mr. Tarken's barbershop. After that night at Collins House he had disappeared, gone home to Los Angeles, Tracy said grimly, and Irini had assumed this would be for good. But here he was again, tipping his hat to her, revealing the unmistakable lines of a Tarken haircut. Now he was stuck in Magrit until his hair grew out.

Irini felt that this was the first chance she'd had to take a good look at him. And even with the chopped hair, darned if Tracy wasn't right. This was a really dreamy guy. "It's swell to see you again, Miss Doyle," he said.

Keep in mind that this is 1947. Who did the teenagers go for? What constituted a dreamy guy? I asked my mother once, and she said she was very much afraid those were the Frank Sinatra years. She didn't elaborate, but I suppose we can assume that just the thought of him made her as squishy and sweaty as summer fruit. We won't dwell on this, and it's not because she's my mother.

It's because it's Frank Sinatra. It's not as if he had a British accent. It's not as if there were four of him. I just can't see it.

I feel differently about Cary Grant. Cary Grant was still the very essence of male heartthrobbishness, but we can't really pretend that anyone else is like Cary Grant. So let's imagine instead that Thomas Holcrow looked just the littlest bit like Tyrone Power, if Tyrone Power had ever worn galoshes and had a bad haircut.

Walter was more the Donald O'Connor type, fair-haired, compact, energetic, and pinkish. It occurred to Irini that she could introduce them and make some point by doing so. But was the point to introduce Walter to Holcrow or to introduce Holcrow to Walter? She couldn't quite work it out and by now Walter was halfway down the block and anyway, she could see Tracy May coming. Tracy would get there before she could and the point would belong to her.

There was a noise overhead, a gabbling, a squabbling, a flutter of wings. Irini looked up, shading her eyes. There were nine Canada geese in the sky, the first squadron of spring headed toward Upper Magrit, rowing through the brightness in their V-shaped constellation. Irini's eyes were filled with tears that she had to blink away and it was just because the geese had come back the way they always did.

12

 Henry insisted Fanny was too old for pranks, but this conclusion was based on statistics and averages, and not on careful observation. It was not a mistake a scientist should have made.

Fanny's age, like everyone else's, was variable. Like everyone else, she had been all grown up during the war and like everyone else, she was sick of it afterward.

Tracy told Irini that the May girls were going a-Maying on the first Sunday in May. This turned out to have been Fanny's idea, a way of forcing spring like a bulb, through the simple expedient of declaring it to be springtime. In Fanny's hands this was a jolly, rousing, piratical approach to the world. She had used it to end love affairs, to start quarrels. She even cooked with it, although the results were seldom fortunate.

She couldn't have imagined that twenty-some years later this same technique would be used to pretend wars had ended; that thirty-some years later it would be applied to the national economy.

Of course, I don't mean to suggest she should be blamed for these later mutations. She's probably not the person who invented the strategy.

But in the almost spring of 1947, Fanny was unmistakably restless.

"We're getting up at dawn and going into the woods to look for flowers," Tracy told Irini as they walked home after work that Friday. "Top secret. No parents informed."

This was because the plan had heathen overtones. Mrs. May would not approve. Irini's father wouldn't care, but after a few drinks, he would look deeply into the daisy mirror at Bumps. He would see his own eyes, bronzed and petaled and repeated many times and it would remind him of the flowers of spring and he would mention it. He wouldn't really tell anyone. It would be a glancing reference, in the middle of a lot of poetry ringingly misquoted, a lot of "rose-lipped maids" and "light-foot lads." His conscience would be clear. But then the Baldishes would figure it out and they'd tell the Tarkens and Mrs. Tarken would be delightfully scandalized. No May wanted to see a Tarken delighted on their account.

"We'll weave crocuses into our hair and dance in our nightgowns. Fanny says it'll be fun. And we'll be back in time for church."

"Who all is coming?" asked Irini.

"Just us girls," Tracy said as if that told Irini something she didn't already know.

It's easy enough to promise to get up at dawn sometime in the middle of a bright afternoon. It may even seem a good idea. It's quite a different matter in the ur-light when the tapping on the frosted window of your bedroom comes from the horrible knuckles of Tracy May. Irini turned her back to the sound, hoping it was all a dream.

She considered the entire plan with a mind cleared of the distractions of consciousness. The trees were ready to leaf and bloom. A troupe of girls dancing in their nightgowns probably couldn't hurt. In any case, it was a gesture. Maggie Collins was a great one for appreciating the gesture. But it might come off as a criticism. A complaint about spring being late. Then it would be rude.

"Irini," Tracy whispered. "I-ri-ni!" as if she could wake Irini by making the name longer instead of louder.

"Irini." Cindy's voice had joined Tracy's and now went on alone. "You made me break a nail. We're going without you."

"No," said Irini guiltily. "I'm up."

A broken nail is the universal shorthand for something so trivial you needn't give it a thought. But not for Cindy May, who'd been born with no fingers at all on her left hand. The hand was round and smooth as a stone under water, with just one small bump where the thumb would have been. It couldn't hold an emery board. It couldn't work a clipper or nail scissors. Cindy would have to gnaw the edge off or else ask one of her sisters to help. Of course they would, but no one likes to ask.

Cindy was usually closer to Fanny, in spite of the twelve-year gap in their ages, than she was to Tracy, although you never could tell. The alliances in the May family were pretty fluid.

She was the quietest and probably the smartest of the May girls. She'd spent the war writing letters to soldiers she'd never met, pretending to be sixteen when she was fourteen and eighteen when she was fifteen. She used a pen with scented ink. Her letters smelled of stale roses.

One day Tracy followed the scent to an unfinished letter locked in a desk drawer. Not only was Cindy lying about her age, she was sending the boys Arlys Fossum's picture instead of her own. Tracy told everyone in the Kitchen on drop-cookie day. It embarrassed Arlys, but Tracy minded more. Why hadn't Cindy used Tracy's picture?

No one doubted that it was patriotically motivated. There was a war on. They were all patriots. The soldiers had to be given every reason to beat the Nazis. And then just in the last year, Cindy had gotten quite pretty herself, in a freckled, rosy, coffee-haired Mayish way, but no one in Magrit had noticed yet.

It was cold out. Irini had selected her nightgown with some care the night before, something suitable for dancing. Now she had to go back and cover it in padded jackets, supplement it with jeans, scarves, boots, and gloves. There was nothing Botticelli-like in the picture she presented and the whole ensemble itched. She was technically in her nightgown, though; no one could say she wasn't.

This had all taken more time. The sun was up, but not really open for business. Irini was the same. "I'm cold," she said, joining Fanny on the Mays' front porch. It wasn't a complaint, just a fact there was no reason to conceal.

Fanny reached into her jacket pocket. "I've got just the thing." She pulled out a flat bottle of rum, uncapped it and took a drink. She passed it over to Irini. "Let's get the sap rising."

Fanny was plenty old enough to drink, but Irini had never seen her do it. Certainly she had never offered Irini a drink before. Irini was surprised, but Tracy was so shocked her voice came out all in a whistle. "Fanny!" she said. "It's Sunday!" Cindy's eyes were round as tea plates.

Irini had been about to refuse the drink. She'd never even liked Maggie Collins's rum cream pies and Maggie was famous for those. But she was still irritated at Tracy for making her get up. Irini took the bottle.

Tracy had not finished arguing. "That's an after-dinner drink," she said.

"Don't whine," Fanny told her. "If this were a proper Maying there would be men. We're just barely making do here. As usual."

Once Fanny had told Irini she didn't like to drink. "I'm always hoping I'll find myself in a situation where I have to think fast," she'd said. "Someday something exciting will happen to me and I want to be awake for it."

The war had rather suited Fanny. There were men to be had, easy pickings, if you could get to any city. Affairs were forced to be everything she liked—passionate, stormy, and short. The period after the war with no men at all was not so good. Irini understood her drinking now to be a sort of giving up. Fanny could go to the woods at dawn in her nightgown and know that nothing exciting would come of it. It was sad.

People talked a lot to Irini about drinking, as if she were some sort of expert. She tipped and swallowed. It was 1947 so who knew alcoholism was genetic? A hot gush slid down her throat and landed near her heart. Her eyes watered. She passed the bottle to Cindy.

"No *thank* you," said Tracy coldly, just in case they didn't pass it to her and she didn't get to make a point of refusing. Cindy swallowed enough to make her cough. By the time it came around to Irini again, she remembered the taste as good. When she actually drank, she remembered that it wasn't. But every time, it got better in the remembering.

While they tippled, they walked. Fanny led them off Brief Street and there they were, two steps into the woods already. Irini took a long, hard swallow. In the growing daylight, it was clear that the dancing was to be redundant. Spring had come. It was there ahead of them, with an exhilarating mix of odors—dirt and water and honey.

As the light increased, the perfumes diminished. A white dogwood was almost in bloom. There were dandelions, blue violets, and wood anemone. Leaves in the thousands, each one shaded a different green, and all colored so delicately. The colors of cake frostings, corsages, and prom dresses.

And there were birds.

Fanny began to hum. Every once in a while, she would sing a word or two. "It might as well be spring." Irini picked up the alto. They extended the final note of the chorus so that Irini could play around with harmonies. It was a subtle sort of tease. Tracy loved to sing. She ignored them both. Fanny handed Irini the bottle.

They went through a boggy patch, where Irini's boots stuck, making sucking sounds as she lifted and planted her feet. Fanny chose a glade of aspens full of deep, wet smells and fiddlehead ferns still encased in silver. She picked two large ferns and put them into the back of her hair. They stuck up like antlers.

On the ground beside her, Irini saw deer track. On another day she might have followed to see if it ate any mushrooms.

Maggie Collins recommends this, because—ask any naturalist—you almost never find a deer with its tongue blackened and its eyes cloudy and its little hooves sticking straight up into the air, and all from eating the wrong mushroom. Deer always know the difference. We don't, which is something to ponder. Anyway, Irini didn't like mushrooms.

Dancing in the woods sounds romantic until you're actually doing it. Actually doing it seems dumb. No one wanted to be the one to start. Irini took another drink, and another. Tracy delayed by making herself a complicated coronet of violets and new leaves. She had begun to hum, the same alto line that Irini had followed, but much fancier, with quavers and trills. She opened her mouth. You could tell she liked the sound of her own singing. She stuck the stems of the leaves into the webby parts of other leaves.

"Make me one, too," Cindy asked.

"It keeps tearing."

Tracy had settled into a complaining tone, which made Fanny push her into Cindy. The two of them regarded Fanny critically. "She wants to be the only one with a crown," said Tracy. "Queen of the May."

"She's not wearing a crown," said Cindy. "She looks like she's got antennae."

Irini was laughing, but she wasn't sure why. Fanny turned her back and began to sing again. "I love Paris in the springtime."

"Queen of the bees." Tracy finished her crown and put it on.

It did look nice. Her hair waved out over her shoulders, dark clouds of hair. "How soon would you let a boy kiss you?" she asked Irini. "Third date? Fourth date?" They'd had this conversation before many times. She knew Irini meant to hold out until the fourth date, at least. The question had become embarrassingly hypothetical. It must be on Tracy's mind again because of Thomas Holcrow.

"Learn to react without thinking," Fanny advised. "Don't make plans. Make a chain." Irini took Cindy's other hand, the one with no fingers. It was hard to grip; she moved her own fingers upward, circled the wrist. Tracy caught Irini's spare hand in her own cold, wet one. "Here we go dancing in May, in May," Fanny said.

She led off, skipping over the dead leaves and pine needles of last year. She made sharp little turns, crack-the-whip turns, so that Irini's arms were pulled at the shoulders and Tracy stumbled and lost her footing. Fanny was usually quite nice to Irini, but never so nice as when she was not being nice to Tracy. There was something familiar about this, therefore. Fanny and Tracy quarreling with Irini's body between them.

"Are you going to play on Walter's baseball team?" Tracy asked Irini, panting slightly.

"*I* am not," said Fanny. "I don't like baseball. And I think this girls' team idea is just a little undignified." Her face was flushed. One of her ferns bent over like a dog's ear.

"It's not ice hockey," said Tracy. "I don't think it'll be undignified."

"Oh, it's fine for you." Fanny cracked the whip so sharply that both Irini and Tracy went sprawling. Because Irini was holding Cindy with her strong arm, she yanked Cindy down as well. The ground was soft with water, but they hit it hard. Only Fanny remained standing. "But I'm an adult," she said.

Irini couldn't get to her feet again and this made her laugh. She lay on the wet ground, with a slug feeding near one of her hands, and the sky spinning. Now she was the May pole, the trees circled around her. "Here you go dancing in May, in May," she told them. In the middle of those greens and all the buds it was impossible not to believe that something good, something exciting was just about to happen. Right there in Magrit. Any minute now.

"Look." Cindy reached an arm over her. Her wrist where Irini had held it was red with fingerprints. Cindy lowered it until it was in front of Irini's eyes.

"Fanny!" Tracy complained. Her voice was a small irritation, like the whine of a distant, summer mosquito. Irini could hardly hear it. She worked to keep this illusion. She brought up the sounds of the birds and the wind and the insects. She tamped down the sounds of the Mays.

"You did that on purpose, Fanny," said Tracy. "What does that have to do with spring?"

"No, that was great," said Cindy. She got to her feet and began to spin again. "We should dance more often. That's my belief." She raised her voice, opened her arms. "Don't forget to dance, world. Leave time for the dancing."

Irini watched her fondly. She was so precocious. So good-natured. So easy to please. It came from being the youngest of three sisters.

"I don't call what we just did dancing," said Tracy. "Do you, *Fanny?*"

"I call it, Falling on Buttocks," Fanny said. "It's my masterpiece."

"Did you write that letter for Maggie?" Irini asked. Her own voice came out very loud. The sky tipped lazily and slid toward her open mouth.

"Who me? Maggie writes her own letters. Put some money in the pig, Irini."

"She already said she didn't." Irini hadn't heard Fanny say this, but Tracy's voice was sharp with the impatience of repetition. "Are you calling my sister a liar?"

"My sister doesn't lie," said Cindy.

"She runs the whole Kitchen," said Tracy. "I'd like to see you try. I wonder how you'd like it if everyone was suspecting you?"

"Anyway, what harm did the column do?" Cindy asked. "I even agreed with it."

"Sorry," said Irini.

She had gotten the information she wanted. She could tell that both Tracy and Cindy thought Fanny had written it. It was enough to satisfy her.

Fanny slid to the ground beside her. "Say, Irini," she said. "Say, Tracy." There was a pause. The pause interested Irini. Fanny was having trouble getting to the point. "What about Maggie's last column?" Fanny asked. "Did anyone but me see a problem there?"

"Which column was that?" Irini wasn't in the mood for problems. She could just begin to feel the cold moisture of the ground soaking through her jacket and into her nightgown. Time to get up. But she wasn't in the mood for that either.

"Jack-Be-Nimble Salad."

In the thirties Maggie had been an enthusiastic proponent of fun foods. She made open-faced sandwiches with olive eyes, she made those little rabbit salads out of canned pears and marshmallows. She thumbed her nose at the Great Depression by suggesting a dinner party where the guests dressed as hobos and took dessert home in their bandannas-on-sticks. Such frivolity was out of place during the war. But not now. If Irini had thought anything about Maggie Collins's Jack-Be-Nimble Salad, it was that this was a return to form.

"I thought that was cute," said Cindy.

"Adorable. I can't find out who sent it in."

"I thought it was cute," Tracy repeated. "I bet Mr. Henry won't have a problem with it. What harm can it do?"

"If it's not a problem, why won't anyone admit to it?"

"Maybe Mr. Henry did it himself. Maybe Mrs. Ada. She's real artistic."

"I can't ask *him,* you know," said Fanny. "He'll know I think it's a problem, if I ask him. If he doesn't think it's a problem, I don't want him to know I think it's a problem."

"Why is it a problem?" asked Irini. "Maggie's done lots of these salads before. Remember Valentine's Day? Heart-shaped peaches and pickle spears?"

"Fine. It's not a problem," said Fanny. "I think Maggie's getting a little out of hand. But just forget I said anything."

Everyone forgot it. Irini put a sudden end to the Maying by being sick twice. She noted that she had never thrown up so effortlessly, but this was just a matter of trying to find the bright side. She would never, never, never drink again.

There was another bright side, which she only thought to appreciate later. This was that none of the neighbors were up yet. No one saw Irini reeling down Brief Street with the Mays, on a *Sunday* morning with violets and fiddleheads in their hair, and all of them dressed for a slumber party in the snow. No one except Sissy Tarken, who looked out from her porch, and they didn't see her, but she asked Irini about it later. No need for the Mays to ever know this. And absolutely no one else except the very first robin of the season, and he kept quiet for two more days.

MAGGIE COLLINS'S JACK-BE-NIMBLE SALAD

Here's an easy way to dress up a humdrum lunch for the girls. Set one pineapple ring per person on a decorative lettuce leaf. Fasten a peeled banana upright inside the ring to resemble a candle. Complete the illusion with a pimiento flame and mayonnaise drips. A great ice-breaker. No one can be too stuffy while eating this!

13

I have warned you of my mother's generous and sunny nature. Here's an illustration. This is her version of an old standard:

Two teenagers are parked on a secluded road. The radio is on. The music is interrupted by a bulletin. A maniacal murderer has escaped from the local mental institution. He can be easily identified by the hook he has in place of his right hand.

A noise startles the teenagers into leaving. The car is just a little slow to respond, just a little sluggish. The boy has to push the pedal into the floor. When they arrive home, they discover a hook, stuck in the door handle on the girl's side.

The next day the man comes looking for his hook. He's traced them through the license plate. Turns out he wasn't the escapee at all. He's a war hero, decorated three times. He just wanted directions. They all have a good laugh about the misunderstanding.

Many things were in short supply during the war—butter, baseball players, body parts. One of the first things the War Production Board did was to outlaw zoot suits and the female equivalent, juke coats. The ostensible reason for the ban was that they required too much material. For the duration of the war, no one would look smoother than anyone else, by government decree. No doubt this had its effect on morale. Good for some.

The national speed limit was thirty-five miles per hour, otherwise known as the victory speed; the gas ration for an ordinary person with an A windshield sticker was three gallons per week, which hardly mattered since you couldn't get tires and then later you couldn't get cars. Nor new bicycles, stoves, household appliances, or anything else made of metal. Paper, including toilet paper, was in short supply. Let's not even think about this.

First sugar, then coffee, finally every food but fruits and vegetables was rationed. You could buy one pair of shoes every six months. There was the black market, and there was also an aggressive advertising campaign against it. "Did you drown a sailor today because YOU bought a lamb chop without giving up the required coupons?" a wartime ad asked. Go live with yourself.

But it was the expressed desire of President Roosevelt that baseball continue to be played during the war. While the Japanese Empire was abolishing baseball, America was saving it. What were we fighting for, after all? Baseball is a protected monopoly. What says America faster than that?

The game was not, however, untouched. There was a war on. Naturally, standards had to be relaxed. Those same shortages that made tires so hard to come by also affected the manufacture of baseballs. For the duration, the balls were made, like wartime pennies, of inferior materials. You could call them victory balls, though they lacked zip.

And the best players were in khaki.

Even so, baseball is in more trouble now than then. You don't need me to tell you this. For the first time since 1904 we skipped a World Series and—this is the real kicker—nobody younger than forty gives a damn. Someone has finally dropped the ball that was handed down carefully from father to son for generation after generation. It looks like it was us. Pretty tacky for the guys who grew up with Sandy Koufax and Willie Mays and Roberto Clemente.

You could blame the owners. You could blame the players. I blame *Sesame Street*. The *Sesame Street* generation morphed directly into MTV. They're a generation evolutionarily adapted to the remote control, which is itself the next chapter in the story of the opposable thumb. Every entertainment ever planned for this group has tried to work within the limits of their tiny little attention spans.

This is a classic confusion of cause and effect. The effect is our children, uniquely capable of watching several games at once, with a movie thrown in for flavor. They've lost the narrative and gained the highlights film. They've lost baseball and picked up hockey.

If *Sesame Street* had felt any responsibility toward baseball, it wouldn't have been an hourlong show. Instead, you would have never known when it was going to end. One day it might be two hours long, the next, three hours and seventeen minutes. If *Sesame Street* had cared about baseball it would have been a leisurely show with a lot of chatting on the mound, like *Mr. Rogers' Neighborhood*.

Margaret Mill applied some flexible standards in order to field a women's team. The starting line-up included Cindy May, who played baseball by imitating Pete Gray—trying to catch, shed the glove, transfer the ball, and throw it back as quickly as he did. Pete Gray was a one-armed outfielder for the Browns. Gray was not a casualty of the war; he'd lost his hand in a childhood accident, but he made it to the majors. In fact, men's baseball has a long tradition of one-armed men. It starts with pitcher Hugh Daily and continues through outfielders Jesse Alexander and Pete Gray straight on to Jim Abbott's no-hitter.

No one-armed woman ever played in the women's leagues. Perhaps this was because, however gifted, a one-armed player still carries the taint of the sideshow, and women's baseball was already a sideshow. Perhaps the same people whose hearts were warmed by the sight of a talented one-armed man would have found an ambitious one-armed woman preposterous. Or perhaps the pool of women ballplayers has always been so small, and the pool of one-armed women so much smaller still, that an overlap was statistically unthinkable.

No one said Cindy shouldn't play baseball. No one even thought it. Cindy did everything her sisters did. She'd always taken her turn at the dishes, same as her sisters. She made her bed, she did the ironing. She'd taken piano lessons, learning to play a baseline of a single note. Chopping and mincing were difficult for her; she didn't work in the Kitchen, but served as Magrit's telephone operator, right from her own home. Norma Baldish had ingeniously modified the control panel so that Cindy could work it one-handed. When Cindy was out for any reason, there was no telephone service in Magrit.

She rarely seemed to think about her missing fingers and neither did her sisters. Irini followed their example. When Irini was twelve or so, Mrs. Baldish asked her once at a recital if she didn't think Cindy was awfully brave to take piano lessons and Irini thought she was referring to Mrs. Gilbertsen's teaching methods. Mrs. Gilbertsen was the sort of woman who would have liked to use a metronome for all of life's activities. "Tempo, tempo," she said sometimes when she saw Irini on the street and this meant that Irini was walking too fast.

Irini had never taken piano herself. Her father said the scales were fascistic when really he just hadn't wanted to have to listen to them. But Mrs. Gilbertsen came to school to teach the girls in Magrit deportment and manners, with a lot of emphasis on gloves and curtsies, so Irini had personal experience.

The boys had never had to go to deportment, back when they'd had boys in Magrit. Boys couldn't grasp the intricacies of good manners. They went outside and worked on blocking and tackling while the girls curtsied and learned to sit with their legs crossed at the ankles and to stand in a position Mrs. Gilbertsen called the Right Hesitation. You teach a girl to hesitate and she'll have a lesson she'll remember all her life.

The concession the Sweetwheat Sweethearts made to Cindy's missing fingers was to play her at first.

This was the starting lineup: Tracy May pitching, Norma Baldish catching, Cindy at first, Claire Kinser at second, Margo Törngren at third, and Arlys Fossum at short.

The outfield consisted of my mother in center, Helen Leggett in right, and Sissy Tarken in left. Sissy Tarken would have been better in the infield, but Walter had lived in Magrit long enough to know that it was best to keep the Tarkens and the Mays as far apart as possible. The Mays, the Leggetts, and the Kinsers were Upper Magrit. The Tarkens and Baldishes were Lower. It was a risk teaming Tracy as pitcher with Norma behind the plate, but there were no options. Arlys, Margo, and Irini were not identified with either faction and could swing both ways. Walter never complained about the added difficulties of coaching a team in which half the lineup didn't speak to the other half. He just worked within the historical context.

"But it's all the same team," Henry said. "Same mill." As the man responsible, Henry had always maintained that the Troubles in Magrit were temporary.

He was firmly blind to these distinctions when hiring. Actually neither Sissy nor Norma nor Cindy worked at the mill, but they could have if they'd wanted to, Henry said, which made it close enough to being a mill team. "Advertising true," my mother used to say sometimes in reference to some of my stories. This was to distinguish them from the actually untrue, of which I've lived long enough now to notice hardly anything is.

My mother could make the throw all the way to home. She was the only outfielder who could do this. Walter called her his grenade launcher. Initially, there was no bench.

The Sweethearts barnstormed all over the small towns of the neighboring states, but they stayed away from the big cities. Partly this was practical. In a small town, the Sweethearts' arrival was a big event.

Partly it was sentimental. Henry had a particular affection for the small-town Midwest. The cereal bowl of America, Henry called it.

Partly it was political. Ada Collins's admiration for the proletariat was more than matched by her horror of the lumpen proletariat. She didn't think good husbands were as likely to be found in the corrupted cities.

Partly it was prudent. There had been race riots in several cities during the last years of the war. The Germans were sometimes blamed. Spies and subversives had convinced the Negroes there were things to be unhappy about. On Hitler's instructions these subversives fanned the flames of discontent. It was all too hot for Magrit.

Naturally none of the small towns had women's baseball. The Sweethearts played friendly games in neighborhood parks against local pickup teams. Henry bought an old school bus and painted it in wheat tones. He paid Norma Baldish to drive and Fanny May went along as chaperone. Fanny was good at this. She performed her function primarily by diversion. Men were so busy sending her flowers, buying her drinks, and bribing desk clerks for her room number that they left the other Sweethearts pretty much alone.

The lack of a bench really hurt the team. Walter had hoped that in a pinch, Fanny might pitch in, but she said there was no chance of that. Henry had bought the Sweethearts' equipment at bargain, because it was war surplus. "That'll be the day when you find me playing with zipless balls," Fanny said.

Tracy May's pitching was also a major weakness. The Sweethearts were to play against men, so they played baseball, not softball, and no one at the mill could do much with the overarm delivery. Tracy was the only one who even thought she could learn to pitch. Walter decided that pitching was largely a matter of self-confidence anyway, which made Tracy the obvious choice. Halfway there already. She and Walter worked out a sort of modified side arm; my mother called it the rug-beating stroke.

The Sweethearts played a tune-up game against their mothers and fathers, and it went three hours and two innings because Tracy couldn't find the plate. The infield was full of dandelions, all in bloom, which meant they were past good eating. The surrounding hills had been painted with large, bright strokes of lupine and hawkweed and buttercups. The air was charged with pollen and very fragrant. It was making Tracy sneeze. Partway through the second inning, seven batters in, she started to cry. She cried and sneezed, cried and sneezed, until her nose went red, white, and blue. Walter had been standing out in right, coaching Helen. He started toward the mound, but Irini ran in to intercept him at second.

"Don't you dare, Walter Collins," she said. She spoke softly so Tracy wouldn't hear. "When she wants to come out, she'll tell you."

"But she's crying. I think that means she wants to come out."

"I think it means she's mad. You'll undermine her confidence if you pull her when she hasn't asked."

"She's walked seven consecutive batters and her confidence hasn't been undermined yet. This is Tracy we're talking about."

"No one else wants to pitch. Leave her alone."

Tracy sneezed three times, one right after another. Each sneeze contained a high and desperate sound.

"This is not working. And these are our parents. They'd be swinging if she were coming within a mile of the plate. What if she beans her mother? What's that going to do to her confidence?" Walter asked.

"She's *not* coming within a mile of the plate. How can anyone get hurt? Leave her alone. I'll see you in Hoboken before I'll let you pull her."

Walter returned to the outfield. Tracy bounced the next pitch in the dirt. Mr. Fossum tried to hit it on the bounce. He took his base with four balls, one strike. It was the best count Tracy had gotten this inning.

She walked one parent after another. By now everyone was coaching her. All the batters, all the fielders. "Calm down, honey." "Loosen up your shoulder." "You're doing fine." "You're doing fine." "Watch the ball all the way into the glove. Give her a target, Norma."

The sun set. A barred owl swooped overhead. Chiggers attacked the outfielders. The game was called for darkness. Tracy May went home and sobbed herself to sleep. In the morning she could hardly lift her arm. But the next time she pitched she only walked eight batters and she went six innings.

The worst player on the team was Helen Leggett, who shouldn't have been on the squad, much less in the starting lineup. Helen was chosen for box office, in lieu of and until Henry could organize the ape. She was chosen for the way she filled out the wheat laurel pocket on the uniform, chosen for her incredible strike zone.

Helen was not an especially pretty girl. Her face was ordinary, but pleasant with a beautiful wide smile she didn't use very often. Her hair was a nondescript brown and wouldn't take curl. It was so thin you could usually see her ears through it. She couldn't bat and she couldn't throw and she couldn't knock down a grounder and she always came in too far on a fly, which was good for at least one extra base. All the same if there'd been cards with their pictures and their stats, she'd have been the card the fans would all have traded to get. One of her would have been worth all the rest of them.

She consistently got on base—walked to first, because the men wanted to see her run to second. She was aware of this. It made her slow and awkward. There was no dignified way to run the bases when she knew all the men in the stands and all the men in the field were waiting to see her try.

The other Sweethearts were protective of Helen. She had developed all at once, over the course of a few months, so fast that Dr. Gilbertsen had had to give her painkillers so that she could sleep at night. It left her with stretch marks and made her shy around men. She never looked at their faces, for fear that they were not looking at hers.

Among the Sweethearts, Helen was loud and well liked. She was a bit like Fanny in that she had a sharp and witty tongue—but not as bawdy. She could keep a secret, not as well as Fanny could, but good by Sweetheart standards. Irini took to playing over toward right when she felt there was a need; and Sissy adjusted when Irini did. Helen was good-natured about this.

After the Sweethearts' first and only season, Helen married a man she'd met on a goodwill tour the Sweethearts made to a rehab center for amputees in Gary, Indiana. He had the Purple Heart. In 1944 he'd been sent on a detail to remove a nest of undetonated shells from a farmer's field in northern England. One of the shells exploded and blew away both of his hands.

14

The week before the Sweethearts' first game Henry tried to keep them busy and loose. He released the fish-stick team temporarily to work on the annual problem of hard-boiled eggs. Easter had come and gone, but it had brought the issue of green egg yolks to Maggie's attention once again. Every year Maggie asked herself why some yolks responded to the boiling process by turning a sad, soggy green color. How could you guarantee the bright, yellow yolk your kids expected every time?

And while they were at it, there must be a way to keep the boiling eggs from cracking. Maggie had discovered that a teaspoon of salt in the cooking water would prevent the contents from leaking even if the shell cracked. This was good for any occasion except Easter, when you must not only keep the contents in, but also keep the dye out. In past years the Kitchen had tried puncturing the shells with tiny pinholes. They had soaked the eggs in vinegar first. They had tried bringing the eggs slowly up to a boil. They had cooked them in salted water. They had dropped room-temperature eggs directly into the boiling water. It was a chemical problem, but it was too much for Irini's father. Nothing guaranteed the hundred percent success rate Maggie had set her heart on.

Two years ago at Eastertime Maggie had created a sensation by blowing eggs out of their shells through a pinhole and then washing, drying, and oiling the shell, and filling it with flavored gelatin. Refrigerate and then peel. Eggs had never been so bright and sweet before.

But she was not the sort to dwell on past triumphs. Maggie Collins would not rest until Easter could go forward without the loss of a single egg.

For the rest of the girls it was muffin day in the Scientific Kitchen. Paradoxically, because she was such a poor cook Irini was much in demand when recipes were tested. If Irini could cook it, well, that said something.

Irini had drawn the recipe card this morning for lemon ice muffins. She put the red kerchief that was part of the Kitchen uniform over her hair and tied on the checked apron. Dinah Shore was on the radio with her comfortable, warm-kitchen voice. "You know what would be nice?" Irini said, measuring the flour. "Muffins that sang as they cooked. Wouldn't it be lovely to come into a sunny kitchen in the morning and hear the voices of six little muffins all singing together? Why doesn't Mr. Henry have us working on that?"

Irini had a fondness for action foods. All her life she craved dishes like jubilees and soufflés and fondues, dishes that flamed or puffed or bubbled.

"Mr. Henry neglects the aural," Helen agreed. "It's because he can't hear." Her own ear stuck out through her limp brown hair like a mushroom in the forest.

"He hears well enough when he wants to. You know what annoys me?" said Fanny. She was wiping down the counters. They glistened whitely behind her sponge as if they'd been glazed. "How every recipe gives you enough for eight muffins, but every muffin tin has six cups. Why is that?"

Fanny was in a bad mood. She had told Margo to pick up Maggie's private correspondence, but she had done it in the presence of Henry

Collins, who made her drop a quarter into the blue pig. Fanny had not actually said that Maggie didn't exist. She had merely told Margo to answer Maggie's mail. She felt this constituted a gray area. As soon as Henry left the Kitchen, Fanny fished her quarter out again. "Notice," she told the girls, "that I am merely recovering my own money. I am not taking anything that belongs to Maggie."

"Because the recipes all call for one egg," said Irini. "You reduce the recipe, you have to work in fractions of eggs." She broke an egg into the bowl, one-handed, lots of wrist. "Of course, they could make the muffin tins with eight cups. I don't know why they don't do that."

"Your average family can't eat eight muffins at a sitting," said Helen. "Your average family consists of a dad, a mom, a son, and a daughter. Two muffins apiece for the dad and the son. One muffin each for the mother and the daughter. Six muffins."

"Show me the girl who can't eat two muffins."

"But she's having eggs, too. And bacon. And toast and coffee."

"And Sweetwheats," said Irini. "Notice how you always forget the Sweetwheats? A cereal that sang while you ate would be nice, too, come to think of it. Pour in the milk and it sings. 'Good morning to you. Good morning to you.'"

Irini's father often sang this same song the morning after a particularly grueling night at Bumps. "We're all in our places, with egg on our faces." It was intended as an apology for whatever he'd done and now couldn't remember.

Danny Kaye came on the radio. They sifted in rhythmic accompaniment, the flour rising in clouds around their hands, red scarves tight over their hair, and sang along until they came to the part where he went too fast, even for Arlys, and they had to stop.

They were waiting for *Wheat Theater,* the weekly radio show sponsored by Margaret Mill. *Wheat Theater* followed the adventures and misadventures of Miss Anna Peal. Anna Peal was a sort of blend of Little Orphan Annie and Fanny Farmer. She lived abroad; her parents were missionaries in an unidentified country whose borders gave her easy access to snowy, Swisslike mountains, humid jungles, the chaparral, and the sands of both beaches and deserts.

In the last episode, Anna had strayed into the jungle, again, and been captured by natives. Naturally they turned out to be cannibals. When we left our heroine last, the cooking water was just coming to a boil.

In today's episode, little Anna took charge of the situation. She convinced the entire tribe to delay her own stewing long enough for her to whip up a squash flambé. The seasonings were so exquisite the entire tribe converted to vegetarianism on the spot. In halting and charmingly garbled English the chief told Anna he had never known that he liked vegetables, because never before had anyone prepared them for him properly. He gave her a necklace of beads. "Steaming, instead of boiling, that's the ticket," Anna told him. "Vegetables have really quite a sweet taste." Listeners learned that a recipe for the squash flambé would be found on the back of any Sweetwheats box.

You mustn't get the idea that Anna was a prissy kind of girl. Her cooking expertise had given her a real feel for backyard chemistry. Tie her up with ropes; she could free herself with a homemade corrosive. Make her walk on hot coals; she would cook up a salve for the bottoms of her feet that would last just long enough. And she would do it all with products you could find in your very own kitchen.

She specialized in explosives. She could make a sort of Molotov cocktail and she could make it fast and she could make it out of ordinary household items. The problem came when it was time to light it. Anna was not allowed to play with matches.

Every week the show was packed with useful information. Never run from a wolf nor stare directly into its eyes. If you are made to walk the plank, slip a hollow reed into your sleeve beforehand. You can breathe through the reed for as long as it takes to convince the pirates you have drowned. Contrary to popular wisdom, puffballs are not poisonous. If the alternative is starvation, go ahead and eat them. Properly prepared, they taste a bit like cattails.

Many of Anna's recipes appeared on the back of Sweetwheats cereal. An exception was the Molotov cocktail. Although instructions would have undoubtedly boosted sales, Henry would not consider it. He had a strong sense of civic responsibility, even beyond Magrit, and lucky for us he did. If Henry Collins had put the recipe for Molotov cocktails on the back of Sweetwheats cereal, we might have skipped the fifties altogether and gone straight into the sixties and how unpleasant would that have been?

Anna's parents never worried much about her weekly brushes with death, because they didn't believe in them. The show's writer, a man who lived in Chicago near the radio station, had a penchant for the *it-was-all-a-dream . . . or-was-it?* ending. Week after week, he managed to walk the knife-edge to the satisfaction of his younger audience. When the girls were ten, they used to argue about it next day at recess. If her adventures were real, then they all wanted to be Anna Peal. But not if she was making them up.

To the fourteen-year-olds, it was obvious the adventures were imaginary. "Anna Banana-peel," they called her, and the writer should have anticipated this bon mot.

As a little girl my mother loved *Wheat Theater*. Later, when *The Avengers* came on television, my mother claimed to see Anna Peal all grown up and to like what she saw.

On this occasion Mrs. Peal tucked Anna into bed. "What an imagination you have," she said fondly. "Now go to sleep and chase some more of those big dreams." She kissed her daughter. But there was the telltale bead necklace, lying on the night stand. "Why Anna, where did you get this?" her mother asked. "Is this your grandmother's bead necklace?"

After each adventure, Anna made an initial attempt to come clean. She never tried more than once and she never tried when she had actual physical evidence to support her story. It gave credence to the Anna Banana-peel camp.

"May I have Sweetwheats for breakfast tomorrow?" little Anna asked instead. "It wouldn't be breakfast without Sweetwheats," Anna and her mother said in unison. Followed by the Sweetwheats' jingle:

> *Every mother's day starts*
> *With Sweetwheats for her sweethearts. . . .*

"Sweetwheats have an appeal," Anna Peal said at the finish of each show. Followed by assorted announcements.

Maggie Collins had come out with a new book, *20 Ways to Cook a Goose.* "Tell your mothers," Anna instructed the little *Wheat Theater* listeners. "Every recipe has been pretested in the kitchens at Margaret Mill."

Free copies had already been given to all the Margaret Mill girls to provide more ammunition in their hunt for husbands. But Irini had no intention of cooking geese. She took the book home and gave it to her father, who amended the title with a ballpoint pen to *20 Ways to Cook* Your *Goose.*

It was a thin, tasteful volume, conveniently organized by body part. There was a small section entitled "Necks!" and a large section entitled "Breasts!" It was lost eventually in one of our moves, but I do remember seeing it.

There was a second announcement: On Saturday afternoon, Maggie Collins's own baseball team, the Sweetwheat Sweethearts, would be playing their first game ever and they would be playing it right over in Yawkey. Balloons would be given to anyone under five. "They're all girls," the announcement said. "And they're all girl."

"Well, that's that," said Irini. "Now the fat is in the fire."

"Is it possible we'll win?" Helen asked.

"We'll be annihilated," Irini assured her. "We'll be humiliated. It will be the most awful day of your life."

"We might meet some swell guys over in Yawkey," Tracy said.

"Isn't that the point? That we meet some swell guy and get married? Who cares about baseball?"

Maggie Collins writes: "To peel a hard-cooked egg, roll it on a hard surface until the egg is cracked all over.

"Never attempt to peel a warm egg."

15

Henry was dickering with a Señora Lagunas over an ape at the Lagunas estate in Havana. He locked himself in the mill office and shouted long distance over the phone. The ape was named Topsy and Señora Lagunas, who professed to love her passionately, was perhaps going to send her to the Chicago zoo to mate with an ape there whose name was Buddy. Señora Lagunas was putting together a trousseau for Topsy, in case she *did* decide to send her to Chicago. The señora had purchased Topsy in Paris several years ago. Topsy had been an infant at the time, so Parisian fashions had apparently imprinted her. The trousseau was mostly imported and it was taking a long time to assemble it.

Or else something entirely different. Between his hearing problems, the long distance, and the language barrier, Henry Collins frequently couldn't follow the drift. "Si, si," the girls in the Kitchen could hear him shouting. Followed by "No, no!"

Perhaps, if Topsy were to be mated, Señora Lagunas would also agree to let Topsy stop in Magrit first. But perhaps not. She did not see Topsy as the sort of ape one experimented on. She did not really see Topsy as the sort of ape who mated with someone named Buddy. Negotiations went forward and backward and round and round. But there was always the chance they would reach a successful conclusion. Then someone would have to fly down and pick Topsy up. This would be Norma Baldish. Norma was the person you sent for if your car wouldn't start, or your pipes had frozen, or you were wiring the back bedroom or you were plagued with raccoons or you needed a stump taken out. Norma was the only person in Magrit capable of going to Cuba and picking up an ape.

The Dodgers were in Cuba in the spring of 1947, and so was the entire women's league, sponsored largely by Philip Wrigley. There must have been more money in gum than in breakfast cereal. The Sweethearts trained right there in Magrit. There was no gym, no locker room, but they did get to get off work early. They brought their equipment to the mill, changed in the Kitchen, and hiked together over to the high school field.

They had to cut across the back half of the Gilbertsen property and through a field of lupine. Up close the lupine was far from the unbroken sheet of purple it appeared at a distance. Still it was intense enough. Irini fell silent, neither saying anything nor hearing anything that was said. She watched her feet making each purple step. When she reached the grasses again, it was as if a spell had been broken.

Initially Henry had opposed the idea of practices. He argued that practicing added an additional muddy variable. The results would be so much cleaner if the Sweethearts could win just through eating Sweetwheats. Walter had to take him upstairs to the ham radio room for a long talk.

After practice, the Sweethearts crossed the other edge of the Gilbertsens' on their way to the Törngrens' steam bath. Margo Törngren was herself a walking advertisement for the benefits of steam. Margo had white-gold hair and pale skin. She looked as delicate as a china figurine, but from kindergarten to graduation she had never missed a day of school. Irini couldn't remember that she had ever had a cold.

Her hair was extraordinary; she was the Rapunzel in Irini's father's fairy-tale Magrit. But her personality was a bit at odds with the extravagant hair. No princess had ever been more practical or diligent or disciplined. Her only sin was tardiness. Her friends had learned to tack on the extra half hour to any plans that included her.

The sauna was set some distance from the Törngren house and downstream from Margaret Mill. There was an old grindstone in the dressing room with the seat and pedals of a bicycle, so it provided an opportunity for exercise, as well as the healthful benefits of steam. This was not an opportunity any of the girls took advantage of. The word "aerobics" had, thankfully, not yet been invented.

While the room heated the girls undressed. They had been stripping together since they were six years old, but instead of becoming more comfortable with it, they had become less so. The past years had seen more towels and less eye contact. If they had lived among the Greeks, this might have been an occasion for boasting. "I am as beautiful as the sea nymphs," they might have said to each other, dropping their towels, just before all hell broke loose. Helen took off her brassiere. "Incoming," she said. Her breasts fell to her waist. Irini looked down at her own legs and saw that they needed a shave.

After a long day in the Kitchen and a long evening on the field, Irini's arm was aching. She couldn't wait to get some heat on it, although she hated the feel of hot air in her lungs or her nose. She pinned up her hair. "Remember how I could put my hair up without pins before I cut it last time?" said Tracy. "It was that thick." She was that close to having her hair turned into snakes.

Fortunately for Magrit, none of the girls, not even Tracy, really felt that they were beautiful. Partly this was because there were no men around, except for a few fathers, to tell them so. "Remember when there were boys in Magrit?" Cindy May asked plaintively.

"Scott Moodey and Wilbur Floyd," Irini reminded her.

"The others. Do you remember when we couldn't come to the sauna without them spying on us every step of the way?"

"As if they were spying on you," Tracy said. "In a pig's eye! When the boys left, you were as skinny as a rail and as freckled as a frog. You were the biggest droon."

My mother said that the Sweethearts never fought. Nine girls, most of whom worked together all day, and my mother couldn't remember that a cross or gossipy or hurtful word was ever spoken, except for the tiniest of quarrels, the smallest of disagreements, only enough dissension to keep things interesting. Of course she was aided in this happy memory by the fact that the Tarkens and the Mays didn't speak to each other at all.

I don't find this picture of excessive harmony and sisterhood to be plausible, and so I'm ignoring it. It's only fair to point this out.

But even my mother would concede that the May girls, being sisters, had a tendency to pick at one another. "This didn't mean they weren't close," my mother said. "Criticize one of them yourself and watch how fast they became the three musketeers."

Margo poured water from the bucket onto the coals. The room began to sizzle and Irini could smell the wet birch overlaying the smell of the wet bodies added to the smell of the damp wood. Arlys and Margo would last the longest. While the rest of them covered their faces with wet washrags in order to survive, Arlys and Margo would whip themselves with birch branches to make it even hotter.

The only explanation for their endurance was genetic. Irini's people had never discovered recreational steam. We've never been a people celebrated for our cleanliness. Irini would take the lowest bench and still she would be the first to leave.

"Walter is spending a lot of time coaching Helen," Cindy observed. She had taken the seat beside Irini. Her freckled shoulders showed above a modestly draped towel.

"Do I care what Walter Collins does?" Irini asked. She and Walter had quarreled about the batting order. He was batting Helen leadoff and nothing Irini said could dissuade him. Cindy was a decent contact batter, although, batting one-handed, she was bound to lack power. She swung the bat like a tennis racquet, and she always hit between short and third. But she was fast and had a good chance of getting to first, while the runner moving from first to second, particularly if she was a slow runner like Helen, was an easy out. Cindy should hit when there was no one else on base, or better yet, when there was a runner on third, but this couldn't really be planned.

Besides, Irini didn't want Helen embarrassed. If the men saw Helen's breasts as freakish or funny or fascinating or whatever it was that men saw when they looked at large breasts, Irini didn't want Helen to have to deal with it.

"If we play smart, we can win," Walter had said to her, as if that were the point of playing baseball. He was being insensitive and Irini could not imagine the circumstances that would induce her to speak to him again.

Margo turned to Helen. "Helen, you need to level out your swing."

"Walter says I don't need to hit the ball."

"But it would be so great if you did. A nice, easy, level swing. Less height, more distance."

"Could we not talk baseball for a change?" said Helen.

"I was talking physics."

"You've got to run faster, too," said Irini. "Cindy's going to be coming right behind you and you're slowing her down. Just try, Helen. You don't look as if you're trying."

"Imagine my gratitude for the advice, because it exists only in your imagination. I don't know why I'm playing at all. I'm going to be terrible."

"You're going to be fine," Claire said. Her light hair was dark with sweat. Two red circles burned in her cheeks. "You'll be great. Won't she, girls?"

"Mrs. Ada has gone to bat for us," Cindy told them. The short hairs around Cindy's face were curling in the steam. She brushed her bangs back with her full hand. They were so wet they stayed there, stuck straight up like the brim of a hat. Irini felt her own hair, sagging limply against her scalp. "Apparently Mr. Henry wanted us to play in skirts, but Mrs. Ada told him not to be ridiculous."

"We'll be sliding into base," said Arlys. "Our legs would be a mass of scrapes and scars. What can he have been thinking?"

"He's still mad at us," said Irini. "Over that Salem thing." (
their suspicions of Fanny and the presence of the two younger Mi
girls, this was a delicate subject. But it was one they all wanted to
discuss. The other girls waited for a sign from Tracy or Cindy, something that gave them permission.

Tracy gave Irini a look instead. It was the opposite of permission.
"We can look just as cute in slacks," said Tracy. "Are you going to
wear a girdle?"

No one else had thought about it. It was an engrossing subject
with much to be said on both sides. They discussed it for several
minutes.

Irini wiped her face with the corner of her towel. She had to
partially disrobe to do so. She tucked the corner away again. Drops of
sweat ran from her neck to the top of the towel and gathered in a little
puddle there. She tried to ignore this, to concentrate on how good
her aching arm now felt. The delicate skin inside her nostrils had
begun to burn. The smell of dried wood became painful. She tried
breathing through her mouth, which quickly scorched her throat.

Cindy was breathing shallowly, too. "Mrs. Ada's also upset about
the fish sticks."

"Little Miss Know-It-All," said Tracy.

"Little Miss Know-Nothing," said Cindy back. It was a fact that
Cindy frequently knew things she had no way of knowing. It was the
two older sisters. And being the town's telephone operator. "Sometimes I hear things," she had once conceded. "Just in that moment
when I'm hanging up."

"Mrs. Ada doesn't see why he can't take it just the one step farther, and make the fish sticks without using any fish. She doesn't want
any fish hurt."

"What next?" said Arlys. Her own tastes in fish ran to nasty, pick-
led things with their heads and their webby little tails intact and one
eye staring up at you.

"Next is India. She's gotten the tickets. She's really going."

"Good for her," said Helen. She stretched out on the wooden

bench with her eyes closed. Her breasts slid to the sides of her body. "Why should the men be the only ones to see the big world?"

"It's not as if they saw the big world at its best," Irini pointed out. Her forehead dripped. She wiped her hand across it. "Helen, it's not fair the way you always make it sound as if they were off on a cruise."

"It's not as if they came back," Margo said.

"Except for Walter," said Claire.

Irini couldn't breathe at all now, but it was the worst possible moment to leave the sauna. It would open her to suspicions. She wiped her face and neck with her hands, wiped her hands on the front of her towel in a hopeless effort to be dry. Her tongue was so parched it was beginning to swell. "Has it ever occurred to you that we're literally cooking ourselves in here? We're being voluntarily parboiled."

" 'Steaming, not boiling, that's the ticket,' " said Margo. "More water, please, Arlys. I haven't broken a sweat yet."

Meanwhile, in India . . .
  Gandhi prepares for Independence.

16

 That spring Henry had a sudden hankering to band some birds. Spring does this to some people. It makes them think of migrations. Everyone in Magrit seemed to be restless that year.

He hired Norma Baldish to string the back of Collins House with nets and bought notebooks and new red pens. He was studying migratory patterns, he told the girls in the Kitchen. He imitated for them the call of the shy yellow rail by tapping his fingernails on the counter. He was good at bird calls and had once done an entire school assembly filled with them. His secret wish was to band the rare and lovely Kirtland's warbler on its way home from the Yucatan. That would be something the Audubon Society would notice.

During the war, what with rationing and all, Maggie had been forced to consider all birds as potential food sources. She didn't want to. But crow, for example, Maggie had found to be no greasier than duck. She recommended it in a recipe book called *Four and Twenty Black Birds*.

Those were dark times. In general, Henry had a fondness for birds, who were, after all, great cereal eaters. There was a bird feeder just outside the Kitchen window, which the girls kept full of Sweetwheats. The birds fed there in the winter. In the spring they ignored it.

Bugs! Seeds! Saps and honeys! There was a red-headed woodpecker nesting loudly in the Doyles' yard. The waxwings trilled among the leaves. Up by Upper Magrit was a large white tree they called Chickadee Pine. Hundreds of the black-headed birds lived there and had for as long as Irini could remember. It was a sort of flying city above the drowned one.

The woods between Brief Street and Collins House were full of robins and wrens and swallows and martins and vireos and tanagers. They swooped and sang and threaded their way above Irini. She was walking over to Collins House to see the nets.

Norma told her father who told her that they were worth seeing. Ada had advised on the placement, so it had a sort of artistic integrity. If Ada had thought of it as art, she might have gone on to bigger projects. She might have strung the nets into a twenty-four-foot fence surrounding Magrit. She might have wrapped the mill in cellophane. She was concentrating on world peace instead of personal achievement, and so, as often happens in such cases, she missed the main chance.

So far the only thing Henry had caught was one of the larger dogs. "Imagine if these nets were meant for us," Ada said gaily to Irini. "I'd arrive in India banded and logged."

Ada was stopping first in New York to buy a travel wardrobe. What one would wear to see Mr. Gandhi was a ticklish question. Modesty was the key, but poverty might be the look. Hopefully someone on Fifth Avenue would know.

She seemed happier than Irini had seen her in a long time. "You win some games while I'm gone," she said. "Win some for Mr. Gandhi. Tell everyone you're playing for nonviolence."

The nets, with their fine threads, lay a delicate curtain of gauze over the vista of hills and trees behind Collins House. They had a surprisingly natural look, more of a shadow than a substance, in the scene. They rippled gently.

Ada left for India by way of New York, on the four o'clock, and Claire Kinser moved into Collins House to do for Henry while Ada was away. Claire was released from work in the Kitchen for the duration. Henry forgot about the fish-stick project, which eventually went belly up. But Claire still made it to practice. Walter drove her over every afternoon.

Two days before their first game, Irini made an appointment to have her hair cut. Mrs. Tarken ran Magrit's beauty shop out of the Tarken home and right next door. In the summer the hair dryers sat on the back porch, where the ladies could read their magazines and look out over the Tarken roses. Mrs. Tarken had a trellis of pale pink Maybelle Stearnes. In the winter the ladies went into the parlor, a small dark room with fuzzy wallpaper and the permanent smell of permanent waves, plus hairspray and tomcat.

This was 1947, when people thought it sufficient to wash their hair once a week. Dandruff was Mrs. Tarken's personal bailiwick and in 1947 it was a large and serious territory.

On her good days, Mrs. Tarken sported a kind of style that was rare in Magrit. Sexy. She wore more makeup, tighter clothes, slimmer skirts, fancier hairstyles than the rest of the mothers. Her lipstick came off on her food whenever she ate. It was a cheap look and the ladies disapproved of it whenever they weren't attempting to duplicate it. But they had nothing but concern for Mrs. Tarken herself.

Mrs. Tarken had always been frail and moody. The loss of her son Jimmy had amplified her moods. They were darker, deeper, and less rational. Twice now since the telegram, she had been found wandering in her bathrobe and furred, high-heeled slippers on Main Street, with no very plausible explanation. Twenty years later she would have been on Valium; fifty years later, Prozac; and maybe then you wouldn't have had to call ahead and carefully gauge her mood before making an appointment. You sympathized, naturally. It broke your heart, but it didn't follow that you were willing to have her despair express itself in some unfortunate way on your head.

Even before the war, there'd been a risk. Once, without asking, Mrs. Tarken had cut and curled Irini's hair à la the Depression era Shirley Temple. The next day at school Scott Moodey bleated at her all recess long. Even her father had said she looked like a dandelion gone to seed, although he contrived to make it sound a compliment. "Wild and wishful hair," he said. "Mrs. Tarken has outdone herself."

"Hair is flat on the sides and the top this year," Mrs. Tarken told Irini over the phone. "And waved in the back." Actually this was the style *last* year, but close enough for Magrit. "I hope you're not going to want that dreadful do where all the hair is combed to the same side. I can't see that on you, Irini. It requires absolutely symmetrical features."

"Just the usual," said Irini. "Just me, looking like me, but trimmed."

Most of the Sweethearts were having their hair done sometime during the week. The Mays had given each other home permanents. Sissy Tarken was a Rembrandt of French braids and ribbons. Helen had cut three inches from the back and gone for bangs well above the eyebrows, like Judy Garland's.

Even Margo was forsaking her usual plaits. She was sitting under the dryer when Irini arrived, while Mrs. Tarken gazed at her lustfully. For as long as Irini could remember, Mrs. Tarken had wanted to cut Margo's hair. "It could be so smart," she said. But Margo's mother had always said no until Margo was old enough to begin saying no for herself.

Something new had been added to the usual chemical and cat smells. Irini could just make out the odor of cooked meat. Margo raised the hair dryer and leaned forward. "Hello, Irini," she said. "Mrs. Tarken? Is your dinner burning or is that my hair?"

Mrs. Tarken went to the kitchen to check the water level in the pot roast. Margo motioned for Irini to come over. The hair dryer stormed and crackled above Margo's head. Her face was pink, and her voice was quiet. "Can you reach my purse, Irini? I left it by the mirror. There's a letter inside. Take it and read it when no one is watching. Don't let anyone see you."

They could hear the *tack, tack, tack* of Mrs. Tarken's heels coming in their direction. Irini put the letter in her pocket. Later, when she was under the dryer and Margo was being combed out, Irini opened a *Ladies' Home Journal* to the Drene Shampoo ad in the middle. For evenings out, the Drene girl was combed into two side loops and a top curl.

The face on the opposite page was that of Babe Ruth. "Medical science offers proof positive. No other leading cigarette is safer to smoke than Raleighs," Ruth said, and let's be fair, he was probably right.

Irini unfolded the letter surreptitiously so as to cover both the Drene girl and the Babe. The letter was handwritten in the rounded, looping penmanship of a young girl.

"Dear Maggie Collins," she read.

> I hope you don't mind me writing again. I felt so close
> to you after your letter and I have no one else. I'm afraid
> you will be mad at me when you hear that I ignored
> your advice and told my best friend how I really feel
> about her. I was hoping she felt the same way. But now
> I wish I had listened to you. She pretended to misunder-
> stand and she hasn't spoken to me since. She has a new
> best friend and they whisper whenever they see me. It
> sometimes seems to me that everyone is whispering.
>
> It helped me so much to have you say that you also
> have such feelings. Now you are my best friend, maybe
> my only friend. I would like to write again sometimes.
> You don't have to answer. I know how busy you are and
> I know you don't have time for someone like me.

It was signed "Lonely in Yolo."

"What does it mean?" Margo asked Irini when they stood together, wavy-haired and rosy-cheeked, on the Tarken front porch. Margo always looked pretty and Irini's hair would be all right when she'd had the chance to comb it out for herself. Mrs. Tarken favored hair that didn't move from one appointment to the next. She used repeated applications of hair spray to achieve this effect, letting each dry before the next coat, as if she were shellacking a table. It would take a boar bristle brush and plenty of muscle to loosen things up.

"I don't know. It could mean anything, couldn't it? It could mean nothing," said Irini. "Don't tell Mr. Henry."

Margo took the letter back. "It must not be Fanny, after all. It must be Claire."

I already told you how Claire Kinser's engagement to the blond soldier from Detroit was mysteriously broken off, but there is more to the story. Claire Kinser had broken it off herself and sobbed out the reason to Fanny over a trio of Manhattans one long night at Bumps. Fanny hadn't told anyone what she said, not a word, but suddenly, quite recently, all the Sweethearts knew. At least they knew what they knew; the concept was so foreign to the girls in Magrit that perhaps only Fanny fully grasped it. "Under the present circumstances," Fanny said, when Tracy and Irini asked her about it, "it seems a pretty reasonable thing to be."

It is highly likely that Claire herself was still working it out. Until her engagement she had spent half her time hoping she didn't feel the things she felt and the other half hoping everyone else felt them, too.

When she did begin, tentatively, to talk about it, she was profoundly depressed by the response. The girls were indulgent—it would be another sixteen years before *The Group* was published—but mystified. They suggested that she had just not met the right boy yet. Had any of them? Claire blushed whenever she saw anyone and wished she had never spoken of it.

Irini had been raised to be a tolerant person; it was, in fact, the one thing her father insisted upon. "It wasn't so long ago that the Doyles were indentured servants in this country," her father said. "The potatoes turned rotten and the Irish sold themselves into slavery for food. You just give everyone their fair chance, Irini. You just judge people by what they say and what they do. That's the only sign of class worth having. That's the only one you'll ever need." Even during the war he never let Irini say Jap instead of Japanese, or Jew instead of Jewish, and when Irini used the old rhyme for choosing, her father made her say "Catch a tiger by the toe."

"Well, I'll answer the letter," said Margo. "We just can't let it go unanswered, the poor little thing. But what if she writes again? She says she's going to. What if she does and neither you nor I can intercept it?"

"We'll have to watch for the postmark," said Irini. "And someone's going to have to talk to Claire."

They agreed that they would tackle this delicate task together. They would ask Claire to the Friday-night pictures. Gently they would lead the conversation around to the letters. They would give Claire every opportunity to confess. No harm had been done. Claire would never, never intentionally hurt anyone; everyone knew that. The first letter had been cute, sort of, and the second letter was a secret. But there was the end to it. The whole thing had to stop.

"Come to the pictures with me," Irini suggested to Claire at practice the next day. "With me and Margo," she added just so there'd be no possible confusion. "It's Andy Hardy. You'll love it." Movies were shown in Magrit once a week in the school auditorium on the back of the map of the world with Norma Baldish running the projector.

And even though it was Andy Hardy, and the advertising campaign had promised a "scene of tragi-comedy in which Mickey Rooney is locked out of the house wearing nothing but a lady's wrapper," a scene unlikely, in fact, to appeal to anyone, Claire said yes, so there they were Friday evening, standing outside the auditorium waiting for Margo, who was late, and instead of Claire confessing to Irini, Claire was, in her gentle way, taking Irini to task over her irritating tolerance. Irini had just assured Claire that everyone liked her anyway.

Claire's normal flush deepened emphatically. "Anyway. Don't you see? You like me because *you're* so nice. I'm supposed to be grateful."

"I didn't mean that," said Irini. "We like you because we like you."

"No. You like me anyway. I'm not complaining. I *am* grateful. You *are* nice. That's the part that really steams me. I don't mean to be critical, Irini. I'm just telling you so you'll understand what it's like for me."

"I do understand," said Irini, who didn't understand any of it. She had never heard of such a thing. She had never read about it in a book or seen it in a movie or heard it in a song or had it covered during a game of Pop-ups. "Gee whiz."

In fact Irini was quite nervous around Claire now. It wasn't the actual facts, whatever they were, that disturbed her. Irini liked Claire. Claire could be whatever she wanted. It was the sense of the secret life. It was the sense of you–don't-know-this-person-at-all. Mostly it was the anonymous letters.

They were interrupted by Thomas Holcrow. "Miss Kinser." He took off his hat. The Tarken haircut had been successfully eradicated. Irini noticed that he had eyelashes as thick and dark as a girl's. He was dressed in dark pants and a dark twill jacket. "Miss Doyle. How exceptionally lovely you two ladies are tonight. Could I persuade you to join me for an ice cream?"

"We're going to the picture," said Claire. Bright red, embarrassed spots the size of quarters flamed in her cheeks. We can assume that Holcrow misinterpreted them.

"Perhaps after?"

"After we have to get home. We have a big game tomorrow. We're in training."

Lucky for Irini that she didn't color as easily as Claire did. Lucky that she had taken the time to put her hair up for the evening. Mrs. Tarken's curls still curved around her face. A bit of breeze passed over the back of her bare neck. It was a sensation much like excitement. Irini, having missed out on one confession, went after another. "Mr. Holcrow?"

"Tom," he suggested. "After all we've been through."

She nodded, but couldn't actually bring herself to say his name. "What are you doing here in Magrit?"

"I fell in love," he said, leaning toward her, "with the place." He paused in the sentence just where I paused. It made the back of Irini's neck prickle and the prickling sensation moved from her neck to her shoulders and her breasts. If this had been a musical, it would have been one of those moments when someone starts to sing.

Irini had a sudden, unasked-for, unexpected, unwelcome desire to kiss him. What would he do, she wondered, if she just fell into his arms?

He wouldn't have caught her. He was already taking in the spring evening with a sweep of his hand. The trees were leafing with the speed of light, and the sky was streaked like marble cake with high swirls of clouds. Everything was absolutely still. Norma Baldish had been hired by the city to repair the potholes, so the sweet scent of tar was carried on the breeze. It was Magrit's loveliest season, and also her loveliest time of day. There in the middle of it was Thomas Holcrow, who couldn't have looked lovelier or more at home.

But Irini had recovered herself and her tone was sarcastic. "Really."

He regarded her for a moment, so intently that she had to look away. "All right, Irini. I'll come clean. I've already told everyone else. It's not a secret. I'm a sort of rocking chair historian. Magrit is pretty civilized now, but it used to be a brawler's paradise. I'm trying to talk to some of the older residents, collecting stories about the old days. Strictly amateur hour. Ladies." He turned away, headed out into the spring evening, in the direction of Bumps.

"Did it seem to you he left a bit quickly?" Claire asked.

You can't be the kind of natural, gifted cook that Claire was without knowing the exact moment when a thing is done.

❀   ❀   ❀

Thomas Holcrow was just beginning to create some problems in Magrit. No one had expected him to come back, but when he did, everyone thought he would choose some girl, at least for the duration of his visit. Tracy had first dibs, but Fanny usually got the guy when there was a guy to be gotten. She was too old for Holcrow, but only by four or five years. If she wanted him, age wouldn't be a factor. She would pout at him once, purse those ripe, full, berry lips. "You know how to whistle, don't you?" she would say or some less inspired Magrit equivalent and he would never look back.

Then there was Arlys, who was the prettiest, with her red-blond hair and her perfect, poreless skin, but she was also shy around men. So was Helen, who was helplessly bound to attract the wrong kind of attention.

There may, in the end, have been too many choices. Holcrow persisted in an absolutely evenhanded flirtation with all of them. Perhaps he hoped in this way to keep everyone happy. If so it was a definite miscalculation. The girls were dressing a little more carefully and quarreling a little more often. Irini thought there was a hint of something special in his voice whenever he spoke to her, but she knew Tracy and Margo and maybe even Claire heard the same thing.

"What do you think of him?" Claire asked after the movie. Arlys and Margo and Irini were walking home. Claire was walking to the Leggetts'. She would have a cup of coffee with Helen and then get a ride back out to Collins House. By now the sun was down, but the moon was up and bright enough to keep the stars quiet. A single bird sang sleepily and monotonously in the distance. A dog barked twice. Somewhere a phone rang.

"A new low for Andy Hardy," Irini said. "What is it about men dressed up as women? Why is that hilarious?"

"Last month at a high school in Ohio all the boys came dressed in skirts. It was a protest over the girls wearing blue jeans," Margo said. "I read about it in *Good Housekeeping*."

"I don't believe it for a minute. And I wasn't talking about the picture," said Claire. "I was talking about Thomas Holcrow. Do you think he's up to something?"

"What do you think he's up to?" Margo asked. Her voice contained more than the usual interest. Claire was not the suspicious sort.

"Nothing bad," said Claire quickly. "He seems really nice. But I was wondering if he might be a treasure hunter. He came to Collins House a couple of weeks ago. Flirted with Mrs. Ada and got Mr. Henry to talk on and on. History, he says. Well, sure. He's looking for the Mather Mine or he's looking for the wreck of the *Griffon*. What else?"

"He's too far south for either," said Arlys.

"He talks a lot to your dad," said Claire. "And, excuse me, Irini, but you Doyles hardly count as old-timers."

"And my dad makes things up," said Irini. "Some night Dad'll tell him we have the Mather map. 'Man gave it to me,' Dad'll say. 'Died in my arms with a potato masher in his back and the Mather map in his hand.' Dad'll think it's a joke."

"Fortune hunters don't think much is funny," said Margo.

"He's too far south," said Arlys.

The girls struck a patch of moonlight. They stopped inside it a moment, searching for flat skipping stones to flick into Glen Annie Creek. Their shadows were dark and squat. Irini had the arm, of course. She threw three stones and the last one skipped ten times, hopping up the creek against the current, ten distinct, solid hops that you could hear as well as see.

"Still the champion," Arlys told her. A cloud passed in front of the moon and picked up its luminescence, became a frothy meringue of light.

"You know who might have had a map of the mine? The Nadeau boys," said Margo.

"They weren't miners," Claire objected. "They were lumberjacks." Her voice was a little stiff, a bit cautious. People from Upper Magrit preferred not to discuss the Nadeaus with outsiders.

"But they worked up north. What if they did have something hidden in the house, something even their mother didn't know about? It could still be there, couldn't it?"

"What if they were all murdered?" said Irini. She made her eyes big and her voice ominous. "And not drowned at all."

"You're trying to make me sound ridiculous," said Margo. "But notice how you're not succeeding. The bodies were never recovered. Why couldn't they all have been murdered?"

"Is this your grandma's bead necklace, Anna-banana? Or was it all a dream?"

"Well, why couldn't they? Do you think no one's ever been murdered in Magrit?"

The question surprised Irini, because it was not a question she had ever asked herself. She couldn't bring to mind a single suspicious death, but it seemed naive to say so. Magrit probably did have its share of adulterers and blackmailers and murderers. Certainly in the old days. And it would be sort of embarrassing to live in a place where no crimes of passion occurred. But who would commit them? The Tarkens? The Baldishes? The Fossums? It was too outlandish. Of course she'd been wrong before, back when she'd assured her father they could none of them be having sex.

Just last year a man and a woman had been murdered in Bloomington, Indiana. I already mentioned this, but there is more to the story. Irini had followed the case in the paper. She was a secretary in a dairy company. He sold insurance. They'd been having an affair on their lunch breaks. One noon they met at an abandoned mill. The bodies were discovered twenty-four hours later; he had been beaten to death and she had been strangled with her own stocking. The police found a packet of love letters from him to her in her purse, letters they had unnecessarily and heartlessly described to the newspapers as childish. The couple themselves were not, in the newspaper photos, particularly attractive. They were middle-aged and married, but not to each other. He directed the church choir; she was an alto. Probably everyone who knew them would have said they were too boring to be writing each other childish love letters, too boring to be murdered.

"Oh, I don't think so," said Claire. "From what I hear, it would have been pretty hard to murder even one of the Nadeau boys. I doubt if Paul Bunyan himself could have murdered all five." They came to the corner of Maple Lane, where the Leggetts lived. Claire said a quick good-night and left them.

Margo waited just long enough to be sure Claire was out of earshot. "So, Irini. Did you get anything?"

"You were there."

"I mean before the picture. Did you get her to say anything?"

"No."

"Did you try?"

"Of course I tried. It would have been nice if you hadn't been late. That would have been a help. We agreed to do it together."

"That was my fault," said Arlys. "I didn't understand the nature of the deadline." Arlys had never been late to anything in her life. Margo, on the other hand . . .

"Why didn't you try after?" asked Irini. "Why did you encourage her to go on and on about the Mather Mine?"

"I thought you'd have it all done."

They reached First Street. The moon gave the trees dark trunks and silver leaves. The aspen glittered like glass. The Fossums lived down the hill. Arlys said good night. Irini waited until she was just out of earshot. "I thought we weren't telling anyone. I thought it was just going to be you, me, and Claire tonight."

"Arlys just wanted to see the movie. Arlys won't talk."

"Of course she will."

"I made her promise not to tell."

"Oh. Well. Then," said Irini crossly. "I made you promise not to tell," she reminded Margo. They had reached the corner of Brief Street. Irini went on by herself without saying good night. She waited until Margo was just out of earshot. "I made her promise not to tell," she said, in one of those mimics that sounds nothing like the person being mimicked and isn't intended to. Now she was quarreling with Margo as well as Walter. Maybe her father would be home. She could go for a triple-header.

Tweed caught up with her at the edge of the Tarken yard. She was not coming from the Doyle home; obviously she had been out on her own errands. But she was pleased to see Irini, her tail wagging, her open mouth closing onto her tongue in the surprise of it.

"Where have you been?" Irini asked her. "Chasing rabbits? Playing cards?" Tweed obviously had a secret life, too.

As a little girl, on her way to school in the mornings, Irini had often walked the Tarken fence. It was a board fence, only three feet high, so walking the railing was easy, but walking across the tops of the planks presented a real challenge. Irini thought it might lighten her mood to walk it now. Irini thought since she was playing baseball again, she could bring it all back—the decoder rings, the games of capture the flag, the jars of lightning bugs, the summer vacations. Irini thought—well, Irini didn't think. She scrambled to the top of the fence. She was much higher up than she remembered being; she could see her moon shadow far beneath her. It had a short torso and skinny little breakable arms and legs. Her feet had widened since her last trip across the boards. She took two or three careful steps. Remembering that, much like riding a bicycle, it had been easier fast than slow, she forced herself to pick up the pace. Tweed whined anxiously.

The Tarkens' porch light was on. Moths and gnats fluttered about it, banged into it. The porch swing rocked gently and there, level with her, were two heads, lit from behind and therefore hard to make out. It must be Sissy and her father.

"Good evening," Irini said. She regretted being on top of the fence, most unfortunate that she was teetering in the air, face level with the Tarkens on the porch, but she reminded herself that Mrs. Tarken sometimes wore her bedroom slippers downtown. They were in no position to throw stones.

"Hello, Irini," said Sissy. There was something in her voice, some tone that made Irini look more closely. Sissy wasn't sitting with her father, after all. Instead Walter Collins was swinging in the moonlight on the Tarken porch with Sissy Tarken.

"Hello, Irini," he said. "You be careful getting down from there. I'm depending on you tomorrow."

The ground tilted and sank beneath Irini; she was about to pitch off. This was not because she was losing her balance. On the contrary, she had been stunned into immobility. It must have been the fence itself that moved, trying to shake her loose. When Walter had told her he had other women now to compare her to, she had never imagined he meant Sissy Tarken.

Just in time she remembered to breathe. It was not easy. Thomas Holcrow and Walter between them had turned the very air around Irini's body into a syrup of sex and confusion. It thickened in her lungs, dimpled and goosebumped her arms, jellied her legs. She was so stirred up she thought it must show, thought that anyone looking at her would see it, like the desperate sparkle of a lightning bug.

Fortunately neither Walter nor Sissy was looking. They had resumed a quiet and private conversation. She took a fumbling step from the top of the planks to the more secure footing of the railing.

She considered dismounting with a bold, unembarrassed leap, but she was afraid she might fall. Just as she had made up her mind to go for grace instead of bravura, to slide slowly, liquidly, sensuously to the ground, the door to her own house opened. The light from the kitchen stretched out along the steps and into the yard in a long yellow corridor. Tweed had gone to inform on her. Now she dashed back down the porch steps and out of the lighted yard into the dark. She stopped at the fence and sat abruptly, staring up at Irini.

Irini's father stood in the door. "Why, Irini," he said. "I didn't recognize you there for a moment. I mistook you for an objet d'art. I thought we had our very own statue of Venus de Milo, perched right up there on the Tarken fence."

"Hi, Dad," said Irini.

Her father had an annoying habit of having the last word, even when he wasn't the last person to speak, which he usually was.

17

Among the standards that were relaxed during the war were the sexual standards. This may have been a slow, smooth sag, starting in the twenties, or it may have been an abrupt spasm, brought on by the war. I don't really know. But clearly, men who were about to be sent overseas, possibly to their deaths, had a powerful trump card to play in sexual negotiations. They can hardly be criticized for playing it. Women were expected to supply morale and motivation to the men. They were expected to dance with them, write them letters, and keep their spirits up. They can hardly be criticized for doing their little bit. The music was hot, the dancing was the best ever, fast and close, and the situation couldn't have been more desperately romantic. No one has ever told me this, mind you. I figured it out for myself.

My biggest clue was the period of retrenchment after the war. Whenever you watch the movies or read the magazines, it's hard to escape the sense of a nationwide conspiracy channeling women toward marriage as fast as possible. Without ever conceding that certain behaviors had been tolerated because of the war, *Women at Home,* among others, made it their business to state unequivocally that such behaviors would not be tolerated now. The shrillness and persistence of the message attests to the magnitude of the problem. But it was 1947, so they couldn't tell you sleeping around would kill you.

Instead they depended on the new demographics. Preliminary estimates suggested that, because of the war, six to eight million women wouldn't get a man; this worked out to one woman out of every seven. All very scientific, all very persuasive. All put to the service of one particular illusion—that marriage was a trap for men, who had to be tricked, cajoled, or flirted into it, but an advantage for women.

No one was saying you were more likely to be murdered by terrorists, but the message was the same. It was not the moment for any woman to give up her edge. Every issue of *Women at Home* ran an inspirational story about some woman who made her man wait and how grateful he was. Even little, innocent Anna Peal was co-opted into the campaign.

Anna had the most exciting life imaginable. She hobnobbed on a routine basis with thieves and cowboys, lamas and llamas. She scaled mountains and bargained for her life with mad scientists. But her greatest ambition was to grow up to be a wife and mother. "Every woman wants to wear white. Every woman wants to care for a husband and children of her own. That's the biggest adventure of all," her own mother assured her periodically.

There have always been women who have made it their business to tell other women to stay home. And a very nice business it's become, too, with lots of travel and guest speaking and dinners that someone else has cooked, on dishes that someone else will wash and a paycheck and everything. Mrs. Peal was not one of these women. But she was a missionary with a flock to look after, and consequently she was never around when Anna needed fishing out of the briny. Plus she was often a bit on the dim side. Sometimes Anna counted on her to be just that bit dim.

Yet this one piece of advice Anna swallowed whole. So, apparently, did everyone else. A poll of high school girls taken in 1947 reported that they expected to be married by twenty-two and to stay at home after the wedding, conceiving, delivering, and raising their four children. When asked if they expected to work, they said no. Raising four children is such a vacation.

Why would the girls at Margaret Mill be any different? What were they going to give up marriage and children for? A better fish stick?

Sissy Tarken was one of those girls whose sexual standards had relaxed during the war. She didn't work in the Kitchen; the Tarkens didn't need the money and Mr. Tarken was afraid to have his wife left alone too often or for too long. Sissy had long black hair that her mother did up for her and large, owlish eyes that blinked slowly at you in a way Irini often found irritating. Irini couldn't remember when she had first realized that, one by one, as the boys left Magrit, they had all gone to say good-bye to Sissy. Naturally this left Sissy with abandonment issues and a reputation.

Irini couldn't imagine when Sissy had become that sort of girl. She hadn't seen it happen, but perhaps, although she saw Sissy on a daily basis, she hadn't been watching. She had a bad conscience where Sissy was concerned.

Technically the same age as Irini, Sissy had always actually been much younger. She was Irini's next-door neighbor. On the other side lived the Mays, a sophisticated trio who knew how and when boys could be safely kissed and what clothes one wore on a date, depending on whether you had been asked out for dinner or whether the evening included dinner and dancing. On many occasions, Irini had awakened in the morning, checked to see what age she was on that particular day, and gone left or right out of the front door accordingly.

In point of fact, Irini preferred the company of Arlys or Margo to any of them, but the Fossums and the Törngrens lived farther away, so seeing them was something that had to be arranged in advance. Margo usually had chores and Arlys was expected to spend the weekends with her family. And although they both liked Irini, they were best friends themselves, which made Irini the expendable one. So Irini, whom everyone liked, and Sissy, whom no one liked, were often thrown together, but the truth was that Irini didn't actually like

Sissy any better than anyone else did and maybe Sissy didn't like Irini as much as everyone else did.

Sissy was a natural follower who tended to follow too closely. When Irini bought a fake-fur coat from Sears for Easter, white and soft as sifted flour, it was only a matter of days before Sissy had done the same. When Irini decided she was really devoutly Catholic and not just formerly Catholic like her father, Sissy said that she was, too. Mrs. Tarken corrected Sissy quickly, corrected her as soon as she heard about it. The Tarkens drove all the way to Rimsey every Sunday to attend the Methodist church there. Still, Sissy's intentions had been clear and Irini's irritation lasted longer than her faith.

Sissy had a good imagination, but it expressed itself in suggestibility. Fun with Sissy usually took the form of seeing how far you could go before she stopped believing you. When Wilbur Floyd told the girls at recess that Madame Nadeau had tied herself to a chair and drowned herself in Upper Magrit and that they hadn't been able to untie one of the cords around her wrist, but had been forced to hack her hand off in order to retrieve the body, Sissy was the only one who believed him.

"Oh, yes," her own brother Jimmy had said. Jimmy was four years older and no more of a torment than most older brothers, which was to say that he tormented them all day long. During the winter he chased them home from school with snowballs. During the summer he made unflattering comments about their bathing suits. His aim was better with the latter than the former. "They tried to dive for the hand, because they wanted to bury it with the rest of her, but the turtles had already eaten it. I've seen the bones myself," Jimmy assured her. "So that's why Madame Nadeau still walks around Magrit at night. She's searching for her other hand."

"Don't let them upset you like that," Irini advised Sissy impatiently. But Sissy couldn't even listen to Wheat Theater until she was twelve. Even little Anna Peal's wholesome and improbable adventures gave Sissy nightmares.

One summer, when they were fourteen years old, Sissy and Irini walked out to the old Sweet cabin together. It was a spooky place and Sissy was naturally reluctant. Irini made her go. Sissy could be talked into anything.

Jacob Sweet had deserted the cabin some twenty years back to live with his sister in Sacramento. No one in Magrit had even known he had a sister. "She'll have to give him a good scrubbing," Mrs. Baldish had said at the time. The joke about Jacob Sweet was that he smelled okay for a dead man, but was a bit ripe to still be breathing.

He had last been seen getting onto the train with no luggage. This was agreed to be suspicious for someone going all the way to Sacramento. Mrs. Baldish had wanted to write the sister, but no one knew her married name. Nothing was done and eventually this inaction came to be classed under the commendatory heading, "Here in Magrit We Mind Our Own Business."

The cabin was west of Magrit. You found it by walking down Glen Annie Creek. Close to Magrit, where the creek was widest and deepest, you crossed on a little wood bridge. The creek was docile and pretty there. Then you hiked along it into the woods as they got darker and closer. Near the cabin the trees grew a dank white mold on their branches and even the spiders were white and bloated. By the time you reached Jacob Sweet's place, Glen Annie Creek was covered with a greasy sheen; when you looked down into it, you could barely make out long strands of algae, undulating from the rocks.

Jimmy had followed them for a while, Indian style. He paralleled their course, leaping out from time to time, or whistling in an eerie way. "Where is my hand?" he said in falsetto from behind a tree. "I want my hand." He quit before they reached Jacob's cabin, made a final, farewell appearance, pulled Sissy's hair, and then vanished.

The cabin had fallen into disrepair and decay. The roof had rotted away. Everything smelled of mold and sawdust. A bag of flour, purchased in Magrit two decades ago, before the war, before the Depression even, had been left on the counter. It had long ago been filled with bugs and eaten up. Next to it was the ghost of a jar of currant jelly, dried to a thin red film of ectoplasm. Properly stored in the cupboard and more resilient were a bottle of Tabasco and a jar of blackstrap. Some sort of rodent had made a nest in the corner and then deserted, just as Jacob had deserted. The nest included strips from the bag of flour and old bits of newspaper and clothes.

Sissy and Irini were far too old to be playing Anna Peal, but that's what they were doing. They pretended that Anna Peal was sheltering here for the night. She had been out, crossing the border on an errand for her mother, when she got lost. She wandered in the dark woods until night fell. Fortunately she came to the cabin. It was deserted. Anna cleaned out the fireplace.

On the radio, Irini told Sissy, they crinkled cellophane to make the sound of a fire. This was hardly necessary in Magrit, where the radio reception was poor and *Wheat Theater* came complete with a constant crackling of static, as if the whole station were aflame. But in Jacob Sweet's cabin, they had to pretend the sound as well as the fire. Anna cooked mushrooms and fiddleheads she had found in the forest. Neither Sissy nor Irini would have taken a single bite of a mushroom or fiddlehead in real life, but Anna could choose a few unexpected seasonings and work miracles.

She had used the penny test to determine the mushrooms were edible. Unfortunately she had used wartime pennies! Now she needed the antidote and there wasn't a second to spare.

The sky outside the cabin darkened. The windows were such a smear of greases on the outside and old smoke on the inside that the girls hardly noticed until they heard thunder. They abandoned Anna Peal to her fate and ran for home. Black clouds poured over the sky, bubbled and boiled. It began to rain, great, frightening sheets of rain, and lightning lit up the whole landscape so that the after-image burned a persistent garish purple under Irini's eyelids. The funny thing was that it wasn't raining on them yet, but off to the side, where they could watch it, like a movie.

Glen Annie Creek was up now, transformed in the short afternoon to a rolling broth of white water. They were running over the bridge, Irini first, when there was a sound above her, like a sudden intake of breath. Irini looked up as a sheet of lightning blinked over the sky. Two ring-necked ducks fell from the air like stones. They splashed into Glen Annie Creek. Irini's mouth opened as she ran. A moment later, less than a moment, she slipped and went into the water. Sissy grabbed her hand just before it disappeared.

Sissy was strong enough to hold on to Irini, strong enough to keep her afloat, but not strong enough to pull her out. There was nothing beneath Irini but water, no place she could find with her feet or her arms. The rain reached them in a torrent of small, stinging drops.

The water in the creek was cold and rough and slapped her around. But what she noticed most was that her hand hurt where Sissy was holding it. "Let me go," said Irini.

"No," said Sissy. Her mouth was pinched shut. Her eyes were wide and vacant. Lightning lit them up momentarily; her hair streamed with water. "I don't know how long I can hold on," she added nonsensically. The pitch of her voice was rising.

Irini made her own voice very reasonable. "I can swim. If you just let me go, I'll swim to the bank."

"I think the water's too strong." Sissy began to cry, so that her words came out in disconnected little spurts. "My arms are starting to hurt."

"Just let me go," said Irini.

Sissy knelt, which dropped Irini deeper into the water. Her grip tightened.

"Let me go." Irini tried shouting. "Let me go, you stupid girl. Let me go! You're a stupid fat cow and nobody likes you. I hate you. I've never seen anyone so fat and stupid. If you don't let me go, I'll hurt you later. I swear I will."

Sissy sobbed loudly. "Help us! Jimmy! Come and help us!"

"Everyone hates you." Irini was screaming now. "You're keep-

ing me here in this horrible water. I'll freeze and it's your fault."
She struggled to pull her hand away. Sissy was bigger than Irini
and Irini had no leverage. There was a crack of lightning. Irini
could see through her open mouth all the way into Sissy's throat.
"Let me go," she said. "I'll be all right if you'll just let me go.
You idiot. You moron. You fat, ugly cow." All the while rain poured
over them so that Sissy must have been as wet and as cold as
Irini.

"Help us!" Sissy's voice was too weak and terrified for anyone to
hear, even if there had been someone else in the woods in the rain.
"Please! Somebody help us."

At last they each of them gave something up. Irini stopped shouting and struggling. She continued to call Sissy names, but her voice
was too low and dispirited for Sissy to hear them over the water. They
weren't much anyway. Her anger was as exhausted as the rest of her.
Sissy stopped calling, and her crying became softer and less spasmodic.
She continued to tell Irini that her arms hurt, that she didn't know
how much longer she could hold on, but Irini no longer believed her.
Even the rain stopped falling. Irini wept, but the only way she knew
this was that the water on her face was warm. Who would have
thought Sissy could be so stubborn? Sissy Tarken, who could be
talked into anything by anybody. There was no way for the thing to
finish until Sissy let go.

Perhaps half an hour passed. It could even have been longer. It was
probably much shorter. But however long it was, at the end of it,
Irini's father came out of the trees, over the bridge, took Irini's hand
from Sissy and pulled her out. The girls continued to cry. Irini's
father picked them up. They were not little girls, they were fourteen
and Sissy was a cushioned fourteen. Still Irini's father carried them
both, one in each arm with their hands clinging to his neck, back up
the path and over to the nearest house, which was the Moodey place.
Mrs. Moodey ran a bath and she made both girls get in together.
Then she toweled them dry with rough towels, rubbing hard to
get the blood flowing. Dr. Gilbertsen arrived in a hurry. He looked

them over, inside and out, gave them each a swallow of something nasty.

Maggie Collins writes: "If medicine has a particularly unpleasant taste, hold a piece of ice in your mouth for two minutes before taking."

Then Dr. Gilbertsen sent them home to bed. Sissy could not move her right arm. She had pulled and sprained the muscles. It had to be splinted for six weeks and she couldn't write to do her schoolwork. Irini had to take notes for her.

Irini slept all night and half the next day. Twice she woke, wet with sweat, and saw her father, sitting in the reading chair, watching her. He was still there, still watching, at noon when she woke up for real.

Later Irini's father told her he'd gone to the Tarkens' looking for her when the rain got so bad. Jimmy had told him where to look and Tweed had actually found them. "We should have taken Tweed along," Irini said, but her father's opinion was that even though Tweed was mostly collie, she was still the sort of dog who, in a crisis, would save herself.

Her father said that if Sissy had let her go, Irini would have drowned. "No question." He coughed to steady his voice. "No question."

Which really made it too bad that Irini had said all those awful things to her. She felt very awkward over what to say to Sissy next. Fortunately, Sissy was prepared to be magnanimous. The Tarken kitchen was filled with cakes and casseroles, all baked in honor of Sissy. There was a short article about the incident in the Chicago paper, using Sissy's name, but sparing Irini's. Miss Cleveland, their beautiful red-haired teacher who looked like no one so much as Glinda, the Good Witch of the South, as depicted on the color plate on the inside cover of Irini's Baum book, made a speech about Sissy to the whole class. If they could all only be like Sissy, she as much as said, the war would be over tomorrow.

Sissy was a heroine, but she was still a slow-witted, uninteresting girl. The kids soon forgot she was the former, while there was always fresh evidence of the latter. Her new status lasted a little longer among the adults. Miss Cleveland might have remembered, but she married a marine at the end of the school year and moved to upstate New York. Only for Irini's father was the change permanent. The rest of his life he never mentioned her name without adding that she was the bravest little girl he had ever known.

Irini herself never forgot, but it was an uncomfortable memory all around. Not only the things she had said, but just the fact of having almost died. She would have preferred never to think of it again. She resented Sissy's bringing it up, although she tried not to say so. Everyone knew that Sissy had saved her by holding her up for an hour, at least, even though Sissy had to have her arm splinted afterward and nearly died of the cold. Well and good. But no one knew until Sissy told them that the whole time she had been saving Irini's life, Irini had been calling her a fat, stupid cow.

"Why were you doing that?" Scott Moodey asked her incredulously.

"She was hurting me."

"But she was saving your life."

"But I didn't know that." Of course, Irini didn't know that. Fourteen-year-olds didn't die in Magrit from anything but polio.

Irini knew she should be best friends with Sissy now, but she still liked Arlys and Margo better. She couldn't help it. It would have been so much nicer to be the girl who didn't almost die, the girl who held on for more than an hour. This would have been just as hard for Irini as for Sissy, since it happened long before she developed her bread-kneading muscles.

It might have been too hard for Irini. Then Sissy would have drowned and Irini would have been the girl who let her. This thought made the uncomfortable topic even more uncomfortable. Whenever she went to the Tarkens' now, Sissy wanted to play some game that required putting her arm in a pretend splint. She had a collection of red and blue bandannas just for this purpose. Irini spent less time with Sissy after the adventure instead of more.

And then, about two years later, Irini became aware of the boys. She didn't know what to feel. She'd known these boys all her life and some of them were going off to war. Was she to blame *them* for the fact that Sissy, who was the bravest little girl her father had ever known, could be talked into anything?

Sissy's unexpected stubborn streak surfaced again after the telegram. She absolutely refused to believe that Jimmy was dead. The telegram said "presumed dead." His unit had engaged the enemy. He had been seen fighting. No one had actually seen him die. He had gone to the same place as Amelia Earhart.

The Tarkens held a memorial service at the Methodist church and many nice things were said about Jimmy afterward. "What a spirit he had," said Irini's father. "What a spirit." Sissy was not there. She had refused to attend, although her mother had cried and pleaded and threatened. It showed an obstinacy and a strength of will only Irini knew she possessed. When Irini talked to Sissy now, Sissy wanted her to pretend that Jimmy was still alive.

But Irini actually believed it. It was not easy, but she did. She could picture him, in his torn and dirty uniform, hiding in the jungle, jumping out at the Japanese. "I want my hand," he said in falsetto. "Give me back my hand." In this fantasy, Jimmy was sort of godlike, almost immortal. It was not easy to imagine Jimmy Tarken as a god. Irini did it for Sissy, to whom she owed her life. It was the best she could manage.

And when she saw Walter there, swinging in the dark, she knew she really should have told Sissy three years ago that you have to keep a boy waiting in order to keep a boy. That boys don't want that kind of girl, even though, under certain circumstances, they tell you they do, so it's best to avoid those circumstances altogether. "Why would he buy the cow, when he can get the milk for free?" Maggie asked the muddled young women who wrote her on the subject. It was just as simple as that.

But Sissy hadn't gotten the message. Sissy had no one to tell her, because her mother was so depressed and the Mays wouldn't speak to her, so it should have been Irini, although, of course, she would have changed the metaphor; that cow business wouldn't have done at all.

And for Walter Collins there were no words.

Maggie Collins writes: "Never dispose of the scum that collects on warmed milk. It contains valuable calcium salts. Whisk it back in."

On the day of her brother's memorial service, after her parents had left the house for the church, Sissy went alone into the kitchen. She pretended that the cookies, the macaroni and cheese, the homemade breads were for her. She got out a tatted tablecloth, embroidered napkins. She polished the good silver. She set the table for five.

It was her wedding day, that was why there was so much food. Sissy Tarken went back upstairs to put on lipstick and paint her nails. She dressed in one of her mother's dresses, pulling the extra material of the bodice around to the back and anchoring it with clothespins. She had to pretend hard. Only the color was bridal. "The food is for the guests," she told Jimmy. "Don't you go eating it now."

Her husband was handsome. Tall. She couldn't get much further than that. He stood outside the door with Jimmy and he wanted to come in, but Jimmy wouldn't let him. Bad luck, said Jimmy, who had to come back, had to be there, couldn't die like this before Sissy had ever even had a chance to like him.

"You boys," said her mother. Such a happy voice. Sissy could hardly remember her mother speaking in such a happy voice. "Don't you tease my Sissy now."

Sissy went back to the kitchen, took the place next to Jimmy's. She lit two candles. She helped herself to the Baldish's cold potato salad. She used a silver fork and laid an embroidered napkin over her white lap. She blew the candles out.

18

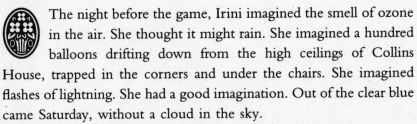The night before the game, Irini imagined the smell of ozone in the air. She thought it might rain. She imagined a hundred balloons drifting down from the high ceilings of Collins House, trapped in the corners and under the chairs. She imagined flashes of lightning. She had a good imagination. Out of the clear blue came Saturday, without a cloud in the sky.

She was surprised at how nervous she was. Baseball was just a game, even when women played it. And because they were women, no one would mind if they didn't win. For girls there were those definite advantages to not winning. She fixed her hair and put on her lipstick, a bright shade from Tangee called Red Drama. Her father was sleeping in, but he heard her in the bathroom. "You go for the fences, Irini," he called out to her. "Go for a husband next time. Go for a home run today."

"It'll have your name on it, Dad," Irini told him. There was a knock at the door. The May girls were ready to walk to the mill. Sissy ran down the steps from her house to join them. Irini automatically took a position between Sissy and Tracy.

She waited for Sissy to say something about Walter, maybe something intended to reassure her or maybe something intended to make her jealous, but something. Instead, Sissy was silent. Her eyes were like broken china; the whites cracked with red. "Is something wrong?" Irini asked and Sissy shook her head.

Norma Baldish was already at the mill, with the bus hood up and her head in its mouth. "Car trouble?" asked Irini hopefully. All you could see of her was her rump. It was a large rump.

"Just checking the oil," said Norma. "Everything looks good." She slammed the hood. Even Norma was wearing lipstick today. Out of inexperience and an unfamiliarity with women's magazines, she had chosen a color too light for her. Her mouth was a ghostly mark in the middle of her face. Irini, already uneasy over Sissy's distress, was saddened even more by Norma's lipstick. She had never thought of Norma as someone who wanted to be married. Norma was twenty-five and already old by Irini's standards.

Norma was too solid and capable to be attractive, but she had always had the dignity of indifference. She didn't read the women's magazines: she read *Field and Stream* and *Popular Mechanics* instead. She kept her hair cut to a sensible length for hunting and other activities involving brambles. It was too curly, even for 1947, when curly hair was much admired. She ran the bar; she could mix drinks, she could unplug your toilet with one hand and bring a deer down with the other. She could wire your house for electricity in her sleep. "I don't miss the young men at all," Irini's father would say from time to time. "As long as Norma never leaves us."

It seemed a safe enough hope. Norma would have Bumps when her parents died and the house by the Falls as well. What did she need to be married for?

She had very pretty eyes. They were light-colored and bright in her face—unclouded as marbles, sky blue. They were her best feature. She had no waist and large thighs. The catcher's pads were a becoming look for her. Her mouth was too narrow, too severe. Still, it was a fashion mistake to erase her lips entirely like this.

Margo and Arlys had cleaned the bus windows, according to Maggie's instructions, as imparted by Henry via Claire, with an ammonia solution and a window-cleaning device Henry had ordered from Chicago and was calling by the unlikely name of squeegee. "Much easier," conceded Margo. "A real advance."

After the squeegee, streaks could be removed with a chamois. "I hope we're not going to do this before every game," Arlys said, but Claire didn't know. The condition of the bus reflected on Maggie, Claire pointed out. Lots of people would be seeing it and making up their minds about Sweetwheats accordingly. Presentation was everything.

Since Claire had moved into Collins House, she had begun to talk about Maggie the same way Henry did. Given the letters and suspicions, it made Irini uneasy. The unstreaked glass broke the early morning sunlight into glints and prisms. Henry had already put the balloons inside the bus. They were untethered and helium-filled, so when Norma slammed the hood, they jumped all at once, a brilliant, leaping rainbow seen through the glittering windows.

Margo's two little brothers defended the Margaret Mill gate, picking the girls off as they arrived with machine gun fire and grenades. There was a constant annoying *ack-ack-ack* coming from that direction and occasional shrill demands that someone fall down. One of them was ten years old and one only six.

Margo was babysitting today and the little Törngren boys had been promised a trip to Yawkey on the team bus and a balloon each if they were good. Irini would have already decided about the balloon, had it been up to her.

Henry was waiting for the girls inside the mill. He was wearing the Sweethearts baseball cap, with the wheat laurel on the brim. His ears floated on the sides like water-lily pads. The girls sat where he had pulled two tables together so each of them could eat a premeasured bowl of Sweetwheats under his watchful eye. He had had bananas shipped in from Cuba for the occasion. He sliced them onto the cereal himself, while a photographer, shipped in from Madison, immortalized the entire event.

It was a courageous show. Gandhi had sworn again that he would never cede an inch of Pakistan, and there had been bloody riots between the Hindus and the Moslems in the Gurgaon District, just eighteen miles from Ada's hotel. Henry hadn't slept all night. But his hand was steady, his banana slicing cool. Every slice was the same size as every other slice. Every girl got exactly the same number of slices.

"You know what I'm thinking?" said Henry. "I'm thinking about a cereal with the banana already in the flake. Maybe the milk as well. What about a cereal you could carry in your pocket? Cereal sticks. All the little bits of cereal held together in a stick with a sort of banana paste."

"How would you keep the bananas from spoiling?" Claire asked.

"How do you keep fish sticks from spoiling?"

"But you can't freeze bananas."

"Why not?" said Henry. "Why can you can an apple and not a banana? What's the difference, chemically speaking?" A product named Pie Quick had just come on the market—premixed crust, just add water and roll; presliced, preseasoned apples, just open and dump. The copy promised a homemade apple pie in the oven in fifteen minutes or less. But the banana cream pie was still an open field as well as being Henry's personal favorite. "Let's work on it next week," Henry suggested. "Fanny, you pick a banana-preserving team. Three girls. Don't limit yourself to freezing. Any preservation method. Think about brine, for instance. Check with Mr. Doyle on the chemistry."

Margo's mother had sent a Thermos of coffee for the team. There were leftover muffins from muffin day, many of them lemon ice, and no one made coffee like Mrs. Törngren. There was a secret to it, a Finnish secret Maggie was dying for, but Mrs. Törngren wouldn't tell. "She spits in the grounds," Margo said once, but she was probably joking. The Finns weren't the French, after all.

Margo unscrewed the lid and a puff of cloud appeared above it, like the mist from Aladdin's lamp. Irini made a wish, but it was only something she felt, not something she could articulate. Even she didn't know what she had wished for. Perhaps a game that went well.

Perhaps a day that went well. She took a large cupful of strong Törngren coffee and left it black, although this was not likely to calm her down.

Arlys picked up a sugar lump in her fingers, lowered it into the coffee, waited until it turned entirely brown, and then, just before it crumbled away, put it into her mouth and started again with another sugar lump. It was a slow way to drink coffee and Irini would have thought Arlys was stalling if this had not been the way she always did it. And then, Arlys had the audacity to claim that she loved a good cup of coffee.

"Irini, you're not eating your cereal," Henry noted.

"I'm very nervous," Irini said.

"In the interests of science, I'm going to have to ask you to put that aside."

Irini attempted to do so. The bananas were overripe and gluey. Arlys was eating even less than Irini.

Henry had a lab book and a stopwatch in front of him. He was observing them carefully and taking notes. No one could have an appetite under such circumstances; even the Collinses' dogs wouldn't eat when they were watched, but when Irini tried to point this out, Henry merely made a note of her objection in his ledger. "No one gets on the bus," said Henry, "until there are nine empty bowls on the table."

It was not an incentive, but Irini's spoon scraped the bottom anyway. "We'll change clothes here in Magrit," Henry said. "When we arrive in Yawkey I want you streaming from the bus, already in your uniforms, smiling to beat the band. I want each of you carrying a handful of balloons. You pass the balloons out to the littlest children. There may well be journalists present. If so, Arlys, I want you to eat a second bowl of Sweetwheats for the cameras there."

"Oh, please not me, Mr. Henry," said Arlys. Her face pinched with distress. "Gee whiz."

"I'll do it," Tracy offered.

"That'll sell the cereal," said Cindy.

"Better than you could."

"Could not."

Irini put the last bite of Sweetwheats into her mouth. Henry thumbed the watch. "Let's get this show on the road," he said. "Remember that you're playing for Maggie today. Make her proud."

He boarded the bus first, leaving the Kitchen to the girls while they changed. Irini hadn't worn a uniform since she'd been a Brownie for about ten minutes once. Back then, as she remembered it, the uniform had been one of the reasons she quit.

Each bus seat held two, except for the large seat at the back, which Henry Collins had taken for himself. He filled the space next to him with charts and magazines and Maggie's correspondence. He was planning to work all the way to Yawkey.

Walter stowed the batting helmets and the bats and sank into the seat next to Helen. He was wearing his Sweethearts baseball cap pulled down so that it shaded his eyes and gave him a furtive look. Inside the dark bus, he folded the brim upward. Now he looked like a goofball. He grinned at Irini, showing his beautiful teeth, the wet, pink strip of gum line.

Irini sat with Arlys, and Margo sat with her brothers. Arlys had the window seat behind Helen. This put Irini directly behind Walter. Sissy walked down the aisle and stopped. Her eyes glassed over with tears. She held out her mitt; Irini could see from where she sat. The mitt was signed with Jimmy's name and molded in the shape of Jimmy's hand. Walter took it.

"Do you think he'll mind me using it?" Sissy asked.

"I'm sure he'd want you to."

"I don't want to do anything dumb with it. I don't want to drop any balls."

"You won't," said Walter. He put his own hand inside for a moment. Then he took it out and handed it back. "He'd be proud of you, Sissy. I know he would."

"I wish he'd come home," said Sissy, the tears spilling onto her nose. She wiped them away and walked on to take one of the seats toward the rear. Irini could hear her in the back, sniffing loudly. Norma started the engine. The balloons hummed in the air above them. The bus had the stale, cramped smell of buses.

Walter turned and offered a stick of gum to Helen. He unwrapped one for himself, folded it into his cheek where it made a lump the size of a buckeye. "Just get in back of the ball when you field it. Think about blocking as well as catching. Think about your whole body, not just your glove. You remember that one thing and you'll be great today." The advice was accompanied by the doggish sounds of smacking and chewing.

Irini could see the side of Helen's face, the rim of her ear sticking out from her hair, her cheek tensing as she chewed. They were all of them on edge. "Helen doesn't need someone coaching her every minute," Irini said.

"Except her coach," Walter answered pleasantly. He snapped his gum. The bus passed beneath the limestone arch and out of the mill parking lot. The balloons rushed from one side to the other as the bus turned onto Mill Street.

Arlys leaned forward. "Walter. I'm so frightened. I don't know that I can do this."

"You're the best player we have. We're all depending on you," said Walter.

"That's the problem."

Walter turned all the way around, hanging his arms over the back of the seat. "Think of it as another part in a play. You're playing the role of a baseball player. No lines, you've got to get the part across physically. You're athletic and self-confident. You're Ty Cobb. That's what I want you to convey to the stands. Grace and self-confidence."

"Didn't Ty Cobb kill his father?" said Fanny, from across the aisle.

"No. His mother killed his father."

"Well, that's a good thing to know, isn't it? Arlys can use that for motivation."

"I wouldn't want to be Ty Cobb," said Margo. "You be Babe Ruth, Arlys."

"I don't think that's the style we want for the Sweethearts," said Fanny. "What's wrong with DiMaggio? Or Musial? He's a dream. I'd walk to Hoboken for a bit of that."

"Just be a baseball player," said Walter. "A gifted, graceful, no-nerves, hitting all-out baseball player."

"You can do that, Arlys," said Irini. "That won't even be a stretch."

The shadow of the Magrit water tower passed quickly over them. Like a blessing. "You have from here to Yawkey to assume the role," said Walter. "We'll all be quiet and let you prepare it. Grace and self-confidence."

"Oh, no." Henry had risen to his feet at the back. Norma hit the brakes in response to his cry, making him stumble forward. The Sweethearts all turned in Henry's direction. In the back window the water tower loomed like a giant jellyfish.

His eyes were as large as his ears. A copy of *Women at Home* was in his hand. "Who is responsible for this Chicken Mole Recipe?"

"That was me, Mr. Henry," said Margo.

"It's been sabotaged," said Henry. "It has chocolate in the sauce."

"No, no, that's right," said Margo. "That's the way it's supposed to be."

"But it's chicken with chocolate sauce. It has chocolate and Tabasco. That can't taste good."

"Mexicans like it."

"Oh," said Henry. He sat again, tense and erect, the magazine still open to the offending recipe. Norma hit the gas. Henry fell back. "Oh, good. Well, that's our Maggie. Always the new and the daring. Always in the vanguard. Claire, perhaps you should fix this for us at Collins House one night. I've no objection to a little experimentation."

They turned onto Country Road B. Norma took the turn sharply and a branch scraped the side of the bus. It unbalanced Cindy, who was edging her way down the aisle, so she grabbed the back of Walter's seat with her hand while Norma corrected the turn. "Walter."

Her voice was intriguingly quiet. Irini leaned forward to hear her over the bus motor. "Walter, I have a visitor."

Walter looked at her blankly. "In Magrit? In Yawkey?"

"My monthly visitor."

Walter looked to Helen who wouldn't look back.

"I'm falling off the roof, Walter," said Cindy.

Walter turned to Arlys who didn't seem to see him. Eventually he got to Irini. "Come on, Walter. You remember the films," Irini said. "Think about it. She's experiencing the monthly glory of womanhood."

"I'm early. It must be nerves. I've been retaining water all week and this morning I've got cramps. I've got pimples." This announcement was hardly necessary. "And look at these white slacks I have to wear. I don't know if I can play."

"We're all on the same clock," said Irini. "Every girl in the Kitchen. We could have told you ahead of time if you and Mr. Henry had consulted with us before you made up the schedule. It really should be worked around."

"It didn't occur to me," said Walter. "We don't have a bench. You all have to play."

"Then let it be on your head," said Irini.

"It won't actually hurt her to play, will it?" asked Walter. "We don't have a bench."

"I'm the only one that cramps," said Cindy.

"It's the white slacks that are really the problem. We should have been consulted about the uniform," Margo said. "Ordinarily white would be fine, but it's going to be hard to play when we're worrying about the white slacks."

"They were a silly choice anyway," said Claire. She was seated next to Fanny. "Did anyone talk to Maggie about it first? Have you ever tried to get grass stains out of white fabric?"

"Oh, I think they'll bleach out," said Walter. It was so naive, such a *boy* thing to say. The girls all shared an exasperated moment.

"Are we there yet?" the younger Törngren brother asked.

"The amount of bleach you're going to be using will destroy the cloth. They'll be white, but they'll be full of holes," Claire said to Walter. Her color was high, her tone patient, but sad. "Do you want to be buying new uniforms every month?"

"Have you ever done a laundry in your whole life?" Irini asked.

"White is not a slimming color," Helen observed. "Why can't the uniforms be navy? Navy goes with anything."

"We're not going to be accessorizing," said Fanny.

"Walter." It was Tracy May. She was looking exceptionally pretty, as if she had already spent a day in the sun. Everything about her was more vivid. Alone of all the Sweethearts, she seemed to know she would do well today. It was inspiring to see this level of confidence. It was awesome. It was idiotic.

She had followed Cindy down the aisle. "Mr. Henry wants to know, when he introduces us, does he do the pitcher first or last?" This was vintage Tracy, but particularly unconvincing, because anyone who turned around could see that Henry had fallen asleep in the back, his pen in his hand, his head bouncing gently on his books.

They were in a quilted countryside of green fields and red barns and round-tipped, bullet-shaped silos. The hills around Magrit were so moderate in slope, they imposed nothing on the engineer; all the roads were laid out on a rectangular grid. The road rose and fell sleepily; the balloons echoed the motion.

For several miles the bus was trapped behind a truck, which threw up a cloud of dirt, coating Margo and Arlys's spotless windows. Finally Norma was able to gun past. A herd of Holsteins looked up at the noise.

"There's still time to change the batting order," Irini told Walter quietly. Every time she turned to look out the window, she caught a peripheral glimpse of Helen's face. Helen held her arms about her, so that they crossed each other and flattened her breasts.

"Cindy May is cramping," Walter reminded Irini. Trust Walter to find a way to work menstrual cramps to his advantage. He looked to Helen again. "Just this once, just for this first game, I don't even want you to swing at the ball. But I want you to smile. Can you look relaxed? Can you look as if you're enjoying yourself? It'll make all the difference."

"Perhaps Sissy could lead off," Irini suggested. She regretted it as soon as she said it. Although Sissy was a decent fielder, once you eliminated Helen, then Sissy was the obvious choice to bat ninth. Irini's tone had been unimpeachably neutral; still it was too obvious a reference to Walter's nocturnal activities, a subject on which Irini had vowed never to say a word.

"You're not serious," said Walter. He turned to look at her. His eyes were steady and he held her gaze longer than she could hold his. "Just let me do it, Irini," he said. "Let me coach the team. Do you have a problem with that? Or with something else?"

"Walter," said Fanny. "We're not going right back after the game, are we? There will be some time to go out with the other team, discuss strategies and the like? Mr. Henry is not going to make us get right back on the bus? I mean, what's the point of a chaperone if we just get right back on the bus?"

"Walter," said Cindy. "Will there be bathroom facilities close at hand? Have you seen the field?"

"It's at a public park."

"Will the bathrooms be open? Did you call ahead and check?"

Irini leaned forward and spoke low so that only Walter would hear and maybe not even him. "Don't get the idea that I'm jealous. Sissy Tarken is a friend of mine. You know what I owe her. I don't like to see her hurt."

Walter spun completely around. His face and his voice were astonished. "Irini! I hadn't been back since Jimmy died. I went to express my sympathy. Jesus, Jimmy was a friend of mine."

"Are we there yet?" the younger Törngren boy asked.

The bus took a perfectly perpendicular turn, leaning Irini into Arlys. She could see out the bus window down the road, all the fields and the tidy dairy farms laid out end to end, the furrows curving off, opening at the horizon like fans. "I'm just saying it might be a good strategy to move our strength to the end of the order," she said hurriedly, with more volume. "Take them by surprise. I'm not trying to coach for you. I'm just throwing out suggestions. I'm just thinking we might be better off not playing everything so much by the book."

"Really." Walter's voice was low. "I can't believe you would think that of me. I don't deserve that from you."

"I think the pitcher should be introduced last," said Tracy. "After a sort of pause."

Irini put her hand on Walter's shoulder and started to speak, but he shook her off. "If I think about this much, I'm going to be even more insulted. Just drop it."

"I think I'm going to throw up," said Helen.

"I think we're going to play a hell of a game." The words came from Arlys's seat, but the voice was too loud for Arlys's voice, and Arlys never swore. They all turned together, turned as a team, to look at her. She had the face of a madonna, radiant and calm. "One hell of a game," she said again.

No one wanted to put that serenity at risk. They were quiet all the rest of the way to Yawkey.

19

The crowds in Yawkey were somewhat smaller than Henry had hoped. The press had given the event a clean miss. The opposing team had to be patched together from kids who were playing ball in the park anyway, plus the two Törngren boys. The average age on the opposing team was eleven.

"Good thing I came along to chaperone," said Fanny, "because I do not like the look of these guys."

Without so much as a glance in Irini's direction, Walter changed the batting order. "Cindy, you lead off," he said. "Tracy, second. Helen, after Sissy. Helen, swing at anything in the zone. Nice level swing."

For three innings, the Sweethearts led. Arlys was flawless. She teamed up with Cindy for two double plays; she picked a line drive out of the air with her ungloved hand. She came up to bat three times and three times she got on base. Twice she doubled. She brought no one home because the bases were empty. Irini, batting just ahead of her in the lineup, had already cleared them.

The opposing pitcher was a big, good-looking, redheaded boy of fourteen named Alex. He pitched faster than anyone Irini had ever faced, but the fast ball was all he had. Irini took a pitch to get her

Peabody timed just right and then she knew exactly where the next ball would come. With the pitch coming so hard and her arms pumped up from kneading dough, she did more than connect. The ball soared out and away from her bat like a small, round bird. The first time it surprised her so much she forgot to run. Fortunately it was an automatic. She stood and watched the ball fly into left field, past the younger Törngren boy and into the duck pond. He insisted on trying to retrieve it. The game came to a complete halt while he made a great show of wading in up to his knees. But the ball was lost. Henry had to pitch out a new one.

The next time she came up they played her deep, but she hit it even farther, all the way to the street, where it rolled under a car. Ka-pow! she thought. Ka-boom! Both times she brought in Cindy and Norma. No one else on either team could hit it so far. Of course, Tracy's pitching was much softer.

But the eleven-year-olds were hitting, too, and in the fourth inning, Tracy started to fade. Margo had made Tracy pitch it easy to her six-year-old brother. By the fourth inning Tracy was regretting this. She tried to put it past him, but he waited out the count and took his base on balls. It was ungentlemanly behavior and Tracy pointed this out by calling him a baby.

"I am not," he said. "You're a sap-head." He began to cry, big, flat, grimy tears that stained his cheeks. When he raised his hands to his eyes, Tracy tried to throw him out. Cindy, who was taken by surprise and had serious scruples about the play anyway, missed the throw, so he made it to second while she was chasing the ball and dropping her glove. He stood with his foot firmly on the bag, rubbing at his eyes while his nose boiled and bubbled.

From this point on the game turned unfriendly. All the boys began waiting Tracy out, so she was pitching five or six pitches per batter, which tired her even more, and walking most of them. The boys had discovered Helen's fielding and when they did swing, they were going for right. Irini played over and she dropped a perfectly routine fly, that even Helen might have caught if Irini hadn't gotten in her way. The out would have ended the fifth. Instead Tracy walked in three more runs. They called it after six innings.

The final score was eleven-year-olds, 16, Sweethearts, 8. The opposing team took their balloons and went home, except for the pitcher, who hung around long enough to ask Arlys if she wanted to go for a malted. "He was too cute," Cindy said. "I don't care how old he was, Arlys, you should have gone."

"Would Ty Cobb have gone?" Arlys asked.

"With a good-looking redhead?" said Fanny. "And how!"

Henry called the team together for a postgame pep talk. There was no dugout; they sat on the grass in right field, out by the duck pond. "I hope no one is blaming me," Tracy said in a voice that would scour pots. "If anyone is they can just pitch themselves next time. I didn't really have the fielding behind me, did I?"

"She's just cranky because her aunt is about to visit," Cindy reminded them.

"Am not, you little droon."

"How nice," said Henry absent-mindedly. "You must bring her to the house."

"No one is blaming you, Tracy," said Walter. "You did swell."

All of Irini's pregame anxieties let go of her at once. She had really enjoyed the game. She stretched out on the grass. The bright sun was making her pleasantly stupid. A big white cloud was puffing overhead, growing like a big loaf of bread in the sky. Her arm hurt in the nicest possible way. She bent it over her eyes, so it could bake awhile. All that she could see now was a small slice of blue. Periwinkle blue, like the crayon. Maggie had a recipe for periwinkle, but Irini tried when possible to avoid eating snails or bivalves. This was not so hard in Magrit.

"I blame myself," Henry said, "for not moving faster on the ape. An ape would have made all the difference today." His voice passed over her like water. A small ant walked among the iridescent hairs of her arm. The sun went suddenly out. Irini raised her arm.

Thomas Holcrow was standing by her head. Irini sat up. Holcrow was dressed more casually than usual, in a red sweater with a bomber jacket over it and his shoulders very prominent beneath. He was smoking a cigarette with a long, ashy tip. He gave Walter's back a friendly tap. "Say, Walter. Excellent game," he said.

He offered Walter a cigarette. "That third inning! That was a whizbanger. I thought you were going to pull it out there." He inhaled and then blew. The smoke curled down into Irini's own hair so that she could smell it. There was something intimate about it that she liked. Holcrow exhaled two gray streams out through his nose. It was 1947, just after a war in which cigarettes had been held to be so indispensable to morale that they were dispensed freely. Irini looked at that coiling nasal fog and thought it was sexy, thought it wrapped the occasion up movie-star style.

And then there was the jacket and the shoulders and her general sun-induced dreaminess. Once again she was ready to kiss someone. Once again there were no volunteers. "Perhaps I could give someone a ride home," Holcrow said. "Arlys? Cindy? Irini?"

Walter sucked in air to light up. He coughed once and cleared his throat. "I want the whole team on the bus," he said. "We have things to discuss while the game's fresh in our minds."

"I think Irini can go home however she likes." Holcrow was considerably larger than Walter. He inhaled. It made him larger yet and the red tip of his cigarette brightened and yellowed in punctuation.

"She made some unfortunate fielding errors. They cost us."

"I thought Irini played a swell game."

"Just look at these pants," said Claire diplomatically, displaying her left knee, which had a grassy blotch about the shape and size of Spain over it. "This particular combination of dirt and grass is never going to come completely clean, I don't care what you do."

Maggie Collins writes: "There are four classes of stain removers: solvents, absorbents, detergents, and bleaches. Every homemaker should have at least one of each group constantly on hand.

"When faced with a tough stain, take your time. Success depends largely on having ample leisure to do the work thoroughly. No amateur should begin a ticklish job with chemicals unless she is prepared to ignore the telephone and doorbell.

"And always try cold water first."

Irini chose to ride on the bus, which didn't please Holcrow. He took Tracy home instead. The bus ride was a penance and no doubt Irini deserved it. They didn't discuss her fielding errors. Henry had fallen asleep again. Walter wasn't speaking to her at all. It was early evening, with the color just falling from the sky and settling its dusky film on the trees and houses.

Norma wound her way back from the park and from there back along the road home. They'd only gone a few blocks when Norma took a turn too quickly. The batting helmets spilled out of the bag, and rolled like drunken bowling balls down the aisle of the bus. Walter rose to gather them up. Norma pulled over off the pavement. They were in a residential area, new houses, old trees. The bus came to a stop. A white dog with liver-colored spots barked at them from the safety of a porch. "It's all right," Walter told Norma. He grabbed the duffel, stuffed the helmets back inside. "It's under control."

"That's not why I stopped," said Norma. "Someone is chasing us."

Irini couldn't see out the back. She shoved her own window open and leaned. The driver's side mirror was round and saucer-sized. Deep inside it was a girl. She ran toward them, a small figure in the exact center of the saucer, with the road twisting behind her and the leaves of the trees tossing above. She was waving one arm in a friendly fashion. They sat and waited until she appeared next, in the bus doorway. She was quite tall, in a print dress that covered her knees and a red bib apron over the dress. Her hair was dark but sun-streaked with red, and curly. She had it tied back from her face with a piece of string. Her legs were bare and surprisingly muscled, like the legs of a ballerina or a long-distance runner. She might have been seventeen or even sixteen years old.

"Are we losing oil or something?" Norma asked, but the girl was breathing hard from her run and it took her a moment to answer.

"I'd like to be on the team," she said. "I'm a good player."

"We're not a real team," Norma told her. "We're not a team like that. We're a mill team. We all live in Magrit. It's a mill town."

"I saw you. You need another pitcher. I can pitch."

"We have a pitcher," Fanny May told her sharply.

"Lots of girls think they can pitch," Cindy said. "And then they try."

"I can play anywhere."

"We all have to eat Sweetwheats," said Helen, glancing at Henry to be sure he was still asleep. "It's not worth it. Trust me."

"Just watch. Will you watch?" The girl stepped down from the bus and searched the ground. There was gravel along the roadside, but nothing larger. Finally she pulled off one of her shoes. It was a brown loafer, creased as an accordion across the toes.

She straightened up and looked for a target. In the yard in front of her the dog was still barking. It came off the porch, toward the bus. Its walk was stiff-legged; its tail wagged aggressively. The barking was steady and annoying.

The girl turned her right shoulder to the noise and kept going, turned her back. There was a slight pause while the dog growled.

Then she swiveled and kicked forward, pitching the shoe, catching the dog right between its eyes. It yelped once, then closed its mouth with a startled click. The girl removed her second shoe. She and the dog stared at each other. It began to back away; she pitched and it dodged. This time she was a little to the right. Same yelp, though. The dog retreated to the porch.

"She hit a dog," said Arlys. She didn't like this. As she spoke, the dog turned its widened eyes to her.

"And it was moving," said Norma admiringly.

"I could do it again," the girl told them, "but I only wore two shoes."

"Can you pitch anything else?" Walter asked. The throws had not just been accurate. They'd been pretty. It was more than pitching; it was dancing.

"You mean besides shoes?"

"I mean besides straight."

"With a ball, I've got a good curve. I've got a slider. I'm the youngest of seven children and the only girl. I can throw any kind of pitch you want, Coach."

"How old are you?" asked Walter.

"Twenty."

Irini didn't believe it. Walter shook his head sadly. "Look, I'd love to have you on the Sweethearts," he said. "Especially if you bat left, too. But we can't just pick you up on the side of the road. You go home, talk to your parents. If you can get to Magrit, I'll take a look. You can stay with one of the girls while you try out."

"You can stay with me," said Helen. "My mother loves company."

"I'll be there," the girl said. She turned to them, smiling broadly, so that the corners of her mouth dug deep into her cheek. It was an effect like dimples and made her look even younger. "See you all in Magrit."

The dog came back from the porch, picked up one of the shoes. It made a great show of offering it to her, laying the shoe down, but when she reached, the dog grabbed it again. It grinned at her, growling, tail ticking, just out of reach.

Norma eased back into the street, started to drive and then stopped again. The girl was waving them down. Irini leaned out the window, looking back. "My name is Ruby," the girl called. "Ruby Red." Actually the name was Ruby Redd, but of course no one knew that just from hearing it.

Back in Magrit, most of the girls went straight to the sauna, even Tracy, who beat them home and might have been expected to feel uncomfortable over her behavior toward the younger Törngren boy, but apparently didn't. "I just told Thomas right off not to get fresh," she said, as if someone had asked. "I just nipped that right in the bud." No one responded. No one, not even her sisters, mentioned Ruby to Tracy. After they had steamed themselves limp, Mrs. Törngren consoled them with more coffee and some icebox cookies, and then they each went home.

"Are you married yet?" Irini's dad asked her.

"I thought I was supposed to hit a home run today. I hit two, by the way."

"You didn't now?" her father said. "And no one married you on the spot? What kind of men do they have over in Yawkey?"

"Not the best kind," Irini agreed. "Not the kind we'd hoped for."

20

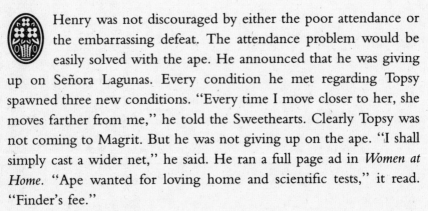

Henry was not discouraged by either the poor attendance or the embarrassing defeat. The attendance problem would be easily solved with the ape. He announced that he was giving up on Señora Lagunas. Every condition he met regarding Topsy spawned three new conditions. "Every time I move closer to her, she moves farther from me," he told the Sweethearts. Clearly Topsy was not coming to Magrit. But he was not giving up on the ape. "I shall simply cast a wider net," he said. He ran a full page ad in *Women at Home*. "Ape wanted for loving home and scientific tests," it read. "Finder's fee."

His response to defeat was to tell the girls to double their daily dose of Sweetwheats. They ignored him.

Summer came and went and came and went that year. One warm day in June would be followed by three cold ones. The birds were quarrelsome and peckish and a robin in the Doyles' backyard went into a nest-building frenzy, starting six nests without ever finishing one. As far as Irini could see, no eggs were laid either. It was an obvious case of acute psychosis and Irini really didn't know what to do about it.

Then there was a tragedy concerning the Collinses' dogs. Perhaps

Henry had fed them one breakfast too many. One night they began a tunnel out of Collins House. It was discovered in the morning, discovered in progress and still so small that only the Pomerian–Boston terrier had gotten through. She was on the loose in Magrit for three days, eluding Norma and her dogcatcher net with, Henry insisted, diet-inspired cunning. It was hard not to think he was rooting for a clean escape. But then she chased the Doyle car one night, and Irini's father hit and killed her. Ada was still in India and hadn't heard yet. Irini's father was devastated. "She came out of nowhere," he said. "Like a little furry tornado. She threw herself at the tire. I never even saw her."

"It's not your fault," Irini tried to tell him, but it drove him to drink.

All in all, summer was not what she had remembered, not what she'd held out for all those snowy Magrit months. Before she was a working girl, summers had been full of slow and sun-stunned days. There had been time to lie on her stomach and eat buttercups, time to read novels that were much too young for her, time to wander up to the falls and out into the woods. What did summer mean anymore, now that she was nineteen and worked for her living? It was nothing but the drudgery of cooking and baseball, baseball and cooking.

The one Saturday they didn't have a game, the Sweethearts were deployed to Collins House. "Although we missed spring training," said Helen, "you'll be happy to hear we're going to make spring cleaning." Henry wanted everything bright as a penny for Ada's return.

"A really deep cleaning," he instructed them. "If it doesn't move, scrub it." He left Fanny in charge, and he and Walter took off at dawn to go fishing north of Upper Magrit. It was 1947 so if you caught a fish you could eat it.

The girls arrived with their aprons and buckets at Collins House about nine. Fanny wrote up a list of chores and then tore it into strips. She dropped the strips into the cut-glass bowl. The one Irini drew said, "Launder bedding. Beat small rugs. Polish copper pots." She had gotten lucky; it was a relatively easy draw. "Anyone want to trade?" asked Margo. She had gotten the oven and the refrigerator. Helen had windows and toilets. "There is no sense of satisfaction in windows," she said. "There is no sense of completion," but Margo said that was only before the invention of the squeegee, so the switch was made.

Irini went into all the upstairs bedrooms and stripped the sheets off the beds. Unmaking was much less exacting and much more pleasurable than making. There was a lesson here and it extended far beyond hospital corners. She tore the bottom sheets loose.

Irini moved quickly through the unoccupied rooms and into Walter's. Ada had redone the room the moment Walter left for boarding school, so it looked like a guest bedroom, neutral colors, navies and beiges. He had set out no pictures, but there was a large abalone shell on the dresser and inside it a number of letters. His duffel bag sat on the window seat. He had yet to unpack completely.

Walter had not forgiven her. It worried Irini a little, but Walter had a forgiving nature and things were sure to return to normal between them. Anyway, his prolonged snit gave her license to snoop as she certainly would not normally have done. She picked up the abalone shell, removing the letters, which were of no interest to her. The inside was pearled with all the colors of water and sunlight. The outside was stony and rough. It was too large and flat to hear the ocean in. There were three mysterious holes along the edge, holes so even and round they appeared drilled. When she went to put the letters back, she dropped them. Naturally she had to pick them up; she was there to clean. She checked the return addresses. They were all from his mom and sister. Then with no provocation, she checked out the sock drawer. This was the place where *she* kept secret and personal items, but Walter was determined to bore her; it didn't even contain socks.

She turned to the bed. The blankets went into one pile; the sheets into another. There was something intimate about dealing with Walter's bedding. She didn't want to be caught at it, but before she could finish, Tracy entered with the Hoover. It roared with the sound of a

P-38, but that didn't stop Tracy from talking. "If anyone else wants to pitch, they're more than welcome to," Tracy said. "My heavens! It's not like I'm just dying to pitch or anything."

"You're doing okay."

"What?"

"You're doing okay."

It was obviously less than Tracy had expected. She flipped off the Hoover and moved the armchair. "It's not that easy," she said. "You can't just put it over the plate. There's a lot more to it than that." There were two pens under the chair. Tracy picked them up and put them in her apron pocket.

"Norma says you're shaking off her calls," said Irini.

"Norma has some good ideas," said Tracy. "But you develop an instinct when you've been on the mound for a while." She flipped the Hoover on again. Irini jumped over its cord and went into Ada's room.

Ada had made a small territory of her own in Collins House. Several of her painted plates were on the walls—the more edgy, arty ones, the ones with roses the color of sand and ashes. Ada tried to make a statement with her art, and probably she did, it was just that no one in Magrit knew what it was. "It's not really piece by piece," she explained to Irini once, at the annual elementary school white elephant sale. Ada was trying to interest her in a gravy boat painted with wilted peonies. "You have to look at the whole body of work. And you have to know something about the tradition. You have to see it as part of a dialogue I'm having with other china painters. Try to see it as both a question and an answer." Irini bought the gravy boat, but she had never understood art.

In Ada's room was a set of sterling silver brushes that would have to be polished along with the dining-room silver; and a set of ivory pillowcases, edged with tatting, that would have to be hand-washed. Irini had scarcely collected the sheets before Tracy arrived, bringing with her her own little storm of noise and dust. "Norma likes to mix it up," Tracy said. "But sometimes it's more of a surprise if you don't.

You learn how to read the batter's face as well as his stance. Norma can't see the batter's face." The vacuum came within inches of Irini's foot. "Has Norma been complaining about my pitching?" Tracy asked.

"Not at all," said Irini. She scooped up the sheets and moved on to Henry's room.

She didn't envy the person who'd drawn the dusting in here. It was the bedroom of a necromancer. There were shells, feathers, skins, rocks, pods, globes, weather maps, and a dozen corked vials filled with nasty-looking fluids. "It's what keeps Mr. Henry young," Irini's dad had told her often. "He's far too interested to die." On one wall Henry had mounted a map. The Sweethearts' upcoming games were marked with green pins, their losses, with pins tipped in black. It saddened Irini to see it. Henry cared more than he was willing to admit.

The Hoover was coming. Irini stripped the bed with lightning speed and started down the stairs with the pile of sheets. She passed Arlys, who was in the hallway wiping down the wallpaper with pieces of fresh bread, according to Maggie's best advice, and Margo, who was scrubbing the toilets with Coca-Cola. The phone rang.

"Irini," Claire called from the kitchen. Irini left the sheets in a wanton pile and went to pick up the parlor extension. Fanny was in the parlor, polishing the brass light fixtures with Worcestershire sauce. "Message from your dad," said Cindy. "He says to tell you he'll make dinner tonight, since you're working all day. He says to call if you've an objection to macaroni."

"Sounds great," said Irini.

Collins House had a completely automatic washing machine. All the women in Magrit had come to look the day Norma hooked it up. It was set in a little stone anteroom off the kitchen, like a throne or a shrine. To get to it Irini had to pass Helen, who was sitting on the kitchen floor surrounded by newspapers. "Don't try to stop me," she told Irini. "Don't try to talk me out of it." She stuck her head into the oven, but there was no room for her breasts. "Good-bye, cruel world," she said.

Claire was mopping the pantry. "Go ahead," she said, before Irini could ask. "But don't let the dogs in."

Norma was working outside with the storm windows and since this was a delicate operation, done with tools and ladders, the dogs had been shut up in the washroom. Norma had been hired on a special contract. You didn't waste a woman with Norma's gifts merely on cleaning. Or if you did, you gave her the death assignments. You put her on point. Norma was there to climb two stories on a free-standing ladder to take down the fifty-pound entryway chandelier and then put it back, after someone else had washed and polished it into mother-of-pearl. She was there to waltz about the roof, cleaning the chimney and the gutters. She was there to remove the second-story storm windows. Naturally she was paid more than anyone else. She earned it.

Irini fought her way through the dogs to the washing machine. Already the air was full of dog hair. She acquired the same layer of dust she would get again, beating the rugs. When she bent down to load the sheets, the Dane stuck his nose in her ear and made a sound like the ocean.

"Can I wash Ada's pillowcases in the kitchen sink?" she asked Claire.

"*May* I," said Helen.

"Little crowded in the washroom?" Claire said.

"May I wash Ada's pillowcases in the kitchen sink?"

"Yes, you may."

The kitchen phone rang. "Irini," said Claire. Irini took the receiver.

"Your dad doesn't like the look of the cheese," said Cindy. "He's thinking if it bakes forty minutes in a hot oven, it will probably lose those green streaks, but he's leaning now toward Italiano."

"Meaning canned spaghetti," said Irini. "I guess I don't care."

"That's not what he says. He says you're the fussiest eater God ever set on two legs. That's a direct quote. He also said to tell you he's making it from scratch. If you don't want Italian call him quick and stop him before he kills another tomato. That's a direct quote, too."

"Is he at home?"

"He's just using the phone at Bumps."

This was ominous. "Italian's fine. Tell him I'll be home by five and that I'll be starving."

Irini filled the sink for the pillowcases. Claire looked at them doubtfully. "Handmade laces should be basted to cheesecloth before washing," she said.

"Good golly," said Irini.

"Good point," said Claire. "And you can bring out the cream color, by soaking it in a light tea. Very light. Very diluted."

"How do you know this stuff?" asked Irini.

"I read Maggie's columns. Don't you? Maybe instead of basting you can wash and rinse in a glass jar. Fill the jar with suds, and let the pillowcases soak. Shake occasionally."

"Do you have a jar large enough?"

"I have an old pickle jar. When you get to the copper, use ketchup and steel wool."

"Really?" asked Irini.

"Cross my heart."

Irini ate the last pickle. She washed the jar and dropped in the pillowcases, where they floated like preserved fruits or discarded gallstones.

She picked up the ketchup and took the pots to the dining-room table. She spread newspapers on the table and used the steel wool and lots of muscle. By the time she finished, the first load of sheets was done.

It was cool outside but breezy. The sheets would dry quickly once she could get them up. Norma was already sliding down from the roof. "There's a nest in the chimney," she said. "I'll have to come back later."

"What kind?"

"Swallow."

"Eggs?"

"Eggs, but no mama. I don't know if she's still around or not. I'm going to go look in Mr. Henry's nets."

The sheets were large and the day was windy. Irini struggled with the corners; the sheets fought against every pin. They twisted and billowed and slapped her wetly in the face. It was a sort of natural semaphore. Irini decoded it as she worked—"Surrender, Dorothy."

Someone had let the dogs escape. The boxer ripped a top sheet from the line and dragged it off while Irini chased. Ten minutes later she retrieved the sheet by feigning disinterest. The dogs were *so* dumb. Fortunately the sheet was so badly ripped and ruined that rewashing it was out of the question. If only this had happened before she washed it.

At two o'clock they broke for a late lunch. Irini shook her pickle jar and ate a peanut butter sandwich. She noticed that Tracy was not speaking to Norma. Apparently Tracy had worked up a temper while vacuuming, and of course this was Irini's fault. Fortunately Norma was oblivious.

After lunch Irini went to collect the area rugs.

"Beat first or vacuum first?" she asked Arlys.

"Beat first."

"Vacuum first or dust first?"

"Vacuum first."

"Just testing you," Irini said.

She covered her mouth and nose with her scarf like a bandit. Beating rugs was a nasty, gritty job. It was a shame that cleaning should make you so dirty. Irini got a bit of sand in the corner of her eye. She was dabbing at it with one grimy hand when she heard Thomas Holcrow behind her.

"Don't shoot, Irini," he said. "You know I'd give you anything you asked for." He pulled a spotless handkerchief from his pocket, cupped her chin with one hand and poked at her eye with the handkerchief in the other. His face was very close to her face. "I see it," he said. "Hold still now. Don't blink."

Tears streamed from her eyes. She needed to wipe her nose, but his hand was in the way. Tears could be attractively feminine. But this other . . .

He pointed at her. It confused her for a moment until she understood that he was merely showing her the black speck he'd found. "Say, Irini. It's as big as your eyeball."

"Thank you," Irini said. She could still feel the spot where his hand had touched her chin. It started a hot current which ran down her neck and into her heart. It set up a shivering inside.

"Is Mr. Henry here?" he asked.

"Gone fishing," said Irini.

"He had some books for me. Maybe I can find them myself." Holcrow winked at her, put his handkerchief away and vanished into Collins House, as if he were the Lone Ranger or something. Irini nailed the rug with a vicious backhand stroke.

By five the house was polished from front to back, from top to bottom. The beds were made, the chandelier was hung, the rugs were back on the floors, the sheets were back on the beds, the dogs were back in the yard. Holcrow had left, although Irini hadn't seen it happen.

She walked home to her own disheveled house. Tweed was waiting to be fed. Otherwise the place was empty. About six o'clock, her father called.

"I'm putting him through," said Cindy.

"Don't make dinner for me," he told Irini. "I'm going to eat at Bumps tonight. Norma defrosted some of her kill and Mrs. Baldish is whipping up a casserole. She won't give me the recipe, but from my bar stool here, it looks to be about four parts wild turkey to one part Wild Turkey. You fiddle with those percentages a bit, and you'll have what I'd call a casserole. Don't wait up, Irini, my darling. I'll be home before dawn and singing as I come."

21

Maggie celebrated India's independence and Ada's return with an all-Indian menu. There was a chicken curry, very mild, served with raisins and red peanuts, a cardamom-flavored yogurt, and a dessert made of batter balls, which had been deep-fried and drowned in a sweet syrup. According to Maggie these balls approximated some Indian delicacy, but Claire had made them more quickly and easily than the Indian housewife by using the hated Bisquick. Only for Ada.

The meal was published in *Women at Home,* having first been taste-tested at a slide show Ada held in the school multipurpose room to educate the citizens of Magrit in the principles of nonviolence. It was the first slide show Magrit had ever seen. Henry was beside himself. Thirty-five millimeter cameras! A real screen. Real-life colors.

Even Mrs. Tarken came, wearing her best bedroom slippers. Walter was there to run the projector. Holcrow turned up, which meant that most of the Sweethearts also attended. Holcrow spilled curry down the front of his white shirt and was given much fluttery advice about Javelle waters and bleaches. In point of fact it was an attractive look for him, sort of helpless and masculine. It would have been a shame to clean him up.

He gave Walter a hand with the folding chairs and they talked about California, all very friendly. Walter had taken too much sun at the last game; his nose was as pink and shiny as a cooked shrimp. It gave him a boyish look again, fourteen-year-old Walter who'd taken her out secretly to let her jump from the boys' tree, where absolutely no girls were allowed, into the waters of Upper Magrit, where absolutely no kids were allowed.

"Hello, Walter," said Irini, and Walter not only refused to answer, but took an ostentatious seat by Sissy. "Hello, Tom," Irini said to Holcrow, who gave her a heart-stopping smile—as if the sight of her was more than he could have hoped for, more than he deserved—but went to sit with Helen. Irini sat between Margo and Arlys.

Ada was dressed in midnight blue and wore no jewelry. She had stopped in New York to get her hair cut. It was now quite short and lifted in a silvery wave up and off her face. She was understated but elegant, which wasn't the usual Magrit style. The food wasn't the usual Magrit fare. In some subtle way, the evening was off to a bad start.

Ada stood before a large map of India and made occasional stabs at it with a pointer to show where the borders between India and Pakistan would be. Even on paper it seemed a very unwieldy arrangement. Then Henry turned out the lights.

Ada was too stiff to be a good public speaker, but she did better in the dark. She described the caste system briefly, and spoke feelingly about the plight of the untouchables. She also spoke on behalf of the women in India. In the Chicago paper last month a Dr. Madison of Mercy Hospital in Cleveland had published the results of a study suggesting that the prime childbearing age for women occured before their sixteenth birthdays. Many of the mothers in India were younger than sixteen and Ada saw nothing beneficial in this.

"Of course Dr. Madison was not advocating young mothers," Henry said. "Of course there are social and psychological considerations. But a scientist must report his findings no matter what they are, no matter what his personal hopes and beliefs. This is the greatness, the grandeur of science. It is absolutely neutral, absolutely without prejudice or malice—"

He was not finished, but Walter interrupted him by advancing another slide. A woman with many arms and a deadly expression appeared. "The goddess Kali," said Ada. Having finished with social issues she was turning to aesthetic ones. The next slides showed the temples, the fields, the statuary. Magrit was shocked to see a naked, large-breasted, round-bellied woman on the screen in the school multipurpose room, even if she was carved from stone. Sometimes Magrit forgot that Ada was an artist. The stone woman's nipples were the size of walnuts and twice as hard.

Walter hurried on to a slide of Nehru, standing with a group of men all in suits, all rather fuzzy and faroff. Ada had not caught up to him yet. "A fertility symbol," she said.

"As if India needs one," said Henry. "You could argue, I think, that India's problems stem entirely from overpopulation. This Muslim-Hindu animosity is merely a symptom. It's called 'the crowded cage behavior.'"

"Then why are you encouraging preadolescent motherhood?" asked Ada.

He turned the lights on. "Of course, I'm not. I was merely trying to say that a scientist must report a scientific finding and not suppress it."

"I think we make far too much of science," said Ada. "Could I have the lights off, please?"

It was humid and close in the multipurpose room. Irini began to envy the thinly dressed Indians on the screen. A cricket had found its way under the stage. It sang ceaselessly beneath Ada's voice. The rhythmical click of the slides, the cricket, and the heat made Irini sleepy. She put her arms on the back of Mrs. Gilbertsen's seat and her head on her arms. A vague recollection of a dream tickled her. There had been a sky with several suns. They rose one after another and hung between the clouds like Chinese lanterns, like home runs. The sky was bright and intolerably beautiful. Irini lay below on the clipped grass of a real outfield. She was not dressed, and it seemed appropriate that she be remembering this in the school multipurpose room, the scene of so many distressingly undressed dreams. But this dream was not like that. Being naked had seemed perfectly all right. An unknown man lay beside her on the grass.

The back of her neck was wet and hot. The skin of her arms turned blue and black in the constant shadow play of the slides. She closed her eyes and the shadows moved to the backs of her eyelids. She thought about kissing someone. She thought about someone kissing her first.

Ada apologized for the fact that there was no slide of Gandhi. It was a conundrum, a poser, a Chinese puzzle from the mysterious east. Irini opened her eyes and raised her head to see the no slide. The screen was blank with light. In a way it was the most dazzling picture yet. Irini could see Holcrow's profile, lit up in the reflected light like a half-moon.

Ada said that she had been permitted to see Gandhi, but not to photograph him. In order to earn the audience, Ada had been forced to learn to spin. Spinning was central to Gandhi's philosophies and Ada announced her intention to continue it at home in Magrit and to teach the skill to anyone else who wished. She proposed substituting it for the Wednesday bridge game. The only thing this accomplished was to give the members of Magrit's bridge group a sudden motive to discredit Gandhi.

"Why spinning?" asked Mrs. Fossum, "as opposed to crochet? Or needlepoint?"

"Or quilting," said Mrs. Baldish. "Or beekeeping? Or collecting spoons," but neither woman had spoken loudly enough for Ada to hear. Ada finished up with a series of slides of a small wooden building and her promise that Gandhi was inside. Henry turned on the lights. Ada retrieved a set of index cards from her purse and began to read off them.

"Satyagraha," Ada read, "means holding on to truth and truth, in the Mahatma's philosophies, is expressed as action, rather than as thought. Satyagraha is a technique for political and social change based on nonviolence and a willingness to suffer in order to find or create truth."

Two rows to the front Irini could see Holcrow leaning over to say something to Helen. He had probably complimented her. Poor, shy Helen was rigid beside him. Irini would have known how to take the compliment. If Henry would just turn out the lights again, Irini might be able to imagine kissing Holcrow. It was hard with the lights on and the stain on his shirt and these constant interruptions. Irini tried, but was forced to give up long before their mouths touched.

"Has Gandhi considered the fact that aggression may be natural to humans? Has he done studies?" Henry asked. "It might be more effective to channel aggression rather than attempt to eradicate it. Does he understand Darwin at all? In the end, we're all animals."

Ada consulted her note cards. "At the core of the Mahatma's philosophies is the concept of ahimsa, but this is not merely a passive refusal to do harm. It is an active, aggressive benevolence. When nonviolence is undertaken simply because the strength for violence is lacking, then it will fail. The mouse can't be said to practice nonviolence against the cat."

"So what are the mouse's options?" Mr. Baldish asked.

"The same as they've always been. The mouse can run and the mouse can hide. The mouse has no obligation to face the cat and be eaten. The truth is not found in this course."

"This course is dessert," said Henry.

"Violence is forbidden to man because man is incapable of knowing the absolute truth. What appears to be truth to you, may appear false to another. You must approach those who differ from you in unending openness of mind." Ada's voice placed a grim emphasis on the last sentence.

Irini couldn't put her head down with the lights on, when everyone would see, couldn't close her eyes, but within these limits she had been drifting, dozing, circling. She thought of a mouse the Tarkens' cat had caught and the disgusting pleasure it had taken in prolonging the kill, tossing it up, over and over, like a furry, squealing pop fly. And because it was Sissy's cat this made her think of Sissy and then of Walter and the fight they were having. The fight was entirely her fault, but it had gone on so long now she was forgetting to feel guilty over it. Just how long did Walter plan to hold a grudge? And then Holcrow spoke and she began to pay attention again.

"It seems naive to me," said Holcrow. "What if we had refused to fight the Germans?"

Mr. Tarken shook his head. "What would we have done without Mr. Churchill? That's what I'd like to know."

"It's become a cliché to suggest that Gandhi's principles of nonviolence would not have worked against the Nazis," Ada said, cunningly accusing Holcrow and Mr. Tarken not only of wrong thinking, but of tired, uninspired wrong thinking. "According to this reasoning, Gandhi is just lucky that he happened to be dealing with the civilized British. In fact, Gandhi has faced many opponents, both in India and South Africa, and among the most difficult are some of the Indians themselves. Mr. Gandhi is no stranger to evil."

Ada told Magrit that the Mahatma had not spoken to her, since her audience coincided with a self-imposed day of silence as well as a day of fasting. This fasting for clarity was not to be confused with the fast as a political weapon.

"An odd weapon to choose in a country where so many are starving," Henry observed heartily. "May we conclude that Gandhi's mother said, 'You clean your plate, young man, before you leave the table' once too often?" Henry had moved from the light switch to the front of the room. Irini could no longer see him. He had dipped behind the rounded hillock that was Mrs. Baldish.

"The argument about Nazis is based, therefore, on a misunderstanding of the Mahatma's theories," Ada said. "There is nothing passive about Gandhian nonviolence. It is an active, positive opposition which includes total noncooperation. It is also dialectical, if I may use the word without offending. Your opponent affects your strategies. The methods you use against the British are not the methods you use against the Nazis. The Mahatma didn't develop the strategies to be used against the Nazis, so we don't know what they would have been. And always remember, in satyagraha you are committed to the long term."

Henry affected an accent. "You finish your breakfast, young man. There are children starving in India." Irini's father laughed loudly. Everyone turned to look at him. He made an apologetic gesture, and probably only Irini knew him well enough to guess that it was the accent he had found so funny and not the joke. The accent was outlandish, otherworldly, perhaps Scottish with some Hoosier highlights. Henry didn't hear well enough to do accents.

Ada fixed Irini's father with a stony stare. "The Mahatma uses no dairy products and drinks no liquors."

"Gandhi could be depriving people of a prime source of calcium. Has he done studies?" Henry's disembodied voice cracked once, giving the word "people" a froggy emphasis. "Does he really understand Darwin? We're at the top of the food chain. It's a scientific fact."

"And isn't that just a pleasant way of admitting that we are food?" said Irini's father.

"Eat or be eaten," Henry agreed. "Bon appetit."

"Eat and be eaten was more my point."

"It's not really a method for an individual, though, is it?" said Fanny diplomatically to Ada. "It seems to require masses of people. I don't see it working in this country. We're not really a nation of followers."

"We're exactly the country which ought to be most interested," Ada argued. "When *must* you practice nonviolence? When the weapons you have are too terrible to be used."

"Who would we use nonviolence against?" Holcrow asked. "The British left some time ago. Not, I might add, without bloodshed. We're a democracy. I don't see the need."

"You don't use nonviolence *against* anyone. You're still not understanding. You use it with, not against."

"It's a doctrine for heroes," said Irini's father. "We're not really a nation of heroes." This was a provocative statement. A shocked silence followed it.

"We just won a war." Mrs. Baldish's voice was clipped and severe. "How did we do that without heroes?" She let her glance linger definitively on Mr. and Mrs. Tarken.

"Oh, the Tarkens are heroes," Irini's father agreed. "The Tarken family is full of heroes. Sissy Tarken was the bravest little girl I ever knew."

"Mr. Doyle spoke without thinking," Mr. Baldish suggested.

"As usual," Irini's father agreed. The awkward moment passed without Irini's father actually retracting the statement.

"Although the Mahatma did not speak to me, he did smile at me." Ada had come to the end of her notes. She tapped the index cards together on her palm, until all the edges were aligned. She might have been blushing. All Magrit, and certainly Henry himself, could see that his wife was in love with another man.

Fair enough, you say, tit for tat. Hadn't Henry had Maggie all those years? What's good for the gander is good for the goose.

But if you really think that, check out *20 Ways to Cook a Goose* and think again.

"Well, it's all too deep-dish for me," said Holcrow.

"Let's have dessert now." Henry gave a brave imitation of good humor. "I think Maggie has sent over a dessert that can't be beat."

22

Magrit had been a mining town before it became a mill town. Its roots were economic; it lacked, therefore, the religious homogeneity of many American towns. But every Sunday morning everyone in Magrit went to church except for Irini and Irini's father. Some families made the long drive to the Lutheran church; some went south to the Catholic; some stayed home and attended Presbyterian. Magrit prided itself on being tolerant of all forms of Christianity.

Irini minded a lot when she was little. It was one more thing that made her different, along with having no mother and a father who drank. Sometimes it seemed as if the only way to ever belong in Magrit was to have been born there.

She knew that while no one blamed her, exactly, this business of not attending church was not considered *nice*. She'd had that brief but devout Catholic period. And for a while in the second grade she went as a guest to the Presbyterian church with the Mays. But one week during Sunday school she was assigned to play the part of the neglected Bible in a tableau and then the next week they read and studied a story from the Old Testament in which God sent a bear to tear apart a group of children for teasing a holy bald man. Irini was too empathetic to tease the bald herself, and she would have thought a good spanking entirely appropriate for anyone who did. But she was deeply shocked by God's behavior. She tried to say so, but Mrs. May, who was teaching Sunday school on that particular occasion, told her sharply that she was not to have opinions about God's behavior, much less express them. Irini had been raised to have opinions about everything. So she didn't show up to perform her part as the neglected Bible, which her father assured her wouldn't hurt the performance at all, but would instead be a very telling detail. Cindy May told her she was going to hell, but Cindy May was only in kindergarten at the time and Irini's father said if it came to that he would take the fall for her.

"I'll give you a religious experience," her father told her and showed her a picture in a book of the face of Mary from Michelangelo's Pietà. It was the most beautiful face Irini had ever seen. When she pictured her own mother, it was also, of course, an image from a photograph. Her mother wore a suit with a fur collar. Her cheeks had been hand-tinted pink. Her eyes were directed downward. She had a slight smile, as if she were being teased.

You could not really say that Irini missed her mother. You could say that Irini's whole life was organized around the absence, but Irini was mostly unaware of this. In fact, for someone raised in a steady glare of pity, Irini managed to be entirely without self-pity. Magrit might have liked her better otherwise.

And you might think, what with her father's drinking and her heathenism and her dinners of soda crackers and jam, that one of the other women in the town would have stepped forward as a sort of mother substitute. I have to assume that the problem of little Irini was discussed over many backyard fences. Probably more than one of the Magrit mothers would have liked to take her in hand, pack nutritious school lunches, hem her skirts at a proper length, so they touched the ground when she knelt, teach her to pray. But Irini was not an easy, affectionate, or grateful sort of child. Instead she was good at fending people off.

And she was intensely loyal to her father. Magrit liked her father well enough, except for those who didn't. Since the war he had the additional stature of being one of only a handful of single men. Still Magrit did not approve of him. In order to have one of the Magrit ladies take charge of her, Irini had only to ask. Irini had only to say, by inference, by the act of asking, that her father could not do it. She had only to admit what everyone could see, that he was an undependable drunk. She had only to go to church on Sundays and leave him at home.

But Irini liked to take care of herself and preferred her father's transparent affections to anything more artful and less heartfelt. And the approval of Magrit depended on Irini's making certain alterations, while nothing was more clear than that her father, from his stool at Bumps, under the spreading arms of Norma's antler collections, in the warped but cheerful daisy mirror, thought she was the best thing since fish sticks just the way she was.

By the time Irini was a teenager she had come to appreciate the lazy Sunday mornings. She would sleep until the sun had tracked across her room and all the way into her eyes. Bumps was closed for the whole day and her father would make her hot chocolate and pancakes or popovers. They read the Sunday paper all morning and went for a drive in the afternoon if Norma had the Oldsmobile running, which mostly it wasn't since even before the war. If the weather was nice Irini might go for a walk with Tweed, into the woods between Brief Street and Collins House, or up to the falls.

North of Magrit there was the beginning of a road. For a while, during the despair of 1942, the government thought an escape route into Canada might be required. The road was never finished and Irini liked to walk out to it and see how the grass and the weeds were taking it back. Sometimes she would think to herself how there were only two roads out of Magrit and one of them led to nowhere, was being slowly erased before her eyes. This was a melancholy thought, but so philosophical and adult that, of course, it had its pleasures.

Sometimes she would think instead how the road was like the war itself. I see this as a particularly American sensibility. No pain is permanent. No act is irrevocable. The day would come when all the damage and all the grief would vanish under new growth. There was a force in the world more powerful than men and she could see it more clearly in the woods than in church.

This was an advantage of Magrit that she didn't learn to appreciate until later, after she left. Magrit was fields and farms and cleared land. But all around it, in a dark circle, were the woods. Hidden inside them were beaver and muskrat, deer and bear. Quiet little mice by the millions burrowed in the fields, breeding with the speed of thought. There was the constant Babel of flickers and waxwings and jays and phoebes and grouse and herons and hawks and toads and cicadas. Never again would she live in a place so busy.

In Magrit she could go out the front door of her little brick house, and within a matter of minutes she could get to somewhere wild. Not a city park—my mother always despised those. But a place where the trees had their own lives and were not clipped and domesticated pets.

"Well, look at this here," Irini's father said, spreading the Sunday *Tribune* over the breakfast table and into the jam. "Mr. Henry's ad for the ape is running here, too. You wouldn't think an ape would be so hard to find. Not for a man with Mr. Henry's money."

Irini was belly-down over the funnies. There was a woman in *Terry and the Pirates* with breasts as big as Helen's, only pointy, like torpedoes. Deadly breasts. You could see the outline of them quite clearly under the woman's satin top. Irini looked for a while. With breasts like those she would have never been able to read the funnies in this way. It would be as much as her life was worth to go up to bat. No matter how far out she stood, she would always be crowding the plate. Irini's own breasts were a source of dissatisfaction to her. She was cross with *Terry and the Pirates* for bringing it up. A girl should not feel criticized while reading the Sunday funnies. She rolled onto her back. "Do you think anyone has ever been murdered in Magrit?"

Her father turned. "That," he said, "is what I would call a non sequitur. Why are you asking me that?"

"Magrit can't be as boring as it seems?"

"Nineteen-year-olds are easily bored. I remember being bored once. Those were the days." Irini's father folded up the paper and gave her his full attention. "And this very Thursday is dish day at the movies."

"But that's what I'm saying. There must be extramarital affairs we know nothing about. There must be seething passions. True love."

"I'm sure we have as much of that sort of thing as anyone. But well-bred people never notice adultery and the Doyles have long been celebrated for their discretion. We don't speculate; we don't pry. Have you and Walter had some sort of tiff?"

"Get over me and Walter. There was never any chance."

"Such a nice boy." Irini's father shook his head sadly. He picked up the paper again. "But I take your point. The whole world's been sugar-coated. It's this labored American blandness. This forced optimism. It happened during the war, somehow. Darndest thing. We've seen the concentration camps. The mass suicides of the Japanese. We've seen innocent hostages shot and hanged, whole cities obliterated in a blink. And we still think we live in a Disney cartoon.

"It's just as if the worse the real world got, the more people believe in the candied one. We've been through the biggest war in history and all we learned was gloss and double-talk, double-talk and gloss."

This was not Irini's point at all. She went on to Brenda Starr. Brenda's apartment had been searched and trashed.

"Not that I ever planned for you to end up in Magrit," her father said. "Look at this. Hoover's in Congress begging for the rights of Germans to fish in the Baltic. The factory workers are on strike in Frankfurt, claiming they're too malnourished to work. Isn't this damnable war ever going to end?"

Brenda's enormous eyes were enormous. "Who would do such a thing?" Brenda was asking.

"We're destroying the fertilization plants in Germany. Just when everyone is starving. Why are we doing that?" asked Irini's father.

"We must have good reasons," Irini said and it was 1947 and they lived in Magrit so maybe neither of them doubted it.

Irini folded the paper and wiped the colors of the funnies off her hands and onto her bathrobe. There was a pile of her father's clean shirts, pressed and stacked on one of the living-room chairs. He'd ironed them himself, but if it was up to him, they'd never make it the last few steps into his closet. Irini gathered them up.

Her father's bedroom was practically bare, as if he didn't expect to be staying long enough to put up a picture in the room where he'd lived for fifteen years. Irini opened his closet door and pulled on the light chain. She stacked the shirts on the shelf, then turned the light off again and stepped inside. She closed the door. She had done this often as a small child. By ducking she could still slide in under the rod, squeeze between the coats and pants. She wrapped herself in the rough arms of her father's suits, the smell of her father's aftershave and his whiskey and his cigars.

23

 The following Monday, Henry called the Sweethearts into the Kitchen to read Maggie's newest column aloud.

Dear Maggie:

The more I see your column "Ways to Welcome Home Your Mate" the angrier I get, and my husband has it taped to our refrigerator, so I see it pretty often. Now when my husband walks in the door from work, he expects to find a peaceful house and me, attractively dressed, lipstick on and stockings straight, holding out an ice-cold martini. Instead our three normal, active boys have overturned the living-room furniture and are clamoring for dinner. "Prepare yourself," you say. I don't have time to comb my hair. "Prepare the children." How? Should I slip them a mickey? Please try to be more help next time out. I begin to wonder if you've ever had children yourself.

Unkempt in Columbus

Dear Columbus:

Your letter touches on a topic that is a real concern of mine. For too long we have willingly blinded ourselves to the very real and prevalent dangers of alcoholism. We've enshrined the institution of the cocktail hour as the very essence of gracious living, with no thought to the consequences. But how many of us are stopping with a single martini? You ask if I can help you. I must tell you no. Only you can help yourself. Stop drinking and encourage your husband to do the same. You owe it to your three little boys.

Maggie

P.S. Perhaps if your husband didn't drink so much he could manage to set the table once in a while. It's not so hard. An ape could do it.

Henry rolled the magazine into a tube. "To use a baseball metaphor, someone has made a good swing, but the pitch wasn't there."

Irini could feel everyone not looking at her.

"Alcoholism is a serious problem and concerned my first wife deeply. Of course, Maggie is also concerned. But I stand by Maggie's original column. It was a good column. Too often women don't understand the pressures of the working world. A man comes home tired." Henry had written the original column himself. "Maggie knows that. I'm forced to wonder if Maggie wrote this letter. It doesn't sound like her."

Ants had invaded the Scientific Kitchen. The girls were trying to trap them with shallow dishes of beer. It was hoped that the pleasantness of this death would be a mitigating karmic factor, but no one was actually checking with Mrs. Ada. The plates were set in many locations so that the girls themselves kept stepping into them accidentally. Sticky beery footprints led from counter to counter. It was hot inside and out. The topic was alcohol and the Kitchen smelled like Bumps on a Saturday.

The project for the day was cheese breads. Irini's hands smelled of aged parmesan. She had washed them twice with dish detergent and the scent wouldn't come off. It was all slightly sickening.

"I didn't write it," Irini said. There was a long silence. Irini could hear the Kitchen clock ticking. It made a clucking, admonishing sound.

"Of course you didn't," said Henry. "I even agree with the gist of it, Irini. Haven't I made that clear? I'm only objecting to the timing. Inappropriate response to the particular stimulus." The skin around his eyes was sagging into shadowy pouches. The skin at his throat drooped. It was a pathetic look. Irini wished he would cut it out.

"But I didn't write it."

"No one has said that you did." Henry managed to make Irini's denials sound excessive. He put his finger deep into his ear, wiggled it viciously. "Everyone can see that the letter was well intentioned. No one is angry about it."

Everyone else was quiet. Irini looked at Margo, who smiled at her, but with obvious embarrassment. She looked at Arlys, who was not looking back, though this could have meant anything. Well intentioned! Irini could not concede this. It was a letter plainly designed to implicate her. And after years and years of not cheating on tests and not reading the answers off Margo's paper when she always sat by Margo and Margo always had the right answer, and not telling lies and keeping her promises and, being, in short, thrifty, helpful, and punctual, still she turned out to be an easy target. Irini, who wasn't born in Magrit, and didn't go to church, and whose father drank too much.

"It was a fine letter," said Henry. "But it came at the wrong time." He had a defeated tone, which angered Irini since it seemed a bit theatrical and anyway, *it wasn't her fault*. "I'm going to have to start reviewing Maggie's letters before publication myself. I should have done so from the start. I blame no one for this but myself. I'm not going to ask if you read it before sending it on, Fanny. I don't even wish to know who wrote it. It was a well-meaning letter."

"Of course I didn't read it and send it on. It made Maggie sound deranged. I wonder why New York editorial let it through," said Fanny. "Everyone knows that Maggie appreciates a fine glass of wine. I don't know how many times she's said so. Mrs. Ada took the packet to the post for me. She said she was going anyway." Fanny looked hot and disheveled. Her scarf was twisted to the side. The strap of her apron was falling from her shoulder.

"Did you read any of the letters?" asked Tracy.

"I read some of them," said Fanny, meaning, of course, no.

"I had a letter in this week, dealing with teenage curfews. I said how, now that the war was over, kids could go back to being kids. I said they should *appreciate* having curfews. We should have had nothing to worry about but curfews. It was kind of a different way of looking at the problem. Why wasn't my letter published?" asked Tracy. "My letters are never picked."

Tracy had to put a quarter in the blue pig. She didn't seem to mind. "Maggie's letter about teenage curfews was better than this letter," she finished airily.

"Irini didn't write it," Arlys said. "Come on, Irini. Let's go get some bread baked."

Irini washed her hands again and sifted flour. She separated eggs so that she could use the yolks to paint the tops of her loaves. She greased her pans and talked to everyone just as if they weren't all thinking she wrote the letter and wouldn't admit it. She listened to the new installment of *Wheat Theater*. Reception was particularly bad, but through the snap, crackle, and pop, she gathered that Anna Peal had had a fight with her mother and that some clown convinced her to run off with the circus. I can teach you to be an acrobat, he told her. But all was not right with the Elastic Man. And then someone cut Anna's safety wires. Someone didn't like her. And Irini had no idea who that was.

Maggie Collins's Atomic Cocktail: Into a large bar glass pour one and one half pony glasses of brandy and a pony glass of red Curaçao. And now for the surprise of the decade: add two generous scoops of ice cream. Mix thoroughly. Fill the glass with ordinary soda and let the games begin!

The cheese breads didn't rise. They could have been used to build houses, to bombard cities. It wasted the whole day's work, all the mixing and measuring the other girls had done, only to turn the dough over to Irini, to Dr. Death. She kneaded and kneaded, draped the loaves in protective towels, set them near the warm, motherly ovens. Somehow she had killed the yeast.

This irritated Fanny, who snapped her towel over the counter tops and scrubbed out the sink in a hasty, abused way. "Maybe we can hollow them out and use them for batting helmets," she suggested. "Maybe we can whittle them down into bats." She was so very much larger than Irini. There was no getting away from her, even in the abundance of counters and corners of the Scientific Kitchen.

"Maybe the water you used was too hot," Irini said.

"All of us?" asked Fanny. "Every single one of us used water that was too hot?"

"Bad yeast," Irini suggested, and no one even dignified this with an answer.

It rained in the afternoon, a funny, warm rain that came in a sheet the girls could see a block away, from the Kitchen window, moving down Mill Street. Claire ran outside to roll up the windows of her car. She came back drenched. She rubbed down with dish towels by the oven and the combination of wet and heat intensified her perfume, a Florida water with citrus overtones. Usually it was lovely; today it merely sweetened the cheese, cut the tang of the beer. The storm, which could have made the Kitchen cozy, made it overheated instead.

The rain played an ominous tune outside on the limestone arch and the gravel drive. There were flashes of lightning, distant percussions.

Practice was canceled, but when work was over it was still light out and not actually raining, so Irini decided to walk to Collins House. Obviously she couldn't talk to her father about the letter. She couldn't talk to anyone in the Kitchen who might turn out to have written it, which was all of them. So she thought of Walter. Of course he wasn't speaking to her, but that was a point in favor of the plan. If she went to him with her troubles, he was going to have to start. At least that much good would come from the whole upsetting incident.

"Aren't you coming, Irini?" Tracy May asked. She sounded almost as if she cared. Irini remembered her, lying on the grass with flowers in her hair. "I wonder how you'd like it if everyone was suspecting you," Tracy had said.

And she didn't like it. But mainly she didn't like it because she hadn't done it. This seemed an important distinction.

"No, I'm just going for a bit of a walk." Irini hoped her own tone was maligned, but not guilty. She watched the others turn right onto Mill Street and then turned left herself. The street ended at the water. She walked along it and then into the woods. The woods were blacker than the town. "Tree darkness," Irini's father called it, "almost as good as the real thing."

As with Claire's perfume, the rain had intensified all the woody smells. When she looked down, Irini saw earthworms. When she looked up, there were chickadees, enjoying the weather. They hopped along the branches, shaking the raindrops loose in a second, tiny echo of the storm.

Tucked into the side of a small hill, Irini found a garden of white violets, quite out of season. Ada had a February birthday; she was partial to violets. Irini picked some to take along, and got her feet wet. Fortunately, when the boys left Magrit, Irini had taken to wearing sensible shoes.

When she came out of the trees, the sky was clouding up again. It was amazing to watch the storm come back, how the whole sky could change and how fast. How transitory good weather was. She began to hurry.

She hoisted herself over the Collinses' fence. It took the dogs only a matter of moments to find her. They were muddy, but delighted. "Hey, it's only me," she told them, but they danced and barked and all but passed out from the excitement of it.

She let herself in through the back porch. "Hello," she called out. "Anybody here? It's Irini."

No one answered. She moved on to the kitchen. There was no sign of a dinner being prepared. Irini took a small cut-glass vase from one of the high shelves and arranged her violets in it. Then she went through the dining room, to the bottom of the stairs. Walter was at the top.

"I called," Irini told him. "But I guess no one heard me."

"Grandpa's gone out. Ada's fasting and observing a day of silence."

"It was you I wanted to talk to," Irini said. Outside the rain began again, softly, at first, then louder. The windows rattled in their frames; the wind whistled and whooped, sliding past the glass. The large clock rang the half hour. All this noise somehow heightened the sense of the house being very quiet.

Walter had changed their relationship, in spite of the fact that it had always worked so well, had been practically perfect as it was, with Walter hopelessly in love with Irini and Irini essentially uninterested, but nice about it. If Walter was not going to be hopelessly in love, then Irini could no longer be essentially uninterested, but nice. This was her favorite role; she couldn't settle into another she liked as much or was as good at. She stood looking up at Walter, who refused to look back, and she could see the exact moment when he stopped being angry. It was a great relief to her. She could still hear and see the storm, but it seemed tamer suddenly, smaller, cut to fit the Collinses' windows.

"Go on into the kitchen," Walter said. "I'll make you a sandwich."

It was only tuna, but Walter put a number of unexpected things into it. Little red tomatoes the size of berries, and dill pickles, and hard-boiled eggs. He toasted the bread. If he had buttered both sides, as Maggie recommended, there would have been less danger of the toast going soggy. Still it was a lot better than Irini would have done. There was something very appealing to her about a man in the kitchen. He set the table with Ada's painted china and the mono-grammed silverware and the linen napkins. The silver was so soft, Irini was afraid it would bend if she used it. She ate her sandwich by hand.

"Maybe you're taking it too personally," Walter suggested when she told him about the letter. He had turned his chair around and straddled it like a horse. His arms hung over the ladder-back. He'd just gotten a Tarken haircut. His hair was so sun-sensitive, the ends were always blond. A haircut darkened his whole appearance, set off the white band of skin on his forehead where his baseball cap sat. Irini had a band just like that. She was thinking of changing her hairstyle, something with bangs she could comb over it. "Didn't the first letter seem to implicate Fanny? Maybe the point wasn't to implicate you, but just to implicate someone."

That made sense, especially if you knew, as Walter did not, about the middle letter. Someone had tried to implicate Fanny, then Claire and now Irini. It was good company to be in. "Everyone likes you," Walter assured her, sounding like the old Walter again. "What's not to like?"

"But Mr. Henry thinks it's me."

"Gramps won't consider any of the Sweethearts. He thinks it's an outside element, an agent provocateur."

"And who would that be?"

"Thomas Holcrow."

Irini was stunned. "It has to be someone at the mill. There's no way he could get to Maggie's letters." She took a bite of her sand-wich. She left the imprint of her teeth in the bread, a neat little semicircle, an inverted image of Stonehenge. Thomas Holcrow was in Los Angeles again and had been for several weeks. He'd promised Tracy to return by the Fourth. "He's not even here," Irini said.

"You don't like for him to be suspected," Walter observed.

"I just don't see how. And I certainly don't see why."

Walter watched her for another couple of chews. He watched her swallow. "I don't either. But the man does poke around. He has been to the mill. At night. It's not as if we lock it. I've seen him there. Smooth as a leek when I asked him about it. Guess what, Irini? I just figured your stats. You're batting .380."

"I'm doing okay," Irini conceded modestly. It was cute of Walter to be running her stats, as if the Sweethearts were a real team and she was a real player. And he was a real coach. She noticed that she was feeling a lot better.

Because of the storm, Walter drove her home. Water streamed over the car windows and bounced on the roof. It gave her a protected, isolated feeling, just her, on an island somewhere, in a cave, at the bottom of the sea. And Walter, of course, but that couldn't be helped.

Then she had to run through the storm from the car to the porch. She stood inside the kitchen, shaking the water from her hair like a dog while Tweed danced around her feet. "Was that Walter who brought you home?" her father asked.

"I'm batting .380," she said. He could hardly believe it. He had to go and work it out for himself. It provided a long diversion.

24

Over the first few games attendance had gone steadily up. Anna Peal plugged the team over the air every Friday. Sometimes she even mentioned home-run hitter Irini Doyle. Henry might accompany them; more often he wouldn't. He was not feeling well that summer; he referred to his health as indifferent. His lack of energy annoyed him, although he was in his eighties, and what did he expect?

By the end of June, the Sweethearts had established a routine. Fanny would select their opponents for the week. She didn't wear the uniform; she refused even the cap, which could be pretty cute, if you'd curled your hair first. Instead she appeared in cinch-waisted sundresses which showed her back. Sitting in the stands had given her what in 1947 was considered a healthy tan. She treated her skin with cocoa butter, which she carried with her and reapplied during inning changes, so she glowed lubriciously and smelled like a large piece of candy.

On an average weekend about thirty men would show, hopeful, high-spirited, and dressed to play. Some weeks were easy. The men who showed would be gentlemen. They would have brought their daughters and their sons along. The game would feel like a family picnic. But sometimes a group of men would show up without their families, and already drinking. Sometimes they would be eyeing Helen and talking baseball, but dirty, as though they were the first to think of this. Would these men make less trouble on the field than in the stands? Fanny had a head for such things. In the process of selecting nine men each week she would break up gangs, separate drunks from their drink, and put together the least talented team available without being obvious about it. She would choose, whenever possible, much older men or much younger men. In this way the opposing team generally mirrored the male population of Magrit.

The best-looking men were invariably left out, but encouraged to join her in the stands to help her score the game. Her score sheets had phone numbers and little compliments scribbled over them. "It turns out I love baseball," Fanny told Irini. "Ain't that the kick? I can't get enough of it."

The Sweethearts would go three good innings. At that point they might be ahead or they might be behind, but the score would be respectable and, depending on the opponents, the game would be fun. Then Tracy's pitching would begin to fail. Fanny would try to cheer them through it. "Good catch," she would shout. "Can o' corn, Arlys. Can o'corn!" But they needed something more than encouragement.

At first Walter wanted Irini to relieve Tracy. Irini was the one with the arm. But Irini lacked control. She loved the all-out aspects of the game. She loved to hit; she loved to run back, jump, and catch a ball on its way over. She was still knocking them out of the park. But she didn't like the pressure on the mound and she didn't have the fine motor skills involved. She didn't want to think about such ticklish matters as hitting the inside of the plate, or of hitting the plate at all. She had a tendency to hit the batter instead.

Arlys could pitch, but not fast and she was too shy for the mound. Besides the infield collapsed without her at short. Cindy could try, and in a gentlemanly game, where people would attempt to hit, she did all right. They might win, they might not. But it would be close enough to keep the game fun. An opponent intent on winning could wait her out, though. It would be a long game of no hits and no fielding. Irini would stand in centerfield and pretend she was in Hong Kong or London or the Sudan, while the opposing team walked around the bases. She would tell herself Anna Banana-peel adventures, only about herself instead of Anna. She would try not to mind losing.

Worse, sometimes, was the batter who hit *at* Cindy. There was no time on the mound for her to use a glove. She fielded the ball barehanded, with her only hand, or not at all.

Irini didn't know how such men could live with themselves. She didn't understand how winning something so small as a ball game could mean so much to anyone. Though current data tells us that the testosterone levels of men—fans, not players—whose teams are winning in sporting events actually increase. The losers' levels sag. These measurements were taken at soccer games, though. This may not be applicable to baseball. In any case, it sure didn't occur to Irini.

The Sweethearts were back on the bus after an awful game in Tomahawk. The opposing pitcher walked Helen, and then tricked her into a pickle between first and second. Both baseman tagged her numerous times with and without the ball; she came to the bench in tears. "I'm not going back out there," she said. She brushed her hair behind her ears and Irini saw a bruise coming out on the part of her arm nearest her breast. "What a gang of horse whistles," she added.

Walter summoned Fanny, who sent another man in to replace the first baseman. "My mistake," said Fanny graciously, but the man stayed to watch, baiting them viciously until Mike Barr, former machinist's mate, first class, U.S.N., and hero of the Battle of Midway, slugged him into silence. It was the only moment of victory. The Sweethearts lost 10 to 5.

Afterward, Fanny introduced them all to Barr. She had accepted a cigarette, tapping it on her oval fingernail. Now she accepted a light. She drew in a long pull, exhaled a dark breath. Her lovely lips pursed and relaxed in little kissy moues. Mike Barr watched her through the rank veil as though he'd never seen anyone smoke before.

"*I* wouldn't mind a cigarette," Tracy said. She removed her cap and shook out her rich-coffee hair, but Barr didn't seem to notice.

"Come by the house," he said to Fanny. "I have something I want to show you. Brought back a little memento from the war."

They gave him a lift on the bus. He lived in a neat little house downtown, painted yellow, with a maple tree and roses, and a small grocery store next door with crates of apples in the front. The apples were little, but the roses were big and filled with the sound of bees. Barr's mother came out to greet them, drying her hands on her apron and patting her hair. "Maggie Collins is just my idol," Mrs. Barr said. "Will you tell her so from me? I do everything she says. I just think she's so smart! I especially liked her defense of larger women. I always know we can count on our Maggie."

I have made it sound as if everyone noticed the apples, the roses, and Mrs. Barr straight off the bat, but this is not at all the case. At the very edge of the finely kept lawn, in just that spot where you might have expected to see a stone gnome or a row of plastic ducks or a metal Negro, there was instead a statue. Head only, like the first manifestation of the Wizard of Oz, it was about the size of a washing machine. It was grinning and snarling, half dog and half lion, but not an American dog, not an American lion.

"Five hundred pounds of solid granite," Mike Barr told them. "And the poundage was nothing compared to the red tape. I had the devil's own time getting it home."

"You were in Japan?" Walter said. "I was scheduled to go, but the bomb went instead."

"My brother's still in the Pacific," said Sissy.

"I took this from a Japanese temple on Saipan." Barr had Fanny by the arm and she was letting him. "You see those brown stains? That's blood. Twenty-five Japanese monks died defending the temple."

"You fought at Saipan?" Walter asked.

"How many Americans?" said Cindy.

"Don't worry. It's not American blood. I promise you that."

"Is it a god?" Irini wanted to touch it, but the stains stopped her.

"I suppose," said Barr. "Didn't help those monks much, though."

Mrs. Barr had taken a scissors from her apron pocket and was cutting roses with it. The roses were old-fashioned blossoms, pink streaked with yellow and each as big as a fist. "You could have knocked me over with a feather, when Mikey showed up with it. *Where* are we going to put it, I asked. Don't expect me to dust that thing." She turned to give her son a smile. "When your boy comes home in one piece, you don't much feel like denying him anything. But now I've gotten used to it. Gives the yard a certain distinction, Mikey's father says. A lot of people come by to see it. We had a fellow from the paper in Chicago."

"A lot of my friends collected samurai swords," said Barr. "And skulls. I just wanted something a little different."

Mrs. Barr handed each of the Sweethearts their own individual rose. "Now who'd like a glass of lemonade?" she asked. Irini took one, but it had been overly sweetened.

"Mr. Henry will be pleased to hear we met a fan of Maggie's," said Margo. "Maybe he won't ask about the score." They were back on the bus, ten minutes out of town. The air inside the bus was a combination of bus fumes, sweat socks, and roses.

"He was a doll," said Fanny. She had twisted the rose into her hair, although it was too large to be graceful there; she might as well have tucked a cauliflower over her ear.

"He was a flirt," said Tracy. "I don't see him as the kind of guy you can count on."

"No?" said Fanny. "Then how about that statue? Don't you think it speaks to his determination? I think Mike Barr is a man who will get things done."

"I don't know about his mother," said Helen.

"I thought she was sweet," said Claire, who always thought everyone was sweet.

"She could get that blood right out with a mixture of bleach and cold water," Margo said. "I wonder why she doesn't."

"I thought she was demented. Roses and blood stains. Too *Arsenic and Old Lace. I* didn't drink the lemonade," said Helen.

Maggie Collins writes: "A hot lemon will yield twice the juice of a cold one. Heat your lemons before squeezing."

Back in Magrit they got a jump on the Fourth by saluting the British, beloved enemies, treasured Allies, with a High Tea Day in the Kitchen. It was a noble experiment in crumpets and scones and lemon curd, which Irini managed to curdle. They played a game in Eau de Lune, which they won by a single run when Arlys stole home while everyone was watching Helen coach first. Walter had given her some new signals to use; they were unusually vigorous, but clearly effective. Maggie published a column entitled "Ode to Vinegar" in *Women at Home,* a piece that stressed the feisty little cider's versatility as a cooking and a cleaning agent. "Add one teaspoonful to lard and the foods cooked in it will absorb less of the fat!"

They played in Shivering Trees and lost. Shivering Trees was far enough away from Magrit to be an overnight. It had a population of about thirty and no electricity or phone lines. But there was a bar, of course, you can't do without one of those, and it had some upstairs rooms the girls could bed down in. After the game the girls were invited down, so that the town could stand drinks for those of them who were old enough, which meant Claire, Norma, and Fanny.

The Sweethearts were a rare treat in Shivering Trees. The opposing team had been made up primarily of the sort of people politely referred to as bachelor farmers. Presumably they had once had mothers, but the memory was dim. Perhaps they had all had the same mother—there was an eerie sameness to them. Redhaired and scrawny, wiry as chickens, they bathed seldom and caught sight of an actual woman only slightly less often. There was no way to determine their ages. They were awkward and shy, but not in a cute way. They couldn't play baseball at all, which meant the loss could only be explained by poor coaching, or a reluctance on the part of the girls to get close enough to anyone to tag him out.

Fanny had expected burly lumberjacks. Perhaps they were in the bar. She accepted the invitation on behalf of the whole team and dressed in a dress with spaghetti straps.

In order to get to the Shivering Trees Bar the girls had to walk through the Shivering Trees Museum of Taxidermy. It was a gauntlet of frozen beaver, fox, weasel, and crow. The feathers were dusty, the fur dim. On the wall of the back room of the bar itself the theme was continued, heads only this time. The crowning piece was a moose, hung morosely over the cash register.

"Look how its eyes follow you everywhere," Fanny complained. She had hoped for lumberjacks. She had gotten weasels. The opposing team was huddled on the other side of the room, under the moose, like adolescent boys at a high school dance. "Baseball is beginning to lose its charms for me."

"I really don't think its eyes are following *you*," Tracy said. "I believe it's looking at me."

"You girls are pretty," someone called from across the room.

"Who said that?" Fanny asked. There was no answer. There was no way to identify the speaker. All possible candidates were soberly examining their drinks.

"Walter, pretend you're with me," Fanny said, although she was in fact much bigger and tougher than he was. "That moose is really beginning to annoy me. Why should it look at me like that? Gee whiz. I don't even hunt. Go look at Norma."

"It's nicely mounted," Norma said. "I know you don't appreciate that sort of thing, Fanny, but really. It's a very nice job." She raised her glass in the direction of the men. "Nice moose," she said politely. Their faces showed the startled fear of trapped animals.

"Perhaps we could discuss the game," Walter suggested. "Arlys, you could have gone for a double play in the fourth. Would have ended the inning. I wondered why you didn't."

"We are not discussing the game, Walter," Fanny said. She spilled some of her beer into her cleavage. It glistened there and she dabbed at it with her fingers. Someone across the room stopped breathing. He'd been breathing through his mouth, so the silence was audible. "Do you want to know why?" Fanny asked, as if she hadn't noticed. "Because the game is over. Let's discuss the schedule instead. We should never have been scheduled for Shivering Trees. What is the possible publicity value of this?"

"So Sweetwheat sales boom in Shivering Trees," Irini agreed. "So what?"

"You know?" Fanny put her empty glass onto the table and stood up. "I'm feeling the need for trophies. Something to remember this occasion forever. A little memento from the war." She held out her hand. "Something like a couple of eyes. Norma, I'm going to need a knife. Someone create a diversion." She walked toward the moose. The men parted and scattered to the other side of the room where they regrouped, watching from behind their drinks.

"Does anyone want to arm wrestle?" Cindy asked them. She was especially pretty tonight. Her hair curled; her cheeks were pink. The freckles gave her a natural charm. "With Irini?"

"I can't risk my arm," Irini said quickly.

"Or dance? Who would like to dance with Irini?"

"Look out the window," said Fanny. "Is that a bear?"

Margo stood up. "You know, you don't really need a special product to keep your—your—"

"Corpses," said Claire.

"—corpses clean. A soft brushing would do the trick. With an ordinary hairbrush. Come back into the museum with me and I'll show you."

The men did not respond. They did not appear to have heard.

"The thing is," said Margo, "to treat them the same way you

would if they were still alive." She looked at Fanny, poised under the moose with a knife hidden behind her back. "Sort of."

SNAPPING TURTLE PIE
À LA SHIVERING TREES

Step One: Let the turtle bite a sturdy stick and then slowly pull the head forward.

Cut it off.

25

 Maggie Collins writes: "An old-fashioned popcorn popper makes a wonderful tool for roasting wieners out of doors.

"A good pie crust always greases its own pan.

"For a safe and sane Fourth, limit the family to those fireworks which do not leave the ground or move. A good time can be had sans risk with fountains, cones, the Ground-Blooming Flowers, and the Egg-Laying Hens."

And then it was the Fourth of July for real.

The Fourth must have been particularly fervent in those days just after the war. Irini's father laid in a record supply of fireworks with fortune-cookie names, like Tiger in the Mountain, Golden Snake of Desire, Forbidden Temple of Water Lilies, Tree Bursts into Blossom in Winter, Mountain Explodes at Dawn. He would be celebrating in style, but cautiously. Everyone took a moment to remember Geb Floyd and his annual Battle in the Clouds display.

Irini had spent her money on sparklers. These, along with the Screaming Meemies, were her favorites. It was, like her preference for vanilla ice cream, too bland and boring to do her credit, especially not in the midst of such riches. But she fancied the way the wands left a lighted snail trail in the air, liked the cold burn of the sparks on her skin. You could use the sparklers to cast spells, conduct orchestras, write poems.

Maggie published a recipe for a red, white, and blue pie—blueberries and strawberries and a whipped marshmallow topping that might have been the world's first Cool Whip, if Margaret Mill had been just a little more perspicacious. Henry seems to have had an almost unblemished record when it came to missing the boat.

Although the phrase "easy as pie" is universally acknowledged as a dastardly canard, the Old Glory Pie was even more complicated than it sounds. In order to keep the berries segregated and their colors pure, they had to be cooked separately first, then gelled. Only a handful of girls in the Kitchen had successfully avoided the color purple. The resulting pie was served cold.

Second only to the fireworks, Magrit looked forward to the mill picnic, an event attended by everyone, mill employee or not, and Henry's swim across the mill pond on Upper Magrit, which was more selective. He had begun the swim in his sixties, an annual demonstration of good health due to good diet. "It's not just the cereals," he told the girls in the Kitchen. "I try to avoid fried foods. Frying destroys vitamins and digestion. And I've cut back on potatoes. Starch is for shirts."

When he hit his eighties, Ada started to worry. Not so far upstream was the spot where old Mr. Kinser, Claire's grandfather and Magrit's reigning dry-fly king, had died in 1941 in a fishing tragedy. When found he was wrapped in his own fishing line like a bug in a web, like a pole on May Day.

Or so they said on the Magrit school grounds. And no one knew how this could have happened. "Vengeful fish," Irini's father suggested when Irini came home and asked him about it. Old Mr. Kinser had been a child of seventy-two at the time.

Each year Henry's progress across the middle, where the water was swiftest, was more suspenseful. Seen from the shore, his thready arms would cycle faster and faster with less and less effect. Each year he seemed to ride a little lower in the water. Each year he landed a little farther downstream. Ada wanted to lay a rope beneath him, across that place where the pond narrowed prior to spilling into the falls. Just under the surface, she told him—it needn't even be visible. She had had Walter bring the rope up. This was not as easy as it sounds. It was a large, heavy coil, big enough for someone to sit in. Walter had to roll it on its side.

Ada also wanted Norma Baldish to swim along with Henry. I don't know if they had the phrase "situational ethics" in those days, but I do know Henry was against them. Visible or not, Henry argued, a rope would have stood witness to a wavering of faith in breakfast cereals in general and Sweetwheats in particular. Norma had enough to do on the Fourth as fire marshall. He could not allow it. Ada spent the whole morning in tense and unhappy anticipation.

Not Irini. Irini had a yellow-striped bathing suit and a matching ribbon for her hair, which had taken on its usual golden summer highlights, even more this year because she had been outdoors so much. For the last two weeks, she had been sunning in her backyard and up at Upper Magrit, trying to write over her baseball tan with something more elegant and Caribbean vacationish.

Since she was still playing baseball, she was only marginally successful. But she had managed to acquire two vivid white lines crisscrossing her back and a gentle sunburn across her shoulders. The burn felt good, hypersensitive to the air and paradoxically cool. It gave her a slight fever, just enough to make her light-headed and a little daring. The day was close and humid enough to keep the backs of her knees and her neck continually damp. She dressed in slacks and a bandanna top that tied at the neck and left her back bare. Although the heat was keeping the mosquitoes at bay, her skin was smeared with insect repellent. She had a sharp smell like kerosene on top of her usual peppermint soap.

Prior to the war, the picnic had been a potentially romantic affair. The girls at the mill had packed baskets for the boys to bid on. The baskets were auctioned off publicly at Nedd's tower and eaten in the privacy of the woods. In the old days, at the Fourth of July picnic Thomas Holcrow would have had to declare himself once and for all. Bidding on a girl's basket was a serious matter and often led to marriage. Holcrow had returned to Magrit just three days ago. "Couldn't stay away," he was reported to have told Tracy, who took it personally. "Magrit is becoming just like home for me."

In the old days Henry had rigged a tent every year to shade the young mothers and their babies. There were no babies at the picnic this year. This was, of course, the echo effect of the missing men. Without the war, several of the Sweethearts would probably have been mothers by now. There might have been little Tarkens, little Moodeys, little Floyds. You could feel bad about this, or you could look at it another way.

The picnic was also a political occasion. Every year the Mays and the Leggetts and the Kinsers responded to Henry's triumphal swim over the prostrate body of Upper Magrit with whispered outrage. In the weeks preceding they would compare it to Attila's romp over Europe, Napoleon's invasion of Russia, Sherman's march to the sea, Hitler's invasion of Poland. On the day itself, they would sit all together, gnawing bitterly on their breasts of fried chicken and their ears of barbecued corn, viciously forking the potato salad. They would speak to no one else, refuse to participate in the sack and egg races, and leave with ostentatious iciness some time before the big swim, always reappearing later for the fireworks. "Mr. Henry takes his chances," they would mutter to each other, meaning nothing for themselves, a sulk was really all they were up to, but no one could discount the dead hand of Madame Nadeau. The Nadeau boys had all been *drowned,* after all. It didn't take a genius to know where they were.

The sky threatened a storm. The air was charged with static. Irini's hair made little wet coils at her neck. She was sweating in all those places where her body folded. "Well, that's that," said Ada hopefully. "I simply cannot understand all this fuss over an Independence Day that happened so long ago, when there's India, just about to celebrate its first Independence Day ever, and the papers can hardly be bothered to cover the event." She was eating a vegetarian box lunch—salted radishes, briny cucumbers, raw tomatoes. A herd of ants sketched themselves in unmolested, fluid lines over her blanket and plate. "And he can't possibly swim if there's going to be lightning."

In case she was right, Irini hurried into the woods with Margo and Tracy to change into her bathing suit and get a dip in before the rain. "Don't you go in now, girls," Mrs. Gilbertsen called to them. "You need to wait an hour after eating," but if the rain wasn't waiting, neither was Irini. Her bathing suit revealed what the slacks had not— that her left leg was bruised in stormy gray and blues all the way from the hip on down. She gave it an unhappy look, then draped her towel over an arm to hide the worst of it. She had damaged and redamaged it sliding into base. Margo had the same bruises and carried her towel in the same way.

The lowered clouds turned the day into a sauna. The girls walked back over a hummock of sand, through the coarse, khaki grasses and mature cattails to the water. At the edges the millpond was green and still and relatively warm. A fog of gnats moved over the surface. In the middle of the pond, the water became a dark, napped blue. Toward the other side it foamed white. It was posted on both sides with signs forbidding swimming.

Irini waded in up to her ankles. The bottom was covered with rounded, furry rocks she could step on if she was careful, from one to the next to the next. Her feet were cold and her shoulders hot. It was an adventure in three dimensions, her feet down in Upper Magrit with the sunfish, her hands and face above with the dragonflies. She could feel exactly that point, that moment where the hem of water bisected her, but it wasn't always exactly the same spot. The surface twitched. Water striders floated away on the delicately bucking skin of water.

Irini walked farther out, three more steps, until she hit the hole where Jim Nedd, years ago, had set his first stick of dynamite. One more step with no bottom to it, a step off a cliff. She leaned forward, breaststroked out to the vanished roof of the Nadeau house, out in the gentle beginnings of the current. A layer of insect repellent swirled from her arms and floated downstream in a rainbow. She paddled upright, her arms and legs moving to get warm. "It's wonderful," she said in the age-old tradition of those who are in cold water to those who are not. "It's not cold at all."

"Don't go out any farther," her father said. His dark face had its customary brooding look. Ever since that afternoon in Glen Annie Creek, he never liked to see her submerged. Besides, he was quite right. Past the Nadeau place, the current was deceptively strong.

She dove and breaststroked down instead of out. The water was hung with flecks of gold so that visibility was poor. But off in the distance, Irini could see the dark streaks of shadows, a row of ghostly posts that allowed her to imagine a drowned city. It wasn't Upper Magrit, though. It was something much, much older; the architecture was dream Doric. If she tried to get closer it would disappear. A flock of minnows pivoted before her with military precision, even their mouths opening in unison. She came up with her hair in her eyes. "Don't go farther out," her father said again.

There was a shriek and a splash. Someone had thrown Tracy in. Another splash. Thomas Holcrow surfaced several feet away, spitting water through his teeth like a Roman fountain. Irini was starting to shiver. She kicked back to the warmer, shallower water. Holcrow seized her foot as she went past. "Miss Doyle," he said. And then let her go.

Tweed appeared on the bank, standing next to her father, barking at the sight of Irini in the water, shifting her weight from leg to leg to leg to leg. Irini stood to show Tweed the water was only up to her waist. Irini was happy. Her shoulders were already warm again, the clouds simmered above her, the water below, lunch behind, fireworks ahead.

Tweed started in toward her, stepped into a small hole, and scrambled out again, shaking. A large perch hung suspended in the water near her leg, rippling its fins. Far upstream a loon dove without seeming to resurface. "Miss Doyle," Holcrow was saying, slowly, teasingly. Tweed shook loose a halo of drops. Irini could feel exactly the place, exactly the moment this all touched her. Now, Irini thought. Now. Now.

"Irini," Mr. Henry called. "Irini! We need you at the ice cream station. No one else can turn the crank." The sun came back out, spreading over the water like syrup.

An hour after ice cream, Henry was ready to make the swim. A group of girls from the Kitchen climbed down, walked under the falls, and climbed back up to set the landing site on the far side. They were equipped with lemonade, sparklers, and towels. The faction from Upper Magrit expressed their opposition this year by standing back and whispering among themselves. They made a sound like the wind in the trees, or the snakes in the grass.

Margo, who was wearing a red scarf over her hair, sat out on a rock as a spot point. She removed the scarf and waved it. Henry waved back. On the other side of Upper Magrit, the girls could see Henry stripping down. His skin was the color of boiled chicken; his chest had a plucked look. He did some knee bends to warm up. They could see Ada speaking to him. He shook his head. Bend, straighten, bend, straighten. The second straighten was slower than the first, the third was slower than the second.

Henry waded in. His footing was awkward. He waded back out again, sat on a rock and examined the bottom of one foot. Ada said something.

"He's picked up a stone," said Fanny caustically. Suddenly she was loud enough for the rest of the girls to hear; the Upper Magrit faction had moved closer to see what the holdup was. "Mrs. Ada is telling him she's very sorry, but now she has to shoot him."

Henry stood, tested his foot. "Oh, good," said Fanny. "He's not lame after all. My mistake."

Ada spoke again. Helen paraphrased. " 'Mr. Gandhi gets his exercise fasting. He doesn't make a fool of himself swimming the Ganges.
Why can't you be more like Mr. Gandhi?' "

Henry waded back into the water. Suddenly he ducked and
windmilled. He ducked again. Bent over, as if facing a strong wind,
his hands covering his head, he hurried back onto the shore.

"What the heck was that?" asked Arlys.

"Bee," Irini guessed. "Big bee."

He and Ada argued with each other. "Henry wants to kill the
bee," said Fanny. "Ada is shielding it with her own body."

Henry waded back into the water. Ada said something. Henry
looked up at the sky. "Mrs. Ada is worrying about lightning," Arlys
guessed. The clouds were high, light, and gauzy.

"Mrs. Ada is worried about aerial bombings," said Helen. "Mrs.
Ada is afraid the Nadeau boys will come in their aerial canoe and
strafe Upper Magrit with their paddles."

"And they could, too," said Tracy. "If they wanted."

Henry waded in deeper. The water was up to his calves now,
which meant he was near Nedd's hole. He took a deep breath which
puffed his cheeks. He bent his knees. He straightened again. He blew
out the breath. No one on either bank moved. Henry's cheeks filled
with air again. Again they emptied. He stared out over the dark water.
Margo waved her scarf.

"Something's wrong," said Irini.

On the opposite bank, Norma Baldish scrambled down to speak
with Henry. He was curling up, growing smaller, aging before their
eyes. He shook his head, waved Norma back. Ada spoke again. Henry
looked at the water. He backed out, up to his ankles, onto the shore.
He dried his feet. Put his clothes back on. Leaned on Norma's arm to
help him up the bank. Went home.

"He just lost it," Irini's father told her later. "Lost his nerve. It was
Mrs. Ada, worrying at him all day. Look at this." Her father had an
S.O.S. Ship in his hand, a cardboard firework in the shape of a boat,
with distressed passengers painted on the sides. He set it in the water,

lit it. There was a desperate shriek, several bangs. The ship took on water and went down. You could see the little painted faces going under.

"He didn't look strong," Irini said. "Mrs. Ada was just being realistic. We should go ahead and string that rope. Just in case. He might not have made it."

"She just loves him," Irini said later. "Would you let me swim it?"

"Aren't there enough ghosts in that pond already?" Irini said, even later. "He's an old man."

Her father was setting out a Python Black Snake on a large, flat rock. "Grows before your very eyes! Three to four feet long!" the box had said. He lit it. It expanded to about four inches. Irini put out a finger. She barely touched it, but it crumbled immediately into ash. "He is now," her father agreed.

At Collins House, Henry had gone straight to bed. Ada put her nightgown on and padded down the stairs to the kitchen, where she made herself a cup of tea. She didn't like tea much, not since she had given up dairy and begun taking it straight, but she was somehow oddly satisfied to eat foods and drink drinks she didn't like. It was purposeless suffering, and she didn't know what Gandhi would say, but it was a kind of practice and might fit her better for the real thing.

What an easy life she had always had. It embarrassed her to think of it.

She sat at the table and stirred her spoon in her cup. The chair was hard. The floor was sticky. The kitchen, all kitchens, were a sort of temple to the body. They trapped you inside the world of the senses. Ada tried to imagine an alternative, a kitchen of the mind, a kitchen of the spirit.

In this kitchen there would be cooks but no one would cook for themselves. The degrading hierarchy of waiting on someone else would vanish when everyone did it. Each cook would serve another; each would be served.

The food would be simple, strictly vegetarian, and with none of those seasonings that excite the senses. Because the food wouldn't be the point.

The point would be the gift of the food. The point would be the discipline of the labor. The point would be to eat, with gratitude, the food that someone else had prepared for you, with love, no matter what the taste, and to give your food away, freely and personally, with your own two hands.

26

 Later that night, when the clouds had blown fortuitously away, under a sky of exploding flowers and screaming stars, Ruby Redd arrived in Magrit to play for the Sweethearts. Irini had completely forgotten about Ruby.

Irini was stretched out on the knobby weeds of the outfield with Walter on one side and Arlys on the other, watching Norma's fireworks. She was covered in Cutter, but there was a bug crawling over her arm. She couldn't see it, but she could feel its various feet, crawling together toward her armpit. Then, while she was trying to track it down, fishing through her clothes, an ominous nothing, no tickle, no further movement. She sat up and at that exact moment, there was shadow in the sky above her, as if a tree had suddenly walked in and set down roots.

"Hi, Coach," said Ruby Redd. She was wearing the same dress as before, the same bib, even the same shoes, which was a bit of a surprise, although they were even more scuffed. When she had been at the mill for a while she would learn to polish her shoes with the inside of a banana peel, the way the rest of Magrit did. "I'm here to try out for the team," Ruby said.

After Ruby, everything was different. "She was so good," my

mother told me. "It was like we had Satchel Paige all of a sudden. She pitched for us and she always went the distance. She could hit. We never lost again. She was so good, I can't even tell you. We never came close to losing again except for just once."

This was a reference to the game that Mr. May attended. The May girls hadn't seen their father since the war. Suddenly he was there in the stands with his gas station–owning slut of a new wife and she was actually calling out their names, cheering them on as if they didn't hate her guts. Naturally Tracy insisted on starting at pitcher and naturally neither of the May girls played their best. Mike Barr offered to beat him up for Fanny, and the new wife, too, if that was what Fanny wanted. He was filled with indignation at the thought of three fatherless girls. Fanny said no, but she thought about it, you could see.

Of course having Ruby on the team meant someone else had to sit out. Walter varied it occasionally, but usually it was Helen, at least for a few innings. The Sweethearts didn't need her now, getting those walks to first. It was enough for her to appear there in the uniform and wave at the men in the stands. It was enough for them to think she might go in at any moment.

Sometimes the person who sat out was Cindy and she minded a lot more. Sometimes it was Sissy. Tracy rarely actually sat out, but she minded most. Walter moved her to third, and put Cindy in right. The opposing teams hit so rarely, and never to the outfield. He could have put anyone anywhere. "We all still batted, of course," my mother said. "It's not as if she could play alone. But I was having trouble connecting. I was in a slump. Not that it mattered."

Anna Peal started announcing the scores as well as the schedule. It was a shame that Henry was in no shape to enjoy it. He never attended the games now, rarely asked how they'd done. He didn't write columns for Maggie, didn't seem to care what the dogs ate. He was undergoing a long, dark night of the soul and he was undergoing most of it in the ham radio room. Ham radio conversations are characterized by an inevitable, effortless cheer. "How is the weather there in Dover? . . . Rained here, too, last week. Pretty today, though."

Walter gave Ruby a job and she moved in with the Leggetts. She was hopeless in the Kitchen, worse than Irini. Claire began visiting the Leggetts almost nightly to tutor her. "We're not going to exploit this young woman's athletic ability," Mrs. Ada said. "After a few years with the Sweethearts, she is *going* to know how to cook. When she leaves us, it will be as a woman with a future."

Soon Ruby was wearing Helen's old clothes. They were a poor fit. Ruby had a muscular build, but thin, just the opposite of plushy Helen. Mrs. Leggett contrived to take the clothes in with oddly placed darts.

"She does sit-ups and push-ups in the mornings before work," Helen told them. The girls were taking their lunch break outside. It was a beautiful day with a high wild wind, so there was sun but only occasional heat. The leaves sawed one against another. It was amazing how much noise they could make, when all those soft sawings were added together.

Ruby had gone for a jog, her hair in a high ponytail, her legs in Helen's old jeans. She was the only one missing from the Kitchen.

Helen stretched out on the grass, wearing cucumber slices on her eyes to reduce shadows and puffing. The road to beauty so often leads first in the other direction. Witness hair rollers. Witness face masks. Helen looked like a praying mantis with breasts. "She does men's push-ups, from the toes. Twenty of them. And she runs in short little bursts. She says it improves her speed."

"Who's chasing her?" asked Fanny. Fanny was patting her throat with the back of her hand in an exercise thought to stave off wrinkles. It gave her voice a strange wobble.

"If she was as good as she thinks she is, it would be something to see. She is so stuck on herself," Tracy said.

"She's just fast," she added when no one responded. "She doesn't have finesse. She's very predictable." Tracy was painting her toenails Ripe Plum. She had cut her hair very short. It was cute, but not as cute as she thought it was.

You would think Irini might have benefited from the example of all these improving activities. But luck, Irini's father always said, would beat out effort every time. Irini lay on her stomach, looking for four-leaf clovers and not even looking hard. If you were lucky, you were lucky. No need to exert yourself.

Irini picked a clover flower, pulled it apart tube by purple tube, and sucked out the honey. She rolled onto her back. Mounds of whipped clouds streamed across the sky above her. The sun flashed in and out, like Morse code. "Irini," it said, and it was probably important, but Irini was too drowsy to work out the rest.

"She is *so* good," Margo said. "She's not the friendliest person. But you have to admit she's good."

"She doesn't pitch with psychology. Pitching is a duel. Pitcher against batter. You have to know a lot about people to be a pitcher," said Tracy. She leaned back on her elbows and waved one finished foot in the air to dry. "I don't think it's possible to be an unfriendly person and also a great pitcher."

"I didn't say she was unfriendly."

"She's just shy," said Claire.

"She's so serious about it," Fanny said. "Like she thinks she's a real athlete."

"She shouldn't wear your old clothes, Helen. That is not an attractive look for her," said Tracy.

"She should think about a different haircut. Long hair is only fashionable if you're eleven," said Fanny.

Irini opened one eye. A giant buttercup bloomed next to her cheek, a buttercup the size of a dinner plate. Much smaller, in and out of her vision, the metronomelike ticking of Tracy's foot in the air. And beyond Tracy's foot, high above Irini, a tiny hawk floated on the wind. Zipping around it, harrying it, was a much smaller bird. A swallow, Irini thought, from the heart-shaped silhouette of its open wings.

Suddenly the sounds of dozens of little birds rose from the ground and the trees. Henry had pointed out this phenomenon to the girls before. The birds were responding to the shadow of the hawk. They were trying to confuse and distract it from its prey by calling to it. "Pure instinct," Henry had said. "Don't confuse it with concern."

Irini watched a moment out of her single eye, while the little bird dove and circled in dangerous proximity. A mother, Irini guessed. This sort of suicide mission was the kind of thing mothers did, and Irini, who had no mother, felt a little sad. She was afraid to watch the ending. She closed her eye again and imagined Thomas Holcrow leaning over her. "Miss Doyle," he was saying, his mouth very very close to her mouth. He put a hand on her breast, startling her so that she opened her eyes. She was not ready to fantasize *that*. What kind of a girl did he think she was?

"I like her," Helen said. "I mean, I don't not like her."

"I like her," said Claire, who liked everyone, so it didn't count. "I think she's swell."

"Did we say we didn't like her?" Fanny asked, in her wrinkle-preventing Elmer Fuddish vibrato.

They heard footsteps. "Did you have a nice run?" Fanny said. "Time to get back to work, girls." Irini sat up.

Tracy and Ruby were smiling at each other, mouths wide, maximum teeth.

Walter asked Irini to walk Ruby over to Collins House one day before practice, when it became clear that Henry wasn't coming in to the Kitchen anytime soon. Their arrival obviously interrupted Ada's spinning. Her hair was flocked like an old sweater with little balls of fuzz. But her smile was gracious and she served them great slabs of marble cake and apple cider with chipped ice, in the gold-rimmed glasses that always gave Irini a guilty start. They took their drinks and dishes into the sitting room. Collins House had a drawing room, a sun room, a smoking room, a library, and a billiard room, so they never lacked for choices.

Thomas Holcrow was there as well. He had been spending more time at Collins House, going over old papers and stories with Henry, who had suddenly started to prefer looking backward to looking ahead. It was more evidence of his rapid aging. There was no further mention of any suspicions relating Holcrow to Maggie's unfortunate outbursts. Indeed, he had become one of the family.

"Walter tells us you're quite the player," Henry said to Ruby. He had taken a seat in the sun. The excessive light showed every spot and crease in his skin. His throat hung loose like a purse and was as napped as corduroy. He was still wearing his dressing gown. He crossed his bare legs at the ankle and you could see up to the two lumps of his knees, but fortunately no farther. "I got Rio on the radio yesterday. Do you know anyone in Rio? I could send a message."

"No, sir," Ruby said. "I surely don't." Her hair was beginning to work free of her ponytail. It curled around her temples. She had finished her juice and her cake. Her hands were folded stiffly in her lap. Irini noticed that she bit her nails. The top thumb had a raw, painful edge.

"They're having a nice sunny stretch down in Rio."

"That's nice to hear," said Thomas Holcrow. "That sounds just swell. I hope they're enjoying it." He was seated across from Irini. He smiled in her general direction.

"Nice weather is nice," she agreed idiotically. She was always nervous with Holcrow, but today even more so with Mr. Henry. She had never seen him stooped like this, bent as macaroni. He had missed a spot shaving. There was a small patch of beard the size of a quarter back by one of his enormous ears. He had combed the top of his hair, but the back stuck out in weedy disarray. He was usually so dapper. Irini swung her legs around so that she didn't face him. She had seen more than enough.

"I'm an old man," he told Ruby, who was, of course, forced to deny it. "No, no. I know what I am."

"According to Hindu tradition the normal human life span is one hundred and twenty-five years," said Ada. "That's how long Gandhi expects to live."

"You have a lot of years left," Thomas Holcrow agreed.

"That's nice," said Henry. There was a subtle popping sound as he stood up. "I wonder if it's raining in Rio today?"

"Have you heard any more about an ape?" Irini asked him.

"Oh, I very much doubt that I'm up to taking on an ape," he said. He climbed the stairs slowly, hands on the bannister, pulling himself from stair to stair. Ada followed. Thomas Holcrow saw them out.

Walter drove them back to the field. Ruby sat with him in the front. Irini took the back. Walter stretched his arm out over the seat. The wind blew a strand of Ruby's hair loose so that it lay against his hand, spread thin like the wing of a dragonfly and the sun caught all the thousands of colors of it. Walter felt it; Irini saw him look over. But he didn't move his hand. "Do you know how good you are?" Walter asked Ruby. "I mean, you're really good."

"It's the only thing I ever wanted to do. Only thing I can do."

Walter accelerated. Wind rushed into the backseat. Irini's hair flew about her head, whipped into her eyes. "Could you roll your window up, Walter?" Irini asked. "Ruby?"

No one seemed to hear her. "You're too good for the Sweethearts," said Walter. "You could play for Racine. They always need pitching in the majors."

"Do you think so?" Ruby asked. Her smile deepened into her cheeks. "I just want to play. I don't care where. I'm happy to be here."

"We're happy to have you here," said Walter.

"It's *nice* that you're here." Irini's voice had a funny tone to it, just a bit cross, perhaps, because when she opened her mouth to speak, her hair blew into it. But no one seemed to notice.

They arrived at the school. The May girls were late. Irini took the field, jamming her hair back into place with her cap. Walter took up his stance at the plate and tagged practice balls around the diamond.

The outfield had become a mass of dandelions, each ripened into the shape of a detonated firework and only slightly more permanent. Irini made a wish and blew one clean. The very next ball came to her. She picked it up smoothly and threw it all the way home.

27

Anna Peal escaped from the circus in clown shoes. The prints they made in the snows of her little island were considered too big to be hers, so no one followed. But her ordeal was far from over. She headed north toward home. The sun was draped and invisible, but she adjusted her directions by the mossy sides of trees.

The farther she went, the snowier it got. She dug under the snow for food, dug into the snow to sleep. She fell into a snowdrift and was forced to build a fire to dry her clothes. She trapped a white rabbit and stewed it with a few simple but aromatic herbs. The story cut delicately away so no one had to picture little Anna tearing a rabbit apart and eating it with her bare hands. Probably she would set a place of leaves.

She transformed the clown shoes into snowshoes by adding a lattice sole made of strips of bark. After stripping the bark from the tree, she had tapped for syrup. Even with her extensive cold-weather training and native good sense, it began to seem possible that she would not make it. She was beginning to go snow-blind, beginning to hallucinate dark shapes in the shining clouds in her eyes. This was Anna, so the difference between her delusional and regular state was a subtle one.

"I'm home," she cried happily, although the music told otherwise.

"There's our little cottage. There's Mother and Father. But why won't they look at me? Mother! Father! Oh, they don't see me. And I'm so sleepy. I think I'll just rest here. It can't hurt to close my eyes, just for a minute." She heard her mother's voice singing softly, ominously, the lullaby from *Hansel and Gretel,* the one that is so full of angels.

"Isn't that funny, Mother?" she said. "It's snowing like everything, but suddenly I'm nice and warm."

"She's cooked her goose this time," Irini's father opined. He was smoking his after-dinner pipe. The curtains were drawn to keep the heat out of the house, so the smoke swirled and settled in the dim light, giving the kitchen an odor somewhat like bus exhaust. In spite of the curtains, there were still beads of sweat on the plate of cheese, butter melting away like the Wicked Witch of the West.

Irini wiped a damp hand across her forehead. She didn't feel like playing. "Nothing is ever going to happen to Anna," Irini said. No doubt housework was a dignified and honorable activity, but barring the occasional laundry-day surprise, it lacked excitement. She resented little Anna for implying otherwise. "A bear will befriend her. She will bake a bear a berry pie." Irini herself was doing the dishes and putting the soda crackers away. How many times had she done this? How many more times would she, while her father sat at the table with his shoes off like a maharajah? She put the crackers in the bread box, just for the variety of it, just so her father would have to hunt for them the next time he wanted them. "She's a sap-head. A buck says she wakes up in her own bed, surrounded by goose feathers from her pillow. As if anyone cares."

"I wish I had your confidence." Irini's father's tone was laced with disapproval.

It almost satisfied Irini, but not quite. "A snow globe falling from her hand, the word 'Rosebud' on her lips."

"I wish I had your composure."

"And, strangely, frostbitten feet."

"And an icicle in her heart," said Irini's father. "Honestly, Irini, there is no point to growing up *too* much. Take it from me."

"Oh yes," said Irini. "We all know you'll never make that mistake."

Apparently Irini was not too grown up to be sent to her room. She lay facedown on her bed, wondering why she had done that. And why she wasn't sorry. She imagined doing it again, doing it worse.

Someone tapped at her window. She sat up. Tracy May stood on the gravel at the side of the house, her face shadowed like a pencil sketch, with cross-hatches from the screen. "Can I talk to you?" Tracy said.

Irini swung her legs around to face the window. The curtains were dusty, a degraded rendition of the Sears catalogue picture. There was a large, dead fly on the sill. Its wings were as thin as silk and as clear as glass. Someone had sucked it dry. Irini hated it.

"You need a new permanent," Tracy said. "I could do it for you." Tracy had recently recut her bangs. They bubbled along the top of her forehead in a blowsy fringe.

"Thanks," said Irini, thinking that of course she would ask Margo or Arlys. Tracy had no sense of timing and you couldn't give someone a permanent without that.

"I think Tommy is about to ask me out. I might say yes. I've been sort of playing hard to get, but I think I'll say yes."

"Good," said Irini. The fly stirred slightly in the breeze of the window, rattled against the screen like a dry, hacking cough. Even after death it was still trying to get out.

"I think I pitch as well as Ruby," Tracy said. She was looking off to the side. She pursed her lips and her nose humped slightly as a result. It was a nervous, rabbity face. Even Tracy had to know she was lying.

"I never saw anyone who pitches as well as Ruby."

"You all field better for her."

"We don't have to field."

"It's not scientific." Tracy traced down the screen with one red fingernail. "I thought this was a scientific experiment. With controls and all." She drew across the top.

T. T for Tracy, Irini supposed. Although it could have been Tom. Tommy. "She's eating her Sweetwheats. I've seen her."

"We've eaten Sweetwheats for years. We were eating them before they were puffed. Now she comes along and she eats them for about a day and suddenly she's the pitcher. I don't call that science. I'm going to talk to Mr. Henry about it."

"We win with Ruby."

"What is the big deal about winning? What does winning have to do with science? Or baseball? Or getting husbands?"

"Winning has to do with everything. Haven't you figured that out yet?" Irini's voice came out high-pitched and irritating. She made no attempt to modify it. "And why shouldn't we win? Just because we're girls no one thinks we need to win. You know what? I like winning. I like going out onto the field and *knowing* we're going to win. Someday I'd like to win at something really big."

"So you don't want her off the team?" Tracy asked. "Even though we were all doing just fine without her?"

Irini thought about that. She thought about the fly, which was scrabbling for her attention. The fly that had lived its whole life in Magrit without ever getting out. She thought about her father going to Bumps tonight just like every night and how she would be doing the dishes tomorrow night just like always. She thought about Ruby's hair on Walter's hand. Then she thought about Ruby smiling so that little dips appeared in her cheeks, almost like dimples, but not quite. She thought about Ruby saying she just wanted to play, Ruby's thumbnail bitten away to below the tip, Ruby dressed in Helen's clothes. She thought about coming in from the outfield, when Ruby had set them down, one, two, three. Sometimes it was hard to know what the right thing to do was, but even now, even in her current desperate mood, this wasn't one of those times. "Nope. I don't think so."

Irini heard her father's step on the creaking board in the hall. He could never stand to fight with her; she could always outlast him. He was going to come in on some pretext to see if she would apologize. Sure enough, there were four timid knocks on the bedroom door.

"You'll have to go now," Irini told Tracy. "I'm being punished."

On the radio, snow falls with the tinkling sound of tiny bells. It is a delicate effect, but even subtler in Magrit, where reception was frequently interrupted by whole seconds of white sound, sounds more like popcorn than like bells.

Against this background, a lovely contralto voice spoke.

> WOMAN: Wake up, Anna. You mustn't sleep here.
>
> ANNA: Where am I? I thought I was home.
> Where's my mother and father?
>
> WOMAN: You are in my kingdom, Anna. You are in
> the land of Winter.
>
> ANNA: Winter's not a land. Winter's a season.
>
> WOMAN: No, no. Winter is a state. A state of mind.
> The state of your heart. Winter is the place
> I rule.

"I have a bad feeling this is going to be a story with a moral to it," said Arlys. "You know I hate those." The Kitchen was exploring new uses for leftover potatoes. Arlys held an egg as if she were about to curve it over the plate, but cracked it smartly against the counter instead. She separated out the yolk, the white falling into the measuring cup in a gluey, translucent clump.

"An allegory," said Margo. The girls all stopped for a moment and looked at her.

"What would that be?" asked Helen, tucking back her hair. "For those of us who didn't graduate top of the class?"

"Like Chaucer," said Margo. "The roosters?"

Everyone was still looking at her.

"I guess I don't remember," said Margo placatingly. The girls turned back to their work.

ANNA: It's a beautiful place. So white and shining.

WOMAN: Thank you, Anna.

Irini stood at the Kitchen window, looking out. The tarry parking lot was swollen with heat. If you stepped on it, the heat would pass right through the soles of your shoes. Hot enough to fry an egg, people in Magrit always said, but it wasn't quite; the girls had tried this once. The egg stiffened and spoiled, but it didn't actually fry. "Wouldn't some cold weather be nice right now?" Irini asked.

"If you can't stand the heat get out of the Kitchen," Arlys suggested. As punishment for wishing winter back, she passed the yolks to Irini for beating.

ANNA: How do you know my name?

The wind came up, howling between the tinkling of the bells.

WOMAN: I know everyone in my kingdom. Come with me. I'll take you to my castle.

ANNA: I guess we *should* go inside. It's so cold here. Just for a little while. Then I have to go home.

WOMAN: Just for a little while.

The wind sawed through the airways like a violin.

"Don't go, Anna," said Claire. "I have a bad feeling about this."

CHORUS OF WOMEN: Every mother's day starts with Sweetwheats for her Sweethearts.

ANNA: Sweetwheats have Anna Peal!

"Mush, Anna," said Helen. "Mush!"

❀ ❀ ❀

Maggie Collins says: "How do you decide what you will eat? Do you follow your own cravings or will you listen to our American scientists, working ceaselessly and scientifically to uncover the secrets of human nutrition? Studies have now shown that our daily caloric intake should be divided into approximately these proportions: ten to twenty percent protein, twenty to thirty percent fats, fifty to sixty percent carbohydrates.

"If your diet is lacking in fats and carbohydrates, consider accompanying tonight's meat with a serving of potato soufflés. This is an economical and delicious use for leftover French fries. And it couldn't be simpler. Just deep-fry the potatoes again. This dish, more French than the French fries themselves, was created for Louis XIV, a man of fabulous appetite. If your fries don't puff on first immersion, don't be discouraged. They may be dipped in the hot fat again and again without adverse effect.

"For those who live in cold climates it should be noted that additional daily fat may be required."

28

Irini's new permanent made her look like a poodle and smell like a flea collar. This was absolutely unavoidable. The hair would relax in a couple of days and the scent would go even quicker, but Margo was apologetic over it all the same. Margo was wearing gloves as if she'd been cleaning ovens or handling uranium. She prodded Irini with one rubber finger. "Your hair takes curl so easily," she said, as if this were something Irini could be proud of, something Margo envied.

Margo's hair was both fine and heavy. She wore plaits to keep her hair out of the food at work, a coronet braid at weddings and dances. This twisting contained and diminished the astonishing golden color of her hair. Irini had always thought her a paler version of the German doll in the Dolls-Around-the-World series. Fair-haired and proletarian. It was a pretty look, but not a sexy one.

When Margo undid the braids, everything changed. Her hair rippled down her back, then straightened again slowly as it hung. Even the sauna didn't curl it. "My Rapunzel," Irini's father would say to Margo. "Let down your hair."

Irini sat at the Doyle kitchen table with a towel over her shoulders to protect her bathrobe, a washcloth over her face to protect her eyes, and a slight burning sensation on her neck where there was nothing to protect her and the solution had stayed perhaps a bit too long. In spite of the towel, rivulets of chemicals and water had run into her ears and down her back, making her damp, smelly, and slightly toxic. Her legs were badly in need of a shave. The bathrobe was an old one with all the fuzz rubbed off the rump.

Although they had started early, they had finished late. Irini heard the screen door and Tweed's welcoming toenails, falling like rain on the linoleum. "What price beauty, eh?" her father said, coming into the kitchen after one of his long hard nights at Bumps. He was as ruddy and elfin as his lupine face allowed. But he was not talking to Irini or to Margo. To Irini's horror, Thomas Holcrow followed him in.

"I apologize," Holcrow said immediately. "I've intruded. Secret girl stuff. I had no idea."

"Nonsense," said Irini's father. He went to the cupboard, got down two shot glasses. "It flatters us to see the lengths to which women will go." Irini gave him a look, one of her best, an unambiguous, incontrovertible look. It did no good. He was so diluted with liquor, he was lighter than air. The look passed straight through him and out the open window, where it hit a passing robin, making it caw, just once, like a crow. "For mere mortals such as we, Irini will burn herself with potions and inhale dangerous gases. Women are the braver sex, make no mistake. They will squeeze, they will tweeze; they will teeter."

"I doubt very much that Irini is curling her hair on my account." Holcrow was wearing a white shirt with the sleeves neatly and precisely rolled up. His dark hair was just slightly too long, and his manner was slow and politely thoughtful. Delicacy of feeling kept him turned slightly away from Irini. She could see his profile from the corner of her eye. He was breathtaking in white. It made her perfectly miserable.

"Norma was in fine form tonight," Irini's father said to Margo. "You should have seen how she handled the rowdy, drunken element. She really laid into them. You have to admire a woman who can

silence a man with just her bare hands." He was having trouble opening the bottle of whiskey. He passed it to Irini. He was having trouble
standing. He leaned against the counter.

Irini considered for a moment the possibility of pretending she
couldn't open the bottle and passing it girlishly on to Holcrow. But
the evening was well past redemption. She twisted off the top, gave it
back. This was 1947 and what they knew about codependency was
nothing.

"Who were the rowdy drunks?" Margo asked.

"Modesty forbids," said Irini's father.

"I should be getting home," Holcrow said.

"Nonsense. We were going to have a drink. We were going to
pursue matters deep and philosophical."

"I feel I've intruded. I feel knee-high to a cockroach."

"Irini is delighted."

"Irini will never forgive me. How am I to live with that?" Holcrow turned to her. He looked straight into her eyes, avoided her hair.
"Anyway it's late."

"The very shank," Irini's father argued, pouring out two generous
whiskeys. "Irini, there are fingerprints on these glasses. What would
Maggie have to say about that?"

Tweed, who had seated herself close to Irini, was scratching behind
her ear. Her leg drummed the floor by Irini's feet. She shifted about,
chewed and licked at her haunch. She moved on to her sexual organs,
and then to her anus, with much evident pleasure. Irini kicked her,
but it brought only a momentary diversion. The moment the pain
subsided, Tweed returned to her ablutions. She licked, she sniffed, she
licked again.

"*I* should be getting home," said Margo. She removed the rubber
gloves and laid them on the counter.

"There goes the bridge game," said Irini's father happily.

"I'll walk you," Irini offered. She stood, turned awkwardly, conscious that the fabric of her bathrobe was at its very thinnest over her
rear. "I'll just get dressed."

"I'll walk you both," said Holcrow.

"You will force me to drink alone," Irini's father warned them. He clicked the two glasses together and raised one to his mouth.

Tweed came along as well. The pavement of Brief Street was still warm, but the air was cooler and scored with the din of insects and frogs. The air was 1947 Magrit clean. Back then there were no street lights, so people in Magrit could still see in the dark.

It was an unnecessary skill on this particular night. The sky was streaked with silver gauze. Moonlight touched Margo's hair so that it glowed. Holcrow, a city boy from Los Angeles, said he could find his way with just that if he had to, just the light coming off of Margo's hair. He was trying to flirt with her, but she was not a girl who flirted. "There's an uneven patch here," she cautioned him politely. "Watch your feet."

Tweed pushed her nose into Irini's leg, herding her around the rough spot. It was a tender gesture and made Irini forgive her for being such a dog. And it helped that Holcrow stumbled a bit, even after Margo's warning, but it didn't help much. They walked on toward the water. Tweed left them for appointments of her own. The sound of the falls rose to cover the sound of the frogs.

They passed the empty, eyeless sauna. The kitchen windows of the Törngren house were golden smears like butter pats in the darkness. In another moment Margo would leave them and they would walk back in the dark alone together. It was a long way to the Törngrens', which meant it was also a long way back. Presumably Holcrow would escort her.

Holcrow in his spotless white shirt. Irini with her hair like an overblown and stinking chrysanthemum.

"I can make it from here," Margo told them.

Then someone screamed. It was a thin scream, an unconvincing scream. There was a second, which was better. Sissy Tarken dashed along the path by the water. Her face was pale; her eyes were huge and dark. She seized Irini by the arm and Irini felt all five of her fingers dig in, nails first. "I saw her," Sissy said. She pointed back toward the falls, upward, in the vague direction of the moon. "She's there! Behind the falls. In her apron."

"Saw who?"

Sissy was breathing too hard to answer. She stood and took in great gulps of air. She shook from head to toe. Irini considered slapping her, but only nicely and only for her own good.

Instead Holcrow put his arms around her. The moment he touched her, she stopped shivering. "Easy now," he said. He kissed her forehead. "It's all right. Everything is all right, sweetheart. Who did you see?"

"In her *apron!* Maggie!"

"You saw Maggie Collins wearing an apron up by the falls?" Margo said disapprovingly. Margo was a girl who didn't like nonsense. "What made you think it was Maggie?"

"Don't I know what Maggie looks like? Doesn't she own this whole town? She had a knife."

"What kind?" asked Holcrow.

"Serrated! And she spoke to me. She told me I would spend the rest of my life cooking and cleaning for some man. She reached for me with her witchy fingers."

"Maggie? Witchy fingers?"

"I'm not lying."

"I'll go up to the falls and look," Holcrow told her. "You stay here with Irini and Margo."

"Don't leave me alone." Sissy clutched at him. "I want to be with you."

"We'll all go," said Margo.

If this were a movie, it would be the moment they split up. You would be in your seat, telling them not to, but they would do it anyway. Nobody ever listens to you. Instead they walked together past the mill and up to the falls with Sissy gasping and gulping and popping like a hooked fish. The closer they got to the falls, the colder the air became.

The cold entered Irini through her lungs, raced for her heart. She would have liked a normal sound, an unconcerned bird, an ordinary frog, and there might have been just such a sound, only she wouldn't have heard it. The falls were a solid wall of noise. She wished that Tweed had stayed.

Behind the wall the rocky path was damp and dark. No moonlight penetrated the water. They walked from one side of it to the other, feeling along the stone interior with their hands. "Nothing here," said Holcrow finally. "Nothing and no one. Do you see, Sissy? Everything the way it should be."

They turned to walk back, Holcrow and Sissy leading, Irini behind Sissy, Margo to the back. Margo knelt suddenly. "Irini," she whispered so that only Irini would hear, gesturing for Irini to come. "What's this?"

She held something up. Something glimmered dully in the darkness. Irini couldn't quite see. She stepped back and Margo placed something in her hand. It was a set of measuring spoons. "You had those in your pocket," said Irini.

Margo looked at her.

"You had them during the permanent. I remember."

Margo grinned at her.

"That's not funny, Margo." Irini laughed. It was an odd laugh, a short gasp, the appropriate laugh for something that was not funny, because it was funny all by itself. Irini was afraid she might not stop laughing. Margo had done that to her once before, during the Christmas concert when Irini had been too nervous because of an upcoming solo and Margo had decided a funny face would relax her. Irini had been given the page's part in "Good King Wenceslas," but then she couldn't sing it, she was laughing too hard, and Scott Moodey had already started the "Hither page and stand by me." Fortunately Arlys had seen the problem and sung it for her.

"Sire, the night grows darker now and the wind blows stronger. Fails my heart I know not how . . ." Irini was shuddering with laughter.

"So give them to me if they're mine." Margo reached for them, shook the spoons so that they rang like little bells.

"Anna Banana-peal," Irini said. She was embarrassed, because she had allowed Sissy Tarken to frighten her and Margo had not. Sissy was waiting down the path, limp in Holcrow's arms.

"She told me I would spend the rest of my life cooking and cleaning for some man." Sissy's face was streaked with tears and eye makeup. Black liner ran in sooty streams from the corners of her eyes to her temples. It gave her a flattened, exotic appearance, like a figure off an Egyptian tomb. "Irini! She made it sound like something bad!"

She rubbed her face. She looked at Irini again. "Did you get a new permanent?" she asked. "You look real puffy."

29

Well, this was an occasion. It had been a long time since anyone in Magrit had seen a ghost. When people tried to work it out, they decided that old man Kinser had been the last. He had seen Opal May, up above the Falls, all decked out in her wedding dress, and then, only seven months later, seven being a kind of magical number—seven brothers, seven swans—he ended up trussed in his own fishing line like a fly in a spider's web, haunting Upper Magrit like all the rest. It couldn't have been the Nadeaus, because the Kinsers were Upper Magrit themselves.

Sissy took to her bed and bloomed there under a steady stream of visitors.

Her mother combed her long black hair artfully over a snowy white pillowcase and rouged her cheeks. Mrs. Tarken was delighted. Sissy was to be married. It was so kind of Maggie to come and tell her, while there was still time for Sissy to finish embroidering daisies on the tea towels in her hope chest. It was better than catching a bridal bouquet. Mrs. Tarken changed her bedroom slippers for pointy-toed pumps and did her own hair. She drew an imaginative shape over her mouth with dark red lipstick, squeezed into a little sheathed number. She walked down to the grocery like a queen, smiling tenderly at all the Magrit mothers whose daughters did not have Sissy's prospects. She purchased a large ham for dinner without accusing Mr. Moodey of having his thumb on the scale. She hummed "If I Loved You" to herself as she walked back home with her ham wrapped in white paper like a wedding gift.

The May girls were the primary skeptics. They could not, of course, visit the Tarkens for themselves and had to settle for Irini and Margo's accounts, which, the Mays pointed out, were as full of holes as cheesecloth. Why would Maggie appear to Sissy with promises of marriage when Mike Barr was obviously gaga over Fanny, coming practically every Saturday now to watch the Sweethearts and sit in the stands? When Helen was seriously seeing her Purple Heart guy.

Claire had the most prospects of all. Out of her own pocket she had bought two train tickets to take Ruby all the way to Kenosha to see the Comets play the South Bend Blue Sox. The game had been eye-opening in a number of ways. "There were people there watching," Claire said. "Lots and lots of them. Like fans. You really can't imagine the excitement. It made me kind of proud to be on a team. And the girls were so good."

"Better than Ruby?" Irini asked.

"Not even close. You should have seen her. You should have seen her face. Like Kenosha was a candy store and she was the girl with a nickel."

Taking Ruby had been an act of such kindness. That it resulted in a reward so immediate was the kind of rare occurence which makes you suspect there's a God. The two of them had gone out dancing with the Blue Sox afterward and Claire had come home with so many phone numbers she couldn't even remember which number went with which girl. The episode had changed her enormously, adding a vivacity to her original sweetness, and both of them so intense as to make her irresistible. So why, Tracy asked, hadn't Maggie appeared to Claire?

Or to Tracy? When Thomas Holcrow was so very close to asking her out.

"What was Sissy doing all by herself up by the falls at night? Taking in the night air? In a pig's nose," Cindy said. No one had shown any interest in Cindy yet. After all those games in the sun, Cindy's freckles had come out very strong. Maggie recommended bleaching them with alpha hydroxy acid, but this was 1947 so she called it lemon juice. It didn't seem to do a thing and it still doesn't. Take it from me. But the freckles didn't make Cindy any less pretty, except for making her feel so.

In spite of the considerable evidence, Irini just couldn't make herself see Sissy as the kind of girl Sissy was. Irini and Sissy used to go into the woods around Collins House and make fairy castles together. They would press bits of slate into the dirt to form the ballroom floor, rub the stones with water until they shone. They would make tiny thrones from large leaves, transplant a mossy strip of carpet to lead up to them. When everything was done, they would pick the fairies themselves—morning glory flowers, with green bodices and petaled skirts. The next day, the flowers would have danced until they wilted. It was a game for babies and Sissy and Irini had last played it about two years ago when they were seventeen.

It was a game Irini had invented. This was the main thing to remember about Sissy, that she was a follower. It was this kind of imagination that Sissy had. If someone else had seen Maggie somewhere else, then Sissy was just the sort of girl to see her too. But not at all the sort to see her first. The more Irini thought about it, the more it troubled her. She remembered Sissy in Holcrow's arms, her eye makeup blacking her face like a pharaoh or a chimney sweep.

Maybe they did all know what she was doing up there by the falls. But who was she doing it with?

Even Ada, preoccupied as she was, with India's independence only weeks away, came to call on Sissy. Holcrow had had a private word with Mrs. Ada after the episode and she drove right over. Everyone must understand, she told Sissy, after the obligatory concerns and respects, that Mr. Henry was in no shape for this news. Maggie had, after all, appeared to Sissy in the exact same spot where Maggie had first contacted Henry through that marvelous aroma. It was the magic that had set everything else into motion—the mill, the millpond, eventually Sweetwheats itself. Sissy's vision was an unfortunate debasement of the original.

It was not so hard to keep a secret from Henry these days. His only informants lived in Rio and Dover, where the weather was shockingly fine. Our Maggie is not in the habit of roaming about at night, threatening young girls with bread knives, Henry would no doubt say bravely, if the story ever did get to him, but it would kill him all the same.

A world away, Gandhi, on the brink of his great success, was in no better spirits. He took no satisfaction in the successful campaign against the British. His thoughts instead were entirely taken up with communal violence and the failure of his philosophies in eradicating four hundred years of racial and religious hatred. He had tried to voluntarily put the Muslims in charge of a United India as a way to avoid the creation of Pakistan. When Congress refused to agree, he withdrew from debate. He blamed himself, searched his heart for weakness, fasted and meditated. Offered congratulations on Britain's departure, he replied that condolences would seem to be more in order. The Congress party was afraid he would quite spoil the party.

Ada had no inkling of this. She imagined that Gandhi was enjoying the culmination of his life's work, that he would be honored and feted on August 15 and that he himself would celebrate hard, in whatever manner it was that ascetics celebrated.

And yet, her own thoughts were running curiously parallel to his. Ada too had been meditating on the problem of communal hostility. Specifically she had been meditating on the fission between Upper and Lower Magrit. The drowning of Upper Magrit had occurred long before Ada appeared on the scene; she had no personal responsibility. But she had profited. It was a shame—she conceded it—that Henry had drowned Upper Magrit for what turned out in the end to be only forty-odd years of milling. Phantasmical odors notwithstanding, Magrit was too far north to be wheat country, and if Lower Magrit hadn't wanted the mill so much, someone might have told Henry so. It had never been a good idea. And then that business with the Nadeaus. Most unfortunate.

But ancient history, after all. Water, as one might say, under the bridge. Henry had been grieving for his mother at the time and had hardly been himself. Much good had come of the mill, many good breakfasts, much good advice. This was because Henry was a good man, a well-intentioned man.

Now Sissy's specter, reminding, as it must, everyone of the original, seemed to give the problem a new urgency. It was time to end the cycle of recrimination and regret. Ada examined the motives of the satyagrahis, in this case, herself. In the past she had tried to stay out of town affairs. She had been afraid that as Henry's wife she would wield more power than she had earned. But her heart was pure. The cause was good. She committed herself to discipline and flexibility. And so, on the first of August, with Irini in a batting slump and Henry deep in a silent depression, with Tracy upset about Ruby, and Sissy either too worn out or too glorious to make practice, and with Maggie stalking the countryside armed to the teeth, Ada brewed herself a cup of tea, borrowed a gelatin drum from the school, and launched Magrit's first satyagraha campaign.

Such a campaign begins with negotiation and arbitration, not to be confused with bargaining and barter. Essential principles cannot be compromised, but demands must be reduced to the lowest acceptable minimum consistent with the search for truth. Ada focused her initial efforts on that point where the rift was deepest—the hostility between the Tarkens and the Mays. This put the Doyles dead in the middle.

Ada typed up a flyer and ran it off for Norma to deliver with the mail. "Anyone who is interested in restoring the peace between Upper and Lower Magrit should come to the school auditorium on Tuesday evening at 7:00," it said in mimeographed purple. "Refreshments will be served." And the Doyles' flyer had a special hand-written message added. "Please be there, Irini. I need you."

" 'Step into my parlor,' said the spider to the fly." Irini's father was reading over her shoulder, although Maggie always said that was rather rude. "Now we'll see the result of all that spinning." He paused and thought again. "Ah well. She's surely less of a nuisance than the first Mrs. Collins. Isabel Collins and her nasty little hatchet."

He stepped out onto the porch for the paper, made a painful, involuntary noise. "It's bright out there," he said, in explanation on his return. "The sun is *beating* down."

By Tuesday night it was pouring great gusts of rain. The Doyles took the car the few blocks to the auditorium. The windshield wipers folded together and fanned apart again with hypnotic precision, sweeping away sheets of water with every metronomish click. Irini ran for the auditorium door, a copy of *Women at Home* held over her hair so that the rain wouldn't amplify the curl. She stepped in a puddle and so much water splashed into her shoes she had to remove and empty them. She walked into the auditorium barefoot as a goose girl.

Thomas Holcrow was already inside setting up the folding chairs. "Where's Walter?" Irini's father asked him. The sentence was accompanied by a thunderous boom. Irini's father had to repeat himself.

"Home with his grandfather. Mr. Henry was feeling peaked. And Walter said it was Mrs. Ada's show." Thomas Holcrow was wearing a pale blue sweater. It darkened his bluish eyes and, draped at his waist, did nothing to obscure the outline of his shoulders.

Norma Baldish and her parents arrived to represent Lower Magrit. They sat in chairs toward the back and talked quietly among themselves. Arlys took the seat next to Irini. "I know the Törngrens were planning to be here," Arlys said. "I guess the rain stopped them." Water streamed down the auditorium windows as if the room were a submarine just surfacing. Thunder popped in the faraway hills, clapped in the downtown street.

Holcrow had been overzealous with the chairs. No one else came to sit in them. At seven-thirty, Norma spoke up. "Do you think we could start? I have a deer to dress."

"I don't mind the poor turnout at all," Ada said. She raised a hand to tuck the side of her silver hair back into place, although it had never been disordered. Her face was bright, but Irini couldn't tell if it was zeal or disappointment. "A single acorn and all that. A small group can move the mountains if it's the right small group."

"I think we should be using *Robert's Rules of Order*," Mr. Baldish said. "We really need to agree on procedure at the outset. If we're going to move mountains we should do it in an orderly fashion. If we can agree on procedure now, it will save us a thousand arguments down the road."

"I'm not really familiar with *Robert's Rules*," said Ada. "The important thing, I think, is that we're all familiar with the principles of satyagraha."

"I move that we adopt *Robert's Rules*," said Mr. Baldish. "Now someone has to second the motion."

"I second it," said Irini's father. "But just for the sake of discussion."

"Now we vote. See, it's easy."

"No, no. Before we vote, we discuss. I'd like to offer an amendment," said Irini's father.

"After we vote," said Mr. Baldish.

"No, before. I'm quite sure. Although technically the meeting was never called to order. Technically we're both out of line here."

The motion was defeated 4 to 3. Holcrow abstained. "I'm not really part of Magrit," he said. "I feel like I am, after all this time now, but I'm not."

"Of course you are," said Ada.

"You're very kind. But I'm really more comfortable as an observer here."

"The meeting was never called to order," said Mr. Baldish, obviously miffed by the defeat. "The vote may not be valid."

"I call the meeting to order," said Irini's father. "Now, let's vote. On Mr. Baldish's motion, as seconded and amended by me."

"What was the amendment again?" Ada asked.

"I'm wondering what gives you the right to call the meeting to order. I'm wondering if we even have a quorum," said Mr. Baldish. "I might still think the vote invalid."

"We have a quorum of the people here," said Irini's father.

"A lot of people aren't here."

"It's the rain," Arlys offered.

"The people who aren't here are irrelevant to the quorum issue," said Irini's father. "I call for the question."

The motion was defeated 4 to 3, with one abstention.

"Good," said Ada. "Now, the thing I wish to have very clear—"

"Just one moment, Mrs. Ada," said Irini's father politely. "Before you say something important, someone should be taking the minutes. I nominate Irini as recording secretary."

"I second the motion," said Holcrow.

"I thought you were observing," said Mr. Baldish. "One minute you're abstaining and the next you're seconding. How would you have voted, if you had voted? The women here seem to think we can muddle through with no set of guidelines."

"Gandhi has laid out our guidelines very clearly."

"I don't want to be secretary."

"Just recording secretary. Someone else will be corresponding secretary," Irini's father assured her. "We'll get to that next."

"I'll be corresponding secretary. Why can't Norma be recording secretary?"

"Norma has a deer to dress."

"I don't want to be secretary," said Norma.

"Irini would be perfect as secretary," said Holcrow. "Irini would be perfect at anything. I call for the question."

"I thought we voted not to use *Robert's Rules of Order,*" said Irini's father.

"I think we need further discussion on that," said Mr. Baldish. "It's going to save us all a lot of arguments down the road."

"The question has been called," Irini's father reminded him. "We can make time for your discussion in the old business section of the meeting, but it's inappropriate now."

"Really I don't see the need for a secretary," said Ada. "I see the need for education and discipline. I see the need for a plan of action. I'd like to get some ideas from you all as to how we can approach the problem in the most loving possible way."

"Excuse me, Mrs. Ada, but the question has been called," said Mr. Baldish.

"I don't want to be secretary," said Irini.

"Don't whine, my love."

There were three sudden cymbal clashes of thunder, each successively louder. The lights went out. They waited for them to go back on. There was a flash of lightning instead. And another. It was Beethoven weather and they sat in the dark and listened to it. It gave them the communal spirit that had rather been lacking.

"We'll get a better turnout on another evening," said Norma diplomatically.

"That would seem to be that," Mr. Baldish agreed.

"The question has been called," said Irini's father. "We can still vote. All in favor? Show of hands please. Keep them up till the lightning comes round."

So Irini was elected during the very next flash, 7 for, 1 opposed.

Minutes of Magrit Committee on Satyagraha,
First Meeting

The meeting was called to order at 7:45 on August 5th, 1947, Ada Collins presiding. A motion to run the meeting according to *Robert's Rules of Order* was defeated. Those present agreed, by a vote of 4 to 3, one abstention, to constitute a quorum. Cookies and punch were served.

Submitted by
the Recording Secretary,
Irini Doyle

30

Irini woke unaccountably early the next morning. The rain had vanished in the night and left only a pine-fresh smell behind. Irini opened the window and the voices of a hundred birds spilled in. One was particularly melodic. Irini traced it to a mockingbird, silhouetted on the telephone wire. Before she had become a working girl, Irini could take sleep or leave it. Now she resented the mornings when she rose even earlier than necessary. It was apparently part of growing up—you began to enjoy nasty things like onions, broccoli, coffee, and sleep. You began to think of those hours you were unconscious as the happiest times of your life.

But there was the consolation of seeing the sun rise. It was not quite dawn. The east end of Brief Street, the mill end, was a bright pearl gray, and far away, at the Moodey place, a rooster was crowing. Why did roosters crow in the morning? What was the Darwinian advantage? Irini made a mental note to ask Mr. Henry just as soon as he was himself again. Cock of the walk.

The Mays' house was shuttered and silent, except for a shadowy figure on the porch. Norma was out delivering the milk. "Good morning, Norma," Irini called, so that Norma came over to her window.

"That was something last night," Norma said. She shook her head emphatically. She was dressed in white coveralls and a white cap. Her eyes, at this precise moment, were bluer than the sky. The sky would get bluer as the sun rose and her eyes would not. If it were a nice day, the vectors would cross sometime before noon. Irini remembered back to high school and crossing vectors, but there was little joy in the memory. Perhaps there were advantages to being a grown-up after all.

"Yes," asked Irini, "but what was it?"

"Your dad and mine. It wouldn't have happened that way if Mr. Henry had been there."

"You think?"

"They have to respect him. He's signing the paychecks. They have to respect her when he's around," said Norma. "Will a quart do you today?"

The sun was coming up now, first red and then yellow, a pale ball blooming in the sky like a stemless flower. Irini put on her bathrobe and slippers, brought the milk in, and picked up the paper. This should have been Tweed's job, but Tweed was not a fetcher by nature. She was a worrier. She stayed at Irini's side, making sure that it was all done right.

The trees cast long morning shadows. The combination of sunlight and leaves dappled the landscape so that Brief Street looked more painted than real. Like someone's illusion set to birdsong. "God's in His heaven, all's right with the world." Had there ever been a moment, a teeny second in the whole history of time, where all had been right with the world?

She heard the porch swing creaking at the Tarkens' and stepped across the wet grass. Sissy sat in the swing, wrapped in a crocheted afghan, her hair ruffled from sleep. Her face was bare of makeup and rather sweet in her usual owlish way. She looked about thirteen years old. "You're up early, Sissy. How are you feeling today?" Irini asked.

Eeek. Eeek. "I got up early so that I could be alone," Sissy said accusingly. It was a bit unpersuasive. The flow of visitors to the

Tarken house had definitely ebbed. It was also a bit unfair. Irini had stayed away entirely.

"I'm so tired of talking about it." *Eeek*. "Everyone asks and asks and then they"—*creak*—"completely misunderstand. My mother completely misunderstood."

"I'm sorry," said Irini. "Of course, it's a difficult thing for people to—"

"Difficult! How difficult do you think it is for me? You were there. You know how it happened." The creaking came faster and faster.

"I didn't exactly—"

"My brother fought in the Pacific, risked his life, for this country. How difficult do you think that was? They all think if they ask me often enough I'll say something different. Like I'll suddenly remember I didn't see her after all. 'Ask Irini,' I'm telling them all. 'She was there, too.'"

A narrow slit of sunlight had reached the Tarken porch. Sissy swung into it and out. If you watched only her face, as Irini was doing, it gave you that stuttering stop-start feeling of a silent movie. What was missing was the silence. "And Mrs. Ada can just forget about us." *Eeek. Eeek.* "We don't have to go to any of her meetings. We don't work in the mill and we never have. We're probably the only people in town who don't owe Mr. Henry anything."

"I thought you liked Mrs. Ada."

"She has no right to come here and tell me what I can and I can't say to people. That's the thing about this country, Thomas Holcrow says. Nobody owns you. This is the greatest country in the world," Sissy said, "and I'd like to see anyone say differently while I'm around."

It would have been a good time for Irini's father to call her. He didn't, but he should have. She went inside and shook him. "You'll be late."

"So I'll be late. Call the *Tribune*. Run a headline." Her father threw an arm over his eyes. "Oh, God," he said. "I'm awake. How did that happen?"

He had the same wounded look at breakfast, but it was more than an expression now, it was an actual fact. He'd cut himself shaving and pasted a bit of tissue to his face with his own blood. It was right there on his chin, a white flag with a round, red center, the rising sun of Japan. "Well, that was inexcusable." Irini's father shook his head sadly. "That was a shameful performance. I can hardly bear to remember it."

He had cooked bacon this morning and then eggs in the bacon grease, so the kitchen had a pleasant odor, a sizzle and pop. He let Tweed lick the frying pan. Grease was good for her coat.

Irini's father liked his meat rare and his eggs soft; they were done quickly. Irini watched as he broke the skin of the yolk so that it spilled onto the plate, pale and slow as honey. "Or maybe I'm not remembering. Did the men talk and talk so that the women couldn't get a word in? Did I personally sabotage every point Mrs. Ada wished to make? Tell me the truth, Irini. Are we all in our places with egg on our faces this morning?"

"I guess you're not far wrong," Irini admitted. "You made me be recording secretary."

"Oh, that," Irini's father said. "I'm not talking about that." He wiped the plate clean with his toast, rose from the table, and put the plate into the sink with the frying pan. He doused the stack with water. "Did I have fun?" he asked her.

"Great fun."

"Well, there's that then." He drew out his car keys, slapped them against the palm of his hand. "No point in putting it off. I've got to go straight to Collins House and apologize. I should go right now. Won't get easier later."

Irini caught him at the kitchen door in time to remove the tissue. "You're my little turtledove," he told her. His breath was yolky, his kiss dry. "Always have been."

Irini combed her hair, put on her lipstick, and walked to work, where she spent the day experimenting with thickeners. They were using a bake-off method in which flour was pitted against cornstarch, and cornstarch against tapioca. It was Walter's idea to enliven the workday with a little friendly competition. The three thickening agents would be tested in gravies, in fruit pies, in sauces, and as cleaning agents. Irini was assigned to the tapioca station, tapioca being thought to require less skill than the other contenders. Ruby was also on Team Tapioca.

Tracy was given cornstarch. "That'll be the most delicate of your thickeners," she'd said. "That's the team I'd better be on." She stood at the stove, stirring and trying to watch over her shoulder to make sure that Ruby wasn't cheating. Ruby worked at Irini's side with her usual silent cheerfulness.

"Would you hand me the paring knife?" Irini asked her once and she passed it over promptly, but without a word.

No one talked about the meeting. Having not attended, the Mays were now expressing their opinion by not asking about it. Not that they would be uninformed. Irini imagined that the Baldishes had phoned a report over to the Tarkens and that Cindy May had probably listened in.

Anyway Fanny had bigger news. Her apron pocket bulged with it. At the right moment, the most dramatic moment, while everybody's gravy thickened except for Irini's, she pulled it out. It was an elegant box, covered in a deep-blue velvet. Mike Barr had sent Fanny a pin in yesterday's mail.

Irini washed her hands when her turn to hold it came. There was accompanying literature to be read first. "BURSTING FURY," it said. "Atomic Inspired Pin and Earrings. The pearled bomb bursts into a fury of dazzling colors in mock rhinestones, emeralds, rubies, and sapphires. As daring to wear as it was to drop the first atom bomb."

It came all the way from Fifth Avenue, New York. Irini pushed the box open with her thumbs. There it was, swirling against the midnight-blue lining, with all its many mock colors. It was quite large. It was lucky Fanny was such a large girl. In fact it was so large that if Mrs. Barr had picked it out, it might mean she didn't like Fanny. If Mike had chosen it himself it was just male clumsiness; it was darling.

"Of course, if she puts it on, they're pinned," Tracy said. "She hasn't made up her mind yet."

"Did he say that?" asked Claire.

"It's a pin," said Tracy. "A boy gives a girl a pin. What needs to be said?"

"It's a step before a step," Fanny agreed. "It takes things in a certain direction." She reached for the box, which shut in Irini's hands with a loud and frightening snap. "I really hate getting gifts." Her mouth made its valentine pout. "Don't you all? It's so, so . . ." She couldn't think what it was and none of the Sweethearts could help her. There was not a one of them who could ever remember getting a serious gift from a boy. It didn't seem as if it would be so bad. There was something they were missing.

"Predictable," Fanny finished.

After work, when tapioca had been bested in the gravy category but took fruit pies, the girls changed their clothes and went to practice. It was too hot. It was sauna-hot. "Don't make us do this," Helen begged Walter, but he did. They were joined by Norma and Cindy, but not Sissy. The outfield had recently been mowed so you could smell it. The ball came off the grass fast and straight. Most of the outfielders liked the flies best, but not Irini. She liked the unexpectedness of the grounders. She liked the surprise of the other team when she threw it all the way in to home to make the play anyway.

It was high summer, which meant that winter was coming. Every step in the grass raised a cloud of tiny bugs. Sweat gathered inside Irini's glove. She pulled her hand out, cupped the ball in it, and smelled the leather. They happened so fast, these summers. You barely had time to complain about the soggy, sodden heat before it was gone. The Sweethearts had only three more games on their schedule. They had expected to play longer; they might play longer. Mr. Henry just needed to make some phone calls, organize some things. "How would you like ten beautiful girls to visit your hometown?" Henry needed to ask. Who would say no? But Mr. Henry couldn't seem to move on it.

"I just hope Sissy makes it Saturday," Cindy called to Walter from first. "Because I'm expecting my aunt again. I don't see why I should have to play when my aunt is visiting, just because Sissy thinks she's getting married to who knows who. I hope she doesn't think just because she missed practice all week that that means she can miss the game."

"I'm going to check on Sissy tonight," Walter told her.

"Fanny is pinned," Tracy told Walter. "To Mike Barr."

"Mike Barr is a good guy," Walter said.

"You could just mention it to Sissy when you see her. Without saying I said to mention it."

Ruby threw one in. Walter popped one up. Norma pulled off her mask and got beneath it. The sun slid behind a cloud.

Irini didn't see her father again until dinner time. The morning's shaving scars were already covered with evening beard. They ate peanut butter sandwiches, hers with milk and his with vodka. He was treating himself to a jar of chili peppers, a gift from Los Angeles via Thomas Holcrow. He passed them to Irini to open. Irini had always suspected that her father ate chilis just because he was the only person in Magrit who could. Moodey's Market didn't even carry them. So they were a rare treat and usually a celebratory, show-offy move, but Irini's father was abnormally subdued.

"How did it go with Mrs. Ada?" Irini asked finally.

"She was very gracious. She was damned gracious. I have never been more embarrassed." Irini's father popped in a pepper. Tears sprang to his eyes and dampened his cheeks.

He coughed and took a drink. "This Indian stuff she's into makes more sense than I expected. And she knows a lot about it. We talked for quite some time."

Outside, on the Tarken side, Irini heard a door slam. She heard Sissy's voice. "You never understand me!" Sissy's voice was full of tears. Then silence.

"You haven't told me what you think about Sissy's latest escapade," Irini said.

"Sissy Tarken was the bravest little girl I ever knew," he answered.

"So you believe her?"

"I think it would be rude not to. I'd die before I was rude to Sissy Tarken."

"But you're rude all the time. You admire rudeness. You've never minded being rude."

"No, you're quite mistaken," Irini's father told her. "I mind every time I do it. I mind all the time."

31

Saturday's game was supposed to be another overnighter. Henry had the Sweethearts scheduled in Willrest, another back-end of nowhere location with a population of fifty. The bus was stuffed like a turkey. None of the Sweethearts had ever been to Willrest so you just never knew. It could be a resort town. This could happen. There might be a place to go dancing; there might be a place to go swimming; there might be one of those traveling carnivals with a roller coaster and a ferris wheel and grimacing kewpie dolls that Ruby could win for them if no man was man enough. When you knew where you were going, then you knew what to wear. Otherwise it was safest just to bring everything.

They got a day off work and left on Friday. The bus was so crammed that Arlys's toilet kit had to be wedged behind Irini's knees. Irini was on the aisle, on the driver's side. She read an Agatha Christie for a while, then dozed. She read some more. It was quite a ghastly murder and she was pretty sure it wasn't the young couple who were so much in love, because things were certainly pointing in that direction. She reviewed the cast of characters, looking for someone suspiciously inconspicuous. "Arlys," she said. Arlys had the window seat next to her. "Are real herrings ever red?"

"Hardly ever. Isn't that the point?"

Norma got caught behind a farm truck with three black dogs in the bed. The road was straight enough to pass, but the truck was occupying the middle of it. The bus inched along while Norma watched for a chance. When the truck swerved, she shot into the open space. The dogs panted at them, bright red tongues, yellow fangs, as they went by. The truck driver honked. He leaned out the window and said something. It was 1947, so it never entered their heads it might be something rude. He waved. They waved back. Norma left him in the dust.

The bus wound through a countryside of fields, not farm fields, not cow pastures, but wild fields, full of high, seedy grass and scratchy mustards and thistle. Then the woods began. Irini looked across Arlys to where acres of small, thin aspens hurled themselves past the bus to shrink again in the distance. It was hypnotic, the dance of the trees. Irini dozed some more and found herself leaning on Arlys's shoulder. This happened in the movies all the time, except the shoulder was of some young man the heroine thought she didn't like. Not a girlfriend. She shifted in her seat, dozed again. "It's a step before a step," she thought she heard someone say.

She woke briefly as they careened across the road, banging her head on the seat back. The bus slammed to a stop, pitching her forward, then rocked sideways and slowly, slowly tipped over. Her vision began to fade, like an old photograph left out in the sun. She could see the suitcases tumbling, but faintly, and then she passed out and it was blacker than sleep.

"Wake up, Irini. Wake up." For a moment Irini thought she must be late to school. She tried to rouse herself, but it was an effort. The inside of her mouth was gummy with salt and stuck together. She couldn't open it to answer. She opened her eyes instead. Things had a hazy underwater look to them. There were bits of all sorts of things where they didn't belong; it was a Picasso of skirts and knees and baseball gloves. "Are you all right?" Arlys asked. Irini's eyes closed and Arlys shook her. "Don't go back to sleep."

Why not? Irini wondered. She forced herself to open her eyes.

Arlys was trapped beneath a suitcase and a seat, both of which were trapped beneath Irini. "I really need you to move," Arlys said. Her face was so pale you could see all the tiny blue veins around her nose. "Can you do that for me, Irini? Can you get off of me?"

Through the window beneath Arlys, Irini could see dirt, reddish-colored like Arlys's hair, and little stones and crushed grasses and pine needles. There was a bat broken across Irini's legs. She tried to remember what it was that Arlys wanted her to do. "What happened?" she asked. She wet her lips.

Coming back a little at a time, as if it were the memory of a dream, she began to hear the other girls. There was Cindy telling Fanny that her arm hurt. There was Sissy crying. She heard Walter talking. "Is everyone all right?" Norma asked loudly. "Please, God, let everyone be all right."

"We've had an accident," said Arlys. Irini grabbed the side of the seat above her and pulled herself upright. This put her out of alignment with the bus itself. It was the oddest feeling, especially on top of her dizziness, her glassy vision. It was a fun-house feeling without the fun.

"There was a deer," Norma said. "Big buck. He came leaping out, across the road. It happened so fast." She burst into tears. "Please let everyone be all right."

"I'm going to call roll," Fanny said. "Tracy?"

"Here."

"Cindy is here. Margo?"

"Here."

"Arlys?"

"Here."

"Irini?"

"Here."

Irini balanced herself on the side of the base of the seat. She leaned down to pull the suitcases off Arlys. She felt stiff when she moved, but she didn't think she was hurt. Arlys had a scrape on her arm. Irini saw blood, but only in small quantities.

"Claire?"

"Here."

"Helen?"

"Here."

"Walter?"

"I'm here. I'm fine."

Arlys stood up. Her feet were on the glass of the window. Irini heard it crack. Arlys reached for Helen who had fallen all the way from the seats opposite. "Are you all right?" she asked.

"I think I am," said Helen. "Scratched and scraped. It's lucky I'm so well padded. I bounced. It's lucky we fell so slowly. Don't you think that was lucky?"

"Ruby?"

"I'm okay."

There was a pause. It was a long pause. Irini had discovered a bump on the back of her head. It was soft and it was getting larger. She rubbed it gently. Sure enough, it hurt. Arlys was examining the blood on her arm, licking her thumb and wiping it away to see what was underneath. Helen was rotating her head slowly on her shoulders, feeling along her neck with her fingers.

There was the sound of sobbing. "Sissy?" Fanny asked finally.

There was another long pause, this one even more awkward. "Here," Sissy said. She gulped and sniffled. "I'm here."

Well, it was a moment. But it was not a moment to be enjoyed. The day was muggy in a threatening, prestorm sort of way. The only door was on the ceiling. The bus had seemed crowded and hot when it was upright. Now with the contents all jumbled together, it was much worse. "I have to get out of here," Arlys said, her voice strung tight. "I can't breathe."

There were batting helmets and balls and canvas bags everywhere, suitcases and people all mashed together, but not as they had been, not with the people on top and the suitcases on the bottom or the helmets and the balls in the bags, but everything the wrong way around.

"Thank You," said Norma. Tears were streaming down her face. "Thank You." She stood with one foot on the dash and the other balanced on the back of the driver's seat and tried to reach the door. Her legs were shaking so that she had to sit down again. "How many deer have I shot in my life?" she asked. "Would it have been such a big deal if I hit one? What's the difference?"

"Don't think like that," said Claire. "Everyone is fine. We've had an accident, but everyone is fine. Who knows what would have happened if you'd hit the deer? Maybe this was best."

"He had a magnificent rack," Norma said. "I was thinking how it wouldn't be sporting to hit him with a bus."

"Don't think about it."

"I have to get out of here," Arlys said. "Please. Right now."

"I'm so sorry," said Norma. "I'm so sorry."

The door on the ceiling was stuck. It took the agility of Ruby to ascertain this. She scrambled up a tower of suitcases, rocked back and forth at the top. She was Errol Flynn, with a rakish gash beneath one eye. She leapt for the door, hung from it like a chandelier, pushed and jerked on it. She did everything but open it. "I need a place to stand," she said.

"So now what?"

"Maybe we could knock out a window," Sissy suggested.

Neither Helen nor Fanny was ever going to fit through a window even if they could climb up to one. Knocking out a window would involve flying glass. "Give her a bat," said Norma. "Maybe she can lever the door."

"You do it, Irini," said Walter. "If you can't do it, none of us can."

Irini stepped from seat side to seat side to the front of the bus. Norma and Claire held a stack of luggage in place; Ruby waited for her at the top. The suitcases were offset like stair steps, but extremely unstable. It was a sort of cartoon escalator—the stairs slid away and disappeared as she stepped on them. She scrambled for a reliable handhold and Ruby offered her one. Ruby's fingers were warm and callused.

Irini was afraid she might fall and hurt herself and this struck her as funny. She looked down to where Norma stood and she could feel herself smiling idiotically. It alarmed Norma. "I'm so sorry," Norma said again, with obvious sincerity.

"Take a deep breath," Walter suggested. "Tell yourself you can do it."

Irini reached up with her right arm. She closed her eyes, breathed deeply and tensed her muscles. They bulged. She pushed. The door opened easily, opened all of sudden, throwing her off balance, tipping the cases. Ruby held onto her with one hand and stuck the bat through the opening with the other. She levered the bat, throwing the door wide.

When Irini had settled, Ruby climbed through. Everything was so easy for Ruby. She pulled up, swung her legs out, and passed over. It was much harder for the other Sweethearts, even with Ruby outside to help them. There was little panache in anyone else's exit.

Getting Cindy out was a nightmare. The only arm she still had use of was the one with no hand. "Here," said Sissy suddenly. She was wearing a printed blue scarf over her thick, black hair. She unknotted it and handed it to Tracy. "You can make her a sling out of this," she said, and she was the one who would know.

Tracy didn't answer, but she took the scarf and fastened it around Cindy's neck for her, just as if she had heard Sissy.

Irini was the last one out. Once she was through the door she still had to get down. It was surprisingly high, the scariest moment of the whole scary episode. She sat on the bus, her feet dangling over the windshield, for the longest time. She wiped her mouth with her sleeve, felt along her head to see how big the bump was now. It was coming right along. "You can do this, Irini," Claire encouraged her. "Come on."

Eventually the Sweethearts all stood in a jumbled row on the ground, with their hair tangled and their makeup smeared, and their scrapes and bruises just starting to hurt for real. "What about the luggage?" Fanny asked, trying to comb her hair out with her pearl-tipped fingers, and Walter told her it was a little late to be asking.

"But I left my cigarettes inside," she said and Helen told her it was time to quit smoking.

They had yet to see another car. "How long has it been since we passed anyone?" Irini asked Norma.

"You remember the farmer? With the dogs? He was it," she answered. They had passed that truck hours ago.

"It's going to rain," said Walter. He was looking up at the sky. He had one red eyeball, a thin red border on the skin all around it. "In another hour we're all going to wish we were back on that bus."

The sky directly above them was blue with large, floury puffs of white. A good luck sky. But far away to the west there was a solid, undifferentiated sheet of gray. A wind swept through their hair and the trees by the road, rattling the leaves, ticking in the pine needles. From somewhere inside the distant gray sky came a faint sound like growling.

"I had a raincoat," said Fanny. "I had clothes for damned everything. I could go dancing if anyone asked. I had two packs of cigarettes."

Cindy threw up. It happened all of sudden and only the once. She kicked leaves over the evidence.

"I'm so sorry," said Norma.

"There's going to be lightning," Walter said. "We have to find a place to get out of it."

They walked ahead since they knew there was nothing behind. They walked single file down the edge of the road, armed with a single baseball bat, and the wrong half of the sky rushing toward them.

After they had walked a long way, with a rest here and there, none of which proved restful, they came to the end of the afternoon. The road was edged with Queen Anne's lace. Yellow butterflies skimmed over them. By now the clouds had spread and thickened like boiling gravy.

They found a side road. It was not altogether promising. It was made of dust, small enough to maybe be nothing more than a driveway, although they could not see through the trees to a house of any kind. But there was a wire fence with a gate swinging open, and this was encouraging. Where there was a gate there had to be a reason.

Cindy was leaning against Fanny and breathing heavily. Her face had become quite pale and she held her arm in the fold of the blue scarf. "I'm afraid it might be broken," Fanny told Tracy. "She says it hurts like the dickens."

"Can she move it?" Tracy asked.

"Yes. I'm fine. I need to lie down," Cindy said crossly. "I can't keep walking forever."

A few fat drops of rain hit the dust and lay round as pearls until sinking in. The ground was the color of cinnamon. "It's starting," said Claire and Irini felt the first drop hit her hand.

Irini was euphoric. It had come over her as she walked. First she was frightened and then she was worried and now she could find nothing to complain of. Everything was perfect. The glassy vision after the accident had been replaced by an exaggerated clarity. She saw the silver undersides of leaves, cut out quite vividly against the black sky. The wind tossed the leaves from green to silver; they sparkled like water. She saw her own feet, the shape of one toe through the shoe, the cinnamon dust coating the leather.

Her feet were tired. They hurt all the way up to her knees. Her head pounded. She treasured every ache in her body. She lifted her wrist, smelling for the rain as if it were French perfume. She wouldn't have changed a thing. They were all alive and she was not about to get upset over something as right as rain. She saw the lovely, furry weeds at the sides of the road—Russian thistles, wild catnip, old man's pajamas. You could eat some of those, she thought, and she would have liked to, just for the sensation of it, just to be sure she was living fully, but she wasn't certain which were the edible ones.

The road rose slowly and the girls walked to the top. Beneath them, through the thickets of thin, leafy trunks, there was a lake, tea-colored like the sky. On its bank was a set of low, cinder-block houses with roofs of corrugated tin. There was no sign of life at the houses—

no lights, no cars, no bicycles, no dogs. But there was a rowboat sunk in the mud of the bank and filled with water. And near it, in the shallow, algaed edge of the lake, a heron trolled, its elastic neck twisting, one leg up, one inside-out knee locked and stiff. A faint and final stream of sunlight rolled down the small feathers of the heron's throat. The light hit the water and broke like a mirror into glittering pieces. The heron paused and looked at Irini.

It was a miracle this bird should be here at this exact moment and that Irini should also be here, seeing it look at her, knowing it had seen her looking back. Of course, when you stopped to think of it properly, it was also a miracle every morning when Irini woke up to find herself in her bed on Brief Street. What were the odds against any one person being in any one spot at any one moment? They must be astronomical. Every step of every day of every life took place against tremendous odds. Irini said some part of this out loud, but only part, so it made less sense than when she thought it. No one else was in the mood. Sissy was sniffling and Cindy was moaning.

"What are you babbling about, Irini?" said Margo. She didn't like nonsense. "Did you bump your head or something?" At the sound of her voice the heron lifted off, and Irini could hear the pump of its enormous wings.

They continued down the road, and while they still had some distance to go, the distance between the bases and back again, the downpour began.

Two minutes later and they could have stayed dry. What were the odds? The rain was a deep, gray veil over the trees by the time they arrived at the first building. There was an overhanging eave, one step up to the door, which was warped, with a screen window and a hook latch that wasn't latched. Walter opened it. "It's perfect," he called back out. "Wait till you see. Like it was made for us."

The girls crowded inside, wiping their faces, drying their hair with their wet sleeves. They stood in a single rectangular room with a stone floor and cracked incompetent windows. The only furniture was fortuitous. Irini saw it all at once, lit up with lightning. Six rows of bunk beds, no bedding, but the mattresses were intact. When the lightning vanished a little pair of eyes shone on for a moment in the corner, then blinked off.

There was a scuttling sound. "Yeesh," said Helen. "I do not want to sleep on a bed I can't see."

"This must be a summer camp," Arlys said. "All these beds."

Irini didn't think so. Nothing of games and comic books and candy bars and sexual misinformation was in the air here. The room smelled of mold and dust and wet stone. Rain thrummed on the tin roof until the whole building vibrated with the noise.

"But it *is* summer," said Margo. "So where are the kids?"

"A work camp," said Irini. "And abandoned."

"Something has been nesting in the beds," said Fanny.

"I don't care," said Cindy. She sat on the closest lower bunk. "Come sit with me, Tracy," she asked. "I just wish I was dry. One wish. Why can't I even have that?" Tracy put her arms around Cindy, rocked her ever so slightly.

"You're all right," she said. "I'm here."

"*I* wish I had a cigarette," said Fanny. "Just one lousy cigarette."

"What now?" asked Margo. She took the bunk opposite the Mays. It creaked loudly when she sat on it. "No one is going to realize we're missing until game time tomorrow."

"Even then," said Arlys, "we can't count on them thinking anything of it. They'll be disappointed, they'll be annoyed. I wonder if they'll be worried, though."

"Someone is going to see the bus," Tracy said. Her voice had a reproving tone. They were all upsetting Cindy and they could all just stop it. "Anytime now, someone will drive by and see that bus and come looking for us."

"Abso-dol-garned-lutely," said Fanny. She gave the word an odd little emphasis, more cross than reassuring. She was drumming her fingers, twitching at her hair, tapping one foot. It was a delayed reaction to the accident, or else it was nicotine withdrawal. She took a bottom bunk and the whole bed shook.

"One thing is for sure. Nobody's been out here for an age," Sissy said and Irini could feel the May girls glaring in Sissy's direction.

"When the rain stops, I'll go for help," said Walter. "Let's just take advantage of the beds and turn in." He chose a top bunk near the door, prepared to vault up to it.

"Walter!" said Helen.

"Yes?"

"You can't sleep here."

"You can't sleep here with us girls," Margo agreed.

"You're kidding."

"It wouldn't be proper. Someone could come by at any moment," Tracy said. "There are plenty of other buildings. Plenty of other beds."

"We have a chaperone," said Walter. "I'll be a perfect gentleman."

"Let him stay," said Ruby.

"Sorry," said Fanny. "As chaperone, I can't allow it."

Walter went to the door of the building. "What if there were no other buildings? Would you make me sleep out in the rain?"

"Don't be pathetic, Walter," said Fanny. "It's not attractive."

"So much for every man's fantasy," he said.

"See you in the morning."

The door squealed when it opened, squeaked when it closed. Irini took the bunk Walter had chosen. It had a stale, spoiled smell. In the sunlight, she was sure to find old stains. She could picture them, yellow and kidney shaped under her back. She left her shoes on, curled herself up so as to touch as little of the mattress as possible. "It can't be later than six. I won't sleep a wink," she thought, and she woke several times during the night with the same thought. Once she dreamed about Walter. He was leaning toward her. "We have got to get you out of those wet clothes," he said. She woke up strangely pleased.

Toward morning, when the rain had stopped, she awoke for good. She was very cold and she had to go to the bathroom. There must be a bathroom, she thought, but it was still too dark to go looking. She had a handkerchief she could wipe herself with, but just the once. She decided to worry about later, later. Desperate times required desperation. She slid down from the bunk as quietly as she could. The door squealed when it opened, creaked when it closed.

The rain had stopped, but the trees still dripped. "Tree rain," her father called this. "Almost the real thing." The ground was covered with wet leaves and pine needles, bundled together, bound at the tops like little whisk brooms, some reddish colored, some old and gray. The slugs were out. Irini's shoes squished. One of the trees stepped toward her. "Irini," it said. It had Walter's voice. It frightened the need right out of her. "You scared me half to death," it said.

There was no reason for him to leap out at her like that. "What are you doing out here?" she asked severely.

"Same as you, I imagine. Come and talk to me afterward."

He waited for her back at the second building. "How was your bed?" she asked.

"Lonely."

They sat on the step together. She shivered and he put his arm around her. "Okay?" he said. "It's just cold."

"It's okay." He had a sort of wet-dog smell, but it was very familiar to her and not unpleasant. She wondered if he could say the same. "Honestly, Walter. How much trouble are we in?"

"None at all." His arm tightened. "We have shelter, we have water. There's got to be some sort of a kitchen here, maybe even showers. As soon as it's light enough, I'll go for help. The worst that can happen is that we all get a bit thinner. We were lucky."

"We were so lucky. It makes you think, doesn't it?"

"What does it make you think about, Irini?" His voice shook slightly. He cleared his throat. She glanced at him, looked quickly away. His eyeball was still cracked with red, but the rim was purple going onto black and had widened.

"You need ice for that eye. You need a big, juicy steak." Irini thought about big juicy steaks. Baked potatoes. Little green peas. Heaps of pancakes. Her father always made her pancakes when they went camping.

"You want to know what my mother used to do when I got

hurt?" Walter asked. His arm was around her, which made it important to keep the conversation impersonal.

"No. What do you hear from your folks these days? What's your dad up to?"

Walter allowed himself to be diverted. "Product development. He's still sure there's a future coming when every American home will have a computer in the basement, down by the furnace. He and Mom'll be in Magrit for Christmas. Of course I may not be."

"Where would you go?"

"Who knows? The season ends, I have no particular plans."

"Now you *sound* like your father." It was about the meanest thing you could say to Walter. It just came out. Irini didn't want Walter around exactly, but this didn't mean she wanted him to leave. Maybe she was just annoyed because he could go in and out of Magrit just like that, whenever he chose.

"What's it to you?" Walter said.

"A bad time to leave Mr. Henry, I think."

"Yeah," said Walter. "Yeah. Something has to be done about Gramps. Anyway I'm not going tomorrow." She leaned into him. He reached around her with his other arm. She could feel his heart beating against her face and also the pulse in his arms against her arms. She was starting to feel warmer.

There was a long silence and Irini was perfectly relaxed, completely unwary. She closed her eyes and more time might have passed than she realized, because when she opened them, it was growing light. She could hear loons calling to each other from the lake. She could see the trees, drenched and dark with water. She could see Walter's normal pink face with its abnormal glowing eye. "Golly," she said, lifting one careful finger toward it. She touched him along the eyebrow. She didn't mean anything. She was just sorry about his eye.

Walter kissed her. His lips were wet and soft. "Hey," she said warningly.

"Hey back." He was grinning at her, revealing the line of his gums.

"Don't do that." She pushed him away.

"Too late."

"Don't make me hurt you."

"Too late for that, too. I'm going for help," he said. "Keep the troops entertained for me. I'm leaving you in charge of morale." He took hold of her arm. "I'm going to kiss you good-bye."

"No, you're not."

"You'd kiss me good-bye if I were Thomas Holcrow." His voice was absolutely neutral, his face with its glorious eye, impossible to read.

"I would not." He was looking straight at her, straight into the black holes of her own eyes. Irini was glad it wasn't any lighter out, glad she wasn't a blusher by nature. Even so she couldn't look back.

"We'll see," he said. He stood up, stretched unconcernedly. "Because he's bound to leave sooner or later."

32

The whole episode left Irini in a state. Only she couldn't identify exactly which state. Perhaps she was in several states. She sat on the step by herself, and already the thrill of surviving the accident was so muted she could hardly hear it under the louder noise of more trivial concerns. Real life in its tedious, hideous quotidian aspect was back. Partly she was feeling guilty and this was not because she had sat with Walter's arm around her, not because she had touched his face when it was so dangerously close to her own. No, these actions still seemed natural and excusable. Irini felt guilty because she had set the stage by dreaming about him erotically during the night.

Somehow he had sensed this. A man might feel nothing but friendship for a girl, but if she introduced the other, he couldn't help but respond. It was a physical thing, a reflex. Men were born this way. Unless he really did still feel something more for her after all the times he had assured her he didn't. In which case Fanny was certainly right. All men were liars. Born to it. Selected for it. It conferred a Darwinian advantage.

And was Walter Collins going to be the only boy to kiss her in her whole life?

The morning air was wet and cold. Irini huddled on the step. There was a chorus of waxwings in the trees. Irini had just spotted them, Quaker gray with their pointy little heads, when she heard the *squeal, squeak* of the bunkhouse door. The sound of the birds stopped like an alarm shut off. "Where's Walter?" Arlys asked sleepily.

"Gone for help."

"Where's the bathroom?"

"I don't know." Irini stood up. Her neck and shoulders were extremely sore. She tried to rub them. It hurt to turn her head. "Let's go see."

"Not a chance for toilet paper, do you think?"

"Not a chance."

"You know, it's a funny thing," said Arlys. "I have listened to *Wheat Theater* many a time and heard Anna spend who knows how many nights in the woods. But I've never heard her address this issue. There's got to be some sort of leaf, or something. Something only mountain men know. Wild-growing Sears and Roebuck catalogues."

They found the bathroom on the far side of the cabins, an outhouse with no front door and an unobstructed view of the lake from the sitting position. It was a pretty scene. The sunlight spread over the lake, turning one side of the tiny waves silver and the other gold. But you wouldn't linger. In spite of its airy vista, there was the usual smell. Irini waited for Arlys and heard the sound of water falling into water. It seemed rude somehow, to have heard it.

Back up the bank was a kitchen, with a few old dishes and a stove you wouldn't dare light. There was a small pot you could cook in, which was a find. They could start a fire and boil water. There were spider webs everywhere, dust and dirt. Behind the kitchen was a small shed with some rusted rakes and trowels, which they took along, too, in case anyone could think of a use for them.

They caught up with Tracy standing on the bank looking at the sunken boat. "It's got a hole the size of a bread box in it," she said. "It's no good at all."

The lake was a busy place in the morning. Under the dazzled

surface, Irini could see bluegills and small sunfish darting about in golden blinks. Mayflies grazed over the surface. Down the bank was a tribe of mallards, the green-headed males and the calmly colored females. They clucked at each other crossly or contentedly. What was the difference to ducks? Surely their moods were ephemeral.

The only thing out of place here was the Sweethearts, but the ducks hadn't noticed them yet. Irini stepped down to the water to wash out her handkerchief. "How's Cindy?" Arlys asked.

"I don't think her arm is that bad. She's just afraid, because it's the only hand she has. She's scared to be without it, even for a little while. You can't blame her."

"It was a miracle that no one was hurt worse, wasn't it?" said Arlys. "It's because the bus tipped so slowly."

Irini couldn't help imagining for a moment what it would be like to have no hands, no hooks even or anything. It was so unpleasant she stopped and took the first possible alternate topic. She pictured the bus sinking to its side like a stiff old dog. This also was unpleasant, surprisingly so. Think of something nice, she told herself, and thought about Walter kissing her again even though this was not what she had meant. It did seem better in recollection than she had found it in fact, though. She noted this as something to think about later.

"I wish there was something to eat," said Tracy. "I'm starving."

"Here you are surrounded by nature's cornucopia. And you say that."

"Fine. What do we eat?"

"For a start," said Arlys, "I spy a fine field of cattails over yonder." Arlys was the best possible person to be in a fix with. "I try to go at life as if I were acting it," she had told Irini once. "It makes things simple. You just try to play the role of the hero." She was rarely out of character, indefatigably cheerful, but it was never an annoying cheerfulness; it never spilled over into perkiness. "Go grab one of those ducks," she suggested.

If Tracy hadn't shown up, Irini might have talked to Arlys about

Walter. Arlys would have had something heartening to say. "Certainly it's not your fault if Walter wants to keep mooning over you," Arlys would have told her and then supported the statement with persuasive arguments. Although Irini couldn't work out for herself what these arguments would have been, she tried to pretend that they had already had this conversation, that she had been persuaded and was now feeling better.

Irini had had suspicions on other occasions connecting Maggie's outbursts with almost every other girl on the Sweethearts, but never Arlys. Of course, if this were an Agatha Christie, nothing would be more suspicious than that. "Red herring," she thought suddenly, because of the Agatha Christie and also the sun shining on Arlys's reddish hair. "Let's wash up," Irini suggested. "Any moment now we'll be rescued by a truckload of burly lumberjacks, and we'll want to be looking our best."

"Burly is a funny word, isn't it?" said Arlys. "Especially in combination with lumberjacks. I think of burls and so when I picture burly lumberjacks—"

"You two are having more fun," said Tracy nastily. "Aren't you? People are back inside the bunkhouse, hurt and hungry, but do you care?"

So Arlys went off to gather breakfast. Irini went for firewood. It had occurred to her that the smoke from a fire might do more than just cook their breakfast. It could be a signal fire. Anna Peal would have thought of this last night.

But the only wood Irini could find was wet clear through. When she returned, the Sweethearts were all about. They were rumpled and gritty, limping and bruised. "I thought there could be nothing worse than sleeping in a bed I couldn't see. And then I saw it," said Fanny. They were hopeful when they learned that Walter was off arranging their rescue. They were hungry. Arlys had found blueberries. She led them to where huge handfuls could be gathered. Glistening spider webs lay over every bush, stretched between the roots of trees. One trunk showed the fresh wounds of a bear's claws.

"No one in Magrit even knows we're gone yet. Isn't that funny to think of?" Sissy asked. Barely awake and already starting to cry; her eyes were as puffy as clamshells from crying the night before. The lids were so swollen she could hardly open them.

Irini chose a spot for her fire. She made a teepee of kindling, took a match off Fanny. The matchbook, she couldn't help but notice, was from a hotel in Tomahawk. It was not hot enough to light her wood. "Let me try," said Ruby. She lit a bit of the grass, coddled it along. The smell of smoking greenery filled the air.

"Maybe we could fish," Fanny suggested. Her lush lips were stained a delicate blue. It was not unattractive. "What could we fish with?"

Irini held out the rusted rake.

"Maybe we could ask one of those men to borrow a pole," said Norma. She pointed out across the water. There was a boat with three men in it, and an outboard motor, headed in their direction. They couldn't hear the motor yet, but it was coming straight at them.

"It's the Nadeaus," said Sissy breathily. Irini turned in shock to look at her. A pulse point was ticking in Sissy's cheek.

"Nonsense," said Tracy sharply. "There're only three of them." She glanced at Fanny, who had a how–dare–she look on her face. But there was really no time to be insulted; there would be time for that later. Tracy began to wave. "Hey. Over here! Help!"

"Help us." Margo gestured frantically. The boat was closer. Its waves were already licking at their bank.

"Hello the shore," one of the men shouted. The Sweethearts gathered along the edge of the water. The boat speeded up. The bow lifted off the lake and pointed right at them. It nosed in. The man in the back cut the motor. He threw the tow line to Norma, who hauled on it. He stepped out, one foot in the algae, then took one big step to the bank. He pulled the boat behind him. "Have you accepted Jesus Christ as your savior?" he asked, with his feet dripping and his eyes deeply, sincerely blue.

"Do you have a cigarette?" Fanny asked back.

So the Sweethearts were rescued by a boatload of fishing Christians. They were taken a few at a time across the lake to the men's campsite and from there in the back of a truck to the big town of Le Coeur, where there was an actual hotel open for the hunting and fishing season, with hot showers and a supper club with hot coffee, and a tow truck and a mechanic named Carl.

The Christian fishermen had spent a short time in a boat and a truck with Fanny and they were ready to fix the bus for her themselves with their bare hands. They glared at Carl. Carl gazed at Fanny. She was wearing Mike Barr's pin now, and you couldn't miss it, but you could miss the significance of it.

The Sweethearts told their story in Le Coeur, where the Le Coeurish were especially interested in the deer. Was it a big buck? they asked, because a big buck had run Mr. Runnberg's truck right into a tree last October. And a big buck had trampled the flowers right there on the supper club lawn. No one had seen him, but he'd left the evidence. And then there was a black stag all surrounded by flame that people saw sometimes, which meant they were going to die, but that didn't sound like the same one Norma had seen, they could thank God for that.

A man up in Canada had been attacked in his truck by flying squirrels. They covered his windshield so thick he couldn't see and the wipers weren't strong enough to remove them. He had to drive the whole way home in reverse. "You were lucky," the denizens of the Broad and Bonny Supper Club concluded.

"You missed the best episode of *Wheat Theater*," the supper club owner sympathized. He was a man with the gestures and facial expressions of a woman. He was the most exotic thing the Sweethearts had ever seen.

"Oh, it was dire. Anna Peal went into this castle made all of snow and she thought it was all beautiful, even though it was so cold. It was because she had a coldness in her heart. Because she was still angry with her mother, even though she thought she wasn't. So she almost froze to death, but once she really forgave her mother, with all her heart, then the castle melted." He poured another cup of coffee. "It was an allegory."

But Irini missed all of this. "We can't just leave," she told the other Sweethearts. "What about Walter? He's off rescuing us."

"We need to get Cindy to a doctor," said Fanny.

"Which way did he go?" one of the men asked.

"Up the road."

"There's some cabins. Not right on the road. There's the Runnberg place. But no towns without crossing the lake. Hard to say when he'd be back. But if you want to wait . . ."

Of course Irini didn't want to wait. Irini wanted breakfast and a shower, same as anyone else would want. But it didn't seem right to just go. How would they ever find Walter again?

"We'll leave him a note," said Margo. "We'll send someone back for him. Come on, Irini."

So Irini went as far as the campsite, where she had a stack of pancakes, but then she didn't get in the truck. "We should take some food back for Walter," she said. "And a sleeping bag. A fishing pole. A frying pan. Toilet paper."

"I thought Walter was off rescuing *us.*"

"We can't just leave him." Irini looked around the circle stubbornly. "Really, someone should stay."

Really, she expected someone to stay with her. She thought Arlys might offer, acting the part of the hero. Or Margo, who was one of her very best friends. Maybe Claire, who was nowhere near so close to her, but was terminally tender-hearted. Surely Claire would offer. She knew she could count on Claire. None of them would meet her eyes.

"We have to get Cindy to the doctor's," said Fanny, as if Irini hadn't heard her the first time, as if otherwise, minus this one detail, Fanny would be right there with Irini, spending another night on those awful beds.

"I'll stay with you," said Ruby.

So the boat took the two of them back and motored away again, its ripples widening in greater and fainter loops. Stillness had already settled on the compound. The bunkhouses, they now knew, had been a prisoner-of-war camp. There had been real Germans up here in the woods during the war. They'd been caught up in Greenland during the battle for the weather stations. Good fishermen. One of them had been an artist. The girls in Le Coeur would see some of his paintings in the diner there. Watercolor scenes of the lake.

The bunkhouses were more uncomfortable now that they knew it was a P.O.W. camp. The quiet seemed less peaceful, more desperate and homesick. Irini would have liked to fill the silence up, but Ruby was not much for conversation. They ate some cheese sandwiches the men had provided. They chose their bunks for the night and lay the sleeping bags out in preparation.

They sat by the water and watched the sunfish. The ducks seemed to expect food. They paddled about in a demanding way, quacking and squawking, then they came right up on the bank and tried to bite Irini's toes. It made Irini even more uncomfortable, thinking about prisoners of war who fed ducks. She and Ruby had very little bread to spare, but really, they had no choice. The ducks were taking no prisoners.

"You're a very quiet person," Irini observed once to Ruby.

Ruby said no doubt it was all those brothers. "Who was listening if I talked?"

"I always wanted a large family. You must miss them very much."

"Yes."

"I always wanted a brother. You're lucky to have so many."

"They're all right," Ruby said.

"I bet they're proud of you. Do you think they'll ever come to one of your games?"

"Maybe."

"I'd like to meet them sometime."

"Sure."

What Irini was really struggling to say was that she was grateful to Ruby for staying with her. Since she couldn't seem to edge up on it, she decided just to say it. Ruby turned to her with that dimpled-milk smile. "I really like Walter," Ruby said. It gave Irini a moment's pause.

"Ruby," she said.

"Mmm?"

"Do you ever worry that you play baseball too well? To attract a guy, I mean. Guys don't really like girls who do things like baseball really well. When you're trying to get a guy, it might be smarter not to be quite so good."

"Oh."

The word was not sufficiently apprehending. This was an important point. Not understanding this could ruin Ruby's whole life. Irini wanted to help. "Guys don't like girls with muscles. They don't like girls who can outrun them, or strike them out, or make them look bad. They like a softer look. They like girls who are more feminine."

"I don't think you can just say 'guys,' " said Ruby. "There are all kinds of guys. I've lived with a whole mess of them my whole life."

It was the longest speech Ruby had ever made. Irini certainly couldn't say the same. She deferred to Ruby's greater experience, although she was still pretty sure she was right.

Maybe there were all kinds of guys. But the better a girl got at just about anything, the fewer the boys who'd be willing to date her. Why narrow your options, when they were already narrow enough?

In the afternoon, while Ruby napped, Irini sat in the camp kitchen. There was a hollow shell that had once been a wood-burning stove. There was a sink with a pump that didn't work; Irini had tried it with her good arm.

There were six wooden tables with benches. The tabletops were scratched with use, but no one had carved into them. No initials. No hearts. Nothing to tell Irini about the men who had eaten here.

They were Germans! Maybe Nazis. The men here were men who

had lost, and a good thing too, but hard to imagine. Hard to imagine losing at something so big.

But how bad could it be? Irini would not feel sorry for Nazis. They had spent the war in the beautiful, remote woods and now they were home again.

She closed her eyes, put her head down, and imagined sounds— soup bubbling on the stove, spoons clicking against the sides of metal bowls, German words and voices. She had a good imagination. Then she made the sounds go away again.

She found she knew a few words that she could say to these men. "Schlaft in himmlicher Ruh'," she told them. "Schlaft in himmlicher Ruh'."

Walter returned next day, in a borrowed truck with a large Thermos of coffee and sandwiches for eleven made on the strangest bread imaginable, a sort of pancake you could open like a purse. When he found that Ruby had waited for him in an abandoned P.O.W. camp when she could have been sleeping in a hotel and eating in a supper club, he just couldn't say thank you often enough. "That's so sweet of you," he told her. "That's just the nicest thing."

The truck was more battered than their bus. It started up with a suspenseful, tubercular noise. Walter had liquor on his breath. Irini was the expert and she could tell as soon as they got into the cab together, even though she wasn't sitting next to him. His eye was green by now, a dark green bloom beside his nose. He looked as if he'd gotten very little sleep; his face had that sort of sag. It was mystifying. Yesterday morning he was kissing Irini, and now, twenty-four hours later, here he was, back again, unshaven and drunk, and looking at Ruby as if he could eat her alive. He was looking at Ruby, but probably when he said thank you like that, probably he meant Irini, too.

33

In fact, Walter had really big news, but he waited to tell them until they had all three squeezed into the truck and taken off for Le Coeur to try to hook up again with the team. The road ranged from very bad to worse than you could believe. It was only wide enough for a single car, but then only a single car, only their car, ever seemed to be on it. It was patchily paved; you never knew what you might find under your wheels. Irini bounced against the door, bounced against Ruby. She had had a headache for two days running now. It was taking a toll.

Yesterday Walter had said good-bye to Irini and left the compound. He walked along the road for several hours. The woods did nothing but get denser. But sometime well after noon, he had finally heard a truck, which he was able to flag down. It was going the other way, back toward the bunkhouses. There were two men inside and neither of them spoke English. They looked Italian, he thought, but he would have understood at least a few words if they'd been speaking Italian. He'd tried to tell them that there were girls to be rescued. They nodded and smiled at him. They made a series of incomprehensible gestures of their own and finally all agreed that he would ride along in the back. He figured that when they reached the road leading to the compound, he could make them take it. To the extent that he had a plan, that was it.

But they turned too early. They turned where there was no road at all, just a space between the trees. They drove toward the lake. They passed a couple of old campsites; Walter could see where the campfires had been. They passed a new campsite, maybe even the one the girls had been taken to. But they kept going, swerving around the trunks of trees, until they finally reached a little set of tents all off by themselves. In these tents were many more people who spoke no English.

And a few who did. Walter was taken to a younger man, a man who still had all his own teeth. "Welcome to Little Persia," the man said.

They were show folk. More like gypsies than like circus people—there were no clowns, no horses. They offered a bit of gymnastics, some card tricks, some dancing. They had a man who could turn himself inside out, or at least that was what they'd told Walter. Probably there was some small snafu in the translation. Probably he was just very agile. They had a woman who could tell the future and she told Walter he had already met the woman he would marry. Irini and Ruby took this news in silence.

The end of summer was their biggest season and they were coming down from Canada for the rich pickings of the United States. Walter told them about the accident and about the girls who played baseball and this was something they all expressed a great desire to see.

"They fed me," said Walter. "They fed me the best meal. Maggie is going to die for that recipe. I don't think it can be traditional. It had venison in it, all wrapped in some sort of leaf. Kind of like stuffed cabbage. They sang for me. I sang for them."

"You were drinking," said Irini accusingly. While she and Ruby were defending themselves from wild ducks.

"Gosh, yes. I had no choice. And then they loaned me the truck. So that I could go and get the baseball-playing girls."

"We're going back there?"

"After we fetch the rest of the team in Le Coeur. I have to. I promised. Anyway, I have to return the truck."

"It sounds like fun," said Ruby.

"And then what? How do we get home?"

"We have to play them. If we win, they take us." Walter kept his eyes on the road. "And of course, we'll win. They had no idea about Ruby here."

"It sounds like fun," said Ruby.

"What if we lose?"

"Cash. But that's not possible."

Irini said nothing. When Walter spoke again his voice was obviously defensive. "It was the best I could do," he said. "These people are professional bargainers. I was the chump from Hoboken.

"Certainly I had no way of knowing you'd be arranging your own rescue and all you'd have to do for it was get baptized."

The road required Walter's full attention for a while. Irini clung to the side of the door and tried not to let the bouncing jar her head. "And anyway, that's not all," Walter told them.

Out in back of one of the tents, leashed to a tree with a chain, was a gorilla. It wasn't even full-grown yet, an adolescent, with the softest hands and the saddest face. Chi Chi. They had traded a bear for her to some schmuck up in Canada. "Can you imagine?" said Walter. "A bear for a gorilla?"

"They all felt very bad about the chain," said Walter. "They said they'd like nothing better than to find a nice home for Chi Chi in the off-season. Here Gramps is, looking and looking for an ape, and here I stumble over her." He paused for maximum dramatic effect and then tried to disguise it with a casual tone.

"They said she bowls," he said.

Hard as it is to believe, utterly unfathomable as it seems to us now, Fanny could not have cared less about the ape. As the chaperone she had considerable authority over the team's whereabouts and plans.

Should things get legalistic, in the case of a dispute, she probably had as much to say about this as the coach. Perhaps more so. She was, after all, much bigger than Walter. "We are going straight home to Magrit," she told Walter in a voice that begged him to just try and argue with her. "The bus will be right and running by tomorrow. We're climbing aboard and letting Norma drive us home as fast as she can. We have no reason in the world to visit Little Persia."

"This is a smart gorilla," Walter said. "She bowls. She's just the thing for Gramps now. You've seen him. Someone has to do something."

"He thinks he wants one, but Mrs. Ada will just end up taking care of it. She has enough to do, what with India's independence and all. And it does not bowl. Take it from me. You misunderstood. Probably it bawls. Our families are worrying about us or they will be once they know the ordeal we've had." Fanny had tried to call, but with Cindy off the switchboard, telephone service in and out of Magrit was spotty. "And Cindy has got to go home."

Cindy turned out to have cracked the bone in her lower arm. For anyone else it would have been a minor injury. For Cindy it meant that for six weeks, someone else would have to comb her hair, dress her, clean her after the toilet, and spoon-feed her. It was a nightmare and she was taking it as such.

Walter was not putting up much of a fight. Perhaps he was returning to sanity from whatever it was besides the liquor that had possessed him in Little Persia. The magic spell Chi Chi had cast. "What about the truck?" he asked.

"Return it," Fanny advised. "It doesn't belong to you."

34

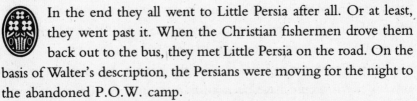 In the end they all went to Little Persia after all. Or at least, they went past it. When the Christian fishermen drove them back out to the bus, they met Little Persia on the road. On the basis of Walter's description, the Persians were moving for the night to the abandoned P.O.W. camp.

"Baseball, baseball," they called to the girls in the back of the Christian fisherman's truck as it passed. "Stick, stick."

Walter pulled them over for some side-of-the-road conversation. He expressed great regrets about canceling the game. He gestured many times to Cindy. Her arm was hurt, he told them. She required immediate doctor's care. Of course she had already seen a doctor in Le Coeur. Her arm was professionally swaddled. Clearly the more he spoke, the less the Persians believed in a team of girls who played baseball. They agreed to help right the bus, but they asked for cash this time, no wagers.

Norma and Carl looked the bus over and talked shop. They had a passionate discussion that ranged from tune-ups to tire rotations to alignments. They weren't in complete agreement on alignments. There was a long argument at the end of which they agreed to disagree. The fishermen talked about Christ and God's role in saving them from the accident. Irini said that He could have spared them the accident altogether. "Sometimes He has to get your attention first," the fisherman told her. Irini was the only one on the bus who didn't attend church at least occasionally. This made it seem as if the accident was for her. Like it was her fault.

While Irini was thinking about this, Walter showed the girls Chi Chi. She was sitting cross-legged in the backseat of a dented green De Soto. She had a regal, disdainful air. She looked at them only out of the sides of her eyes. It was impossible to imagine her bowling. She was more the tea-party type.

Eventually the team limped home to Magrit. This required enormous effort, especially on the part of Carl and the Christian fishermen, but they proved equal to anything. Under Norma's direction, they patched tires and greased axles and hitched and towed. Whatever was needed they gave like Christians.

No one in Magrit knew they had done anything but play a game in Willrest that weekend. The girls knew this, and yet they couldn't help coming home, expecting a welcome, a little fuss, a little hoopla. Instead everyone expressed a faint surprise that they were back so soon. It was in many ways, Irini thought, the story of her life.

Most of the Sweethearts were not planning to be at work on Monday, so when Collins House called to give them the day off, it was a bit redundant. Norma took over for Cindy on the phones. Irini cleaned up, wrapped herself in her old robe, took her father's usual chair—the comfortable one—and told him about their adventures. She wasn't really much of a storyteller, but her father was good with questions. He didn't want to hear about the bus rolling off the road, with Irini trapped inside like a seed in a maraca; he motioned her quickly past that part. But he liked Little Persia. He liked Chi Chi and he liked especially the part about the watercolors painted by the German prisoner of war that now decorated the walls of the Broad and Bonny Supper Club. He went off to Bumps to wait until Norma got off the phones and hear her version.

He would have loved to hear about Walter kissing her, but Irini didn't tell him that part. She didn't really think he could handle it.

Consternation was greater at the Tarken place; the weeping was loud enough to be heard over at the Doyles. "You girls just shouldn't leave Magrit," Mrs. Tarken said to Irini in the yard the next day. Mrs. Tarken was so upset she hadn't put lipstick on, so upset she had gone after her eyebrows with excessive pluck. Without lipstick and eyebrows, her face was unfamiliar, worn away like a stone, smoothly moonlike. It rose over the pea patch at Irini. "I just said to Sissy, you have better things to do than play baseball, young lady. I just said to Sissy, you are off that team. We don't owe the Collinses anything." She was pulling up carrots, shaking them by their throats. The loss of Jimmy was the only thing left on her face.

"Now, now, Mrs. Tarken," said Irini's father. He had come out behind Irini, dressed for work, coffee cup in his hand. He never drank liquor in the morning on a workday. It was a point of pride with him. "No one was hurt. They were all in Norma's hands. You can't find a safer place than that."

"She is off the team," Mrs. Tarken repeated. "She can just as well find a husband right here in Magrit." And, right on cue, here came Thomas Holcrow walking down Brief Street. He was wearing a light blue short-sleeved shirt and khaki pants. He could have been coming to the Mays or the Doyles. Irini held her breath, but sure enough, he turned in at the Tarkens'. Mrs. Tarken disappeared inside, her bare face as smooth as cream.

"Never mind, Irini," Irini's father said. "He was never your type."

"Too gorgeous for the likes of me?" Irini asked, irritated with her father for knowing that she liked Holcrow, just the same as Walter knew. But how? The mere presence of Holcrow had heated the air so hot it singed her from a whole house away, but when had she done anything to betray this to anyone?

"Not nearly gorgeous enough."

Irini went inside so that she would not appear to be waiting when Holcrow came back out. As a result she had no idea how long he stayed. She didn't know that he went straight from the Tarkens' to the Mays', and she wouldn't have ever known it if Tracy hadn't boasted to her about his visit. It made her so upset, the thought of him calling in on every girl on Brief Street with the exception of her, that she told Tracy he had been to see Sissy first. Even though she knew she was setting the reconciliation of Upper and Lower Magrit back by decades.

Her father went to work. She lay on her bed and finished the Agatha Christie. She hated it when the murderer turned out to be a child. Not much scared Irini, but there was something so evil in that. She was surprised that a lady, a real lady, such as Mrs. Christie, would even make up such a thing. She was alone in the house. She glanced around her bedroom, and sure enough, thanks to Mrs. Christie and her demented mind, the dolls had all assumed debauched expressions.

She decided to go outside, but there were ghosts with knives at the falls and shadows in the woods. She walked downtown to the grocery, for a Dixie cup of ice cream. Her father said those Dixie cups were half air, but she thought that might be the half she liked best anyway. "You girls had the adventure," Mr. Moodey told her when she brought the ice cream to the counter, and she said she knew, she'd been there while it happened. "It's a miracle no one was killed," he said, "but then that's our Norma behind the wheel. We thank God for our Norma."

Irini browsed through the magazines. She looked at hair styles, she read snatches of the fiction. A toothpaste ad made her wonder briefly if her teeth were yellowing. Would anyone be enough of a friend to tell her so? Perhaps dandruff was her problem. Perhaps that was why Holcrow was ignoring her. She glanced at her shoulders, widened the glance to make sure Mr. Moodey was not going to come up behind her. She reached for *True Life*. "My Fear of His Love Almost Cost Me My Husband," the cover said. There was a drawing of a woman with a lovely, agonized face. It was just the thing to put murderers who were children completely out of her mind.

The woman had married at just nineteen, just Irini's age, after a brief but sweet courtship. He'd been a pilot in the war, an officer and a perfect gentleman. He had kissed her when he asked her to marry him, kissed her deeply. But he had never tried to tempt her down any other path but purity, no matter how hard this had become for him.

Then the first night of their honeymoon everything changed. He asked her to undress when she came to bed. He said that he liked to see her body when they made love. He said that her body was beautiful. Irini read faster and faster.

He slid the straps of her nightgown down himself when she wouldn't. He lowered his body over hers. She pushed him off. You're my wife, he said. He pulled her to him, kissing her neck, sliding her nightgown away, *licking her breasts,* first one, then the other. Something unbearably pleasurable shot through her body in just that instant before she could refuse.

Then she ordered him to stop. This was unnatural, she told him. What he wanted, she would never do. His blue, blue eyes went cold. He said he would never ask her again. He turned from her in the bed they shared . . ."

"Are you finding what you want?" Mr. Moodey asked her. He was only an aisle away, over in sundries. Irini hastily picked up a copy of *Women at Home,* fumbled through the pages, groping toward a recipe, any recipe. She flipped past Maggie's column straight to tuna casseroles. Mr. Moodey came around the canned goods.

Maggie was calling for a nationwide strike of housewives. That couldn't be. Irini flipped back again. She looked at the column. Stop cooking, Maggie was saying. Stop cleaning. You, quite frankly, don't have the time. It's just us girls talking now, so let's be honest. As I keep telling you, any trained ape can do the dishes. Why are you the only ape in your house?

Life is for the living and you've only got the one time through. Dance on the tables. Dance with the chairs. Order the lobster. If he doesn't appreciate you, leave him on his sorry buttocks and find someone who does. Children and marriage may not have been the right thing for you. Don't let one mistake hold you down. If it feels good, said Maggie, then it's the thing to do.

There it was, the word "buttocks," right there in *Women at Home.*

The shock of it froze Irini into whole minutes of inaction. She had never seen so many un–Maggie-like sentiments in one place at one time. Her first impulse was to hide all the copies of *Women at Home* behind the *Good Housekeeping*'s where no one would ever find them.

She did so, keeping out one copy only, which she bought. She tore out Maggie's column, folded it several times, and put it in her sleeve. She abandoned the rest of the magazine by poking it through the wire in the schoolyard fence. Then she walked as fast as she could to Collins House, ran the usual gauntlet of dogs, got the usual stuff on her shoes, walked past the pissing cupids, through the porch, through the kitchen, and called up the stairs.

"It's Irini Doyle," she called. "Is Mrs. Ada in?"

Walter came out of the parlor. Holcrow came out of the library. Ada came down the stairs. "Walter tells me that Sissy and the May girls spoke to each other on the trip," Ada said. Her voice, her face were full of light. "Come and tell me all about it."

Irini was dreadfully conscious of the two men. A brisk walk had been just what she needed after the grocery store. That and her concern over Maggie had quite calmed her down. But now there were these men. They came to stand with her, one on either side. They stood very close; they loomed beside her, even Walter, who was hardly big enough to loom. They sandwiched her in. She couldn't move her arms without touching one of them. Walter was breathing on her shoulder. She could feel the little puffs of hot air.

"Maybe two words," she told Ada with some difficulty. "And they're already mad at each other again." She didn't mention that this was her fault. The men reached out and slipped the straps of her nightgown over her shoulders. "Even by the end of the trip, they already weren't speaking." Her voice was so uneven she had to cough. Holcrow leaned in and kissed her neck. Walter reached for her breast. "So we were right back where we started," she finished woodenly.

"But that's wonderful," said Ada. "That's all we need. A beginning. We can build on that."

Ada was making far too much of things. She was imagining things that weren't occurring. Fortunately Irini could make that stop. Irini had just the way to bring her down. "It's happened again," she told Ada, handing her the column. "I don't know how. Fanny was screening everything. There's no way this could have gotten through."

Ada unfolded and smoothed out the page. She read it over. She folded it up and gave it back to Irini. "The thing is," she said sadly, "that the really good life is a life of self-sacrifice. That's where lasting happiness lies. This will take people in the absolute wrong direction."

Walter reached over and took it from her. "Olé," he said, reading the page.

Holcrow leaned in close, trying to read it, too. Holcrow smelled of bay leaves and Ivory soap and cigarette smoke. Walter passed the column to him, across Irini. His arm brushed her arm. "Oh for goodness sake," said Irini crossly.

Holcrow straightened away again. "What? What did I do?"

There was no answer to that question. Irini turned back to Ada. "Will Mr. Henry see it?" she asked.

"We'll have to see that he doesn't. That will be my job," said Ada. "Your job is to figure out who is doing this."

"Why?" said Irini.

"And why," Ada agreed. "Where is Maggie going with this? Look for the pattern. Motive and opportunity. Those are the keys."

"I meant, why is this my job," Irini said.

"Not just you, Irini. You young people." Ada shook her head. "Well, I can't do it, can I? I have these problems between Upper and Lower Magrit to settle."

"Dog my cats!" Holcrow was still reading. He seemed to be a very slow reader. "I can't see anyone being swayed by nonsense like this. Imagine a country without mothers. It's not America. It's not what we fought a war for. Let's not get too upset over this garbage."

"Oh, people are gullible," said Ada. "They believe everything they see in print."

"Did you see this part?" Holcrow asked. He pointed to the household tips column.

"Maybe Maggie's reached that time of life," said Walter. He took the page back from Holcrow, looked at it again. "It sounds as if our Maggie has a lot of regrets," he said.

Maggie Collins writes: "Make your toilet bowl into a handsome terrarium! Maybe the problem is not that you have things growing in your toilet, but merely that you have the wrong things growing. With a little planning and a little planting, your toilet bowl can become a restful sanctuary for you and a delightful conversation piece for your guests."

And underneath that was a paragraph entitled "New Uses for Old Pipe Cleaners." Irini really didn't dare read further.

35

Indian Independence Day was almost upon them and Ada had yet to settle on the appropriate way to celebrate. Of course she would have to have a party at Collins House, a big party, the whole town and then some. Miss Schaap had agreed to visit again to see the flowering of the seeds she had sown that long-ago evening around the Collinses' dining-room table. And Ada knew the party would have to be inside. This was a shame. With so many people the house would overheat unbearably, but outdoors would be hot as well, unless it were actually raining. And outside there would be mosquitoes, which people would kill right before Miss Schaap's eyes or else do it secretly and wander around with those telltale bloody smears on their bare arms.

So she knew the day and she knew the location. But what would she serve? They had already had curry once this summer. And what kind of entertainment would she provide? They had done the fireworks thing on the Fourth; it was too much to make Norma do it over again. Ada took the classic etiquette misstep of inviting people to a party she hadn't yet planned and now she was suffering for it.

She asked Claire for menu suggestions, and they spent an entire afternoon huddled over the dining-room table with cookbooks and magazines and notebooks, but neither of them came up with anything that satisfied. The day was to be strictly vegetarian, no dairy even, which quite tied Claire's hands. And Ada wanted something different. Ada wanted something so different they couldn't even begin to imagine it. She told Claire she felt as if it were the first party she had ever given. Every other party, she had said, everything else she had ever done in Magrit, had always been for Mr. Henry. Only this was entirely her own. She was so excited she glittered.

The day grew nearer and nearer and she never called Claire back to finalize the food, but she did have the girls in to sweep and dust. She had her heart set on perfection. The big chandelier, cleaned only months ago, was lowered and cleaned all over again. It took the team: it took Norma on the ladder, Irini and her right arm on the rope. Henry came down the stairs to say hello to everyone and then went right back up. His ascent was painful to watch. He stumbled on the one high step. It was as if he had forgotten it was there.

Ada had the bird-banding nets taken down. They had outlasted their original function and also their aesthetic appeal. They were torn and sagged. Weeks had passed since they had fooled a single bird.

Meanwhile, back in the Kitchen, where Irini was supposed to be conducting her investigations, she was not Miss Marple and had never aspired to be. Fortunately Margo had quite taken over. Without any explicit instructions from Ada or anyone else, Margo began to interview the girls and write everything they said down in a spiral notebook.

"We can handle this latest," Fanny told her. "It was so overboard. Next issue, we announce that it was all a prank. Maybe it could even work for us. The one thing Maggie never had was a sense of humor."

"So, Fanny." Margo noted the suggestion, but was not diverted by it. "You read everything that went to New York and you're ready to swear that this was not among that lot."

It turned out, according to Fanny's recollection, to have been one of those weeks when no one had written a column for Maggie. With Henry benched, there were frequently weeks in which no one wrote her column. They were depending more and more heavily on letters. But since they had just run a column entirely of letters the week before, Fanny herself had collated the results of the thickener research and written them up. She had done this prior to actually finishing the tests. This meant that she had projected the results in a most unscientific way, but she had included a chart in red and blue ink, which was both quantifying and clarifying. Like anything else with numbers, it certainly looked authoritative. You would never have read this chart and thought someone was making it up.

The chart had taken her most of one night. It was a useful sort of chart, the kind you could tear out and keep on your refrigerator.

And then, because there was still space, there were also a number of letters and Maggie's answers. There was the usual spate of girls wanting to be complimented for their good judgment in refusing to have sex with their boyfriends. Maggie was always happy to oblige there.

There was a letter from Milwaukee where a woman had found a sweet potato at her local store with poor late President Roosevelt's profile. She enclosed a picture of the potato, a cigarette holder plunged into its side like a dagger.

There was an interesting letter from a university professor at Brown suggesting that population growth was a bigger threat to mankind than the bomb. He also had sent a chart, and his numbers were considerably bigger than Fanny's.

"I mailed the pickings myself," said Fanny. "And there was nothing in the package about buttocks. Although I myself have seen them on many a sweet potato."

Irini thought that Fanny was taking the whole thing a little casually. Not as if she were guilty herself, but as if she knew who was and didn't want them exposed. If Fanny *did* know, it wouldn't help Margo's investigation at all. Nobody could keep a secret the way Fanny could.

"Who took the package to the post?" asked Margo.

"Who appointed you Erle Stanley Gardner?" Helen asked. "Aren't you as much a suspect as the rest of us?" She stood with one arm around Claire.

"I took the package," said Claire. If Fanny was underplaying everything, Claire was overdoing it. Her face was pinched; her color high and her voice low. "I had letters of my own to mail. I offered to take it."

"Was it ever out of your sight?" Margo asked.

"I met Mrs. Ada downtown. She took it and some of my personal mail to the box for me."

The Sweethearts were young enough, most of them, to think that a wife would never hurt her husband. We, of course, know so much better. But they thought that suspecting Ada was out of the question. So who would have picked the letters out of the box? In Magrit, where the mailman had gone off to war and never come back, Norma Baldish handled the mail. Motive and opportunity, Ada had said. Fanny and Claire and Norma had the second. But which of them had the first?

Norma seemed especially motiveless. What could she have against Maggie? She didn't work in the Kitchen. She liked Mr. Henry, as they all did. She wasn't even Upper Magrit. And tampering with the mail before it was put into the box was merely dishonest. Tampering with it afterward was a federal offense. Surely no one in Magrit could be guilty of a federal offense.

"I'll have to talk to Norma later," Margo said, making a notation in her book.

There was a long silence except for Louis Armstrong on the radio. No one was quite ready to get back to work.

Suddenly Claire began to cry. "I did write a letter. A couple. Not for publication, some of the private ones. I only meant to be kind, but I knew all along that Maggie wouldn't like it."

"Everyone knows you wouldn't hurt anyone," Fanny said sharply. She looked around the Kitchen. She stopped at Margo's face. "Of course we don't suspect Claire, do we? Do we, Margo? Why, I wrote a letter, myself. I wrote that first one about overweight women. I didn't mean any harm, but I guess I gave someone else ideas. I didn't write any of the others." She continued her look around the circle of girls. "Oh come on," she said. "You all knew I wrote that first one."

And it seemed as if they sort of had. They turned to Irini, waited.

"No," she said. "I didn't write that one about martinis. I told you that at the time."

"*I* confessed," said Claire, wiping her eyes.

"*I* confessed," said Fanny.

"But I didn't do it."

"Whenever you're ready," Fanny said. And then she said that she would handle the column for next week, the one in which Maggie announced she had a sense of humor, and they all returned to their sinks. The schedule for the day was omelets and they fell to it with forced enthusiasm. Irini could see quite clearly that they were angry at her. Something new had entered the Kitchen, something like suspicion and maybe even almost fear—anger, at least—and somehow this was Irini's fault. Because it wouldn't be there if Irini had only confessed. That would leave just the final column unaccounted for and surely someone would admit to that column, too, if Irini only stepped forward. The Maggie Collins episodes would turn out to be something they'd done together, something they'd done as a team. Instead of this way, with someone hidden and possibly vengeful.

Irini looked around the Kitchen and she saw Arlys stabbing potatoes, Claire beating eggs, Tracy whipping cream, Fanny pulverizing toasted bread. Helen was chopping onions. Margo was mincing mushrooms. Ruby was shredding cheese. It was the excessive normality of it all that disturbed Irini. Every single one of them deep in their own private mayhem, *just like always.* What did she really know about what any of them might be capable of? Sissy had turned out to be capable of heroism and also of sex, and who would have predicted either of those?

When the girls looked at Irini she imagined it was with resentment. Irini didn't feel like practicing with them today so she began at noon to complain that her headache had returned and by punch-out time was being ordered home to lie on her bed with the curtains drawn. It was a good decision in any case; it was much too hot to play baseball. Irini walked home, and the acorns swelled like beads of sweat along the branches of the trees.

She went home and lay down, just as she'd told everyone in the Kitchen she would. Her arm and shoulders, still stiff from the accident, hurt all over again. Her father had heard about her headache and came in to check. He sat on the side of her bed and rubbed her temples gently and told her that the achievement of independence in India was a large step for all mankind. Mankind just had to be made to recognize it as one.

"I don't think people are nice enough for nonviolence," said Irini. "In their hearts, it's not what they want. They want drama and excitement. They *want* evil, if it comes to that."

"You don't understand yet. Satyagraha is more sophisticated than that. Gandhi knows what people are like." He stopped, as if surprised to find himself arguing with her. "I haven't believed in anything for so long," he said. "I think it scares me a little."

Sometime in the last week he had begun a directed reading course. "It's more active than you realize at first," he said now. "I thought it would just be the same old turn-the-other-cheek stuff, but it's quite confrontational, quite revolutionary." The question that interested him now was whether or not the movement was specifically Indian. Could it be transplanted?

"For what purpose?" said Irini.

He really didn't see how she could ask that, with the bomb hanging like the sword of Damocles over their heads. As far as he could see, it was nonviolence or it was nothing. Darned right he would celebrate it.

"I meant," said Irini, "who do you want to confront?" but he didn't seem to hear her. He went on for some time about the threat of nuclear annihilation, about the desolated cities. "Dust to dust," he said and it wasn't Irini's favorite topic, even when it was just dust and dusting, so she only listened occasionally. Her head had decided to make an honest woman of her. It really was hurting by now.

"You know there won't be liquor served," Irini told him finally.

"There never is at Collins House," he said. "My goodness, do you think I can't get through a single evening without drinking? Do you think I can't have a good time unless I'm lit up like a Tannenbaum?"

Fortunately the question appeared to be rhetorical.

36

The sun came up a murderous red on August 15 and had bleached out by noon. The day was steamy and sticky. Magrit arrived at Collins House dressed to the nines, or at least the eights, which was all Magrit could manage. The dresses were home-made or catalogue. Buying off the rack was a luxury Magrit seldom enjoyed.

Mrs. Tarken was honoring the Indians with a seriously scooped neckline. If she twisted just right you could just see the line that marked the top of her nipple. Magrit tried not to look, but naturally this was hard, especially if you had to wait for her to twist just right in order to not look.

Mr. Baldish was wearing one of those wide, short ties you see in the forties movies. It was a bright indigo, and it was 1947, so no one thought it was wide or short, although everyone thought it rather blue.

Ada herself wore a deep purple sari with a silver band. It was surprising how well it suited her. She drifted down the stairs as grace-ful as if she'd been born in it, as graceful as if it didn't, every once in a while, bare a sizable strip of her stomach. The silver set off her silver hair. Ada had solved her menu problems by deciding to fast. They would all fast. It was new, it was different. It was so Indian.

It was a surprise. Irini had not eaten all morning in anticipation of party food and there must have been many others who had done the same. Without anything to eat, it was hard to find anything to do. You think of eating at a party as something that happens while everything else is going on, you think of it as background noise to the real party. This did not prove to be the case. By early afternoon Irini's stomach had begun to gnaw loudly on itself. She thought it best to keep moving.

It was hot inside, hotter still, out. Henry was seated in the smoking room, slumped but splendid in a bow tie. Claire was on one side of him, Norma the other. Claire was animated and lovely. Perhaps it was because she had cleared her conscience. Or perhaps she had not enjoyed providing the food for every party in Magrit as much as people thought she had. Perhaps she was really relishing the chance to be a guest. She had her hand on Henry's arm and she was telling him a joke. It had fish and cannibals and psychologists in it and really, none of this was like Claire.

Irini interrupted long enough to pay her respects to Mr. Henry and left the smoking room. She went into the parlor. There she saw Holcrow and Tracy talking with their heads bent together slightly. Tracy was facing her. She also looked very pretty. She gave Irini a don't-even-think-of-it look and Irini backed out again. She went to the kitchen where she considered getting herself a glass of juice. She glanced around to see that no one was watching. She put a hand on the refrigerator handle.

Someone knocked. "Hello?" someone said. "Hello?" Irini dropped her hand and turned.

Two blurred figures stood on the outside of the screen door. "Hello?" said the closest. He swung the door open and the vague, screened shape of him came into sharp focus. It was Mike Barr and right behind him a strange young man. Irini thought they were together, but Mike came in and went past with a quick greeting and no introduction. The other man stopped.

"Excuse me," he said. "Excuse me for intruding. I have no invitation. I'm looking for Ruby Redd." His eyes were large, and one of the irises was slightly clouded over. This made it hard to see in. Irini wondered what it was like, looking out.

His hair was curly and dark. He was so tall he had to bend slightly to speak to Irini. "I got off the train in Magrit, but it was like a ghost town," he added. "It gave me the oddest feeling. The conductor told me to try up here. Do you know Ruby?"

"Yes. She's on my team," Irini said.

"I'm her brother." He held out his hand. It was a working man's hand, hard and rough. His hand was older than his face. Irini guessed his age at eighteen, which made no sense. Ruby had said her brothers were all older than she.

Irini took him inside. Suddenly no one could find Ruby. She had been there a moment ago, wearing one of Helen's hand-me-down dresses in a pale tangerine, with some lace at the collar Mrs. Leggett had added to make it seem new. They looked for her in the kitchen and the smoking room and the parlor. They checked the ham radio room upstairs. They called and called.

"We've been looking for her for weeks," her brother said. His name was Horace. "Mama is desperate for her."

"She told us she had her parents' permission," Walter said.

"What kind of parents would give a fourteen-year-old girl permission to gallivant about the country with people they'd never met?" Horace sounded angry. "We may be poor, but we love each other."

"She said she was twenty."

"And you believed that? She'll be fifteen in November." This made her a Scorpio, and secretive by nature, although it's all complicated by rising signs, as you don't need me to remind you, and moon signs, too, but in 1947 in Magrit, who cared? And anyway, if her parents loved her so much, why did they stick her with a name like Ruby Redd?

"How old are you?" Cindy asked him. He didn't have a handsome face, but it was a friendly one, even when angry. Now the anger vanished instantly, like someone switching off a light. He turned to

Cindy, smiling, looked her over. He held out his hand. She nodded down to her sling; it was an excuse and also an explanation, but he ignored it, reached over and took the other hand.

"Old enough." He didn't let go.

With the sudden, unexpected appearance of a new man, the party picked up. It was better than food; it was better than liquor. It was the perfect way to celebrate Indian Independence Day. The muscles in Horace's bare arms were as distinct and defined as Irini's. Cindy, Tracy, and Sissy clustered like grapes about him. Holcrow, Walter, and Mike Barr formed the second tier.

"She's an excellent player," Tracy said. "We're very fond of her. And we've taken good care of her." Except for that time we nearly killed her in a bus accident, Irini thought, but there would be time for that later. Next lifetime later.

"No doubt. Her mother wants her back."

"You must be proud of her," Walter suggested.

"Proud of her? Because she runs away from home to play base-ball?"

"She's really good," said Walter.

"So what? She's a girl. If you people cared about her, I don't think you'd encourage her. And we're tired of doing her chores."

"Is it true there are six more of you?" Cindy asked.

"The six Redd boys. Yes."

"Are they all as good-looking as you are?" This was Fanny, of course, shouldering her way through to stand next to him. No one else would be so bold. No one else could make it work the way Fanny did. No one else could make it sound as if she'd just now made it up.

No one else wouldn't care that her actual boyfriend was there to watch. Fanny had abandonment issues with men. She was afraid that, once encouraged, men would never go away.

Horace was taller but thinner than she, so she looked the bigger as they stood together—Cary Grant and Mae West. Mike Barr took hold of Fanny's elbow. It was a clear statement of possession, but if it was aimed at Fanny she didn't seem to get it and because she didn't, neither did Horace, if it was aimed at him.

314

"I don't know how to answer that question," Horace said. "I guess you'll have to come and see for yourself." A look smoldered between them and because she was so much older than he, it was not an appropriate look. Fanny wet her gorgeous lips. It made Mike Barr swell like a toad, but neither Fanny nor Horace broke eye contact long enough to notice.

"I always wished I had brothers," Cindy said coldly. Sometime back Horace had dropped her hand.

"Isn't it lovely to have men around?" Fanny agreed.

"I'm to stay right here until I find her," Horace said. "I can't go home without her."

Irini felt Walter's hand on her arm. It was not a gesture of possession. It was a request. She turned. He was wearing a shirt and his usual pants. He'd not really dressed for the party. His feelings concerning Ada had always been a bit complicated. So he looked the way he always did, blondish and pinkish and regular. Come with me, he was asking, through pressure and gesture. She followed him to the dining room.

"Don't worry," Irini said. "She won't leave without saying good-bye to you. Your under-age sweetheart."

"Capital S? Or little s?" asked Walter.

"What?"

"My Sweetheart? Or my sweetheart?"

"Both," said Irini, who had no idea what he was saying. "You were in love with her."

"You wish. Golly gee," said Walter. "I knew she was younger than twenty. I never dreamed she was fourteen. But, hey, Irini. Ruby'll turn up. This isn't about that. You know how worried I've been about Gramps?"

"Yes."

"I've been thinking and thinking what I could do. I had a long talk with him after our trip. I told him about the ape. Nothing. No reaction. An ape who bowls right there for the picking."

"Yes?"

"And then I knew. He's never going to be better until he swims

Upper Magrit." Walter stood with his arms folded, waiting for her response.

Irini thought it a surprising idea. "He doesn't believe he can make it anymore," she pointed out. "And I'm not sure he's wrong. You'll never talk him into it."

"He would do it for Ada. To win her back from Mr. Gandhi."

Irini thought it an unlikely idea. "She doesn't want it."

"That's why it has to be a surprise. She can't know until it's over. 'Guess what I did for Indian Independence Day, darling,' he can say over dinner. 'Guess what I did for you.'"

Irini thought it a very bad idea. "He might not make it."

"He made it every other year. Just last year he made it."

Irini looked at Walter, with his straight earnest hair and his pink scrubbed face and his eye, still richly hued but fainter, like a watercolor, and thought how he always just drove her nuts. In fact, she was a bit insulted. "You've already talked him into it, haven't you? I hate it when people ask me for advice and they've already made up their minds and it doesn't really matter what I think. Why ask? Go away and do whatever it is you're going to do. I'm looking for Ruby."

She left with as much passionate dignity as she could put into the mere act of walking out a door.

Which was a lot. I saw it many times in later years and I can promise you it was good. It's one of those things I miss. Isn't that a surprise?

I'm not so bad at it myself. It's worth practicing till you get it. It confers a Darwinian advantage.

Irini expanded the search to the yard. The sun was keeping the mosquitoes down. She tried the porch and out by the fish pond. The clouds were stationary overhead but rippled below, reflected in the smoky water. Ada had stocked the pond for the party. Brilliant orange fish, the little ones that came in Chinese-food containers, flickered beneath the lily pads. The pond had to be restocked from time to time, since the dogs apparently drank up the originals. Everyone did them the courtesy of assuming this was unintentional.

No one else in Magrit had a fishpond like that. It was shaped like a cereal bowl, Mr. Henry had always said, and if that's what it was meant to be, why was there a stone cupid peeing into it?

No one else had a yard with statuary and sundials. No one else had a yard this size unless they farmed it. Ruby could be anywhere. Ruby could easily be among the trees. Irini stepped through the gate and called to her.

She thought she saw something bright up ahead, a piece of skirt in a tangerine color like the one Ruby had been wearing. She called again, ran in that direction. The wind was beginning to rise, a hot wind moving sluggishly through the heavy air. Overhead, the clouds began to race, promising shade, but somewhere else. Irini stopped, searched among the tree trunks for just that bit of color. She left the path and made straight for the road.

She heard a car, but by the time she had come out of the trees it was already past her. She could still see it, though. It was Walter's car and there were three men inside. Walter, Mr. Henry, and Holcrow, she thought. On their way to the mill parking lot, then under the limestone rainbow, and up to Upper Magrit. The end of the road shimmered in the distance. It was set in fairyland. Irini was at the wrong end, in the heat and the grit of Magrit.

She stood and watched the dust from their tires settle again, and because of the wind it didn't ever quite. Dust devils continued to spin down the sides of the road. Dust to dust to dust to dust . . . She walked after the car. She walked faster; she began to run.

Long before she reached the mill parking lot she was convinced Henry was going to die. And it wasn't just him. The guilt of it would take Walter with him. And maybe her, too, because she could have stopped it. If she had thought more about the danger to Mr. Henry and less about her own feelings, there were so many things she could have done. She could have said no forcefully. She could have told Mrs. Ada on them all. She could have cried. She could have taken Walter upstairs to the ham radio room, and kissed him so hard he would have forgotten he ever had a grandfather.

She could have gone back and taken a car. By the time she thought of this it was too late. She was going to be too late. She had a cramp in her side and couldn't get a decent breath. She was covered with sweat; it pooled and poured off her.

She had a vision as she ran, but it was filled with large, black, empty spaces brought on by the heat. The vision was of Mr. Henry stripping out of his party clothes, unknotting his bow tie, and standing in his bathing suit, with his sad little frog body—sticks of legs, round white Buddha belly. She could imagine it quite clearly, except for those dark spaces. He would do a few knee bends. He would talk to Walter and Holcrow in a serious way about the conditions, as if these things could be quantified, and once quantified, understood, and once understood, controlled. He would defer to Walter's expertise. Walter was the wave forecaster.

He would wade out. Walter would give him last-minute instructions, which he wouldn't hear over the noise of the Falls and the constant ringing in his ears, but they wouldn't be important anyway. He would take a deep breath, so that his cheeks puffed.

She had to stop. The black spaces were spreading over the whole picture. She stood and rubbed the sweat out of her eyes. She was breathing again, but it seemed to have no oxygen content. Her face and her neck and back were drenched. By now Mr. Henry might be just short of halfway across and losing momentum. His strokes would cease to move him forward and between each stroke he would drift downstream. He was trying to correct this by angling his body more and more against the current. He was pulling his head too far out to breathe. The stroke had a panicky look to it. He would float downstream and then crawl back, float and crawl, float and crawl. Every time he would lose a little more ground.

They should have strung the rope. Irini had said they should have done this, said it back on the Fourth of July. And then never followed through. Henry would surface one last time, his eyes flickering white and rolling like a frightened horse's.

By now he was so far out; it was the distance between centerfield and home and then considerably more. If she were there, she could have thrown him the rope. It would have been the throw of her life. Walter couldn't do it. Holcrow couldn't do it. No one else in Magrit, no one but Irini Doyle, the human grenade launcher, could make this throw.

Irini had begun to run again. She made it to the mill parking lot. She saw Walter's car, an inert lump shaped like a large toaster, in the mill drive. She started the climb. Somewhere above her Henry was floating, spinning in the current, flailing, flying. His legs were too heavy to kick now. His own legs were sinking him. Walter was trying to reach him.

She ran through the cold air in back of the falls, over the dim shelf of the rock. It cooled the sweat on her face.

Then there was a moment when she thought there was something in the water. In her peripheral vision she saw something large and colorful plummet over the falls. Irini screamed, but no one would hear it, not with the din of the water. She ran the rest of the way through, came out, and climbed back out into the heat to where she could look down.

She was still dizzy. Her eyes stung and wouldn't work. There was nothing in the pool beneath her. Nothing moving downstream. She wasted valuable moments, looking, waiting for something to surface, trying to focus, praying as earnestly and naturally as if she believed in prayer. Maybe prayer wasn't a matter of belief after all. Maybe it was instinct.

Then she raised her eyes to the falls themselves. There, hovering inside the water, she could just make out the liquid figure of a woman. She wore an apron tied in the back with a bow, like Maggie, but was otherwise naked. Her breasts, behind the striped bib, were large and maternal. She gazed upward, her arms curved out beyond her breasts, the way you would catch a large ball, the way you would hold a small child. She wavered there in the water, all motherly anticipation.

It calmed Irini down, even as it frightened her. Irini was not too late, not yet anyway, because there Maggie was, still waiting for her son to come to her. Expecting him. It was a race now, between Irini and Maggie Collins, herself.

Irini ran on. She made the top of the falls at last. She stood, panting, up by Nedd's tower, dizzy from sweat and fright.

There was no more need to hurry. Henry lay in the cattails of the bank, coughing up water. Walter lay beside Henry, shivering uncontrollably. His blond hair was dark with water. He was making an awful face. Holcrow was wet as well. All three men were in their underwear.

"What happened?" Irini called. Her relief was vivid. It brightened the colors of the scene and sharpened the edges. She could see the little teeth on the leaves on the trees above Henry's head. Someone else had saved him. She was embarrassed to feel just a touch of disappointment. She put it quickly aside.

"He didn't make it," Holcrow told her. "Walter paced him and then had to pull him out. I think he nearly sank Walter. I had to go in, too. Scared us all."

Irini walked down the bank. Henry patted Walter's arm and coughed. "It's all right," Henry said when he could speak again. He was remarkably chipper. His voice bounced from word to word. "I can hear again. Isn't that the most remarkable thing?" He cupped a hand beneath one large ear, tapping the water out. The water filled his palm, spilled over the sides. "I'm perfectly all right, Walter. Stop shaking, boy. I'm perfect. Say something to me."

Walter raised his ghastly eyes and looked at his grandfather. "I'm sorry," he said. "It was a stupid idea."

"Heard it. Heard every bit of it. I'm wonderful," Henry insisted. All the little hairs stood out on his pale, skinny chest. "Don't you see?" He coughed again. "The thing is, I haven't eaten a bowl of Sweetwheats since the Fourth of July. You didn't know that. But this is a very gratifying result. Nothing proven yet, of course, we'll have to do more tests. But this is a gratifyingly suggestive beginning. Help me up."

He held out his hands to Walter. Walter raised him. The two men stood together for a moment, holding each other tightly and it was

Henry who provided the support. "There are birds in the trees!" he shouted, from behind Walter's shoulder, so loudly that the birdsong he was hearing stopped suddenly and then started again.

They stayed at Upper Magrit for some little time and then they went back to the party. The men had dressed, with Irini averting her eyes, as if she hadn't already seen them all. She could just as well have looked. There was nothing very thrilling about men in their underwear. She hoped they didn't think otherwise.

They walked single file behind the falls without incident. Irini was careful to be in the middle. She couldn't help but feel that the air was extra chilled. "It's deafening in here," Henry shouted happily, and it was. Someone could come right up behind you with a serrated knife and you would never hear a thing.

They got into Walter's car. Back at Collins House Ruby had not yet been found, but Horace and Mike Barr had exchanged blows. No permanent damage had been done unless you counted Mike Barr asking Fanny to marry him right in front of everyone and her saying yes. Unless Irini was much mistaken, neither of them looked very happy about it. Fanny's large Atomic Pin spat sparks from her shoulder.

Horace had a split lip and a mess of female sympathy about him. "You missed everything," Tracy told Irini coldly. She looked from Irini to Holcrow. "So did you. Where have you been?" she asked and he bent over to tell her.

It was a secret, he said. Until Mrs. Ada was informed. She must come in very close to hear. Tracy was softening before Irini's eyes.

When Ada was included, she did not take the news well. In deference to Walter's feelings, the story Henry told was stripped of all drama. It was more of a parable; its focal point was the moment Henry could hear again. Even abstracted this way, it was enough to make Ada's eyes pop out like a freshly caught fish.

"Why don't you just leave Upper Magrit alone?" Claire asked when Henry had finished. She was flushed and tearful. Loving Mr.

Henry as she did, and being Upper Magrit as she was, put her so often in an uncomfortable place. Now she was clustered with the Upper Magrit faction. They whispered together.

"That's it," said Ada. "That is absolutely it. We will be draining Upper Magrit this winter. We'll raise it from the dead. We'll put everything back the way it was."

"Except the Nadeaus," said Claire as if they were a family she'd actually met, people she actually missed.

"What's Upper Magrit?" asked Horace.

"A memory," said Sissy. The Upper Magrit faction whirled to look at her and then away again.

"I don't think that's possible, my love." Henry's voice was mild. "You can't undo dynamite. You can't unring a bell, you can't implode an explosion. Anyway, I'll need to swim it again after Sweetwheats have been restored to my diet. Today's results will mean nothing without that."

"Until Upper Magrit is raised, I will continue to fast. There will be no Sweetwheats in *my* diet. Nor anything else." Ada turned, baring a white band of midriff briefly, and went upstairs. The party, it seemed, was over.

On the way home, Irini told her father about seeing Maggie Collins in the water of the falls. Her father took some time responding. He didn't like it. Irini knew him. He was trying to find some way back to the point in his life before he had heard this.

"It seems more like something I would see," he said first. "The things I've seen after a good night at Bumps!" He spent a moment lost in memory.

"Maybe it was dust that you saw. Dust does some strange things. Makes sunsets, makes clouds. The sky wouldn't be blue without dust. You think of that next time you're dusting.

"Of course, you'd just run all that way," he tried next. "On such a hot day. On an empty stomach. I'm sure you were seriously dehydrated. Dangerously dehydrated. These things are bound to happen."

He twisted the steering wheel, putting them safely back on Brief

Street. Since the bus accident, Irini had felt a little differently about Brief Street. It was home. It was where she belonged. The car slipped beneath the shadows of the trees like a fish through the weeds. Her father shook his lean and feral face. "Fistfights, and engagements, and missing persons, and ghosts."

Tweed came off the porch to meet them. Her toenails scraped the paint of the door before they'd even come to a stop. Irini opened the door and Tweed put her head in Irini's lap. She looked up at Irini. She was the best dog in the whole world.

"You've got to expect these sorts of things will happen when you give a party and you don't serve drinks," Irini's father said.

37

The last thing the Sweethearts did together as a team was to lower the big chandelier at Collins House before the party. They had played their last game and the rest had to be canceled. Ruby couldn't be found. Cindy's arm might take six weeks to heal; the season would be over. The bus had limped home to Magrit but needed expensive repairs, many of them cosmetic. This didn't mean they weren't necessary. What kind of an advertisement for Sweetwheats would it be, Claire pointed out, if the Sweethearts arrived in a rusted, dented bus?

And now that Fanny was engaged, she had less enthusiasm for her chaperoning duties. "It's not as much fun as it was. I'm turning my attentions to the other kind of diamond," she said. Helen, too, had become engaged soon after Fanny.

Also there were Maggie's tirades. Hard to keep that old team feeling when the person throwing you the ball and pretending to be so nice and ordinary was really no such thing.

At first, because Irini didn't know who was responsible, she had tried to suspect no one. Now she suspected them all. And they all had to suspect her—in fact, they suspected her strongly, all but one of them anyway. She didn't have a friendship untouched by Maggie's outbursts.

That was the cruelest part, not knowing who. Mike Barr picked up on the tension. "Girls don't really have team spirit," he said. "That's why they're not great athletes. They're not really team players."

"As if we don't cook together every day of our lives," Fanny told the girls in the Kitchen. She was taking exception to everything Mike said these days. She was planning her wedding.

The yellow greens of spring had become the gray greens of late summer. Summers passed so quickly in Magrit, and there was a sense of more things coming to an end than just the season. It was horrid. "There'll be next year," Arlys told Irini, who was strangely tearful.

She retired to her bedroom, where she progressed from tears to great gulping sobs, crying in a way she hadn't cried since she was twelve. And it was all for baseball. There wouldn't be a next year, and Irini knew it. She would never get over her batting slump; it would be permanent. Mr. Henry was already off searching for Chi Chi, the bowling ape, and once he found her he would have no more need for the baseball-playing girls.

Back in Magrit, one early evening shortly after the party, when Irini should have been at practice, except there was no more practice, ever, Irini's father knocked on her bedroom door.

"Get your mitt," he told her. "My own chick. My little chickadee. Let's go out back for some pop-ups." It was almost dark, late to be beginning a game. He must have something that just couldn't wait.

They often played catch, but they hadn't played pop-ups for years. Irini had a dreadful, dizzy feeling. She remembered being twelve again, the great shock sex had been to her. First her period and then sex, all casually conveyed to her while the ball was high in the air. But the games had gotten fewer and fewer and she had let herself imagine she pretty much knew it all.

Her father had clearly fortified himself with drink for this occasion. Was it possible there was something else now, something worse than sex, some new surprise so utterly appalling she had never had a clue? Something that couldn't even be hinted at until she was at least nineteen?

"Move in," her father said. "I'm going to throw them really high." The ball disappeared into the branches of the apple tree and came back down with several apples. It was a trick throw. Still, Irini had great powers of concentration; Irini caught it and an apple as well. "How would you like to go to college?" her father asked. "Get a teaching credential or something. You're a smart girl. You don't want to stay in Magrit your whole life, do you? It's not what I want for you."

"How are we going to pay for that?" Irini asked.

"I thought we could sell the house," her father said. "You'd have to get a place anyway, of course, on campus. Don't move to the right. Catch it across your body."

"Throw me a really high one. Where will *you* live?"

"There's a couple of rooms above Bumps. The ones Holcrow's been in. He's got to move on eventually and I think they could make quite a comfortable apartment."

"You're going to live above the bar? I'm not sure that's such a good idea. Have the Baldishes agreed to this?"

"Yes. Yes, they have."

"I don't like to think of you living by yourself above a bar."

"Mmm-hmm. It's still Magrit, Irini. You conjure up a picture of the Bowery. *Don't* move like that. Practice catching it across your body."

"Why? Why should I practice? When am I ever going to play baseball again?"

"Don't be sad, Irini. It's the one thing in the world I can't bear. Think about going to college. All the things you'll learn. All the people you'll meet. I really think it's the right move for us now."

"Anyway, we'd have two rents then. Would we really be any better off?"

"Actually I wouldn't be paying rent."

"The Baldishes are letting you live above Bumps for free?"

"Yep. Give me a nice high one back. That's my girl."

"And who would buy our house? People aren't streaming into Magrit."

"I rather think Helen might. Her and her beau. Mr. Henry has offered him a job in sales. He'll qualify for a V.A. loan plus his disability. I really think we could do it."

"Have you talked to Helen about this already?"

"Mmm-hmm."

"I just don't think I can let you do this. It's so awfully sweet of you, Dad, but I can't accept. The house is all we have. And you'll be lonely all by yourself. What if you got sick and I had a job in some other town and I couldn't come and take care of you?"

"I guess my wife would have to take care of me. Oh, unlucky. You took your eye off the ball." The game came to a stop. Her father's voice was casual, but his face was as white as an egg. "The thing is. The thing is, my love. My own Irini. My only, darlingest child." Irini's father began to play catch with himself. Little tiny pop-ups, like juggling. He was just drunk enough to make it exciting. "I rather thought of asking Norma to marry me. Only if it's all right with you."

Norma Baldish. Norma Baldish! "Have you asked her already?"

"I may have hinted at it."

"Did she hint at her answer?"

"She said yes."

"So that stuff about it being all right with me, that's just for form. Really I can't do a thing about it. You know how I hate it when people ask me for my advice, but it's really already done."

"Irini, you're the love of my life. If you say no, then I'll instantly become the sort of despicable heel who makes promises to a woman and then breaks them." He caught the ball and looked at her. In some lights, from some angles, he was a handsome man. His face was thin and toothy and hairy, but it was quite a masculine look. He wore it well, except when drunkenness slackened the whole facade—except for that eighty percent of the time.

He was much better-looking than Norma Baldish. Of course, he was considerably older. Much, much older. Horribly older. Norma was not all that much older than Irini. Irini hated this part.

"Do you love her?"

"The woman can fix a car, snowplow a street, pump a septic tank, bring a deer down with a single shot, and make a martini so dry it'll suck your heart right out through your throat. Of course I love her. Good golly, Irini. Who wouldn't? I'm the luckiest man in the world."

Norma Baldish was also a primary suspect in the Maggie Collins case. A suspect with no possible motivations, so if she was responsible for Maggie's tantrums, then she was probably mad as a hare. A mad, capable, sharp-shooting hare.

"Of course, you're surprised," her father said. "I know, I know. I told you once that true love was the worst thing that could happen to a man. When it hits you, I said, you go home and have a few stiff drinks. Have more than a few. In the morning, when you wake and you feel that sick, slugged-in-the-stomach feeling, at least there'll be some confusion as to the cause. I remember saying that."

He had never said this to Irini in her whole life. Irini held out her mitt, so that he threw her the ball. His eyes were on her. They were standing close enough together that she could see his inky, pleading pupils. "I'm so happy, my love."

She forced herself to smile at him. "Then that's all right," she said. "Then that's exactly what we'll do."

38

Ada only fasted for a day or so. "Stewing in her own juices," Irini's father called it. He went to see her. According to his reading of Gandhi, blackmail of this sort was a gross misuse of satyagraha. They compared texts until she admitted it.

She began instead to call on the Mays and the Tarkens at tiresome intervals, all in the pursuit of truth, to meet weekly at Collins House with the rest of the satyagrahis. Irini's father often joined her at one of the next-door sessions. Norma Baldish and Mr. Baldish began to attend. Then the Leggetts, who as Quakers were naturals at this stuff.

Soon they had quite a little study group. They read Gandhi and they read about Gandhi. Together they began to dislike Churchill, first Irini's father, and then Norma, and then the rest. It was a hard step to take. The rest of Magrit strongly disapproved.

Irini's father began to read Tagore. He just couldn't help himself. In the midst of a group of rebels he was forced to be rebellious.

And they followed events in India. This was extremely depressing. India was awash in blood. The desire to inflict pain was still greater than the willingness to endure it. Somehow Gandhi had to tip the balance. Ada and Irini's father fretted because the news came to Magrit so slowly and in such little detail.

If only Gandhi could see the progress being made in Magrit. One day Cindy May attended a session held at Collins House. She and the Leggetts were Upper Magrit, of course. The Baldishes, Lower. They all sat at the same table together and admired the same man.

It was the beginning Ada had hoped for, and even Fanny May's relentless opposition couldn't spoil it for her. Fanny made it a rule in the Kitchen that anyone who mentioned Gandhi had to put a penny in the blue pig. "Don't ever mix politics and baking. All you'll get is bread that won't rise," she said to the girls in the Kitchen.

The blue pig had been retired from its original function as Maggie's piggy bank. Henry emptied it out one day—there was more than a dollar there—and bought Ada some potted chrysanthemums.

Maggie had never existed. She was a fictional construct and everyone was free to say so. This was because of Maggie's last column. It came only one week after Indian Independence. During that week, Fanny had applied herself, at the expense of her wedding plans, to the delicate job of suggesting that the previous column, the one telling you to leave your husband on his sorry buttocks and plant a victory garden in your toilet, had been a joke. Maggie Collins, she tried to suggest, had always had her larkish, whimsical side, even if no one had ever seen it before.

Fanny had rewritten the column many times, trying to get it just right. She read it to the whole Kitchen for criticism and advice. Then she sent it off to New York. No one touched the mail except for her, putting it into the mailbox, and Norma, taking it out. But the following appeared in *Women at Home* under Maggie's usual softly smiling portrait instead.

> Girls!
> A woman's life is bounded on three sides by three
> constraints. We may think of these constraints as the
> three R's: Religion, Reputation, and Romance.

Under Religion we include all those considerations a woman makes to lead a moral, upright life. Although they may come from the external agency of a church or synagogue, we here make a distinction between them and Reputation, which is entirely external. By Religion, we mean the little voice inside that says, "You mustn't do that." By Reputation, we mean instead the voice that says, "What will people think of you if you do that?"

Romance is perhaps the most potent of the three R's. In Romance we include the compromises you make and continue to make in order to capture the heart of a man, the sacrifices you make for husband and children. You think you want Romance, you have been made to think you want it, but it is, in fact, merely a tasty sauce poured over an unappetizing dish.

Taken altogether the three R's form the powerful prison in which most women find themselves trapped.

But it takes four walls to make a prison. Flee through the open space with only the clothes on your back. What you need most, after food and sleep, is silence and time. You will not find these in your little house with the white picket fence and the screaming children and the glowering husband. Live in the woods, eat like the birds. Wear your feather dusters as hats; make hammocks of your aprons. Warm yourself at the primitive fires. Be nameless.

Life is a smorgasbord. Take many lovers. You will be surprised how many people are edible if you prepare them properly.

The ad on the facing page was for tooth polish. The original for the column, recovered from New York and examined, proved to have been typed on the mill typewriter.

✿ ✿ ✿

Somewhere in Northern California in the fall of 1947, a small sect of menopausal women abandoned their families for the redwoods, where they built small huts and held moonlight dances. It was 1947, but it was still California. These women called themselves the Harpies, picking the name quickly before anyone else could bestow it on them. They favored clothes with feathers.

They supported themselves first by making the drip candles you see in restaurants, and later by growing and selling marijuana; they had special contracts with the Mob regarding both products. Every once in a while they showed up at bake-offs, dressed in gorilla suits. You yourself must have a vague memory of these women. They were an intermittent embarrassment to breakfast cereals in general until the sixties, when the strident noise of the general culture swelled to drown out their shrill eccentric voices.

Otherwise the response to Maggie's column was characterized by the three D's, Disdain, Disapproval, and Disappointment. It was an advertising disaster. There was too much damage this time; it could not be repaired. The only possible response was triage, tragic in 1947, though a concept we seem more willing to embrace now. Margaret Mill was forced to distance itself from Maggie Collins, and just before the fifties, just before that time when her household prowess might have let her rule the world.

It was, the regulars at Bumps decided over beers, the final revenge of Upper Magrit on Henry Collins, although none of them knew how Madame Nadeau had brought it about.

Maggie's portrait was quietly removed. Her column space was given over entirely to recipes and beauty tips, all published by the editors of *Women at Home* without attribution. The very name Margaret Mill had to be changed. I won't tell you what it was changed to, but you would recognize it, if I did. You might have seen it this very morning on your very own breakfast table. You might still have some of its dangerous flakes dissolving in your blood stream, into your very bones. Are you discontented, vaguely nostalgic for times you never had? Well, all right then. It's in the flake.

All evidence had to be destroyed, and this included little innocent Anna Peal. *Wheat Theater* was too closely tied in the public mind to Maggie Collins. One day Anna was wandering through the snows of her island paradise, on her sweet way back to hearth and home. The next, she had been replaced by three cats who could speak among themselves, though not to humans, and solved mysteries. Siamese cats, but that goes without saying.

Little Anna was left permanently out in the cold. "I try to think of her in Shangri-la," my mother told me once. "I try to think of her happy."

Irini had not told anyone else in Magrit that she had seen Maggie on Indian Independence Day. But there were other sightings, sightings that went on for years. Maggie survived her fictional death as a rumor, a bogeywoman that Magrit parents threatened their children with if they didn't clean their rooms and clean their plates. "Maggie Collins will get you," Magrit parents said and it never failed to convince.

Henry managed. He persevered. He found Chi Chi and brought her back to be the new spokeswoman for the new Sweetwheats, whose name was changed to the one I won't tell you. It turned out she didn't bowl after all. There had been some communications snafu, just as Fanny had predicted, and Henry had already gone to all the trouble and expense of having Norma build her a lane to practice on at Collins House. What she did was bow. It was well done: she put one hand in front of her waist and one behind and bounced. It was cute as could be, but it was over so fast.

She never could be taught to bowl. Henry had a special ball made with very large finger holes. She used to hide her Sweetwheats in them and pretend she'd eaten them. She was all charm and guile and big brown eyes.

He was quite heartsick about Maggie, and all the apes in the world couldn't make it up to him. But he was one of those old-fashioned self-made men, and not like today's breed. He had never asked for a life without setbacks and he would not have enjoyed one. Maggie had betrayed him and he left her behind and he never spoke her name aloud again.

The leaves began to turn. Irini met Henry one day in August, wandering up by Upper Magrit. "Look at this, Irini," he said. He held out a yellow aspen leaf and a red maple. "The yellow is caused by xanthophyll, same as egg yolks. The red is sugar." He shook his head. "There's food everywhere I go," he said, with anguish. "Makes it hard to forget."

He gave a toast at the wedding of Irini's father and Norma Baldish. It had been a long time since there was a wedding in Magrit, so they pulled out all the stops. It was an evening affair, very formal. Somewhere in the sky above, Cassiopeia whirled about in her chair and she was beautiful, beautiful whether Irini could see her or not.

The bride wore a white veil, in a pattern that spiraled out like Queen Anne's lace. Irini was a bridesmaid in powder blue, although really, she thought, she ought to be giving him away. She thought she was entitled to this. They took over Bumps for the reception, removing the tables for dancing, and there was a wedding punch with champagne and orange juice and sherbet that Maggie had once concocted during her happier days.

"It has been a summer," Henry said, incontrovertibly. He held his glass high. He didn't drink, but he pretended to for the sake of the toast.

Not everyone was listening. He tapped his glass and began again. "Quite a summer for us here in Magrit. And somewhere in the midst of it all, these two kids found the time to fall in love. Let it be a lesson to the rest of us. There's always time for love."

Magrit drank to that. Thomas Holcrow came to stand at Irini's side. She had never seen him in a tux. Words failed her. Her lungs filled with the smoke of his cigarette. She breathed in deep. She felt that same shuddering inside. "I'm leaving Magrit," he said. "Hitting the road. I don't expect I'll be back, but you never know."

Now she couldn't breathe at all. "I'm leaving, too. I'm going to college." Was the tone casual enough? Apparently not. Holcrow took her hand. Days later she would still feel the touch of it.

"That's peachy. I never wanted to hurt you, Irini," Holcrow said. "I really hope things work out for you. I always thought you were swell."

"Did you get what you wanted here in Magrit? Your research? You're not leaving just because Dad and Norma want your room?"

"No, I'm done here. And if we do meet again, I hope you'll forgive me. I would always want to think of you as a friend." He was still holding her hand. He dropped it, touched her cheek.

Then he made a graceful exit, a Hollywood exit. He stopped briefly beside Arlys, Margo, and Cindy. He spoke to them, leaning in close. He took their hands, one after the other, and kissed them, even Cindy's, which had to be removed from its sling first. Irini watched his backs in the daisy mirror above the bar. It was the very same place she had first seen him. Irini's eyes filled with tears.

And yet, that speech he'd just made. It was a little presumptuous. How could he possibly know that she was feeling all the things that she was feeling? Why should he apologize when he'd never distinguished her by any particular attention? How dare he think she cared for him? The whole thing made her feel distressingly naked. Walter didn't help. "There goes the man of your dreams," Walter said. He was in a tux as well, but who cared?

"Thomas Holcrow is nothing to me." Irini had the usual tone she adopted with Walter. Starchy.

"Then come and dance." Mrs. Gilbertsen was playing the piano. It was not dance music, but all Mrs. Gilbertsen's selections had a steady tempo. Walter put his arms around her.

"No, no," said Irini's father, taking her out of them again. "This dance is with me."

His first whirl was so extravagant he nearly lost her. Irini had worried that the whole improbable marriage scheme was something he had cooked up just to get her out of Magrit. But tonight she was believing in it. Tonight he was clearly a happy man.

He looked across the room to where Norma was dancing with her own father. "Isn't she a beautiful woman?" he asked his daughter, and fortunately, the question was rhetorical. Norma was a woman with the shape of a bear. Irini's father was a man with the face of a wolf. Irini could see how this could be a good match. She thought that now that Norma was her mother, maybe she could offer a little advice about lipsticks and blushes.

There was, of course, a shortage of men at the wedding. Her father went to dance with Claire and Irini danced with Margo. Margo was wearing calico. Her hair was down about her shoulders, thick as amber, full of lights and colors. Then she danced with Walter while Margo and Arlys danced. Behind them, Irini could see her father dancing with Sissy now. No one had told Sissy yet that Holcrow was leaving, or she would not be keeping time. But Tracy knew. Irini had caught a petaled glimpse of her reflection and it was enough. She was rushing from the room. She had looked so pretty, had dressed so carefully for the wedding. She had planned on catching the bouquet.

And then Irini had to go back to Brief Street and spend the night alone. She couldn't ever remember having done that before. Tweed didn't like it either. She paced and whined and kept Irini up. Irini tried to keep her thoughts on the new life she would be starting. There would be so many boys at college. She had never liked the old life so well that she should cry about it.

39

In September, Gandhi stopped the riots in Calcutta by fasting. It was a triumph for nonviolence. Irini's father phoned to tell her about it. They were rioting riotously in the streets in Magrit, he said. Or anyway, he was.

My mother told me that when I was born, he wanted me named Ahimsa. She refused, even when he threatened to fast, or at least go on an all-liquid diet, and a good thing she did, says I. Let's not ask ourselves what kind of story I might be telling now if I'd gone through the fifties named Ahimsa. But it shows the level of my grandfather's commitment.

Irini had gone downstate to college. There was no baseball team for her, but there was a good program in education and she was studying to become a nursery school teacher. She didn't get back to Magrit often. At first it was because she didn't fancy sleeping with her father and Norma in the two little rooms above Bumps. Someday they would have the whole Baldish place and a bedroom for her to come home to. But not for years, and Irini didn't want to consider her father's situation. It wasn't romantic, it was ridiculous for him to be living in a cramped little place as if he were a young married man just starting out. Of course he had done it for her. And for love. And maybe to be close to the spigots.

So when Sissy came on the train one day that next winter to visit, Irini was unexpectedly happy to see her. They tramped around the campus together, snow caking in the crevices of their boots, the shape of each snowy flake distinct and intricate against the black of Sissy's hair. They went into the student union for hot chocolate. "I'm so starved for news from home," she told Sissy. Home. Dear old Magrit. And she heard how Helen was expecting a baby, and that all Magrit was knitting booties. It had been so long since Dr. Gilbertsen had delivered a baby, he was telling everyone he might have forgotten how.

The Fanny May–Mike Barr wedding was on again. "Not that I'm invited either way," said Sissy. Cindy May was seeing Horace Redd, which made Tracy the only May girl without a beau, and pretty darned cranky, too. There were rumors that Ruby had shown up at the end of the summer to try out for the Belles. When the Redds heard, Horace went straight to Racine to fetch her, but she'd fled again. She'd played two games though. One of them was a no-hitter.

"At least that's what Cindy says," said Sissy. Which is how Irini knew that Upper and Lower Magrit were beginning to talk.

Claire had been hired, with Mrs. Ada's recommendation, as cook to a wealthy family from Chicago who traveled all over Europe. This family was having an enormous party, an opera-night party, sometime in May. It was going to be *Carmen,* and they had sent Claire to France to learn Spanish cooking. Just for the party! They were paying for everything and Claire was seeing the world. Irini and Sissy drank their hot chocolate and tried to imagine Claire in Paris. "Le chapeau de ma tante," they said, by way of a toast. "La plume de mon père."

The student union was becoming too hot. Irini took off another layer of clothing. She had plenty left. "I owe you an apology," she said finally, awkwardly, still struggling out of her sleeves. It should have been said in Magrit, it should have been said weeks ago, but it had to be said.

"Oh, goodness, Irini. I got over that years ago."

Possibly Sissy was thinking of the storm at Glen Annie Creek. Or something else. Sissy and Irini had known each other too long not to have behaved offensively on multiple occasions.

Irini didn't want to stop and think of how many other things she should be apologizing for; she would never finish. "I didn't believe you when you said you saw Maggie up by the Falls that time. I thought you were making it up, just to get Thomas Holcrow's attention. But then I saw her, too. On Indian Independence Day. Right in the water. I never told anyone."

Sissy put her hands into the steam over her cocoa. Her fingers were red and rough just as if she worked for a living. Her large eyes blinked at Irini slowly. Then she looked away from Irini and she didn't look back. "No, you had it right. I *was* lying." Her voice was hoarse and whispery. "I *was* trying to get his attention. I saw you and him and Margo leave your house that night, so I ran out to get ahead of you."

She switched hands, put the other one on top. "But then it got Mom so excited. And Tom really didn't seem to care. And I felt so guilty about it afterwards. I got it into my head that Madame Nadeau would come and punish me for it. I never go up to the falls alone now."

"It wasn't your idea in the first place," Irini suggested.

Sissy nodded eagerly. "I would never have thought of it. I got it from *Wheat Theater*. Remember when Anna Peal faked a ghost?"

"To scare the headhunters? That ghost?"

"To punish the pirates. Tom was so interested in Maggie. He used to come over and ask about her. What was she like? What did I think she *stood* for? Do you know, for the longest time he thought she was real. No one told him she wasn't. But even when he knew, I could tell he didn't like Maggie much. He was very suspicious of her. I thought if I actually saw her he would come over even more to hear about it.

"Oh, Irini, I'm sure you didn't see Maggie up there. I'm sure it was just Opal May again. Don't you think?"

Irini supposed it could have been. She hadn't really seen a face. It wasn't like Maggie to appear topless, but it wasn't really Opal May's style either. Irini had been influenced, perhaps overly, by the apron.

"Do you think he ever really liked me?" Sissy asked.

"I'm sure he did," said Irini, thinking, of course, he didn't. She remembered Holcrow putting his arms around Sissy to calm her down, kissing her forehead.

"He always wanted to go into Jimmy's room. He said he had a good view from there."

"A good view of what?"

"Of your house," Sissy said.

"Why would he want to see that?" Irini asked, startled, but Sissy didn't know.

Nothing was left in Irini's cocoa cup but a dark, cold, and bitter residue. It could probably have been salvaged for something—put into a devil's food cake, or used as a starter on the next cup of cocoa or soaked into a rag for shining shoes. Maggie Collins had always opposed waste. In honor of Maggie's ghost, Irini forced herself to gulp it down.

40

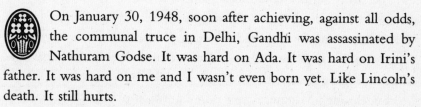 On January 30, 1948, soon after achieving, against all odds, the communal truce in Delhi, Gandhi was assassinated by Nathuram Godse. It was hard on Ada. It was hard on Irini's father. It was hard on me and I wasn't even born yet. Like Lincoln's death. It still hurts.

Meanwhile, back in America, a former marine, Joseph McCarthy, had been elected to the U.S. Senate from the same state that once gave us the La Follettes. J. Edgar Hoover had already gone before HUAC, attempting to have the Communist party outlawed. "They have developed one of the greatest propaganda machines the world has ever known," Hoover warned America. "They have been able to penetrate and infiltrate many respectable and reputable public opinion mediums."

In February of 1948, in congressional committee, Thomas Holcrow, an agent for the FBI, denounced Ada Collins as a Communist spy and her husband, prominent capitalist and civic leader, as a dope. And Irini's father, in what was very much a sidebar, as a fellow traveler.

Holcrow had been collecting evidence all summer and the file was too thick for anyone to read all the way through. No need; its mere size was overwhelmingly persuasive. It contained affidavits and recipes and doubtful housecleaning tips. There was an inclination toward bananas that Holcrow found suspicious enough to mention. They were not an American fruit. The entire minutes of the Magrit Society of Satyagraha were also included. Holcrow noted that, although he had been present, whenever decisions were made he had abstained.

Ada had unabashedly declared herself a Communist during the war. She had never denied or apologized for it. She had access to ham radio equipment. She had taken trips abroad. Her ideals and heroes were dark-skinned and foreign.

Her artwork was examined by members of the House of Representatives. They looked at those blue period teacups with their ashy flowers, their dusty colors, especially the set with the withered stems, and said no American could have painted them. They were, in short, the kind of art that was bad for people.

It might not have mattered so much, but the Collinses were rich. Why would a rich person be a Communist? It was the most un-American thing the members of the House could imagine.

Plus, through Maggie, Ada was in a position of considerable influence and power. In a poll conducted by the editorial staff of *Women at Home* Maggie had once been voted the most admired woman in America. And if you lined the recipes in *How to Cook a Goose* up vertically on the page, as Holcrow had done, if you put the middle one first, the last one second, the first one third and so on, and then eliminated every fourth letter the first letters of the first word of each recipe spelled out "Stallgn" and that was just far enough removed from "Stalin" to be cunning. It maintained deniability, that was the cunning part.

Holcrow testified that he believed Maggie's recipes to be full of such coded information. It had been a convenient way for Ada to send information abroad. Two teaspoons could easily refer to two missiles. A tablespoon might well decode into an armed submarine. The Bureau had their top men working on it in secret kitchens in Washington.

Women at Home had an international market and the whole New York staff could well have been implicated if they had not cooperated fully with Holcrow. They had received Maggie's final columns direct from Holcrow himself and had run them unhesitatingly, disregarding any possible legal ramifications or First Amendment issues. This was, Holcrow implied, the mark of the true patriot. As a result the magazine's reputation had suffered along with Maggie's. Holcrow was glad of this opportunity to set the record straight.

It was a shame, Holcrow told the committee, that a dangerous woman like Ada Collins should have used and abused the reputation of a fine woman like Maggie. Because he loved this country, he'd been left with no choice but to destroy them both.

It was the headline story in the Chicago paper: SPY RING EXPOSED. RED MAGGIE COOKS FOR COMMIES. Norma Baldish folded the issue inside out so nothing but the personals showed when she left the paper on the porches of Magrit. It was 1948, and the personals were pretty sedate.

Down at college, Irini read the headline and phoned home. "Hey, Cindy," she said. "How's my dad doing? Do you think I should come back?"

"Whatever for?" said Cindy. Irini tried to pretend that Cindy's tone was not just a little bit cool.

Her father, in contrast, was cheery. "I'm ignoring the whole thing," he told her. "It's not as if Mr. Henry's going to fire me over it. I'm okay as long as the mill survives."

No one in Magrit was surprised to learn that he was a dangerous revolutionary. They had always pretty much assumed it. Those people who had already disliked him now liked him less. But Magrit, along with the rest of the country, was not as casual about communism as they had been. The suspicions and whisperings that had once been confined to the Kitchen now spilled out. Magrit was seeing Communists the way they had always seen ghosts.

They wondered about Claire, who'd told a number of people she never would marry. This didn't seem American. They wondered about the Leggetts with their unnatural Quaker doctrines. They wondered about the Törngrens with their sauna and their foreign cooking. They snubbed Ada completely. It was not a pleasant place for Irini to come home to. In fact, it was not home at all.

The Baldishes were the most tangibly hurt by the accusations, because of their association with Irini's father. Business at Bumps fell off and never recovered, although Irini's father did his best to personally make up the difference.

Suspicions were trained particularly on the Magrit Society of Satyagraha. None of the satyagrahis turned out to have the moral courage to keep coming to meetings. The movement for nonviolence in Magrit was obliterated, wiped out as if it had never been. But Irini's father refused to allow a petty bureaucrat like Thomas Holcrow to bully him out of his admiration for Gandhi. Or for Mrs. Ada.

Who was ecstatic. There was no one in Magrit more ready to serve jail time than Ada. She went to Washington at her own expense to let them know before they even asked that she would name no names. She began an immediate fast. She wrote letters, she circulated petitions. She did serve some jail time, about two months. She emerged more committed than ever. She urged the FBI to join with her in the search for truth and they did so, whether they realized it or not; that was the beauty of satyagraha. If they'd only been paying a little attention, Martin Luther King Jr. might not have had to do it all over again.

She was, according to Irini's father, the bravest old woman he had ever known. It irritated Irini that he said this, not the brave part, but the old. In point of fact, Ada was not so much older than he was. At nineteen herself, Irini really couldn't see the difference. Ever since he had married Norma, he had completely lost track of his age.

Ada considered going back to jail, but Irini's father talked her out of it. It seemed unnecessarily cruel to force Thomas Holcrow to comprehend himself this way, as a man who put old women, in whose houses he had been a welcome guest, into jail.

And her hard time was hard on Henry. His first wife had been in prison often enough, but he'd been a younger man. Now he'd lost

Claire. And his radio show. And his baseball team. And Maggie. Most of all, Maggie.

There was more to the story, but it didn't come out for several years. Then, sometime when I was about five, my mother had a visit from Margo who told her that Sissy Tarken had told Arlys, who told Margo, who told my mother that Cindy had told Sissy that she had written Maggie's final columns.

In fact, with the exception of the letters Claire wrote, the columns were all authored by various Mays. The alcohol column was written by Tracy. She'd become concerned at the way suspicion was directed toward Fanny. She'd been angry at Irini for voicing this suspicion. So she chose alcohol as her topic, because no one would think this was Fanny and Tracy didn't care if they thought it was Irini.

I almost remember the conversation. I'm going to pretend I remember it better than I do. My mother and Margo sat at our dining-room table, playing big casino and drinking coffee. I sat under the table, between the two pairs of shoes, legs in nylons, the tablecloth around me like a cave. The cards fell onto the tabletop like rain. *Slap, slap, slap.*

Margo said, "At first he just wanted her to listen in on Mrs. Ada's phone calls."

"I always knew she listened to us," my mother said. At the time, I assumed this was a reference to me. I didn't think Margo knew I was there, crouched by her feet, eavesdropping silently, but I knew my mother did. "She was such a precocious little thing." My mother's tone was affectionate. The sound of the cards was cozy.

"When that didn't give him what he wanted, he escalated." Maggie had her initial outbursts. Holcrow found out that Cindy had written fake letters to servicemen during the war. It all fell together so neatly. He told Cindy she had the experience and the brains her country needed. He appealed to her patriotism, both for America and for Upper Magrit. He told her she would be a secret operative of the FBI. She was seventeen years old. It was more exciting than being a telephone operator.

"Tracy was always so sure he was coming over to see her," Cindy said to Sissy, who passed it on. "No one ever thought he could be interested in me." She began to attend the Committee on Satyagraha meetings, strictly in an undercover capacity.

My mother refused to blame her. This is so like my mother.

It made Margo just as nuts as it used to make me. The cards were falling faster and harder. "Cindy May knew she would end up hurting Mrs. Ada and Mr. Henry. They were always kind to her. She spied on your own father. She wrote those demented columns."

(Well, actually those columns contained some pretty good advice. Those final columns, in my final grown-up opinion, had the real Maggie whipped like an egg.) But didn't Cindy May completely destroy the movement for nonviolence in Magrit? Set the Sweethearts to suspecting each other? Kill innocent little Anna Peal?

"That period where she had no hands was so hard on her," my mother said.

"I think she faked the injury," said Margo. The bus turned over and she had hurt her arm, all right, but just badly enough to give her an idea. She could slip into the mill, type the columns on the mill typewriter, and with no hands, no one could possibly suspect her. It was one of those lies you show rather than tell.

My mother was still not persuaded of malice. Cindy had a love of drama, perhaps. A yearning for importance. Perfectly understandable from the youngest of three girls. "You've forgotten how it was. We were all patriots then," my mother said. "We'd just won the war. You and me, we might have done the same if he'd asked us."

"Never," said Margo. "Never me, never you." She reached under the table with one hand. She opened it somewhere by my ear. There was a Toll House cookie in it. I remember that part for sure.

Cindy May went on to become a mystery writer. Quite successful. Her specialty is kitchen cozies, that line of books with murders and really great dinners and sometimes a recipe or two. My mother always maintained, if you read Cindy's books carefully, you find a subtext of regret and contrition. Those books are practically an apology.

My mother always hated mysteries in which the murderer turns out to be a child.

Eventually all of the Sweethearts managed to marry, except for Sissy, who was, as we know, damaged goods and could hardly have expected to.

Tracy and Cindy both married into the Redd family, and even so the Redds had boys to spare.

Claire became modestly famous and had her own television show for a couple of years—*Claire in the Kitchen.* It ran in the Boston area, where she lived up until her death in 1982 with Fanny May. The exact nature of their relationship was never known. Not for lack of speculation, but you'll get none of that from me. I come from a family celebrated for its discretion.

Fanny had jilted Mike Barr at the altar. I think it was because of the Atomic Pin. In the end she just couldn't make herself wear it. He haunted Magrit, shattered and shaken, for several months, until Margo Törngren finally told him to stop his whining. Margo's practical, sober, industrious ways stood in stark contrast to Fanny's. They were married in the Lutheran Church and settled in Los Angeles. "I think they were very happy," my mother used to say, though never without the "I think."

Arlys, the prettiest and nicest of them all, had the last Sweetheart wedding. She went to visit Margo, where she met and married an ex-marine. He knew an athlete when he saw one. My mother had a wedding picture of them standing under two crossed bats. Her husband coached basketball at a high school in Ventura, California. She had more children than any of them, although in Magrit fashion, they were mostly girls. She still lives in Ventura, surrounded by her daughters and granddaughters and the occasional flukish grandson.

Irini married Walter. This is no surprise. Haven't I been tipping it that way all along? It happened while Irini was in college. She was working in a diner and Walter walked in. "Who's the cutie at the counter?" one of the other waitresses asked and Irini turned around to see. And that's what she saw, a really, really cute guy and only seconds later realized it was Walter. He looked exactly the same as always.

"Just a Coke, please, miss," he said.

"Strictly coincidence, me walking into that diner," Dad used to tell me. "Of all the gin joints in the world," and Mom used to say to give her a break. And then my Dad would drop his voice. He would whisper to me so that Mom wouldn't hear. "Your mother begged me to marry her," he would say to me, smiling so that I could see that little bit of his gum line. I have, so people tell me, the same smile.

When I was about five, my parents took me to a minor league game and told me to watch the first baseman in particular. He was a thin, graceful, pretty man and he made a couple of good plays. "He's batting .298 this season," my dad told me. "He used to play for the Sweethearts."

In Magrit Ruby had passed as a twenty-year-old. Now she was passing as a man. Because the days of women's baseball were over, and anyway, it had always been so complicated, being that good and being a girl. It just couldn't be made to work.

"But what is she really?" I asked my mother, who told me that she was really a baseball player.

"I wish," my mother said. She was watching the ball go into the catcher's mitt. "Peabody, Peabody, Peabody," she said.

"What do you wish?" my dad said.

And she told us she couldn't remember, but I always thought it must have had something to do with baseball.

That is where the story, if my mother were telling it, would end. You are welcome to stop reading here, if you like. In fact, I recommend it. It is 1948. The war is over. We won.

Afterword

In my own kitchen I now have many of my mother's things. There is a hutch with Ada's painted dishes in it. A toucan napkin ring that my mother used to use. An oak table that Norma built for her. A Chianti-bottle candle from some dinner I was never told about.

I have done my best with my mother's story, although it was hard to get her to talk about Magrit. I think it had all been spoiled for her by the FBI and she was the kind of person who, lacking anything good to say, said nothing at all. I had to fill in a lot. I warned you about that part.

If I have made Magrit seem simple or naive, I apologize. Because of my own age, I was forced to set the story not in the real World War II years, but in those fictional World War II years I knew growing up. A story set in storyland.

My first introduction to World War II was to play it. The game was much like cowboys and Indians, only the names and the sound effects were different. When I had children of my own, the *Star Wars* movies came out and all the kids were on the streets fighting storm troopers again. It is apparently the mythology we are most comfortable with. It's the game we were given to play, but not the story we ourselves were given to live.

My mother's story has everything I would want for her—a romance and work and games, a loving father, and a happy ending. Not only because she believed she'd had all those things. But also because she believed in them for everyone else as well. Even when her own marriage failed, she still believed in them for me.

I've always tried to believe in the same things she did. I can't explain why it's so much harder for me.

My mother believed in a good breakfast. She thought it was the most important meal of the day. This one is easy; I can believe this. But I was recently told that, in other towns than Magrit, in 1947 or thereabouts, Americans were being fed irradiated oatmeal in an experiment designed by their own government and kept a secret from them.

My mother believed in baseball. What made 1947 such a special year? I told you that the Dodgers had spring training in Cuba instead of the South, as was customary, but I didn't remind you of why. This was the year that Branch Rickey and Jackie Robinson integrated the major leagues. This was the year that baseball ceased to be merely a game and became a morality play. This was the year that many people who didn't care about baseball at all followed the Brooklyn Dodgers as if their lives depended on it. There was a brief time when baseball really did matter as much as people are always saying it does, and that time was 1947.

No black woman ever played professionally. The All American Girls' Baseball League has said it was because there was no black woman good enough.

My mother never believed that. When she told me the story of Cassiopeia, the queen so beautiful she made the goddesses jealous, my mother made sure I knew she was from Africa.

My mother knew that there were race riots in the forties, just like in the sixties. She knew about mobs. She knew about lynchings. She knew about the concentration camps and she still believed in the innate goodness of other people. This one is tricky. It's easier when you don't think about it.

My mother believed in the good war. I can't dispute it; I wasn't there. But I also know that wars are insensate, savage, and racist affairs. Every single one of them. Ask Gandhi.

I've given you my mother's end to the story, and it's her story, I kept telling you that, so really I should have stopped by now. Except that I can't quite believe it.

It's not only the 1940's style romance that makes me stumble. There are also those final columns of Maggie's. They just don't read to me like the work of a seventeen-year-old girl.

I'm sitting here in the kitchen of the dead, and if my mother were here with me, she would tell me to go on as long as I wished. My mother would say to do whatever I wanted.

So here's my own ending. Hers is nicer, but mine is more modern: When Cindy wrote Maggie's final columns, she did it in a single night. "They just poured out of me," she said. "I didn't even think about them. Usually it was so hard for me to type, but my hand just flew over the keys." Years later she read the columns over and she couldn't remember writing them at all.

This happened in 1947, in Magrit, where they had never heard of channeling. But now it's the nineties; we're a little more sophisticated. So, on the basis of the evidence of the columns themselves, and on Cindy's own perceptions of inspiration, I can suggest the obvious. That the columns were written by Maggie herself.

In 1949 Magrit was troubled by a series of grisly incidents we would recognize now as quite ordinary cattle mutilations. Eventually the citizens of Magrit decided to blame Chi Chi, who had to be sent back to Little Persia, even though anyone who had spent ten minutes with her knew that Chi Chi was too refined for this.

Nor was the nocturnal surgeon an extraterrestrial. Nineteen forty-seven saw the first epidemic of UFO's, starting with pilot Keith Arnold's sightings above the Cascade Mountains that summer, but Magrit was behind the times and only saw the occasional old-fashioned ghost.

This leaves us with only one possible explanation. That this, too, was the fury of Maggie Collins, scorned and abandoned by the man who loved her, *pissed off* about those radioactive breakfast cereals, but silenced forever, secreted with the other drowned things in Upper Magrit. No wonder she surfaced from time to time, filleting everything in sight.

She was seen on many occasions and the people in Magrit knew who she was, all right, because of the apron, but now she had the eight arms of Kali as well. She scorched the earth like an overheated iron wherever she set her foot. Her hair crackled with the static of electrically dried clothes. She stirred the waters of Upper Magrit like a cauldron.

She was a cold wind, a hot flame. She ushered in the fifties as the fifty-foot woman, the unfortunate product of gamma rays and the bite of an irradiated ant. In the sixties she dressed as a guerrilla and carried a flamethrower. No one saw her at all in the eighties, but she struck with the precision and the training of a ninja.

We all get the goddesses we deserve. Sooner than you think, she'll be enhanced with bionics and then just watch her beat and bake! She is coming on line and you have never seen a virus like her.

Time for you to get out of the kitchen.

She is the mother of us all, the mother of birth and death, queen of the circle, with the circle just coming round again. But she is a bit disappointed in us; we are not the people our parents were. It doesn't mean she doesn't love us. She is preheating her ovens, sharpening her knives. She is waiting, waiting, waiting, and this woman is a professional, she knows *exactly* how to prepare you.

Acknowledgments

Special thanks are due to Mikki and Phil Adams, who gave me space, time, and love when I needed it. Also to Marlis Runnberg, for her helpful letters.

And the usual gang—Debbie Smith, Alan Elms, Sara Streich, Clint Lawrence, Darcy Campbell, Kevin Mims, Don Kochis, Nina Vasiliev, Stan Robinson, Ursula Le Guin. And always Marian Wood. And always Wendy Weil.

The Sweetheart
Season

KAREN JOY FOWLER

A Reader's Guide

A Conversation with Karen Joy Fowler

Q: Henry James used to talk about the "seed" of his stories—the source that served as the basis for his plot. Sometimes he created a story out of a bit of gossip he overheard or from an account reported in the newspapers. Where did you get the seed for *The Sweetheart Season?*

A: Probably the initial trigger was the stories I grew up with about my mother's experiences during World War II. I didn't use the actual stories—my mother was in La Jolla, California, during the war, and her stories all involved spear fishing to supplement the rations, watching the ocean for submarines, and everyone pooling their gas to drive to Mexico for a steak dinner. But I had my mother very much in mind when I was trying to picture Irini. My mother died while I was writing the book and I spent as much time with her as possible in her last years. I comforted myself with memories and surrounded myself with pictures of her as a young, vibrant woman. I wrote the book, at least partly, to deal with my grief and to try to be close to my mother by meditating on the differences between World War II and my mother's generation, and the Vietnam War and my own generation.

Q: Why do you suppose that Americans who grew up in the forties and experienced the Holocaust, race riots, lynchings, and other hideous acts of inhumanity and suffering still managed to, as a reviewer for *The New York Times Book Review* so aptly put it, "retain the kind of hopeful, heads-up innocence that seems to elude us"?

A: Well, that's really the central question of the book. The whole book can be organized around that single issue and best understood as me fumbling to answer that very question. In the end I really can't answer it. It just makes no sense to me. My generation's tendency toward despair, pessimism, and whining seems a more sensible reaction to the facts as they have been presented to us. But I very much admire the other response. I think perhaps one factor was the earlier conviction that they themselves were good people, and I think that their conviction stemmed partly from believing that their role in World War II was an admirable one. I can understand that such assurance would put everyone in a sunnier mood.

Q: If optimism and a naive innocence was the mind-set of your mother's generation, what characterizes the mind-set of your generation and the narrator of *The Sweetheart Season*'s generation?

A: I never said they were naive or innocent. I don't think they were. I just think they all liked their war better than we liked ours. Vietnam really stamped my generation irretrievably. When I was a teenager, the Civil Rights movement was underway. It was something I watched on the evening news—Martin Luther King Jr. and the sit-ins, the marches, voter registration—a nightly demonstration of passion, courage. I was very caught up in the drama of it. And it was absolutely clear who the good guys and who the bad guys were. Although I was white, I never for a moment felt implicated. If anyone on the screen represented me, it was my government, the federal government. To the extent that I understood its role, I was proud of it. The Supreme Court was absolutely unified on school desegregation, no dissenting opinion, and that made me very proud.

So I could see that horrible things were happening, that innocent people were being hurt and even killed. But my government and me, we were trying to stop that. We were moving in the direction of justice and equality and brotherhood. So imagine my surprise when this same government lied about our reasons and our role in Vietnam. Just a few years later, and I was seeing pictures of napalmed children and knew my government had used the napalm. And suddenly I could see that

I had no power or voice, never did have. The pride I'd felt was replaced with a vision of my country, my government, and ultimately myself, since it *was* my government, as vindictive, petty, small-minded, mercenary, dishonest, and uncaring. As well, it pointed out to me that my own politics were those of a despised minority. This country will never resolve Vietnam and the culture will never pardon those of us who protested and dissented.

Q: **Is Martha Stewart the modern day Maggie Collins? How are they different?**

A: I did not once think of Martha Stewart when I was writing the book. But, yes, I can see the lineage. I think that maybe Maggie Collins would argue that her expertise extends to a wider range of areas. She has aspects of Miss Manners and Dr. Joyce Brothers—she'll advise you on your marriage and your menus and your morality, too.

Martha Stewart is more about presentation than about substance. She's more appropriate to this time period. But I think Martha Stewart is an interesting icon. She emphasizes domesticity, but it doesn't feel antifeminist. She does her homemaking and her entertaining with such élan and precision and energy that it becomes a kind of revenge feminism. Try to shut a woman like her up in the home and she'll decoupage your socks and then you'll be sorry!

Q: **What does the narrator mean when she says at the end of the book, "We all get the goddesses we deserve"?**

A: The World War II generation was hearty and sensible and hard-working so they get a hearty, sensible, hard-working goddess. But if my own generation chooses instead to emphasize victimization and entitlement and self-pity, then we can expect to see a different aspect. We'll find our goddess checked into the Betty Ford clinic.

Q: Did you start writing *The Sweetheart Season* before the movie *A League of Their Own* came out? If so, how did it affect you and the book?

A: Actually my original plan for the book involved the professional women's league. I had already done a lot of research when I began to hear about the movie, and it was very distressing. First I thought, Maybe it will be just a really tiny movie and nobody will notice it. But when I heard that Madonna had signed on, I knew I had to change my plans because Hollywood was not cooperating.

Initially I had thought I would write a book about female athletes, the issues involved in being physically gifted and female, and the ways in which women are sometimes discouraged from being good at something when competence is almost always admired in men. I thought I would be writing about the league and about women who played baseball very, very well, but when *A League of Their Own* came out I thought, All right, I'll write about women who don't play baseball so well after all, and so the whole issue of being athletic and being female was largely lost in this revisioning. Not gone entirely, but very peripheral.

Q: Did you like the movie *A League of Their Own*?

A: No, not much. There's so much to be said about the professional women's league: where it came from, what happened to it, what it meant in the context of the war, what it meant for the women in it, what kinds of women were in it. The movie didn't touch these issues. I thought it was a very safe movie and, therefore, not a really interesting one. And there were a few, just a few, things in it that struck me as mean-spirited. For example, I intensely disliked the portrait of the team chaperone. Very stereotypical, very tedious. I wanted my own team chaperone, Fanny May, to play against type.

Q: Why do so many of your characters distrust science? Are you saying that we rely on or trust science too readily?

A: I wish we relied on science more. Actually, I think as a species we seem to have a predilection for magical thinking instead. That makes fools of us. But so does science. Early results look promising. Snake-oil salesmen pass as Ph.D.'s; Ph.D.'s pass as dispassionate, rigorous practitioners. I mean, both my novels have dealt with historical periods and one can't help but notice that last year's science is often this year's nonsense; it's not real science, but whatever is passing as science. So let's say that I distrust scientists, not science. But often it's hard to know where one stops and the other begins. I especially object when the language of science is adopted in the social sciences to feign precision and reproducibility. The very words "studies have shown," or worse, "studies have proved," arouse my instant ire.

Q: What do you want people to get out of reading *The Sweetheart Season?*

A: *The Sweetheart Season* is intended to be a comic novel. I am most pleased when people tell me it made them laugh. And I wouldn't mind at all if people thought just a bit about Gandhi again.

Q: How much research went into writing *The Sweetheart Season,* and how did you go about doing the research? Did it require reading old cookbooks and advice columns, traveling to the Midwest, investigating the life of a cereal magnate?

A: Yeah, all of the above. I read a lot of old magazines, which was great fun. I talked to my aunts about whatever they remembered. They provided me with a lovely list of euphemisms they swear women used whenever it was necessary to talk about menstruation, "Falling off the roof" being my favorite. I mean, what was the derivation of that? I had baseball experts to advise me. I read old housekeeping books and actually tested out some of the housecleaning tips—I tried cleaning my toilets with Coca-Cola and wiping my walls with fresh bread. I made many unauthorized uses of vinegar. My home was lovely to look at, but a bit sticky to the touch.

Q: Was this, your second book, easier to write than your first?

A: No. Harder.

Q: What's the subject matter of your third novel?

A: It's a sort of secret history of San Francisco. I really can't say much more. I'm making it up as I go. Anything could happen.

Reading Group Questions and Topics for Discussion

1. Why does the narrator of *The Sweetheart Season* state up front that the story she is about to tell is "told by two liars"?

2. The narrator is a child of the 1960s—a person labeled a "baby boomer" by popular culture. How does her perception shape the story, and what shaped her perception?

3. How do you think World War II shaped the ethos of the country in the 1940s?

4. Irini Doyle and her daughter, the narrator of the book, both came of age during a time of war—World War II and the Vietnam War—yet their experiences, opinions, and attitudes are vastly different. Why?

5. Do you think women today are anything like Maggie Collins, whom the narrator describes as "a tidy, indefatigable, even-tempered, ageless woman...She shared the scientist's obsession with reliable, predictable results...and she was as interested in innovation as she was in codification"? What about women of the 1940s?

6. What does the narrator think about the culture and climate of the 1940s?

7. Conservative social critics frequently call for a return to the simpler values of America's past—particularly the values of the 1940s and '50s. Do you think things are better now or were they better back then? Why do many of us tend to romanticize the past, whether it's our own past or that of our ancestors?

8. Which mind-sets and behaviors have changed since the 1940s? Which do you wish had stayed the same?

9. Do you think the Vietnam War and World War II had differ-

ent effects on the young Americans who lived through them? If so, why?

10. Why do you think the author has chosen to make Irini Doyle motherless with an alcoholic father?

11. Why does Fowler make Upper and Lower Magrit in dissension? And what role does the sunken part of the city play in the story?

12. Is Henry Collins anything like today's business tycoons? How does he compare to modern captains of industry such as Bill Gates, Lee Iacocca, Donald Trump, and Ted Turner?

13. Is Ada Collins, genteel bohemian and former Communist turned follower of Ghandi, the antithesis of Maggie Collins? Explain how Henry Collins could be in love with two such dissimilar women.

14. What's the significance of the fictitious radio character little Anna Peal? What purpose does she serve?

15. Discuss the following quote from Irini Doyle's father: "The whole world has been sugar-coated. It's this labored American blandness. This forced optimism. It happened during the war, somehow. Darndest thing. We've seen the concentration camps. The mass suicides of the Japanese. We've seen hostages shot and hanged, whole cities obliterated in a blink. And we still think we live in a Disney cartoon." Do you agree?

16. Why did men consider it so undesirable for women to be strong and competitive in the 1940s? Do you think most men still feel threatened by women who excel in sports and things that are physical?

17. Why do you suppose the author chooses the character she does to be responsible for writing Maggie's final columns, which urge women to "Flee through the open space with only the clothes on your back. What you need most after food and

sleep is silence and time. You will not find these in your house with the white picket fence and the screaming children and the glowering husband. Live in the woods, eat like the birds. Wear your feather dusters as hats; make hammocks out of your aprons. Warm yourself at the primitive fires. Be nameless. Life is a smorgasbord. Take many lovers, you will be surprised at how many people are edible if you prepare them properly."

18. Karen Joy Fowler is a cocreator of the James Tiptree Jr. Memorial Award, which is presented, in her words, "to a short story or novel that explores or expands our understanding of gender...to remind the field of its own importance in the continual struggle to re-imagine more livable sexual roles for ourselves." How does *The Sweetheart Season* accomplish this goal?

© Shannon L. Fowler

ABOUT THE AUTHOR

KAREN JOY FOWLER, born on February 7, 1950, lived in Bloomington, Indiana—where her father was a professor of psychology—until she was eleven years old. "Bloomington lives in my mind as a sort of Oz-like place where I caught fireflies and watched lightning and ran around. None of the yards were fenced, so we could play games that covered massive amounts of territory." She then moved to Palo Alto, California, and was outraged to find that all the yards were fenced. "As part of growing up, I suppose, the things I was expected to do got smaller and smaller anyway, in the same way that the territory I was allowed to occupy got smaller and smaller because of the differences between California and Indiana."

Fowler majored in political science at the University of California at Berkeley, and had her first baby at twenty-three during the last year of her master's program at the University of California at Davis. After completing her master's degree, she entered what she refers to as her "child-rearing years." Though she loves her two children with an intensity that still amazes her, Fowler—then thirty years old—began to feel restless. She decided to take a dance class to reclaim some territory of her own. "And it was only after I realized that I wasn't going to make it as a dancer that I took a creative writing class in Davis."

Fowler began to publish science fiction stories. She soon made a name for herself in the sci-fi community with the publication of *Artificial Things*, a collection of short stories. She then wrote her first novel, *Sarah Canary*, a critically acclaimed book that she hoped would bridge the gap between mainstream and science fiction. Fowler considers her second novel, *The Sweetheart Season*, to be "a romantic comedy with historical and fantastical elements."

In 1991, Fowler, along with science fiction writer Pat Murphy, created the James Tiptree Jr. Memorial Award which, in Fowler's words, "is presented annually to a short story or novel that explores or expands our understanding of gender...both to honor Alice Sheldon [the science fiction author who used the pen name James Tiptree] and to remind the field of its own importance in the continual struggle to re-imagine more livable sexual roles for ourselves."

Karen Joy Fowler, who lives in Davis and now writes full time, is currently at work on her third novel.

Excerpts from reviews of Karen Joy Fowler's
The Sweetheart Season

"Ms. Fowler's willingness to take detours, her unapologetic delight in the odd historical fact, her shadowy humor, and the elegant unruliness of her language all elevate her story from the picaresque to the grand."

—*The New York Times Book Review*

"A combination of inquiry, skepticism, and sympathy voiced with a zany appeal, a hint of magic...Its flavor is tart, comic, and unreliable."

—*The Los Angeles Times*

"Smart, wry, and just this side of insane...A remarkable treasure...Enchanting."

—*The Washington Post*

"*The Sweetheart Season* is the sort of novel that makes the reader want to meet the author....The characters are entertaining and well-defined. The plot twists are unexpected, and Fowler's witty writing is a joy to read."

—*USA Today*

"*The Sweetheart Season* is full of sparkling wit and flat-out good writing about a town where someone can be suspected of putting on airs simply by sporting an 'out of town haircut.' In territory long staked out by Garrison Keillor, Fowler's book reads like the best of Lake Wobegon and then some."

—*The Philadelphia Inquirer*

"*The Sweetheart Season* is a brilliantly evoked re-creation of the post-war period in small-town America, filled with well-drawn characters....A complex mixture of generosity and skepticism, a warm meditation on and paean to those most romantic

American traits: the propensity for optimism in reduced circumstances, a gullible faith in the unexpectedness and persistence of
love, and an unshakable sense of irony that is large enough to
embrace both humor and affection."

—*San Francisco Chronicle*

"Fowler loves raising questions about where reality ends and imagination begins....If you're willing to take chances on writers who
color outside the lines, try Fowler. She's a true original and one of
the funniest people currently writing in the English language."

—*Minneapolis Star Tribune*

"Fowler's authentically detailed and clever novel is frequently
digressive, but the digressions charm. Deadpan irony ('The
Baldishes had been among the first to explore decorating with
deer') and quirky characters worthy of Dickens raise the entertainment quotient....Fowler depicts our nation's past as more surreal
than real while at the same time slamming her book out of the ballpark."

—*Publishers Weekly*